35th
Mystery
Annual

ELLERY QUEEN'S

CRIME CRUISE
ROUND THE WORLD

26 stories from
Ellery Queen's Mystery Magazine

Edited by
Ellery Queen

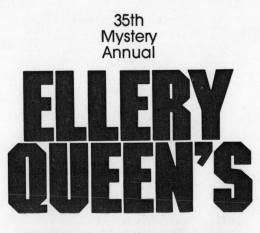
THE DIAL PRESS
DAVIS PUBLICATIONS, INC.
380 LEXINGTON AVENUE
NEW YORK, N.Y. 10017

ACKNOWLEDGMENTS

The editor hereby makes grateful acknowledgment to the following authors and authors' representatives for giving permission to reprint the material in this volume:

T. M. Adams for *Short Week,* © 1979 by T. M. Adams.

Julian Bach Literary Agency, Inc. for *Behind the Locked Door* by Peter Lovesey, © 1979 by Peter Lovesey.

Bonaparte Holdings Pty. Ltd. and Hope Leresche & Sayle for *Wisp of Wool and Disk of Silver* by Arthur W. Upfield, © 1979 by Davis Publications, Inc.

Georges Borchardt, Inc. for *On the Path* by Ruth Rendell, © 1978 by Ruth Rendell.

Curtis Brown, Ltd. for *The Ledbetter Syndrome* by Stanley Ellin, © 1979 by Stanley Ellin.

James Brown Associates, Inc. for *The Boiler* by Julian Symons, © 1979 by Julian Symons.

Borden Deal for *You Understand?,* © 1979 by The Borden Deal Family Trust (Borden Deal, Trustee).

Editions OPTA for *The Prisoners* by Jacques Catalan, © 1976 by Jacques Catalan.

Celia Fremlin for *A Lovely Morning To Die,* © 1979 by Celia Fremlin.

Brian Garfield for *Scrimshaw,* © 1979 by Brian Garfield.

Laura Grimaldi for *Affirmation of Truth,* © 1973 by Laura Grimaldi.

Edward D. Hoch for *The Theft of Yesterday's Newspaper,* © 1979 by Edward D. Hoch.

International Creative Management for *Is Anyone There?* by Timothy Childs, © 1979 by Timothy Childs.

Clements Jordan for *Mr. Sweeney's Day,* © 1979 by Clements Jordan.

Seicho Matsumoto for *The Woman Who Took the Local Paper,* © 1979 by Seicho Matsumoto.

Florence V. Mayberry for *When Nothing Matters,* © 1979 by Florence V. Mayberry.

Scott Meredith Literary Agency, Inc. for *A Place of Her Own* by Joyce Harrington, © 1979 by Joyce Harrington; and *Mr. Fixit* by Ernest Savage, © 1978 by Ernest Savage.

Robert P. Mills, Ltd. for *The Oldest Law* by John F. Suter, © 1979 by John F. Suter.

Frits Remar for *The Photo,* © 1977 by Frits Remar.

Georges Simenon for *The Man from Out There,* © 1963 by Georges Simenon.

Larry Sternig Literary Agency for *The Midnight Strangler* by Jack Ritchie, © 1978 by Jack Ritchie.

Janwillem van de Wetering for *The Deadly Egg,* © 1979 by Janwillem van de Wetering.

Kathryne Walters Literary Agents for *The Big Ivory* by Victor Milán, © 1979 by Victor Milán.

Donald E. Westlake for *The Girl of My Dreams,* © 1979 by Donald E. Westlake.

Donald A. Yates for *The Two Kings and the Two Labyrinths* by Jorge Luis Borges, translated by Donald A. Yates, © 1962 by Davis Publications, Inc.

4

ITINERARY

5

INTRODUCTION

Dear Reader:

Be a modern Magellan of mystery. Circumnavigate the globe and discover a new world of excitement, wonder, suspense, and surprise.

Here is the itinerary of your Round-the-World 'Tec Tour. Bon Voyage!

You start by visiting five cities in the United States—Hoch, Ritchie, Savage, Westlake, and Harrington.

Then a quick side-trip to Mexico—to Deal.

Before spanning the Atlantic, there is a stopover in Argentina—at Borges.

Then overseas to England where you will stay in Lovesey, Rendell, Fremlin, and Symons.

From England to Remar, in Denmark.

Then hop south to van de Wetering, in The Netherlands.

South again to connect with Simenon in Belgium.

Still farther south to Catalan in France.

You continue your Grand Tour by visiting Italy where you have reservations at Grimaldi.

By air to Milán in East Africa.

On to Mayberry in Israel.

Then the long journey to the bush in Australia, sightseeing in Upfield.

Next you head north to Japan where, after enjoying the hospitality of Matsumoto, you cross the Pacific, stopping over at Garfield in Hawaii, and finish your globe-trotting back in the United States—in Jordan, Childs, Adams, Suter, and Ellin.

Six continents—13 countries—26 stops—and welcome home from your Crime Cruise Round the World!

ELLERY QUEEN, Travel Agent

North America

UNITED STATES

Hoch
Ritchie
Savage
Westlake
Harrington

MEXICO

Deal

Edward D. Hoch

The Theft of
Yesterday's Newspaper

*Nick Velvet is a unique thief—and in a sense, a unique detective.
As a thief, Nick steals only the valueless, the worthless—"never
money or jewels or art treasures"—and for a minimum fee of
$20,000 (inflation has not yet reared its ugly head). But to be a
successful thief it is usually necessary for Nick to solve a mystery,
thus becoming a detective with a unique purpose—a detective
whose aim is not to uphold the law but to break it.*

*In this caper-case Nick is hired to steal a copy of yesterday's
newspaper—and usually there is nothing so dead (worthless) as
yesterday's newspaper. But then there was the mystery to solve:
why should a copy of yesterday's newspaper be worth $20,000? . . .*

Nick Velvet slid a stack of chips across the green felt of the roulette
table on the top floor of London's Playboy Club and waited for
the wheel to be spun by a pert blonde girl with long legs and perfect
teeth.

"So much, Nicky?" Gloria asked cautiously at his side.

"I've a hunch black is due to come up."

But as the girl spun the wheel, Nick's attention was distracted by
a stout man on his right. The man thrust something into his hand
and when Nick looked down he saw it was a check drawn on a
London bank in an amount approximately equal to twenty thousand
American dollars. It was payable to Nick Velvet and signed by someone named Felix Poland. "That's better than a calling card," Nick
commented.

"I thought so," the man said with a smile. His eyes were deep and
alert, though the wrinkles around them hinted at an age past 50.
"You see my name there. May we talk business?"

"It would be a pleasure, Mr. Poland."

Gloria was tugging at his sleeve. "Nicky, we won!"

"Great! Scoop up the money and keep playing. I have to go chat with this man." He slipped the check into his wallet and followed Felix Poland to a lounge area at the end of the room.

It was only eight o'clock, but Nick already knew it would be a profitable evening.

Actually, their luck had been running well since Nick and Gloria arrived in London three days earlier. It was a vacation for them—replacing the dampness of January in Westchester with the dampness of January in London—and Nick had no thought of doing any work. But the weather on their arrival was unusually good, almost balmy, and their good fortune was compounded at the hotel which discovered it had no double room reserved for them and promptly put them in a three-room suite for the same price.

Nick had been to London before and he enjoyed showing Gloria the sights, especially places like Buckingham Palace and the Regents Park Zoo which had figured in a previous adventure. They'd registered at some of the casinos when they arrived, and observed the two-day waiting period before being allowed to gamble. Finally this was their first gambling night, and judging by the unexpected check from Felix Poland their lucky streak was continuing.

"How do you know my name?" Nick asked when he and Poland were settled at a corner table in the lounge.

"I have contacts around London. Someone told me you were here and you're just the man I need." He sipped his drink and added, "The check is quite good, in the event you're wondering."

"That's my usual fee, as you must know," Nick said. "The only thing untouched by inflation. But I steal only the valueless—never money or jewels or art treasures."

"Exactly. And are you available tonight?"

"What do you want stolen?"

"Yesterday's newspaper. The *London Free Press,* to be exact."

"Certainly a valueless item," Nick agreed. "I'd suggest searching through some of the rubbish barrels around town."

"I believe the one I need is at the home of Hope Trennis, the actress. Certainly if anyone has one, she has. She's throwing a party tonight and I was invited weeks ago. You and your lady can be my guests."

"Wouldn't she be suspicious?"

"No, no, the party's to view her film '100 Minutes' on BBC television tonight. I distributed the film to British theaters last year and she'd expect me to bring guests. She'll be pleased to see fellow

Americans—a great deal more pleased than she'll be to see me, really. Our relations aren't too cordial these days."

"But you're still going to her party?"

"As I said, I was invited weeks ago, before our falling out."

"Just where is the newspaper?"

"No idea. Somewhere in the house. In her study safe, if she hasn't already destroyed it."

"Why is it so valuable?"

"It wouldn't be, to anyone but me."

"You're telling me that a copy of yesterday's newspaper is valuable to you only, and that it's in the possession of Hope Trennis and nobody else?"

"There might be a few other copies around, but I'm sure hers would be the easiest to find."

"Very well," Nick agreed. "When do we leave?"

Felix Poland glanced at his watch. "We should be getting along."

Nick went back to the roulette table where he found Gloria with a new stack of winnings. "This is our lucky night, Nicky!"

"It certainly is. We're invited to a party." He started to gather up the chips. "Let's turn these in."

"Do we have to?"

"We'll come back tomorrow. This party might be fun. There'll be some movie people there."

"Like who?" she asked suspiciously.

"Hope Trennis, the actress. It's at her place."

Gloria's eyes widened. "Really?"

As Nick cashed in the chips he hoped their luck would hold through the night.

Hope Trennis' home was an exquisite townhouse within sight of Belgrave Square—the sort with a fireplace in every room and a cluster of quaint chimneys on the roof. Though Hope was an American actress she had resided in London for well over a year—ever since she finished filming the highly successful "100 Minutes." Nick was hardly a movie fan but he had seen that one, a suspenseful chase film in which the entire action took place during the one-hundred-minute running time of the picture itself. Now, about a year after its London theatrical release, the film was being shown by BBC television.

"It's generally the type of thing the commercial channel would carry," Poland explained as they entered the house to be met by a uniformed butler. "But with Hope living here now, she managed to have it shown this once without interruptions."

Nick and Gloria handed their coats to the butler. "Look at this place, Nicky!" Gloria squealed. "It's like a palace!"

Nick, who had seen the inside of Buckingham Palace, was less overwhelmed. Still, he had to admit the lady had taste. He was staring up at the multi-tiered chandelier when Hope Trennis herself appeared, sweeping down on them in a cloud of pink chiffon. "You must be one of the BBC gentlemen," she greeted Nick. "So good of you to come."

"Actually, I'm—"

"He's a friend from America," Felix Poland explained. "Nick Velvet. And this is his wife Gloria."

Gloria was used to that introduction by now and she didn't change expression. She was too busy bathing in the vision of Hope Trennis from three feet away. Nick had to admit she was a lovely woman—perhaps a bit older-looking than on the screen, but every bit as charming. Even when she turned to Poland with a brusque "I didn't expect to see you here," there was no noticeable bitterness in her words. Whatever had passed between them would not be allowed to ruffle her composure this night.

"Am I still invited?" Poland asked her with a smile.

"Of course. Come in and have a drink before the film gets under way. I promise not to poison you."

He shot her a look of anger, but she'd already turned away. They followed her into a large living room where perhaps 30 people were chatting in small groups while a maid passed a tray of drinks in the best tradition. "This is really living," Gloria whispered.

Nick felt a bit like the society thief in those old Raffles books. Glancing at the necklaces and diamond rings adorning the women, he had to remind himself that he'd come to steal nothing more valuable than yesterday's newspaper.

Hope Trennis led them to a slender man wearing mod glasses and dark hair long enough to cover his ears. "This is my friend Eric Noble from the BBC. You know Felix, Eric, and this is Nick Velvet and his wife Gloria, over from America."

They shook hands all around and Hope flew off to greet more late arrivals. "Your first visit here?" Noble asked Nick. No doubt it was his stock conversation gambit with visiting Americans.

"No, I was over in '71."

Nick lit one of the infrequent cigarettes he'd been indulging in during their vacation, ignoring Gloria's pained expression.

"You'll find some things changed since then." Noble motioned toward the color television set. "I suppose you've already seen the film?"

Nick nodded. "We caught it back in the States."

"I'm a big fan of Hope's," Gloria added.

Nick left her to converse with Eric Noble while he took Poland to one side. "Where should I look first? You mentioned a safe in the study. Or should I check the dustbins first?"

His client snorted. "Picking up our British phrases so quickly, Velvet? No, it's more likely in the safe, or somewhere else in her study. I'm sure she was sent one yesterday morning by a columnist on the paper, and I don't think she would have destroyed it so soon. Be careful, though. If she discovers you're after it, she could burn it quickly enough."

"Don't worry."

Hope Trennis was at the front of the room, flanking the television set and calling for attention. "It's about to begin, ladies and gentlemen. Do be seated. After the show we'll be serving a buffet supper in the study."

Nick glanced at his watch as the lights dimmed. 9:15, exactly. That meant the film would end its hundred-minute run at 10:55, since it was playing without interruptions. He wondered why the British TV schedules always seemed so irregular. Nothing would ever begin at 9:15 back home. He settled back in his chair to watch the beginning of "100 Minutes," keeping an eye on the study door which was slightly ajar. A light was on in there, and he saw the butler and maid pass across his slender line of vision from time to time, preparing the buffet supper for later. He realized he might have no chance to slip into the study unobserved.

The film droned on and he watched a surprisingly agile Hope Trennis scale a board fence while pursued by the villains. She played the middle-aged wife of an important presidential advisor, sought by kidnapers who hoped to force her husband to deliver certain top-secret documents into their hands. It was predictable but exciting.

Nick glanced at the glowing numbers on his digital watch.

9:39.

The light in the study was still on. He had a glimpse of the maid carrying a tray of cups.

On the television screen Hope had eluded her pursuer for the moment and taken refuge in a gas station where she'd met a handsome mechanic. While Gloria watched the screen as if she'd never seen the film before, Nick grew increasingly restless. He was missing the perfect opportunity to search the study.

9:52.

As the minutes passed he decided the butler and maid intended to remain in the study until supper was served. But then, as if in answer to his silent prayer, the study light went out and the door opened. The servants slipped into the living room to watch the last half of the film.

The time was 10:05.

In the darkness no one but Gloria noticed him leave his chair and slip quietly to the back of the room. For the most part the audience watched the film in polite silence, though occasionally Hope would cause a ripple of laughter with some remark directed to her image. During one suspenseful moment Nick slipped into the darkened study and closed the door. He was certain not even the servants had noticed.

10:08. He turned on the desk lamp and set to work. He had 47 minutes to find the newspaper. Plenty of time.

If it was in the study at all.

10:15.

The desk had yielded nothing, nor had the cabinet with drawers that stood against the far wall. His eyes passed over the fireplace and a crowded bookcase, searching for the most likely hiding place for a safe.

Nick found it behind one of the paintings, in the best British tradition. As he twirled the knob experimentally he really did begin to feel like Raffles, the famous gentleman crook.

The safe was an old one, not very good. But then he wasn't a very good safecracker, either. He pressed his ear against the cold metal and listened for the sound of the tumblers.

It took him ten minutes to get the first number.

He began to sweat a bit. The time was 10:30. Could he do it in twenty-five minutes?

The second number came at 10:38. He was working close to the line. He heard a cheer go up from the next room and he knew the moment of the grand climax was approaching.

Just a few more minutes . . .

The safe came open at 10:51. Four minutes to spare.

He was reaching inside it just as the door opened and Eric Noble stepped into the study. The man from the BBC eyed him for an instant and quickly closed the door before others could follow. "Well! What have we here?"

The safe held nothing but a satin-covered jewel box. Nick closed the door, spun the dial, and replaced the painting. "Just keeping my hand in," he said.

"So I noticed."

The study door opened again and the butler hurried in to complete the food arrangements. The guests were crowding behind him. Nick tried to keep cool. "So the BBC dropped four minutes out of Hope's triumph?"

"Not at all," Noble said. "Oh, I see! You were working against the running time of the film. You didn't know—"

"Food's ready, everyone," Hope Trennis announced. "Be sure to pick up a glass of champagne at the end of the table."

Felix Poland came in with Gloria. He glanced over to where Nick stood, a question in his eyes. Nick ignored it and stepped to one side with Eric Noble. "You're the first thief I ever met," the BBC man said. "Out of loyalty to Hope I really should turn you in."

"I stole nothing. And there's only your word that the safe was open."

"True enough," Noble agreed. "What's your game, Velvet? You're not the usual run of thief. And you did arrive with Felix Poland." Even as he said the words a light dawned. "Of course! That rascal hired you, didn't he?"

"Did he?"

Gloria came up to them with a plate of food. "You'd better get in line, Nicky, before it's all gone."

"I don't think Hope Trennis is likely to run out of food," he said, but he joined Noble in line nevertheless.

"I'll give you a tip for next time," Noble said. "An engineering quirk of British television transmission causes an imperceptible speed-up of projection. A twenty-five-minute film loses one minute on our TV. And Hope's '100 Minutes' is a fast ninety-six minutes here."

"So you didn't cut anything."

"Oh, no. You saw it all. Or I should say you would have seen it all if you hadn't been busy cracking Hope's safe."

Nick gathered up a plate of food, feeling depressed. He'd been caught in the act by this man who taunted him, and he still had no idea where the newspaper was.

He watched Hope approach the butler and wave toward the fireplace. "Didn't I tell you to burn that right away?" she asked. The butler murmured an apology and picked up a long match.

The fireplace!

Nick's eyes shot to it, saw the folded newspaper lying on top of the wood, and knew instinctively it was the one he sought. It was valuable only to Poland, not to Hope Trennis, and she wanted it burned.

He turned quickly to Gloria and whispered, "Sorry, my dear"—and upset his plate of food down the front of her dress.

"*Nicky!*" she screamed.

The butler, half bent toward the fireplace, heard her cry, and straightened up. He blew out his match and hurried over with a napkin.

"I don't know how I could be so clumsy," Nick murmured. He stepped behind the butler, and while all eyes were on Gloria quickly scooped up the newspaper from the fireplace. Before he tucked it under his coat he verified the date. It was indeed yesterday's *London Free Press*.

He went back to Gloria's side while the butler and maid finished wiping off her dress. "How could you do that to me?" she asked.

"I'll explain later," he said softly. "It was necessary."

"I don't think this is our lucky day any more."

"We'll see."

They departed soon afterward, with Hope Trennis seeing them to the door. She seemed suspicious of something, but uncertain of what it was. "I hope you enjoyed the evening," she said.

"It was most profitable," Felix Poland assured her. "You'll be hearing from me."

The actress smiled thinly. "Not too soon, I trust."

In the taxi back to the hotel Nick handed over the paper. "Is this what you wanted?"

Felix Poland quickly opened it to an inside page. "I'll tell you soon enough. Yes, this is the one! You do good work, Velvet."

"What's this all about?" Gloria asked.

"Your husband is an extremely accomplished thief. And you are quite an actress to distract their attention the way you did."

"What does he mean, Nicky?"

"I'll explain later."

But for Felix Poland the time for explanations was now. "You see this item in the 'Mayfair Gossip' column? The light's dim so I'll read it to you. *'Actress Hope Trennis is still mourning the apparent suicide of her best friend, Rena Poland. Trennis refuses to accept the verdict and tells friends that Rena wasn't the sort to kill herself, saying, "If there was poison in that wine, her husband probably put it there."'* End of item, beginning of lawsuit. This is going to cost Hope Trennis and the *London Free Press* one million pounds!"

"Why did you have to get that particular paper?"

"They stopped the presses and yanked that item at the very beginning of the run. They insisted no copies were distributed, but when I heard about it I knew Hope would have one if anybody did. And just one is all I need to prove publication."

"She must have known it was a foolish thing to keep. That's why she told the butler to burn it."

"The editor was asleep, allowing such an item to slip through in the first place. The British libel laws are quite strict, and no one is going to print that about me!"

Gloria and Nick got out of the cab at their hotel. "A pleasure doing business with you," Nick said.

"And you, sir."

Nick stood on the curb watching the taxi pull away. After all, his luck had held. Now if only he could explain it to Gloria . . .

In the elevator she said, "You always told me you worked for the government."

"Sometimes I do."

"Stealing things?"

"I—" The elevator doors slid open on their floor and he cut short the conversation. Eric Noble, the man from the BBC, was leaning against the wall by their door, obviously waiting for them. "How did you get here so fast?" Nick asked.

"My taxi driver knew a short cut. You lit your cigarette with matches from here, so I knew where to find you. These American-owned places always have free matches."

"A regular detective!"

"That's why I'm here. May we talk inside?"

Gloria produced her key and unlocked the door. Once inside, Nick asked, "Now what's this all about?"

"Poland intends to sue Hope for libel, doesn't he?"

"You'll have to ask him."

"He really did poison his wife, you know."

"Then he won't win his case, will he?"

"The libel laws here are tricky. Sometimes truth is no defense.

But that's beside the point. I'm a close friend of Hope's and I want to protect her. I don't want to see her dragged through a long libel action by that swine Poland."

"And yet you didn't sound the alarm when you found me at her safe."

"You weren't taking anything. Later, when I realized what happened while your wife diverted our attention, it was too late. Poland needed that paper, and you stole it for him."

"What about his wife? *Was* she poisoned?"

Noble nodded. "Two months ago. She and Hope were great friends and she told Hope everything. Poland wanted a divorce so he could go off with some young bird from one of the gambling clubs. They had bad scenes over money and Rena wouldn't consent to a divorce. Then one afternoon in his office she drank a glass of poisoned wine and died. The police decided it had to be suicide."

"Why?"

"Because she was alone at the time. Poland was attending a meeting on the next floor, and I was at the meeting myself to vouch for it. She poured herself a glass of sherry from the decanter in his office. His secretary heard noises and rushed in to find Rena dying on the floor. The police found poison in the glass but not in the decanter. There was no way that Poland could have poisoned the drink before it was poured, and he was still in our meeting when the news reached him."

"Yet Hope accused him."

"She shouldn't have said it, and the *London Free Press* shouldn't have printed it. But she feels strongly on the subject. She knew Rena well enough to rule out suicide completely, so she knows Poland must have killed her somehow. If he wasn't in charge of film distribution over here for her producer she never would have invited him tonight. Oddly enough, we were discussing the BBC showing of '100 Minutes' in that meeting two months ago, the afternoon Rena died."

"Tell me what happened."

"Well, I had a couple of chaps with me, and so did Poland. The meeting was scheduled for three, and the wall clock was chiming the hour as he walked through the door. I remember checking my watch against it. Poland sat at the head of the conference table and we started our meeting. It was just ten minutes later when his secretary phoned from the floor below to say that Rena had been stricken. I went with him, but by the time we arrived she was dead."

"Did he marry the girl from the gambling club?"

"Not yet, but I expect he will after a decent interval."

"All right," Nick said. "I've listened to your story. Now what do you want of me?"

"Your help in preventing this lawsuit. I want you to go to Felix Poland tomorrow and persuade him to abandon it, or else I'll have Hope file burglary charges against you."

Gloria rushed to Nick's side. "He's no burglar!"

"When I caught him he seemed quite skilled at it."

Nick weighed the possibilities. He was certain the burglary charge would never stand up, but Hope Trennis was an important woman with important friends. He didn't want to be stuck in England for weeks or more while the charges were pending. "I'll go see Poland," he said. "That's all I can promise."

"Tomorrow morning."

"Agreed."

"And don't try sneaking out of the country."

When they were alone, Gloria said, "Nicky, you haven't been honest with me."

"Let's wait till this is over. Then I promise to tell you everything."

In the morning Nick went to Felix Poland's office. He was there shortly after ten o'clock, stopping only long enough to cash Poland's check and have the money converted into American dollars for transfer to his New York bank. The film distribution office occupied two floors of one of London's newer buildings. He found Poland on the lower floor, checking the ad layouts for a new American movie about to open in Leicester Square. The stout man seemed annoyed to see him again and sent his secretary scurrying from the office.

"Our business was concluded last night, Velvet. You have no reason to come here."

Nick glanced around the office, taking in the expensive wood paneling and the little bar where some decanters stood. That would have been where Rena Poland poured her last glass of sherry. "I'm in a bit of difficulty," Nick began. "Eric Noble caught me in the act. He threatens to have me arrested if you institute that lawsuit."

Felix Poland folded his hands before him on the desk. "That's a danger in your trade, I suppose. I can hardly come to your aid."

"Noble thinks you really did poison your wife."

"Would I be foolish enough to drag this into court if I had?"

"A clever man would. Or a man who thought the law couldn't touch him."

"Scotland Yard investigated the case and cleared me without question. No one—not Hope Trennis or Eric Noble or Nick Velvet—can say differently. If anyone does, I'll sue each one for a million pounds. Is that clear?"

"Certainly. But I was wondering about the exact circumstances of your wife's death."

Poland jabbed impatiently at the call button on his desk. When his dark-haired secretary appeared he told her, "Run through your testimony about my wife's death, will you, Carol? Mr. Velvet here has a great curiosity."

She glanced at Nick, perhaps wondering if he was from the police, and began. "Your wife arrived just before three, as you were leaving for your meeting upstairs. She said she'd wait in your office. I was in the outer office with two other girls, stuffing envelopes for a mailing to exhibitors. We all remember your leaving the outer office and walking to the elevator just as the clock chimed three. About five minutes later we heard a gasp or cry from in here, and we all ran in. Mrs. Poland was on the floor, apparently in great pain. I phoned a doctor on one of the lower floors and then I phoned you in the upstairs conference room. But she was dead by the time the doctor and you got here."

"The poison was in her sherry?" Nick asked.

Carol nodded. "She must have put it there herself. I'd just washed all the glasses and filled the decanter from a new bottle. There was no poison anywhere but in her glass."

"And in Mrs. Poland," Nick added.

"Well, yes."

"Satisfied?" Poland asked Nick.

"You might have left a glass of sherry already poured for her."

"But I didn't. Carol and the other girls were in and out of the office, putting together their mailing. They verified that the glasses were all empty when I left."

"The decanter could have been poisoned, and a second unpoisoned one substituted later."

"Again—no. Neither Carol nor I nor anyone else was alone in that office after the poisoning. And the police took the decanter with them at once. There was no second decanter, or hidden bottle."

"Can I go now?" Carol asked, looking uncomfortable. "I've been over this so many times before."

Felix Poland nodded. When they were alone once more he asked, "Satisfied, Velvet?"

"I suppose I have to be."

"Rena was upset because I wanted a divorce. I've never denied that. She came here as I was leaving for a meeting, went into my private office, poured herself some sherry, and dosed it with a fast-acting poison. I suppose the idea of killing herself in my office appealed to her."

The buzzer sounded and Carol said, "The gentlemen from Thames Television are here for their eleven o'clock meeting."

"I'll be with them in a moment," Poland said. He stood up. "You can go out this way, Velvet. You do understand, don't you? Our business association is ended. Take the next plane home."

As the wall clock chimed the hour Nick found himself shuffled quickly out a rear door. He stood for a moment in the corridor, then sighed and headed for the elevator. It was time for a return visit to Hope Trennis' townhouse.

Though it was nearly noon when he arrived, the actress received him in her dressing gown. The servants from the previous evening were still busy cleaning up after the party, polishing silverware and vacuuming the carpets. "An unexpected pleasure, Mr. Velvet," Hope Trennis said. "Please sit down. Eric has been in touch with me, of course. You were very unlucky to be caught."

Nick smiled. "I wasn't caught, only detected. There's a difference. By this time tomorrow I'll be on a plane back to the States."

Her expression hardened at his words. "I thought Eric made your position quite clear. Have you persuaded Felix Poland to abandon his threatened lawsuit?"

"No."

"Then I'm afraid you'll be charged with burglary, Mr. Velvet."

"Of what—a day-old newspaper?"

"Eric found you with your hand in my safe."

Nick nodded. "Because your film ran four minutes shorter on British television. A few minutes can make a big difference."

"It can for you, Mr. Velvet. I have many friends at Scotland Yard."

"I'm glad to hear that, because I want you to go to them."

"With the charges against you?"

"No—with new evidence against Felix Poland in the death of his wife. Your perfect defense is to go on the offensive. Prove that he poisoned his wife and he won't be in the mood to sue you."

"And how do I go about doing that?"

"As I pointed out, a few minutes can make a big difference—the few minutes less your film ran on British television, or the few minutes' difference between two clocks. I haven't checked the actual testimony covering the time of Rena Poland's poisoning, but if Scotland Yard looks at it again, they'll find an important discrepancy.

"According to his secretary, Felix Poland left his office as the clock was chiming three. And Eric Noble told me Poland walked into the meeting on the floor above as the clock was chiming three. He could hardly have gone up on the elevator and walked into the other office in a matter of two or three seconds. No, one of those clocks had to be a couple of minutes wrong. And it was most likely Poland's, since Noble remembers checking his watch against the conference-room clock.

"But if Poland's office clock was just a couple of minutes fast it demolishes his alibi. He could have left his office, headed toward the elevator, and then turned and reentered his private office through the rear door down the hall. Using the pretext that he'd forgotten something, he could have said a few words to his wife, poured her a glass of sherry, and gone back out the same rear door. Then up to the next floor. Total elapsed time, two or three minutes."

"It could have been that way," Hope said, her eyes alight.

"The testimony of the chiming clocks will only prove that his office one was fast, but that may be enough. Most electric clocks, especially office ones, have a high degree of accuracy. If it was fast, it was probably set ahead deliberately. If Poland set it ahead, that's evidence that he was planning an alibi."

"Thank you for this, Mr. Velvet. You have solved the mystery. Can I pay you for it?"

He shook his head. "I'm no detective. I'm a thief. And Felix Poland has already paid me. It's been a pleasure meeting you."

He went back then to Gloria, because he knew after all these years that the time had come to tell her the truth. He sat with her over drinks, explaining what he did, telling her about the minimum fee he charged and the unique things he stole. And even after 13 years of living together he wasn't certain what her reaction would be.

She sat for a long time in silence, staring at her drink, and finally he asked her, "What do you think?"

She lifted her head and smiled. "I think you should be charging at least twenty-five thousand."

Jack Ritchie

The Midnight Strangler

*This may be the strangest case in the career of Henry Turnbuckle,
"the bonded and licensed private detective from Milwaukee." One
might say that Turnbuckle was involved up to his eyebrows—but
not over his head . . .*

I had been just about to enter my automobile when a half dozen
flashlight beams were directed on my person and I was peremp-
torily admonished not to move or I would have my head blown off.
In an instant more I was surrounded by at least 20 men, half of
them in police uniform.

I realized that this was certainly not the proper time to argue, but
I did pose a question. "Gentlemen, what is this all about?"

No one chose to answer. Instead I was thoroughly searched, handcuffed, and whisked into a waiting patrol car. In another moment
we were off, sirens wailing, despite which it took us nearly fifteen
minutes of threading our way through the congested evening traffic
to reach police headquarters.

There I was pushed and pulled through a horde of what appeared
to be newspaper reporters with questions, hustled into an elevator,
and finally ushered into a small room on one of the upper floors.

A huge florid individual in mufti, who had been at my elbow
throughout my journey, glared at his entourage. "How come I find
all those reporters waiting downstairs? I'll bet one of you clowns
phoned the papers ten seconds after we picked him up."

No one met his eyes and I thought I detected some anonymous
shuffling of feet.

"All right," he snapped. "Now all of you get the hell out of here
and somebody find Sergeant Wiggins and tell him that we caught
his Midnight Strangler. If he doesn't know already."

It was a bit warm in the room, so I reached into my topcoat pocket
for a handkerchief with which to dab at my forehead. I found no
handkerchief, but my fingers did close on a small card. I brought it

23

out and discovered it was the business card of one Clarence Darrow Theobault. Attorney-at-law. Trial work.

Evidently the welcoming throng down below had included at least one lawyer who had taken the opportunity to slip his card into my pocket as I was being muscled through.

The huge man sat down on a chair opposite me. "I am Captain McGillicutty. Of Homicide."

I took off my topcoat and sat down. "I gather you are under the impression that I am the Midnight Strangler?"

McGillicutty allowed himself a tight smile. "So you *have* heard of him?"

"Of course."

And as I remembered, the Midnight Strangler had so far claimed seven victims, all of them men. The group had included a sociology professor, chiropractor, dentist, school bus driver, tool and die maker, sewer inspector, and linoleum layer—all of them between the ages of 46 and 54.

Actually the appellation Nine O'Clock Strangler would have been more apt, though not as catchy. All the victims seemed to have been pounced on by the strangler after they parked their automobiles for the evening in their respective driveways, garages, or breezeways, the deaths occurring between the hours of eight and ten. And on each of their foreheads there had been imprinted—apparently with a rubber stamp—the words, "Sinners must pay."

The door opened and a tall thin man whose expression indicated a headache, entered the room.

McGillicutty introduced him. "This is Sergeant Wiggins."

Wiggins regarded me curiously. "Has anybody read him his rights?"

McGillicutty thought about that. "Come to think of it, no. In all the excitement we forgot." He turned to me. "You have the right to remain silent. You have . . ." He faltered. "How does it go, Wiggins?"

"It's on that little celluloid card, Captain. The one we're supposed to carry on our persons at all times."

McGillicutty smiled patiently. "I haven't personally made an arrest in ten years and I don't know where my damn card is."

Wiggins handed his over and McGillicutty read the words. That over, he returned the card and said, "Well, do you want a lawyer?"

"I don't think that will be necessary."

Wiggins showed teeth. "Believe me, it will be necessary." He seemed rather happy about my situation. "Is there anything we can do to make you feel more comfortable? Care for a cigarette? Coffee? Can I hang up your topcoat? Should we send out for sandwiches?"

I declined the food, drink, and cigarette, but handed him my topcoat, after first removing Theobault's card from the pocket. "Gentlemen, I am not your Midnight Strangler. My name is Henry Turnbuckle and I am a bonded licensed private detective based in Milwaukee, as you have no doubt ascertained from the credentials in my wallet."

Wiggins blinked. "Is that right, Captain? Is he a private detective?"

McGillicutty nodded. "That's what his wallet says. But I don't take that as a guarantee that he can't be the Midnight Strangler."

I examined Theobault's card once more. "I am utterly innocent and therefore do not require legal aid. However I am rather curious about what I could get. Would I be going wrong if I sought to retain a Clarence Darrow Theobault of your city? I believe that he's downstairs at this very moment."

McGillicutty scowled at the mention of the name. "All right, Wiggins, see if Theobault's downstairs. And he probably is. This is his kind of case."

Wiggins returned in ten minutes with a tall loping individual whose arms seemed a bit long for his body.

His large powerful hand enveloped mine in a pressure grip. "My name is Theobault. Clarence Darrow Theobault. Perhaps you've heard of me? I *do* hope you haven't told the police anything? And if you have it was undoubtedly under duress."

"So far I have had the opportunity to give hardly more than my name and occupation."

He rubbed his hands. "Excellent. Very clever and clear-headed of you." He turned to McGillicutty. "I would like to speak to my client alone."

Theobault watched them leave and then regarded me with a somewhat sharkish smile.

"One moment," I said quickly. "I have not officially retained you as yet. Let us first establish that this is a preliminary conference and that it does not cost me one red cent."

"But of course, of course," Theobault said. "You are under no obligation."

"How much do you charge for defending a man accused of murder?"

He chuckled. "My dear sir, there are no set fees in matters like this. One cannot anticipate the expenses involved. My fees are elastic, but one must not really be concerned with mere money at a time like this. Your life is at stake. We must see that you receive at least a lengthy trial. By the way, what *is* your profession?"

"I am a private detective."

He gave that dubious thought. "You are the head of an agency? Or at least an executive in the firm?"

"No. I don't even have a secretary. Frankly, the private detecting business hasn't been going all that well. Maybe I should plead indigence and have the court appoint an attorney for me?"

He quickly closed the gap. "Nonsense, nonsense. All is not lost. This is much too important a case to entrust to some fledgling lawyer. We will come to some mutually acceptable monetary arrangement, I am sure. Now, we will plead not guilty by reason of insanity."

"But I am innocent. And sane."

"Of course you are. Of course." He sat down beside me and lowered his voice slightly. "Now, I don't want you to say a single word to any newspaper reporter, or to any writer for a magazine, and don't talk into anybody's tape recorder. Tell those people to come to me first. I'll be handling your affairs and we've got to keep exclusive rights. There's no point in handing out anything for free. We get a cut of all the action and that includes interviews, tapes, television, and the movies."

I frowned. "It was my understanding that a murderer is not allowed to profit from his crimes."

Theobault laughed lightly. "Of course a murderer is not allowed to profit from his crime. But, after all, he's got to have money if he wants to be defended by a competent, experienced attorney and that isn't *really* profiting from his crime, now is it? Besides, there are all kinds of technicalities involved. A *sane* murderer obviously shouldn't be allowed to profit from his crime. But does this hold true for an *insane* murderer? After all, can he be held responsible if somehow he picked up a buck or two? It's just something that happened to him. Like an act of God. Leave everything to me."

"Do you think you can get me an acquittal?"

He winced. "That would kill our movie sale. Who cares about the life story of an innocent man?"

There was a knock on the door and it opened. McGillicutty looked in. "Are you two through yet?"

I nodded. "I rather think so."

Theobault patted my shoulder. "Don't answer any questions unless I give you the nod."

McGillicutty and Wiggins brought a third man into the room. "This is Oscar Vandermeir."

Oscar Vandermeir was a hulking pot-bellied man with large baby-blue eyes. He stared at me curiously. "So this is the Midnight Strangler?"

McGillicutty nodded. "Have you ever seen him before?"

Vandermeir walked first to one side of me and then to the other. "Well, he's not one of my customers. Unless maybe he wore a beard. But actually he's not the type which comes into my store at all. Mostly they're late middle-age and ninety-nine percent of them are men. But what with this Women's Lib, who knows but what that might change. And usually they're single, though I suppose once in a while I get a married man."

Theobault spoke up. "Just who is this man and what does he have to do with the case against my client?"

McGillicutty smiled. "Mr. Vandermeir is the proprietor of the AAA Acme Adult Book Store. Perhaps you've heard of it, eh, Turnbuckle?" He turned back to Vandermeir. "All right, Oscar, tell them all about it."

"Well," Vandermeir said, "I'm not the type of person who goes to the police. Usually they come to me. Or at least they did a lot. But times change." He side-tracked in reminiscence. "In the old days I had to fill my store with those dusty second-hand books that were classics and so on. I kept the real stuff in the back room. And you never knew which customer might be a cop. I'd get arrested half a dozen times a year and my place was once shut down for sixty days. But things are different now. More honest. More sophisticated. No hypocrisy." His blue eyes were thoughtful. "Except maybe for the word adult."

McGillicutty prodded him back. "Get on with the story."

Vandermeir nodded. "Anyway, I don't read the papers much. All that print is bad for the eyes. But I heard people talk about the Midnight Strangler and so when he wipes out his fifth man, I get hold of a newspaper and lo and behold the picture on the front page is that of one of my best customers, though I don't know his name until I read it. My clientele don't usually volunteer names unless they want to get on a special mailing list.

"So I think, what a coincidence, and nothing more. Then comes the sixth murder and I see that I lost another good customer.

"But still two coincidences don't make enough coincidences for me to go to the cops. But I wait for number seven. And sure enough, again it's one of my regulars who's deep into flagellation among Transylvanians. So I decided that I ought to tell the police, even though they never done anything for me. And here at headquarters I look at pictures of all the other victims and I recognize all but two."

I rubbed my jaw. "Why would the strangler kill five people who were your customers and two who were not?"

Vandermeir shrugged. "I'm not saying those two weren't my customers. I'm just saying I didn't recognize them. A lot of my people feel that they got to wear false beards and mustaches and wear dark-green glasses."

"Ah, yes," I said wisely. "Apparently the strangler feels strongly about the kind of people who patronize adult bookstores and thus make them profitable to operate. He feels justified—possibly even cosmically called upon—to rid the world of sin. This particular kind, anyway."

McGillicutty regarded me pointedly. "Why didn't this strangler just kill Vandermeir and get it over with?"

I shrugged. "I rather suspect that he was saving Vandermeir as the *pièce de resistance.*"

McGillicutty folded his arms. "We've had a stakeout on Vandermeir's store for two days now. We saw one of his customers come out of the store, and we saw you step out of a dark doorway and follow him."

"That was Homer Schleigel," I said.

"And who is Homer Schleigel?"

"Once a week, on Thursdays, Homer Schleigel goes bowling. Or he claims to. Only last week he forgot to take his bowling ball along. When he got back home at about eleven that night, his wife asked him how the bowling had gone, meaning to twit him on forgetting his ball and assuming that he had been forced to use one of the balls provided to the public by bowling alleys. He said, fine, fine, that he'd rolled a 600 series, and that the old ball was operating better than ever.

"His wife lapsed into silence and suspicion. The next day she phoned Hanlon's Pizza, which was the name on the back of her husband's bowling shirt, and discovered that Homer had quit the team some six months before. She would have followed him the next Thursday—which is today—except that they aren't a two-car family. So she hired me to find out what he's been up to."

I called to mind Homer's movements. "He left Milwaukee at six-thirty. It is a half an hour drive south to this city. He put his car in the Apex Parking Lot. He then walked to the Tivoli, where he saw *Deeper Esophagus,* which I understand is a sequel. At its conclusion he stopped in at Mac's Malt Shop for a pistachio sundae. He then resumed walking with a purpose, eventually entering Vandermeir's establishment. He did some extensive browsing and then made a few purchases. He returned to the Apex Parking Lot and reclaimed his auto. I was about to do the same for my vehicle and follow him when you people descended on me. Homer is probably back in Milwaukee by now."

Sergeant Wiggins had been listening hostilely. "I got no use for private detectives."

I sighed. "I had hoped to ride out this storm on my own strength, however I see that I do need help. Actually I am a member of the Milwaukee police department. I believe that should carry some weight. At the moment I am on educational leave. I am working on my masters degree and my subject is the function of the private detective in our society and it seemed to me that I could hardly learn more about the field than by becoming a private detective myself."

McGillicutty turned to Sergeant Wiggins. "Check that out."

Wiggins left the room and McGillicutty also excused Vandermeir.

He got back to me. "Just because you're a regular cop doesn't mean that you automatically can't be the strangler. We'll check you out and we'll check you out good."

My eyes had been drawn to my topcoat hanging on the wall peg. I distinctly remembered reaching into the right-hand pocket for a handkerchief, finding none, but instead finding Theobault's card. That pocket should now be empty, and yet there seemed to be a slight bulge there. It rather piqued my curiosity.

I rose and went to the coat. I slipped my hand into the pocket and it closed on an object. I pulled it out. It was a small rubber stamp. I tested it on the back of my hand and could just make out the faint words, "Sinners must pay."

"Well," I said accurately. "Well, *well.*"

McGillicutty had, of course, been watching me. So had Theobault. The latter rose to his feet. "Turnbuckle," he commanded. "Don't say another word."

"Shut up," McGillicutty said, and I rather agreed with him. McGillicutty and I sat down again, facing each other. McGillicutty began darkly to think.

"Captain," I said, "when I was arrested, I was thoroughly searched, was I not?"

He agreed reluctantly. "I searched you myself. No stamp." He sighed. "The strangler knew that we were watching the store. Hell, he probably saw us—there were enough of us scattered around. He saw us pick you up. He realized that if we were watching Vandermeir's store that we must have found the key to the string of murders. He decided he might as well call it quits. He also figured that was a good opportunity to nail the case down so that we wouldn't be looking for the strangler any more. He rushed over to the station, waited in the crowd, and while you were being hustled through he planted the stamp in your pocket. Just like Theobault planted the card."

McGillicutty eyed Theobault.

Theobault flushed. "I am not the strangler. All I slipped into Turnbuckle's pocket was my card." Nevertheless, he looked down at his huge hands and seemed to be trying to think them small.

"No, Captain," I said. "Theobault did not slip the stamp into my pocket. When I came into this room, I reached into that pocket for a handkerchief. I found no handkerchief, but I did find his card. However, *only* his card. No rubber stamp."

McGillicutty frowned. "You mean that the stamp was planted in your pocket *after* you got into this room?"

"That's right, Captain."

His eyes narrowed. "Are you saying that *I* planted that stamp in your coat?"

"No. I have been sitting here in this chair and the topcoat has been in my sight continuously. I know that you did not approach it."

"Vandermeir? He murders his own customers because he's got a guilt complex about how he makes his money?"

"No. Not Vandermeir either."

"Then who the hell else is there?"

"Captain, was Sergeant Wiggins on the stakeout at Vandermeir's store?"

"No, this was strictly a homicide show."

"Isn't Wiggins in Homicide?"

"No, he's with the vice squad. But naturally he's got an interest in the case and so I sent for him when I brought you in."

"Captain," I said, "the only person who touched my topcoat after

I entered this room was Sergeant Wiggins when he so graciously hung it on that peg."

McGillicutty closed his eyes.

I nodded. "Wiggins was here at headquarters when you brought me in and he realized that this was a perfect opportunity to frame me and close the case. Evidently he didn't have the opportunity to slip the stamp into my pocket as I was being pushed through the crowd downstairs. Or he simply didn't have the stamp on him. But it must have been near somewhere, because between the time I arrived here at headquarters and the time he appeared in this room I doubt if he would have had time to drive home, retrieve the stamp, and return."

McGillicutty sighed. "He lives way out near the county line—at least an hour round trip. And he's been pretty upset about the new porno laws. And he's got those damn headaches all the time . . ."

"He was hoping I would be searched again as a matter of routine and the stamp found. Or he might have even planned to suggest another search himself."

I put the stamp back into the pocket of my topcoat and returned it to the wall peg. "However, I wager that now Wiggins will attempt to *unframe* me."

That got McGillicutty's attention. "Unframe?"

"Yes. Because it is one thing to frame a simple private detective for murder, but it is quite another to attempt to do the same to a legitimate policeman who has the rank of detective-sergeant and an unblemished record. Too many questions would be asked, there would be too much probing, and the truth would probably come out. No, Wiggins has to unframe me now."

"And how is he going to do that?"

"When he returns and sees that we have apparently not yet found the stamp, he will invent some reason for approaching my topcoat. He will surreptitiously remove the stamp."

Wiggins returned some five minutes later. "He's a cop all right, Captain. A detective-sergeant." Wiggins licked his lips. "Well, I suppose we'll just have to hand him his topcoat and let him go. Right? We all made a mistake." He moved to the topcoat and for perhaps two or three seconds his back effectively shielded it from our view.

He turned and brought me the coat.

McGillicutty and I studied the contours of Wiggins' suit and probably arrived at the mutual suspicion that the small bulge in the right side pocket of his suitcoat was now formed by a rubber stamp.

"Wiggins," McGillicutty said, "what is that bulge in your right-hand pocket?"

Wiggins did not look down. "Nothing, Captain. Nothing. Maybe my key ring or something."

McGillicutty was insistent. "Let's see it, Wiggins."

"Captain," I said. "When one finds a rubber stamp, can a stamp pad be far behind? You don't suppose that if we looked in his locker, or perhaps in his automobile, we might find a stamp pad and that if this stamp pad were subjected to laboratory scrutiny we might even find on this pad several vestigial impressions of the words, 'Sinners must pay'?"

Wiggins lost his color. "Damn you, nobody has the right to search my car." Then he stared at the revolver Captain McGillicutty had pointed at him and he pulled himself together. "I refuse to say another word until I see my lawyer."

Theobault rose and rubbed his huge hands. "If you don't mind, Captain, I'd like to speak to my client alone."

Ernest Savage

Mr. Fixit

*She didn't even know who Dr. Mortimer was, but he had phoned
and given her Mr. Fixit's name. "For that leaky sink, and any
other problem you've got. Yes, Mr. Fixit's your man."*

*A touching and delicately woven story that will take you up to
but not through "that light-filled door" . . .*

He hadn't wanted to take the job, but she'd been so persuasive
over the phone and had—somehow—sounded so much like Millie that he'd agreed to at least talk to her about it.

But the next morning at her front door he still didn't want the job
and was prepared to tell her so when two things occurred at once—he
got his first good look at her eyes, and the left-rear tire of his van
parked in her driveway blew out with a loud bang.

"Good heavens!" she said, recoiling a ladylike distance, her eyes
wide and luminous. "How clever you are."

He had not, of course, staged the event, and either her naivete or
wit—whichever it might have been—annoyed him. But there were
those eyes. How was it that frail and delicate women of a certain
vintage had eyes of that special provenance?—from, say, Cartier's?
As Millie's had been toward the end. Jewels glowing with a deep
inner fire. You never saw them in the young or the fat or the healthy.
Ah, the healthy.

"Come in," she said, pulling the door wide, but he still didn't want
to. And if that damn tire hadn't blown out just then, he would've
excused himself and driven away. But willy-nilly now, he was stuck
in her driveway for at least a half hour and he might as well see
what she wanted. He followed her into the dark hall and through
a door to the kitchen. She had mentioned the kitchen over the phone.

"There," she said, pointing. "The sink. And cabinets."

Well indeed, there was work there—too much of it. He could see
the stains of dry rot where the old linoleum butted against the
cabinet base; which meant, of course, that he'd have to tear out
everything down to the joists below and replace it *all*. Four or five

33

hard days of work for one man and he didn't want it; it was too soon, too soon after Millie's death. He'd not yet found the new path to follow with his life—but surely, he kept thinking, it wasn't more of this, more of the same. He turned, hard-faced.

"I can recommend a man to—" The eyes stopped him cold, staring from the door. Did they never blink?

"I wanted you," she said firmly. "*You* were recommended. You are Mr. Fixit, are you not? Your van says so."

The legend MR. FIXIT was painted on the side of the van clearly visible through the kitchen windows. Yes, he was Mr. Fixit and had been for the five years Millie had spent dying. Before her affliction, he'd run his little store downtown, but when she began needing his attention every several hours day and night, he tailored his work to suit that need. He could not have afforded outside help, and wouldn't have wanted it anyway. Luckily he had, in earlier years, developed the skills necessary to do almost any household-repair job and he'd become a handyman, Mr. Fixit.

But he did not intend to remain one, and with Millie gone a month now there was no need to. There were other things he could do, other places he could go, a whole world out there, and at 60 he still had time to explore it, to find his intended path. He knew it was not merely repairing kitchens.

"Please," she said; and he thought, well, this one last time, but by God she'll pay for it.

"It'll be expensive," he said gruffly, "and perhaps not worth it to you. I mean, the sink *works* at least, doesn't it? So what if it leaks a little? I mean, why not just let it go? None of us live forever, ma'am, and no offense intended, but you—" Well, no, he couldn't tell her her hold on life was palpably weak, even to a lay eye, that the new sink might not even arrive before— No, there were limits.

"I want you to do it," she said, almost imperiously, the large eyes blinking twice now, as though to hold back tears.

"I charge seven dollars an hour," he continued, thinking to blow her out of the water with the sheer cost. It was two dollars more than he'd ever charged before.

"That's all right," she said.

"Eight dollars if you watch me."

"That's all right."

"Nine dollars if you talk to me."

"Please—" She seemed frightened.

"Ten dollars if you tell me how to do it!" His voice had crescendoed in unexpected anger and she backed slightly out of the room. "And I get paid every night before I leave," he said. "In cash. Not a check, but cash."

"It's all right," she whispered.

"Too damn many people have cheated me," he said. "The laborer is worthy of his hire, but some people don't seem to think so. You'd be surprised how many people in this town owe me money for work done!" His voice was rising again. "I collect in cash at the end of every day—do you understand?"

"Yes—it's all right."

She had remained just outside the kitchen door in the gloom of the unlit hall and it was amazing how much she looked—just then—like Millie. Those glittering eyes set in the tightening silvery skin of the drawn face. The narrow shoulders hunched up against his anger—or some implacable inner pain. The formless dress, hanging straight as laundry on a line on a windless day. Lord God, how he had loved her! Can anyone understand how much love it had taken to do what he had done?

"And I'll want two hours for lunch," he said, more gently now. "I go home for lunch."

"It's all right," she said again.

They sometimes didn't understand that he had to have two hours in the middle of the day to tend Millie and do the chores. He had discovered early that if he let the dishes go, even for one day, or the endless laundry, or anything, that it seemed to become almost insurmountable and would bury him alive. And Millie's flowers— Always, every noon, he gathered flowers from the garden and arranged them in the vase by her bed. He was good with flowers—he had the hands both to grow and to arrange them. Artist's hands, Millie had said. Creative.

He smiled at the memory and the woman saw it and stepped tentatively back into the kitchen.

"When?" she said.

"I'll start tomorrow."

"And finish—?"

"When I'm done," he said. "It won't be soon. Do you like flowers?"

"My husband—when he was alive—we had a garden."

"And now?"

"I can't." Her hands, he saw, were lumpy, like gnarled pink clubs. She drew them behind the edges of her dress out of his sight, and her eyes closed for a moment.

She had been a beautiful woman once; not, he thought, so long ago.

"When did he die?"

"Three years."

Her eyes closed again, slowly, as though of their own inexorable weight, and he stared at her until they opened again.

"I'll start this afternoon," he said.

He could not understand the flat tire on the truck. Outside, he looked at it as though it had betrayed him, which it had, he thought. If it had not blown when it did—and for no visible reason—he would be home by now sorting out his life, or trying to. More important to get your life sorted out than to replace some leaky sink.

He got out the jack and changed the tire. It took him twenty minutes. He would put it on her bill.

He brought her roses, a dozen or so mixed long stems from his yard. He'd always liked the way a random color-mix of roses looked in a tall slender vase—the vase was important—and even though the one she gave him was too fat, his arrangement looked fine on the kitchen table in a patch of sun there. It was the first thing he did when he returned that afternoon and it amazed her. His arrangement of the flowers was exquisite, a Renoir still life, and she could not believe the roughness with which those same hands attacked the sink a few moments later.

"Eight dollars an hour if you watch me," he said, his old gruff self.

"I'm looking at the flowers," she said spunkily.

"Nevertheless you're in the room."

"I'll pay it," she said.

He amazed and frightened her. He *must* be the man because he was the man Dr. Mortimer had recommended, and Dr. Mortimer had called her, not vice-versa. She didn't even know who Dr. Mortimer was—someone from the Coroner's office, had he said?—had never even heard of him until he'd phoned and given her Mr. Fixit's name. "For that leaky sink," he'd said, "and any other problem you've got. Yes, Mr. Fixit's your man."

"Who are you—?" she'd started to say, but he'd cut her off.

"Oh, and remember," he'd said sharply. "Mr. Fixit works only for cash. No checks, just cash. Every night."

He was on his back now, under the sink, his legs sticking out onto the worn linoleum of the floor, his big battered work boots lolling there for a moment as though asleep. David had had a pair of boots like that—she supposed all men did—and he'd be doing this job now if he were still alive. Tears welled in her eyes, rendering prismatic the roses in the vase. Dying suddenly like that—in full stride—as it were—and leaving her to struggle on alone. What a blessed way to go!—all at once instead of one crumbling pain-wracked piece at a time.

The sink was older than God, he thought; cast-iron, heavy as a battleship. He would replace it with stainless steel and the corroded metal pipes below with plastic. He'd done a hundred jobs like this, his hands and tools moving almost without conscious direction. It was easy—and dull, deadly dull, and no way to spend your life. Before—with Millie alive—he'd had no choice and thus no nagging doubts. He'd never thought about his work, he'd just done it and then hurried home. But now— He had no sense of vocation. This was not really what he was meant to do with these hands and this life, and it depressed him now as it never had before.

He quit at five that afternoon. It was no longer necessary that he quit at five and rush home to Millie, but the habit of years wouldn't be broken overnight. Besides, the job was not going right, fighting him at every turn; an unfriendly job, almost an enemy job.

He wiped his hands clean on a rag and said, "I'll take my money now."

She was still seated at the kitchen table, reading. She got up awkwardly, painfully. "It's in the bedroom," she said. "Come."

"Bring it to me here."

"No!" She faced him, dander up, cheeks pink with the rush of blood. She'd thought that it might happen now, at the end of the first day, and she didn't want it to happen in the kitchen. She felt firm and righteous about it. She had some say in the matter after all, didn't she?—and she'd been a fighter all her life. "In the bedroom," she said stoutly, and turned and walked through the open door to the hall. He shrugged and followed.

After talking with Dr. Mortimer, she'd closed her savings account at the bank and brought the money home, several thousand dollars in small bills. It was in a gray metal box on her bedside table, the lid open.

"That'll be four and a half hours," he said, "including changing the tire. Times eight. Thirty-six dollars—even."

The unfairness of it riled her suddenly. "But I didn't *talk* to you after that first minute or two."

"You were in the room—it's the same thing."

"It isn't! And the tire had nothing to do with me!" She stamped her foot and felt pain rush through her body and gather in her neck and head, as it always did. She could have screamed with it, her eyes wide with it, the pain burning in them like fire.

"Lie down!" he ordered quickly, and she almost fell onto the bed. He rolled her onto her face and his hands seemed to circle her neck, pressing gently, and the pain receded at once, a light airy sense filling her mind, as though she'd drifted free from her body and all that it was. She groaned. It was a wonderful relief.

But then his hands lifted and she returned to her body and its pain, and she groaned again and said, "More," a whisper, a prayer.

He was taking money from the box, counting off three tens, a five, and a one. He looked at her angrily. "You shouldn't have anything like this much money in the house," he said. "What about burglars?" He was angry at her because he didn't love her—and what right had *she* to need his hands on her as Millie had? You had to love a person to help them in that special way and he couldn't just turn it on, could he? "There must be thousands here," he growled.

"Take it," she said. "It's for you. Dr. Mortimer—"

"What do you mean 'Take it'? What do you think I am, some kind of crook?" He stuffed the $36 in his pocket and strode to the door of the room, whirling there to look back at her. He was going to tell her he quit, but she was so frail and thin as to seem almost printed on the surface of the bed, and his anger waned.

"I'll be here at nine tomorrow," he said, and then amended it to "eight tomorrow," remembering he needn't spend so much time at home any more.

In the four hours before noon the next day he got a great deal done and was well pleased with himself. And not at all displeased with her. She had sat in perfect silence all morning at the kitchen table, reading, and now again sniffing at the roses, which, even though just half open, nearly filled the window frame behind them.

From the little distance away she looked pretty sitting there, her misshapen hands hidden in her lap, and he felt a surge of sympathy for her, almost of affection. He asked her if she liked pizza and she said she did and he went out and got one for their lunch while she made coffee. She could make coffee, at least, and open cans with the electric opener, but not much else.

The afternoon went as well as the morning had and he didn't quit until nearly six o'clock.

"Couple more days at this rate," he bragged, "and I'll have 'er done."

"Oh?" she said, surprised. "All of it?"

"Of course all of it. I don't leave loose ends, lady."

"Thursday then," she said, looking at the roses, and then out the window for a moment—at infinity. "Thursday will be fine. Thursday." She repeated it quietly to herself, getting the sense of it. Just two more days. After so many thousands of them.

She got up and led him to the bedroom again and asked him how much this time and he hemmed and hawed before answering, less assertive today. "Seven," he said finally. "Times seven. Forty-nine dollars."

"But you worked longer than that," she said. "Nearly nine hours. And then there's the matter of the pizza."

"My treat," he said. "Forty-nine is enough. Fifty. Make it fifty even."

She took five ten-dollar bills from the gray metal box and handed them to him. She would not argue tonight, one way or the other. But she would ask, "Would you—please—the neck again? It was such a relief. It was almost as though—a kind of preview." She closed her eyes and swayed a bit in delicious recall and he caught her arms in his hands and then dropped them as though they'd turned hot.

"I know," she said, her eyes open again, and hurt, almost ashamed. "It must be—repellent—to touch me. Anywhere."

"It's not that," he said angrily, and caught her fleshless arms again in his hands. "I'm used to it. It's just that—I have no right, only love gives you the right."

"Love! What has love to do with it? You have the gift—it's in your hands—I felt it there. Is not pity enough? Is not money? Empty the box, but for God's sake give me your hands! Dr. Mortimer did not say you'd fight me! You are Mr. Fixit, aren't you?"

"Who's Dr. Mortimer?"

"He recommended you."

He could remember no Dr. Mortimer, but he'd had dozens, even hundreds of customers down through the years. It didn't matter. "Of course I'm Mr. Fixit," he said, and drew her gently against his chest, his hands sliding up her spine to the neck, and that detached feeling starting almost at once for her, that sense of flight, of freedom—

"Oh, God—" She sighed against his chest, slumping there, her body almost empty of feeling, her knees melting. He caught her and put her on the bed and her big eyes flinched as the pain surged back again. "More," she pleaded, almost inaudibly, but he was standing now, his hands at his sides. He took the comforter from the foot of the bed and drew it up around her chin. Then he kissed her lightly on the forehead and told her to sleep, and she tried, searching for that distant point of balance where the pain would be like a fire at which she could merely warm herself.

He was there earlier the next day, and stayed later. He brought enough lunch for them both and ate his while he worked. He felt committed to being done with the job—paint and all—by Thursday night. He'd promised her and he saw in her eyes the need for that promise to be fulfilled. Besides, he felt a growing affection for her, for her courage, for her Millie-like qualities.

During the long painful years of Millie's decline he had not realized there must be other women out there in similar agony, but alone, with no loving husband to serve and protect them and finally, when the time came, to guide them through that light-filled door. Now he knew; and simply knowing was a source of love.

That night, before he left, he took just a few dollars from the gray metal box. He didn't really need money any more, with Millie gone. Then he eased her pain for a few moments with his hands, covered her with the comforter and kissed her. He didn't leave until he knew she'd found sleep again.

He was finished the next day by five o'clock and sat down at the kitchen table with her, tired. It was almost, he thought for a moment, like being home, like being with his wife again. He smiled at her and reached across the table and touched her hands, which she no longer felt the need to hide from him. The roses, alongside, had reached their peak of perfection and were awesome in their beauty. But already several petals had fallen to the table below.

"They too," she said to him, and felt a chill sweep her flesh. *He was through now.* Her eyes were enormous. She got up and walked from the room and he followed.

She insisted on paying him full count for the day's work, eight dollars for each of eight hours. $64. She made him put it in his wallet. She wanted no laxity now, nothing less than full measure, either way.

He took her shoulders in his hands and pulled her against his chest. He was happy with her there, she belonged there. He felt love for her, unforced, natural. His lips brushed her forehead and his hands moved up her spine for the last time to her neck. Her knees buckled then and he picked her up and placed her gently on the bed, his hands barely pressing her throat, the sinewy sides of her neck, softly probing, knowing more in themselves than he knew or wanted to know. He could almost feel her leaving, as Millie had left, almost feel her slip between his fingers and brush by as she rose.

He remained over her for three or four minutes and then straightened, exhausted. Her eyes were half open and he closed them and kissed her once more on the pale brow. Then he covered her with the comforter, tucking it carefully beneath her chin.

Then he went into the kitchen, gathered up his tools, and went home.

She had the same kind of voice and he told her over the phone that he'd come by at eight in the morning.

It was the same kind of house, too, old, the shingles curling on the roof, the peeling paint. He stopped for a moment in front and then pulled into the driveway.

And the same kind of eyes—huge, aglow with the heat of a ceaseless fight. The same loose shapeless dress.

He didn't enter when she bade him. Instead he said, "Who recommended me?"

"What does it matter?" The same spunky voice.

"Was it Dr. Mortimer?"

"Yes."

"Is he your doctor?"

"No. I'd never heard of him before. He called me. He said he was with—" She paused, frowning.

"Yes?"

"The Coroner's office, I believe. I talked to him but once, yesterday. You *are* Mr. Fixit, aren't you?" The big eager eyes glanced at the truck with the name on the side.

He nodded; and once again refused her almost imperious demand that he enter. "Later," he said, his eyes flicking at the truck as though to say, "Quiet—patience," to the tires. "This afternoon at one. I get seven dollars an hour, in cash."

"I know what you get. Plus one if I talk to you."

It pleased him that she knew. He grinned. "Yes. I'll be back at one."

At the Coroner's office a lady clerk said to him, "Dr. Mortimer? Just a moment, please." She went away and returned in a minute with a man in a full-length white smock. She said, "This is Dr. Jackson."

Dr. Jackson put out his hand, had it shaken, and said, "Dr. Mortimer is not a member of our staff. Perhaps I can help you."

"Do you know Dr. Mortimer?"

"Of course. He's one of the finest pathologists I've ever seen work."

"Here? He's worked here?"

"Why, yes, of course. As a specialist. He assisted on a case just last week."

"A little old lady found dead in her bed?"

"Why, yes. How—?"

"And before that?"

"Well, last month—"

"Another little old lady?"

"Why, yes, I believe so. But—"

"Where can I get hold of Dr. Mortimer?"

"Ah—well, let me see. I believe he's with the University."

"Here in town?"

"Well—no, I believe another branch. Or perhaps—"

"What?"

"Well, come to think of it, I believe he mentioned an eastern school—Dartmouth? Harvard? I'm not sure."

"What does he look like?"

"Ah, well now— let's see, he's—"

"Tall? Short?"

"Hmmmm."

"White? Black? Brown?"

"Not brown, if I remember, but—well, maybe. By George, what color was the man?"

Mr. Fixit smiled. "I guess we'll never know," he said, and turned and walked away.

When he got to the little old lady's house that afternoon, he had a dozen long-stem roses in his hand, and, for the first time in his life, a sense of vocation—a calling.

And a partner.

Donald E. Westlake

The Girl of My Dreams

The unusual—even extraordinary—tale of a mugging, of a beautiful girl in danger, of a shirt salesman in a clothing store who becomes a shining knight . . . Why unusual, even extraordinary? Well, read the story and judge for yourself. We promise you won't forget it, perhaps never . . .

Yesterday I bought a gun.
I'm very confused; I don't know what to do.
I have always been a mild and shy young man, quiet and conservative and polite. I have been employed the last five years—since at 19 I left college because of lack of funds—at the shirt counter of Willis & DeKalb, Men's Clothiers, Stores in Principal Cities, and I would say that I have been generally content with my lot. Although recently I have been finding the new manager, Mr. Miller, somewhat abrasive—not to overstate the matter—the work itself has always been agreeable, and I have continued to look forward to a quiet lifetime in the same employment.

I have never been much of a dreamer, neither by day nor by night. Reveries, daydreams, these are the products of vaulting ambition or vaulting desire, of both of which I have remained for the most part gratefully free. And though science assures us that some part of every night's sleep is spent in the manufacture of dreams, mine must normally be gentle and innocuous, even dull, as I rarely remember them in the morning.

I would date the beginning of the change in my life from the moment of the retirement of old Mr. Randmunson from his post as manager of our local Willis & DeKalb store, and his prompt replacement by Mr. Miller, a stranger from the Akron branch.

Mr. Miller is a hearty man, cheeks and nose all red with ruddy health, handshake painfully firm, voice roaring, laugh aggressive. Not yet 35, he moves and speaks with the authority and self-confidence of a man much older, and he makes it no secret that some day he intends to be president of the entire chain. Our little store

43

is merely a stopover for him, another rung upward on the ladder of his success.

His first day in the store, he came to me, ebullient and over-powering and supremely positive. He asked my opinion, he discussed business and geography and entertainment, he offered me a ciga-rette, he thumped my shoulder. "We'll get along, Ronald!" he told me. "Just keep moving those shirts!"

"Yes, Mr. Miller."

"And let me have an inventory list, by style and size, tomorrow morning."

"Sir?"

"Any time before noon," he said carelessly, and laughed, and thumped my shoulder. "We'll have a great team here, Ronald, a first-rate team!"

Two nights later I dreamed for the first time of Delia.

I went to bed as usual at 11:40, after the news on channel six. I switched out the light, went to sleep, and in utter simplicity and clarity the dream began. In it I was driving my automobile on West-ern Avenue, out from the center of town, It was all thoroughly realistic—the day, the traffic, the used-car lots along Western Av-enue all gleaming in the spring sun. My six-year-old Plymouth was pulling just a little to the right, exactly as it does in real life. I knew I was dreaming, but at the same time it was very pleasant to be in my car on Western Avenue on such a lovely spring day.

A scream startled me, and my foot trod reflexively on the brake pedal. Nearby, on the sidewalk, a man and girl were struggling together. He was trying to wrest a package from her but she was resisting, clutching the package tight with both arms around it, and again screaming. The package was wrapped in brown paper and was about the size and shape of a suit carton from Willis & DeKalb.

I want to emphasize that everything was very realistic, down to the smallest detail. There were none of the abrupt shifts in time or space or viewpoint normally associated with dreams, no impossi-bilities or absurdities.

There was no one else on the sidewalk nearby, and I acted almost without thinking. Braking my Plymouth at the curb, I leaped out, ran around the car, and began to grapple with the girl's attacker. He was wearing brown corduroy trousers and a black leather jacket and he needed a shave. His breath was bad.

"Leave her alone!" I shouted, while the girl continued to scream. The mugger had to give up his grip on the package in order to deal with me. He pushed me away and I staggered ineffectively backward just as I would do in real life, while the girl kicked him repeatedly in the shins. As soon as I regained my balance I rushed forward again, and now he decided he'd had enough. He turned tail and ran, down Western Avenue and through a used-car lot and so out of sight.

The girl, breathing hard, still clutching the package to her breast, turned to smile gratefully on me and say, "How can I ever thank you?"

What a beautiful girl! The most beautiful girl I have ever seen, before or since. Auburn hair and lovely features, deep clear hazel eyes, slender wrists with every delicate birdlike bone outlined beneath the tender skin. She wore a blue and white spring dress and casual white shoes. Silver teardrops graced her graceful ears.

She gazed at me with her melting, warm, companionable eyes, and she smiled at me with lips that murmured to be kissed, and she said to me, "How can I ever thank you?" in a voice as dulcet as honey.

And there the dream ended, in extreme closeup on my Delia's face.

I awoke the next morning in a state of euphoria. The dream was still vivid in my mind in every detail, and most particularly I remembered the look of her sweet face at the end. That face stayed with me throughout the day, a day which otherwise might have been only bitter, as it was on that day Mr. Miller gave the two-week notice to my friend and co-worker Gregory Shostrill of the stockroom. I shared, of course, the employees' general indignation that such an old and loyal worker had been so summarily dismissed, but for me the outrage was tempered by the continuing memory of last night's wonderful dream.

I never anticipated for a second that I would ever see my dream girl again, but that night she returned to me, and my astonishment was only matched by my delight. I went to bed at my usual hour, fell asleep, and the dream began. It started precisely where, the night before, it had ended, with the beautiful girl saying to me, "How can I ever thank you?"

I now functioned at two levels of awareness. The first, in which I knew myself to be dreaming, was flabbergasted to find the dream picking up as though no day had elapsed, no break at all had taken place in the unfolding of this story. The second level, in which I was an active participant in the dream rather than its observer, treated this resumption of events as natural and inevitable and obvious, and reacted without delay.

It was this second level which replied, "Anyone would have done what I did," and then added, "May I drive you wherever you're going?"

Now here, I grant, the dream had begun to be somewhat less than realistic. That I should talk with this lovely creature so effortlessly, without stammering, without blushing, with no worms of terror crawling within my skull, was not entirely as the same scene would have been played in real life. In this situation, in reality, I might have attacked the mugger as I'd done in the dream, but on being left alone with the girl afterward I would surely have been reduced to a strained smile and a strangled silence.

But not in the dream. In the dream I was gallant and effortless, as I offered to drive her wherever she was going.

"If it wouldn't be putting you out of your way—"

"Not in the least," I assured her. "Where are you going?"

"Home," she said. "Summit Street. Do you know it?"

"Of course. It's right on my way."

Which wasn't at all true. Summit Street, tucked away in the Oak Hills section, a rather well-to-do residential neighborhood, was a side street off a side street. There's never any reason to drive on Summit Street unless Summit Street is your destination.

Nevertheless I said it was on my way—and she accepted pleasantly. Holding the car door for her, I noticed my Plymouth was unusually clean and I was glad I'd finally got around to having it washed. New seat covers, too, very nice-looking; I couldn't remember having bought them but I was pleased I had.

Once we were driving together along Western Avenue I introduced myself. "My name's Ronald. Ronald Grady."

"Delia," she told me, smiling again. "Delia Wright."

"Hello, Delia Wright."

Her smile broadened. "Hello, Ronald Grady." She reached out and, for just a second, touched her fingers to my right wrist.

After that the dream continued in the most naturalistic manner, the two of us chatting about one thing and another—the high schools we'd attended and how odd it was we'd never met before. When we reached Summit Street, she pointed out her house and I stopped at the curb. She said, "Won't you come in for a cup of coffee? I'd like you to meet my mother."

"I really can't now," I told her, smiling regretfully. "But if you're doing nothing tonight, could I take you to dinner and a movie?"

"I'd like that," she said.

"So would I."

Our eyes met, and the moment seemed to deepen—and there the dream stopped.

I awoke next morning with a pleasant warm sensation on my right wrist, and I knew it was because Delia had touched me there. I ate a heartier breakfast than usual, startled my mother—I have continued to live at home with my mother and an older sister, seeing no point in the additional expense of a place of my own—startled my mother, I say, by singing rather loudly as I dressed, and went off to work in as sunny a mood as could be imagined.

Which Mr. Miller, a few hours later, succeeded in shattering.

I admit I returned late from lunch. The people at the auto store had assured me they could install the new seat covers in 15 minutes, but it actually took them over half an hour. Still, it was the first time in five years I had ever been late, and Mr. Miller's sarcasm and abuse seemed to me under the circumstances excessive. He carried on for nearly half an hour, and in fact continued to make reference to the incident for the next two weeks.

Still, my hurt and outrage at Mr. Miller's attitude were not so great as they might have been, had I not had that spot of warmth on my wrist to remind me of Delia. I thought of Delia, of her beauty and grace, of my own ease and confidence with her, and I weathered the Miller storm much better than might have been expected.

That night I hardly watched the eleven o'clock news at all. I stayed till it ended only because any change in my habits would have produced a string of irrelevant questions from my mother; but as soon as the newscaster had bid me good night I headed directly for my own bed and sleep.

And Delia. I had been afraid to hope the dream would continue into a third night, but it did, it did, and most delightfully so.

This time the dream skipped. It jumped over those dull meaningless hours when I was not with Delia, those hours as stale and empty as the real world, and it began tonight with me back at Summit Street promptly at seven, and Delia opening her front door to greet me.

Again the dream was utterly realistic. The white dinner jacket I wore was unlike anything in my waking wardrobe, but otherwise all was lifelike.

In tonight's dream we went to dinner together at Astoldi's, an expensive Italian restaurant which I had attended—in daylife—only once, at the testimonial dinner for Mr. Randmunson when he retired from Willis & DeKalb. But tonight I behaved—and felt, which is equally important—as though I dined at Astoldi's twice a week.

The dream ended as we were leaving the restaurant after dinner, on our way to the theater.

The next day, and the days that followed, passed in a slow and velvet haze. I no longer cared about Mr. Miller's endless abrasiveness. I bought a white dinner jacket, though in daylife I had no use for it. Later on, after a dream segment in which I wore a dark blue ascot, I bought three such ascots and hung them in my closet.

The dream, meanwhile, went on and on without a break, never skipping a night. It omitted all periods of time when I was not with my Delia, but those times spent with her were presented entirely, and chronologically, and with great realism.

There were, of course, small exceptions to the realism. My ease with Delia, for instance. And the fact that my Plymouth grew steadily younger night by night, and soon stopped pulling to the right.

That first date with Delia was followed by a second and a third. We went dancing together, we went swimming together, we went for rides on a lake in her cousin's cabin cruiser and for drives in the mountains in her own Porsche convertible. I kissed her, and her lips were indescribably sweet.

I saw her in all lights and under all conditions. Diving from a tacketa-tacketa long board into a jade-green swimming pool, and framed for one heartbeat in silhouette against the pale blue sky. Dancing in a white ball gown, low across her tanned breasts and trailing the floor behind her. Kneeling in the garden behind her house, dressed in shorts and a sleeveless pale green blouse, wearing gardening gloves and holding a trowel, laughing, with dirt smudged on her nose and cheek. Driving her white Porsche, her auburn hair blowing in the wind, her eyes bright with joy and laughter.

The dream, the Dream, became to me much finer than reality, oh, much much finer. And in the Dream there was no haste, no hurry, no fear. Delia and I were in love, we were lovers, though we had not yet actually lived together. I was calm and confident, slow and sure, feeling no frantic need to possess my Delia now, *now*. I knew the time would come, and in our tender moments I could see in her eyes that she also knew, and that she was not afraid.

Slowly we learned one another. We kissed, I held her tight, my arm encircled her slender waist. I touched her breasts and, one moonlight night on a deserted beach, I stroked her lovely legs.

How I loved my Delia! And how I needed her, how necessary an antidote she was to the increasing bitterness of my days.

It was Mr. Miller, of course, who disrupted my days as thoroughly as Delia soothed and sweetened my nights. Our store was soon unrecognizable, most of the older employees gone, new people and new methods everywhere. I believe I was kept on only because I was such a silent enduring victim for Mr. Miller's sarcasm, his nasal voice and his twisted smile and his bitter eyes. He was in such a starved hurry for the presidency of the firm, he was so frantic to capture Willis & DeKalb, that it forced him to excesses beyond belief.

But I was, if not totally immune, at least relatively safe from the psychological blows of Mr. Miller's manner. The joyful calm of the Dream carried me through all but the very worst of the days in the store.

Another development was that I found myself more self-assured with other people in daylife. Woman customers, and even the fashionably attractive and newly hired woman employees, were beginning to make it clear that they found me not entirely without interest. It goes without saying that I remained faithful to my Delia, but it was nevertheless pleasurable to realize that a real-world social life was available to me, should I ever want it.

Not that I could visualize myself ever being less than fully satisfied with Delia.

But then it all began to change. Slowly, very very slowly, so that I don't know for how long the tide had already ebbed before I first became aware. In my Delia's eyes—I first saw it in her eyes. Where before they had been warm bottomless pools, now they seemed flat and cold and opaque; I no longer saw in them the candor and beauty of before. Also, from time to time I would catch a pensive frown on her face, a solemn thoughtfulness.

"What is it?" I would ask her. "Tell me. Whatever I can do—"

"It's nothing," she would insist. "Really, darling, it's nothing at all." And kiss me on the cheek.

In this same period, while matters were unexpectedly worsening in the dream, a slow improvement had begun in the store. All the employees to be fired were now gone, all the new employees in and used to their jobs, all the new routines worked with and grown accustomed to. Mr. Miller seemed also to be growing accustomed to his new job and the new store. Less and less was he taking out his viciousness and insecurity on me. He had, in fact, taken to avoiding me for days at a time, as though beginning to feel ashamed of his earlier harshness.

Which was fine but irrelevant. What was my waking time after all but the necessary adjunct to my dream? It was the dream that mattered, and the dream was not going well, not going well at all.

It was, in fact, getting worse. Delia began to break dates with me, and to make excuses when I asked her for dates. The pensive looks, the distracted looks, the buried sense of impatience, all were more frequent now. Entire portions of the dream were spent with me alone—I was *never* alone in the early nights!—pacing the floor of my room, waiting for a promised call that never came.

What could it be? I asked her and asked, but always she evaded my questions, my eyes, my arms. If I pressed, she would insist it was nothing, nothing, and then for a little while she would be her old self again, gay and beautiful, and I could believe it had only been my imagination after all. But only for a little while, and then the distraction, the evasiveness, the impatience, the excuses, all would return once more.

Until two nights ago. We sat in her convertible beneath a full moon, high on a dark cliff overlooking the sea, and I forced the issue at last. "Delia," I said. "Tell me the truth, I have to know. Is there another man?"

She looked at me, and I saw she was about to deny everything yet again, but this time she couldn't do it. She bowed her head. "I'm sorry, Ronald," she said, her voice so low I could barely hear the words. "There is."

"Who?"

She raised her head, gazing at me with eyes in which guilt and pity and love and shame were all commingled, and she said, "It's Mr. Miller."

I recoiled. *"What?"*

"I met him at the country club," she said. "I can't help it, Ronald. I wish to God I'd never met the man. He has some sort of hold over me, some hypnotic power. That first night he took me to a motel and—"

Then she told me, told me everything, every action and every demand, in the most revolting detail. And though I squirmed and struggled, though I strained and yearned, I could not wake up, I could not end the dream. Delia told me everything she had done with Mr. Miller, her helplessness to deny him even though it was *me* she loved and he for whom she felt only detestation, her constant trysts with him night after night, direct from my arms to his. She told me of their planned meeting later that very night in the motel where it had all begun, and she told me of her bitter self-knowledge that even now, after I knew everything, *she would still meet him.*

Then at last her toneless voice was finished and we were in silence once again, beneath the moon, high on the cliff. *Then* I awoke.

That was two nights ago. Yesterday I arose the same as ever—what else could I do?—and I went to the store as usual and I behaved normally in every way. What else could I do? But I noticed again Mr. Miller's muted attitude toward me, and now I understood it was the result of his guilty knowledge. Of course Delia had told him about me—she'd described all that to me during her confession, relating how Mr. Miller had laughed and been scornful to hear that "Ronald the sap" had never been to bed with her. "Doesn't know what he's missing, does he?" she quoted him as saying, with a laugh.

At lunchtime I drove past the motel she'd named, and a squalid place it was, peeling stucco painted a garish blue. Not far beyond it was a gunsmith's; on the spur of the moment I stopped, talked to the salesman about "plinking" and "varmints," and bought a snub-nosed Iver Johnson Trailsman revolver. The salesman inserted the .32 bullets into the chambers, and I put the box containing the gun into the glove compartment of my car. Last evening I carried the gun unobserved into the house and hid it in my room, in a dresser drawer, beneath my sweaters.

And last night, as usual, I dreamed. But in the dream I was not with Delia. In the dream I was alone, in my bedroom, sitting on the edge of the bed with the gun in my hand, listening to the small noises of my mother and sister as they prepared for sleep, waiting for the house to be quiet.

In last night's dream I had the gun and I planned to use it. In last night's dream I had not left my Plymouth in the driveway as usual but half a block away, parked at the curb. In last night's dream I was waiting only for my mother and sister to be safely asleep, when I intended to creep silently from the house, hurry down the sidewalk to my Plymouth, drive to that motel, and enter Room 7—it's always Room 7, Delia told me, always the same room—where it was my intention to shoot Mr. Miller dead.

In last night's dream I heard my mother and sister moving about, at first in the kitchen and then in the bathroom and then in their bedrooms. In last night's dream the house slowly, gradually, finally became quiet, and I got to my feet, putting the gun in my pocket, preparing to leave the room. And at that point the dream stopped.

I have been very confused today. I have wanted to talk to Mr. Miller, but I've been afraid to. I have been unsure what to do next, or in which life to do it. If I kill Mr. Miller in the dream tonight, will he still be in the store tomorrow, with his guilt and his scorn? If I kill Mr. Miller in the dream tonight, and if he is still in the store tomorrow, will I go mad? If I fail to kill Mr. Miller, somewhere, somehow, how can I go on living with myself?

When I came home from work this evening, I didn't park the Plymouth in the driveway as usual, but left it at the curb, half a block from here. My mind was in turmoil all evening, but I behaved normally, and after the eleven o'clock news I came up here to my bedroom.

But I was afraid to sleep, afraid to dream. I took the gun from the drawer, and I have been sitting here, listening to the small sounds of my mother and my sister as they prepare for bed.

Can things ever again be as they were between Delia and me? Can the memory of what has happened ever be erased? I turn the gun and look into its black barrel and I ask myself all these questions. "Perchance to dream." If I arranged it that I would never awake again, would I go on dreaming? But would the dream become worse instead of better?

Is it possible—as some faint doubting corner of my mind suggests—even remotely possible, that Delia is not what she seems, that she was never true, that she is a succubus who has come to destroy me through my dream?

The house is silent. The hour is late. If I stay awake, if I creep from the house and drive to the motel, what will I find in Room 7?

And whom shall I kill?

Joyce Harrington

A Place of Her Own

*"She looked like a great big bundle of old clothes," crouched down
in her little sheltered corner next to the bank. And there but for
the grace of God . . . Another of Joyce Harrington's penetrating
insights into the hearts of people and into the heart of society, a
story full of sharply observed details, each true to life, each on
target. Look around, as Joyce Harrington does, and see how some
people live—if you can call it living . . .*

If you asked me when she first showed up on the corner, I couldn't
tell you. One day she just started being a regular part of the
scenery, like Carvel's and Waldbaum's, and then she was always
there. Summer and winter, rain or shine, she was there sitting on
the sidewalk like patience on a monument. In the good weather
she'd sometimes go across the street to the opposite corner where
there was a tree and a mailbox and sit between them. But most of
the time she would be scrunched down in a little covered-over space,
like a shallow cave, right between Carvel's and the bank. That was
her place.

I was surprised that the bank let her stay there where everybody
going in or coming out could see her. Not good for business, if you
know what I mean. I thought about saying something to the manager, but it wasn't my bank.

Once in a while she'd be gone. The first time I went by and she
wasn't there I said to myself, "Oh, boy! A good thing. Somebody
picked her up. The police or the loony squad. Either way, a good
thing. She's not making a disgrace of the neighborhood."

But the next day she was back, crouching in her cave, drinking
coffee from a paper container and staring around with her crazy
eyes. I can tell you, it gave me a shock to have those eyes staring
at me when I wasn't expecting it, but I just walked on as if nothing
had happened. I never missed a day of work in my life, and the only
times I was ever late was when the subway got itself messed up. By

the time I got to the station my heart had stopped pounding and all I could think about was squeezing onto the train.

After that I was always ready for her. I could see from a block away if she was there, and I could walk fast and keep my eyes looking the other way. Or I could walk on the other side of the street. But ready or not, something always made me look at her. Not right in the face, but at some part of her clothes or her feet or the top of her head. I couldn't go by without one quick look.

She always wore a coat, summer and winter. Sometimes she had it all buttoned up, other times slung over her shoulders like a model in a magazine. Underneath the coat she wore sweaters. Even on summer days when the temperature got in the nineties and everybody else was dying from the heat, sweaters. And baggy dirty slacks. I got the impression she wore a couple pairs of slacks at once. She looked like a great big bundle of old clothes. If you didn't look at her face, you could just walk by like she was some pile of garbage waiting to be picked up.

I took my vacation in August and went to Ohio to visit my married daughter, Ellen. I have to go to her. She won't come to visit me. When she got married, she said to me, "Momma, I hope you won't be hurt, but I'm getting out of this crummy town and I'm never coming back."

Well, I'm not hurt. Why should I be? It's pretty where she lives. Grass and trees around the house. Everything clean. She has a nice new car to drive around in. The kids, God bless them, almost grown up and never sick a day in their lives. Only they hardly remember me from one visit to the next. Their other grandmother lives nearby. She's a nice lady, I guess. The kids show me all the presents she gives them—ten-speed bicycles, a record player for Kathy, Timmy's racing-car setup in the basement. Those are nice things to give your grandchildren. I brought them presents, too—small things I could carry on the plane. Nothing special.

This time Ellen said to me, "Momma, you've been working over thirty years in that store. You could retire anytime you want. Wouldn't you like to stop working and come and live with us?"

She doesn't understand. It's not just a store. After her father died, rest his soul, I was lucky to get a job there. Ellen was only five years old. What does she remember about that time? But I remember how frightened I was the day I walked into the Personnel Office. Artie was a good man, but he didn't leave any insurance or anything else.

He never expected to be taken off so young. So I had to get a job, quick, and I'd never worked a day in my life.

I was so nervous that day when they showed me how to work the cash register. Artie used to give me just enough money to buy food with and everything else he took care of himself. So it scared me to have all that money that wasn't mine passing through my hands every day. But I got used to it after a while, and I got used to having money of my own, too. So much for the rent, so much to live on, so much to save. And it's a good thing I saved because when Ellen got grown up, she wanted to go to college and that's where she met her husband. So it all worked out. If it wasn't for the store, Ellen wouldn't be living in her pretty house, with a dentist for a husband and two fine kids, and she ought to understand that.

Sometimes I think she's a little ashamed of me. Once, when I was there visiting, she had some of her neighbors over for coffee in the afternoon, and when she introduced me, she said, "This is my mother. She's a buyer for a big New York department store." Well, it was only a little lie, but I felt my face getting red. I couldn't correct her. That would only have made things worse. So I just smiled and hoped nobody would be interested enough to ask me any questions about my job. They weren't. Fact of the matter is, I am a saleswoman in the Ladies Foundations Department and that's where I've been for over 30 years. I'm not ashamed of it even if Ellen is.

When my vacation was over and she was driving me to the airport, she brought it up again. "You're too old to keep on working, Momma," she said. "Peter and I talked it over and we'd be happy to give you a home with us. I worry about you all alone in that awful little apartment. There's so much violence these days. You'd be safe out here with us."

Well, I had to bite my tongue to keep from saying what I wanted to say. The "awful little apartment" had been my home for more years than I had worked in Ladies Foundations. It was the home that Artie and I made together when we were young and I wasn't about to leave it now that I'm old. It had been Ellen's home, too, although she didn't seem to want to remember that she'd had some happy times there and there was always good nourishing food on the table.

What I said was, "I still have your bedroom suite. Good as new. Maybe Kathy would like to have it for her room. I could ship it out."

She laughed. "My God, Momma! Get rid of it. Give it to the Salvation Army. All pink ruffles and flounces, wasn't it? I can't believe

I used to pretend I was some kind of movie star in that room. No, thanks. But whenever you're ready, you just get rid of all that junky old furniture and we'll set you up with a room of your own, a television, everything you need. Peter says we might be able to put in a swimming pool next year."

I thought about those things on the plane, and I thought about what I would really want to do with myself when the time came that I wouldn't be getting on the subway every morning and going to the store. It wasn't yet, but it would be soon. Three more years? It would be nice being right there to watch Kathy and Timmy grow up and get married. But the fact of the matter is that outside of Ellen herself, I've never been around teen-aged kids very much. They seem kind of large and noisy. And I have a television. Small, but perfectly good. I got it on sale at the store, which, with my discount, made it a very good buy. And what would an old lady like me want with a swimming pool? I haven't been in swimming since Ellen was 15 and we went for a week to the Jersey shore, and even then I only got my feet wet up to my knees.

I took a cab from the airport. Expensive, but I was tired and the next day was already Monday and the end of my vacation. I'd have to go back to work. It was a heavy evening, humid and overcast, and the whole world was a dirty gray color. By the time we got off the expressway, it had begun to rain and the cab driver, like everyone else trying to squeeze through the weekend traffic, was scowling and muttering curses. For a moment I thought maybe Ellen was right and I ought to pack up and leave all this behind.

But then we swung onto a familiar street and home was only a few blocks away. I leaned forward to give the driver directions and through the rain-streaked windshield I saw her. She was crouched down in that little sheltered corner by the bank, a sheet of plastic tucked in around her knees. All around her she had boxes and shopping bags tied with string, and parked at one side she had a Waldbaum's shopping cart piled high with God knows what kind of rubbish. And right in the middle of all this she squatted, staring out into the rain. She stared right into the cab as we drove by and I felt sure she recognized me. It seemed as if she shouted something, but I couldn't hear her.

The driver said, "Which way, lady?"

So I told him where to turn, and in less than a minute I was paying him off with a good tip because he helped me carry my luggage up to the door. Before he left, he said, "How do I get out of this crummy neighborhood?" So I told him that and then I dragged my luggage indoors.

Home. I looked around the lobby and it was just the same as it always was. But for some reason I began to remember that years ago there used to be a red-leather settee and a couple of armchairs over against the wall. There was nothing there now. I couldn't remember when they'd been taken away. Then I remembered that on the wall, over the settee, there used to be a picture. Horses, I think. Or sailboats. Something outdoorsy. Now, if you looked very closely you could just about make out where it had hung, but the wall was so dirty everything had blended into the same shade of grimy green. The floor was dirty, too, and not just because it was raining and people had been tracking it up with wet feet. Whatever happened to the rubber mat the super used to put down when it rained? I guess a lot of things had changed over the years, and I'd just never noticed.

I pushed the button for the elevator, and while I was waiting I glanced over at the mailboxes. My neighbor across the hall, Mrs. Finney, had been picking up my mail while I was away, so there was no reason for me to check my mailbox. Still, I noticed that some of the little metal doors were bent and hanging loose. Not mine, but some of the others. How long had they been like that? And why didn't the super get them fixed?

Next to the mailboxes a sign had been taped to the wall. From where I stood I could read the big print at the top. It said: ATTENTION ALL TENANTS, and there was a lot of small print underneath. I was about to go and look at it, but the elevator door opened, so I dragged my luggage on and pushed the button for the sixth floor.

I don't know if it was because I was so tired, or because of the change coming from Ellen's pretty house with the trees and grass around it, or because I was finally seeing things the way they really were, but when I got inside my apartment and turned on the lights I could have cried. Nothing had changed in my apartment. Everything was just as I had left it. It wasn't even dusty or bad-smelling because Mrs. Finney, when she brought in the mail, would always open the windows and give the place a quick once-over, which I would do the same for her when she was away. No, it was something else, something inside me that turned on like a searchlight and made everything look shabby and old. Worn out. Like Ellen said, junk.

The living-room suite, that Artie and I bought with the money his folks gave us for a wedding present, was covered with summer slipcovers just like every summer. The slipcovers weren't as old as the furniture. I got new ones every few years or so from the store. How long ago did I get these? Whatever, there were holes in them and the brown plush underneath was showing through. That made me think of the places on the couch cushions and the arms where the brown plush was worn down to the shiny material. Old, right? Junk.

Same thing with the rug, the coffee table, the bookcase with Ellen's old books in it, even the draperies at the windows. Everything was old, shabby, faded, chipped, ready for the junk collector. Even the television was an old black-and-white set that I'd bought back in the days of Uncle Miltie and Howdy Doody. For Ellen.

I went into Ellen's room. I don't know what made me keep her room just the way she'd left it. Maybe I always thought she'd come back for a visit, in spite of what she said. The bedroom suite was a present I got for her when she started high school, so she'd feel like a young lady, no longer a baby, and have girl friends over to visit. I remember how proud she had been of her room.

This time I didn't turn on the overhead light. Maybe that's what made the living room look so awful. I walked into the room to where there were two little pink-shaded lamps sitting on the vanity table. I turned on one of those instead. The room was small, I have to admit that—smaller than the room I'd stayed in at Ellen's house. And most of it was taken up with the bed. I'll never forget the look on her face the day the delivery truck from the store came and the men carried that furniture upstairs and even helped put the bed together. When she saw them put the canopy on top, I thought she would never stop smiling and dancing around and squealing. "Oh, Momma! It's beautiful! I love it!" Those were her exact words. I guess people change.

Now, in the rosy glow from the vanity lamp, I could see that the canopy was sagging and the pink quilted bedspread and dust ruffle had turned the color of old underwear. The pink net skirt on the vanity table, which I'd made myself, was droopy and frayed at the bottom, and the white paint on the bedposts and on the chifforobe was dingy and gray. Maybe if I scrubbed it down . . .

The door buzzer sounded. I got my face ready with a smile because right now it would be very good to have some company and forget all this gloom that was making me feel like a worn-out piece of junk myself. But before I got to the door I took the smile away just in case it was some creep going through the building looking for old ladies to molest. Don't laugh. It happened in the next block. Thank

God the landlord put peepholes in all our doors. I looked through and it was Mrs. Finney from across the hall.

Right away when she came in she said, "Did you eat yet, Lillian? I brought some Danish."

That's Grace Finney. Always worrying about whether people got enough to eat. A good person.

"I ate on the plane, but I could have some Danish. Why don't I make some coffee?"

She followed me into the kitchen, and again I noticed things, like the worn spot on the linoleum in front of the sink and the scars on the table that made it look like it had been through the wars. But I put it all out of my mind so I could tell Grace about Ellen and her family and how well they were doing. She put the Danish down on the table while I filled the kettle and got out the instant coffee.

"Did you read your mail yet?" she asked. "No. I can see you didn't. Wait a minute."

And she raced out to the living room where the mail was stacked on the coffee table and came back waving an envelope.

"Wait'll you see this," she said. "And there's nothing we can do about it. Not a damn thing."

It was unusual for Grace Finney to swear. She prided herself on being a lady and got her hair done every Saturday morning at Gwen's around the corner. So it must be something really bad.

I looked at the envelope.

"Open it. Open it," she said.

It hadn't come through the mail. There was no stamp on it and no address. Only my name, Mrs. Lillian Curry, written out in big black letters.

"We all got one," she said. "It came right after you left. It's a shame. A crying shame. Read it."

I opened the envelope. Inside was a single sheet of paper. I pulled it out and right away across the top I saw: ATTENTION ALL TENANTS.

"What is this?" I said. "I saw it downstairs but I didn't stop to read it."

"Read," she commanded. "You'll cry. If I tell you, I'll get so mad I don't know what I'll do. Old Mr. Zukowski in 2D, when he read it, he had a heart attack and he's still in the hospital. Nobody knows if he'll ever get out alive."

So I read. And then I turned the kettle off. And then I sat down on a kitchen chair, the one that wobbled a little. Coming on top of the way I was feeling, I didn't know whether to laugh or cry over what the piece of paper said. I guess it's safe to say I was stunned, because I just sat there with my head going around and the words on the paper getting all blurry when I tried to read it again to make sure it was really true.

What it boiled down to was this. The building had been sold and the new owner was going to tear it down. All the other apartment buildings on the block, too. In place of a lot of rundown little buildings he was going to put up a brand-new giant building with lots more apartments. We all had to get out within two months, because after that all the services would be shut off. We could all come back if we wanted to and get apartments in the new building. At the end they tried to take the curse off it by saying what a great thing it was for the neighborhood and how projects like this would help put an end to urban decay.

Urban decay. Junk. Everything was turning into junk. They wanted to turn us all over to the junk collectors. Buildings, bedroom suites, people, even an old dog wouldn't be safe. Could they give me a new body, a new life to live in the new building? I could feel words choking in my throat, and I must have made some kind of noise, because Grace was shaking me and bending over to stare in my face.

"Are you all right?" she demanded. "Don't you go having a heart attack on me. Here, I'll make the coffee."

She rattled around and pretty soon a cup of black coffee was on the table beside the Danish.

"Eat," she said. "It's from Dubin's."

So I ate a bite of Danish and I sipped some coffee. And I have to admit I felt better, but still not clear in my head.

"I'm leaving," said Grace. "I'm not waiting around while this place turns into a ghost building and the scavengers start breaking the windows and stealing the pipes off the walls. The moving truck is coming in the morning. I found a place out in Queens. The rent is more, but at least it's clean and they won't be tearing it down around my ears. You ought to leave, too."

"But I just got back."

"Yeah, I know. It's a shock. You need a little time to get used to the idea. But don't wait too long. You know what happens to empty buildings. It's not safe."

"Where is safe? Ellen wants me to go out and live with them. She says it's safe."

"She's a good daughter, Ellen. You ought to go. I wish I had a daughter like that. All I have is that bum, my son, who can't even hold a job. Forty years old and still trying to figure out what to do with his life. Well, I have to go. I still have a lot of packing to do. I just didn't want you to be alone when you got the news. You'll be all right now? Have the rest of the Danish for breakfast."

I sat there at the table for a while. The coffee got cold and a roach got brave and ran across the drainboard. I didn't even get up to chase him. I always keep my kitchen spotless, no food lying around, so the roaches won't come. But they come anyway. You can't get away from them in these old buildings. Maybe the new building wouldn't have any roaches. Maybe I could find a place to stay in the neighborhood, a room somewhere nearby, and move into the new building when it gets finished.

That's what the piece of paper said, that we could all move back in and have nice new apartments. But what about the rent? New apartments don't come cheap. And what would I do with my furniture in the meantime? How long does it take to build a giant apartment house? A year, two years? Come to think of it, how would my junky old furniture look in a brand-new apartment? Come to think of it, would I live that long?

I shivered. It wasn't cold, only like the old saying goes, somebody was walking on my grave. Wherever that would be. I'd never thought about that before, but now it came through like a *Daily News* headline. A place to die. I wouldn't be looking for a place to live. I'd be looking for a place to die.

It was crazy, but the thought made me feel better. I wrapped the Danish up in plastic and put it in the breadbox. And then I went to polish my shoes. Tomorrow was Monday, and I never went to work on Monday without polishing my shoes.

In the morning I put on a black dress. I know things are different now, but back when I started working in the store we all had to wear black dresses and I never got out of the habit. Sometimes I'll wear brown or navy blue, but that's as far as I'll go. Not like some of the other girls who wear pantsuits in turquoise or lavender. It wouldn't be right.

I ate the rest of the Danish I had started and had a cup of coffee. There wasn't much else to eat, and I would have to stop at Waldbaum's on my way home. There was one Danish left over, so I put it in a bag to take with me for my coffee break. When I left the building, the moving truck was already in front and Grace Finney's upright piano was standing on the sidewalk. She could only play *Chopsticks*, but she'd bought it years ago when her boy said he

wanted to study music. He'd never even learned *Chopsticks,* but
Grace hung on to the piano and used to let Ellen play whenever she
wanted to. I walked away fast. I didn't want to be late for work on
my first morning back from vacation.

The subway station was three blocks away, and as soon as I turned
the corner I saw her. I didn't see her exactly, but I saw her shopping
cart parked in its usual place outside the bank, so I knew she was
there. I kept on walking fast, and I kept watching the toes of my
shiny black shoes going one, two, one, two in front of me. I didn't
look up when I passed her, and I don't know what made me do it,
but I put the bag with the Danish in it on top of the mound of old
junk in her shopping cart. I was trembling so bad when I got to the
change booth, I could hardly pick up my tokens.

The only thing different about the store when I got there was that
they had the new fall merchandise on display. When I had left, they
were getting rid of the last of the summer stuff. But Ladies Foundations doesn't change much from season to season. A girdle is a
girdle, even though they keep coming out with new kinds of fabrics
and new styles. It felt good to be back, and right away before the
opening bell rang I started checking over the shelves and drawers
so I'd know if we were running low on any sizes.

Miss Kramer, the floor manager, came by before I'd gotten very
far, and she said, "Good morning, Lillian. Welcome back. Did you
have a good vacation? I'd like to see you in my office if you have a
few minutes."

So I said, "Good morning. Thanks. Yes. I'll come right now."

I followed her across the floor and into the corridor behind the
fitting rooms where her office was, all the way wondering what she
wanted to talk to me about. It had been over a year since my last
raise, so maybe that was it. I could sure use a raise if I was going
to have to find a new apartment. I had a little money saved up, but
the way prices were going higher all the time, it was getting harder
and harder to save anything.

"Sit down, Lillian," she said.

So I sat down in the little straight chair in front of her desk and
she sat down in the swivel chair behind her desk. She looked at me
for a second and then she started flipping through some cards in a
metal box. She pulled one out.

"Lillian," she said, "you've been with us for over thirty years."

"Yes," I said, feeling proud and smiling a little. It was sure to be
a raise. It always started like that; how long you've been there and

what a good employee you were and how you've earned a little extra in your paycheck.

"And you've been in Ladies Foundations all that time," she went on. "You've received five letters of commendation from the President, your attendance record is perfect, and your sales record is steady."

I just nodded and held my breath. I couldn't say a word. It was coming now. I just wondered how much it would be. My hands were getting clammy and I wished I had brought a handkerchief.

Miss Kramer took a deep breath, bulging out her chest, and looked at the wall behind my head. "Lillian," she said, "you're sixty-two years old. Have you thought about how you will spend your retirement years?"

"What!" I said. "No! There's plenty of time for that."

"Well, that's just the point," she said. "There isn't plenty of time. We're cutting back on staff, and we'd like you to take early retirement."

It was like a knife cutting into my heart, cutting off the blood, cutting off the air to my lungs. I couldn't breathe. I got cold all over. There was a pain somewhere inside that wouldn't stay still and wouldn't let go.

I must have scared Miss Kramer. She must have thought I was going to faint or have a stroke or something. She got up out of her chair and ran around her desk and held me by the shoulders.

"Lillian," she whispered, "are you all right? Do you want to lie down?"

"No," I said. And I shook myself a little, so she would let go. I couldn't let her see that I was weak enough to fall off the chair, so I held on to the seat with both hands.

She backed off a little but kept her eyes glued to my face. "Do you understand, Lillian?" she said. "You've worked a long time and you've been a good employee, but now it's time for you to take it easy. You'll get your pension and you'll always have your discount. And we'll keep up your medical insurance. We're not going to throw you out and forget about you. You'll always be a member of the family."

"No," I said. "I won't go. You can't make me. What about my regulars? They always ask for me."

"Lillian, nothing lasts forever. If I were you, I'd be glad to have a chance to rest and do what I want to do. Don't you have a daughter and grandchildren somewhere out west? Think how glad they would be if you could spend more time with them."

"No. I don't want to go out there and be an old lady stuck in a room with nothing to do. I've always worked. I'm a good worker. You said so yourself. These young kids, what do they know? Here one day and gone the next. Not me. I'm not going. You can't make me go. I'll talk to the President. He knows you can't run that department without me."

She sighed and sat back down in her chair. "Lillian," she said, "don't make it hard for yourself." She picked up a sheaf of papers and handed it to me. "Here's your retirement computation all made out and signed by the President. He'd like to wish you well himself, but he's out of town this week. Now if you'll just hand in your identification card, I'll give you your final paycheck and you'll be free to pursue a life of leisure."

"Just like that? Out?" I couldn't believe it. "You don't even want me to work today? Out on the street? No place to go? Nothing to do? After I polished my shoes?"

"There'll be a Christmas party for retirees. You'll get an invitation. Now if you'll excuse me, we're getting ready for Labor Day and you know what that means."

"You couldn't let me stay and help out?"

She didn't answer. Now I really wished I had brought a hand-kerchief. But I held back the tears and we walked back to my counter. I got out my pocketbook, handed her my I.D. card, and she gave me the check and that was that.

I stood there behind the counter for a minute, but then I started feeling funny, like I didn't belong which, of course, I didn't any more. I walked around to the other side of the counter, trying to feel like a customer, but that didn't feel right either. I wanted to say goodbye to the other girls in the department, but I was afraid that if I did I'd start crying and that wouldn't do any good. So I just drifted away across the floor as if I was only going to the ladies room or the cafeteria for a cup of coffee.

That was the way to do it—a little bit at a time. I walked around the floor, through Sleepwear and Daywear and Robes, and I saw a lot of familiar faces behind the counters getting ready for business. But I might have been invisible for all the notice they took of me. I guess the word had got around.

By the time I got to the escalators, customers were beginning to spread through the store, so I just went along following this group or that group. All morning I wandered through the store, up and down the escalators, visiting all my favorite departments. But I didn't buy anything and I didn't speak to a soul. At lunchtime I ran out to the bank and cashed my check. I couldn't eat in the employees' cafeteria any more, but I did the next best thing. I ate in the restaurant on the fifth floor.

In the afternoon I spent a lot of time looking at things that Kathy and Timmy would like. And then I went to Home Furnishings and thought about how I would like my new apartment to look. I stayed there until quitting time.

After I got off the subway, I stopped at Waldbaum's. I bought a barbecued chicken, some cottage cheese, a head of lettuce, and two tomatoes. The street was full of people going in and out of shops and hurrying home from work. I was hurrying home from work, too, but not so fast that I didn't notice her. She was in her usual corner by the bank, staring and smirking at the people going by. I stopped, and for the first time I looked right at her. She didn't like that. She shook her fist at me and growled some words I couldn't understand.

I said, "Do you want something to eat?"

I didn't wait for her to answer. I think she was as surprised as I was that I had spoken to her. I pulled the barbecued chicken out of the bag and stooped to lay it in her lap. Getting that close to her was a revelation. She smelled. Well, of course, she did, poor thing. There aren't any bathtubs on street corners. Then I went home.

The moving truck was gone, and that meant Grace was gone. There really wasn't anyone else in the building I was on friendly terms with. No mail in the mailbox. Who was there to write to me except once in a while Ellen and once a month Con Edison? The building already seemed deserted. My footsteps made a hollow sound in the lobby and the elevator groaned like it had rheumatism. I wondered how many besides Grace had already moved out. Maybe I was the only one left.

I made a little cottage-cheese salad for my supper and went to bed as soon as I had washed my plate and one fork. Ellen was right about one thing, I wasn't getting any younger. My black shoes were good and strong and had low heels, but even so, my feet hurt and my legs ached clear up to my knees from standing up and walking around all day. I fell asleep thinking about the Labor Day sales and how busy we would be at the store.

In the morning I got up and took a shower just like always, put on my black dress and my black shoes that still had a good shine to them, and got ready to go to the store. I always put on a little makeup, not a lot because an old lady with a face full of makeup looks like death warmed over, but just enough to show I cared about my appearance. This morning I took a good hard look at myself. I had gray hair, and so did she. Blue eyes, both of us. My skin, wrinkles and all, was pale and soft with only a few age spots, while hers was coarse and red. Otherwise, we might have been sisters. I wondered if she'd eaten the chicken.

When I left the building, a man was hauling in the garbage cans. He wasn't the regular super, but I stopped to talk to him anyway.

"Where's Victor? Is he sick?"

"Who?"

"Victor. The super."

"Gone. All the supers gone. The whole block. They fired all the supers. Me, I just come around and do the garbage cans. But not for long. Another week or two, then no more. You got garbage, you gotta get rid of it yourself. Better you should get out, lady. You got a place to go, go. It ain't safe around here no more. Last night they broke in next door and cleaned out the empty apartments. Light fixtures, toilets, it's a wonder they don't take the wallpaper off the walls. Damn ripoff artists!"

He sent the garbage cans crashing down into the areaway as if they were the thieves in question. I walked away toward the subway. I certainly didn't want to be late today, not with Labor Day coming up next weekend. A place to go. I always had a place to go. The store was my place. I would always be safe there.

When I got to the corner by the bank, she was standing up. I think she was waiting for me. I had never seen her on her feet before, and I was surprised to see how tall she was. Somehow I'd always thought of her as bent and stunted, a dwarf, but she was at least as tall as I am, maybe an inch or two taller.

"Wait," she croaked. She rummaged in her shopping cart and came up with a bright yellow bundle. "Take it."

"No," I said. Even though it was a summer morning and already hot and sticky, I felt a chill.

"Take it," she growled, and shoved it into my hands.

I shook it out. It was one of her sweaters, a yellow orlon cardigan, wrinkled and raveling, with buttons missing.

"Put it on."

She looked so fierce that I didn't want to risk making her angry with me. I put it on. The surprising thing was that my flesh didn't crawl from contact with the filthy thing. Instead, I felt a kind of warmth spreading all through my shaking body.

"Nice," she said. "You keep it."

I said, "Thank you. I have to go now." And I went on to the subway.

The guard wouldn't let me go in the employees' entrance. I had to go around to the front and wait for the store to open. That was the first thing. The second thing was that after I'd been in the store for about an hour I noticed one of the store detectives following me. I knew her, a nice girl who'd helped me out several times when ladies would try to put on two or three girdles and walk out.

I stopped and said, "Why are you following me?"

"I'm not following you," she said.

"Yes, you are. Do you think I'm going to steal something?"

"No," she said. "Look, Mrs. Curry, why don't you go home. They're afraid you might do something crazy. They saw you walking around yesterday and we all have orders to watch out for you."

"Do I look crazy?" I asked her.

"No," she said, but her voice wavered and I could see her taking in the yellow sweater. Then I realized that I'd forgotten to put on any makeup that morning and maybe I hadn't even combed my hair.

"Okay," I said. I wasn't going to wait around for a third thing to happen, and I could see Miss Kramer sailing across the floor with a hard look on her face. I got on the down escalator.

It was strange getting on the subway in the middle of the day. No crowds, I even got a seat. I noticed that people avoided sitting next to me. The yellow sweater was like some kind of magical cloak that made a little wall of privacy between me and everyone else. I thought that over all the way home, that and the fact that the store really wasn't my place any more and I would have to find some place that was mine.

When I got to the corner near the bank there she was. Some kids were teasing her, bouncing a ball off the wall and making it go as close to her as they could without actually hitting her. She crouched in her corner with her eyes closed, trying to ignore them, but her lips were moving a mile a minute and she sure wasn't saying her prayers. I felt sorry for her and at the same time glad, because for some reason when I stopped at Waldbaum's I had picked up double what I needed for my dinner. Two little steaks instead of one, not sirloin or anything like that. Just minute steaks, but they taste okay if you put some steak sauce on them. Two nice potatoes to bake in the oven and some frozen peas.

I guess I was thinking that I could eat one steak today and one tomorrow, but now I thought, "Why not have some company? Mrs. Finney is gone and there's nobody to talk to, and maybe this one could do with a decent meal. It would be my good deed for the day."

I shooed the kids away. They went, but not before they called me some names I'd never heard before and I thought I had heard everything. When I turned back to look at her, she was looking at me. And smiling. At least, I think it was a smile, but it was hard to tell because one side of her mouth went up and the other side went down and there were a couple of teeth missing in the middle. But she seemed friendly enough.

I said, "Hi. Was the chicken okay?"

She growled something and started rummaging in one of her boxes. What she pulled out was a plastic bag, the kind that hot-dog buns come in, and she handed it to me still growling and smiling and getting very excited. I looked in the plastic bag. It was full of chicken bones, big ones and little ones, all the meat chewed off clean as a whistle. I guess she was saying thank you and wanted me to know that she had really polished off that chicken.

"Well," I said, "that's nice."

I didn't know what to do with the chicken bones. I didn't want to put them in the trash barrel on the corner right in front of her eyes, just in case she meant them as a present for me and I would hurt her feelings. So I put them in my Waldbaum's shopping bag. Her smile got even bigger, and she started nodding and making gobbling noises and pointing at my shopping bag. I got the idea.

"You want something else to eat?"

Oh, boy! Talk about hitting the jackpot! Her eyes got bright and nearly bugged out of her head, and spit started drooling down the corners of her mouth.

"Well, okay," I said, "but you'll have to come home with me so I can cook it."

That stopped her. She closed her eyes, sank back into her corner, and pulled her coat collar up around her ears.

"Suit yourself," I said. She was acting like a little kid, so I'd just have to treat her like one. "Come or don't come. It's up to you. I'm going now."

I crossed the street, but I hadn't got more than half a block away before I heard the shopping cart rattling and bumping along behind me. And that's the way we went home, me walking along in front pretending I didn't know she was following, and her pushing her shopping card loaded up with everything she owned, which was junk.

When we got inside the lobby of my building, I kept on pretending she wasn't there, and when the elevator came I got on it and so did she without saying a word. But when we finally got inside my apartment I couldn't keep it up any more.

"Well, here we are," I said.

She didn't say anything, but she started looking around and picking things up and putting them down. I didn't mind because it was all going to have to go anyway, and if she broke something what did it matter because it was all just as much junk as what she had in her shopping cart. Which was parked just inside the door.

"I'm going to cook now," I said. "The bathroom's over there if you want to wash up."

So I went in the kitchen and did what I had to do. Potatoes in the oven, set the table, get out the frying pan. I had some sherry left over from Christmas. I'm not much of a drinking person, but every once in a while I liked to have a glass or two with Mrs. Finney. Might as well get rid of it, I thought. So I went into the living room to ask if she'd like some. She wasn't there. I thought maybe she got nervous and left. Nothing to be nervous about. But then I saw the shopping cart still there, and not only that, but she had put my pair of china robins that I'd won at the bingo at church years ago right on top of the heap of stuff in the cart.

"Well, that's okay," I said to myself, "if it makes her happy. It all has to go and it might as well go that way."

She came out of the bathroom and her face was about ten degrees cleaner, although the rest of her still didn't smell too good.

"Want some sherry?" I asked her.

She smiled that crazy crooked smile and croaked out a word that sounded like "Yes."

So back in the kitchen I went and got out some glasses and the bottle, and while I was doing that I got so angry because a couple of roaches crawled out of the breadbox.

"Dammit!" I said, although I hardly ever swear, and I quick got the roach powder out from under the sink. Boy, did I let them have it! I buried them in it. And I watched them curl up and tip over on their backs with their legs waving in the air. And then I poured the sherry. I had to stir hers around a lot because the way it is with oil and vinegar, it's the same with sherry and roach powder.

It wasn't that I thought she was a roach or something horrible.

She was really kind of nice to have around. She didn't talk too much, and she had a sense of obligation which she showed by giving me her yellow sweater. The only thing was, there wouldn't be room for the two of us in the corner by the bank, and I didn't want to leave the old neighborhood, not even to go to Queens where Grace Finney was.

Well, she drank her sherry up right away, in one gulp, and held out her glass for more. So I went back in the kitchen to get her some more. And then some more. Pretty soon the bottle was empty. So was the roach-powder box.

I threw them both in the garbage and checked on the potatoes baking in the oven. They weren't done yet. I went back in the living room and she was sort of toppled over on the couch kind of snoring and blowing bubbles out of the side of her mouth.

I said, "If you're tired, why don't you come and lie down?"

I pulled her up and made her get off the couch. It wasn't easy, what with her being almost a dead weight and the smell and all. But I took her in my bedroom and let her flop down on my bed. She looked at me once, and I think she looked kind of happy. She gave a little growl and closed her eyes and that was that.

The potatoes still weren't done, so I decided the least I could do was make her look halfway decent. I took her shoes off. She was wearing an old pair of sneakers with holes at the toes, tied with string. No socks. Her ankles were crusty with dirt. I got a basin of hot water and soap and towels and a scrub brush. It was hard work, getting all those clothes off her and cleaning her up. And it was sad how thin she was underneath everything. I washed her like a baby and when I got finished she was as clean and fresh as a baby. I even washed her hair. And then I dressed her in one of my own flannel nightgowns and straightened her out on the bed and covered her up. She looked like she was sleeping, so I tiptoed out of the room.

Boy, was I hungry! By then the potatoes were done, so I put both steaks in the frying pan and boiled up the water for the peas. And believe it or not I ate everything. Every bite. Then I cleaned up the kitchen, because you never can tell. I wouldn't want to go off and leave a mess behind for someone else to see. I'd been thinking about it all, you see, and what I thought was this. She had a place in the world and now she didn't need it any more. I had no place in the world and I needed one. Now I would take her place, and she could have my old place, which was no place.

And what would happen when they find her? Who can tell the

difference between one old lady and another? Who cares? They'll write to Ellen and tell her, "We found your mother." Maybe she'd come, maybe she wouldn't. Maybe she'd cry a little, and have the body shipped out there to be buried. I don't want to be buried out there, dead or alive. If she comes here and says, "That's not my mother," they'll say, "Then who is she? We found her in your mother's apartment." But she won't come. Anyway, maybe they'll never find her. If I know them, they'll just tear the building down and cart the rubble off to New Jersey, her included.

And all the time I'll be laughing. I'll be there in my corner. She'll be there. We'll be there. I never knew her name. That's all right, though. We'll have a new name. Or no name. Who needs a name? I have this nice shopping cart and a place to go to.

She's always there, crouching down in the little covered-over space next to the bank on the corner. Rain or shine, winter or summer, she's there watching the people go by. It's not a bad life, and you learn a lot about human nature. It's amazing, the good stuff that people throw away. If it gets cold, there are places to go to keep warm, but after a while you get so you don't feel the cold. One thing, though. I always keep my shoes polished.

Borden Deal

You Understand?

Join two Americans in the cantina of the Inn of the Two Roosters (or maybe it was the Twin Roosters), in the little Mexican fishing village of Venta Prieta, and hear the story of a fugitive from the law . . .

I left the yacht in Venta Prieta because things were getting pretty sticky aboard, and bound to get worse. The owner's wife had extended the invitation for the entire three-month cruise, but I hadn't realized at the time just how fervent she would feel about the prospects of those days and nights in romantic waters. As a result, the owner, drinking more every day, was beginning to talk to himself.

Venta Prieta was only a fishing village, high above a white-sand beach that, closer to Acapulco, would have been a national fortune. I thought philosophically, *Any port in a sexual storm,* and leaving a diplomatic note prominently displayed in my stateroom, I had the mate take me ashore before daybreak. I walked up the single dusty street and stepped into the cool of the inn, where a smiling, mustachioed *bandito* welcomed an American customer.

I had got a good look at the local prospects and found them bleak. Yet, in the mood for a span of foreign solitude after shipboard intimacy, I decided to remain at least a week to knit up "the ravell'd sleave" of my cares before I even inquired whether it was possible to return to civilization from Venta Prieta.

The one street was lined with fishermen's shanties; their boats were pulled up on the beach. There were only two metropolitan-type buildings—the police station and jail, the inn and its accompanying cantina. The Inn of the Two Roosters, it was called. Or maybe Twin Roosters.

I watched with satisfaction as the motor yacht upped anchor at midmorning and put out to sea. I was so pleased with myself that I pulled out the old portable, which hadn't been out of its case since we'd left San Francisco, and worked with great accomplishment until the middle of the afternoon. At which time, along with every

72

man and dog of Venta Prieta, I took a siesta under the droning sound of a ceiling fan and a lonely fly on the window.

I found the food at the inn quite good—though thoroughly Mexican, of course—and the bartender smiled when I entered the cantina for an after-dinner *Dos Equis*. He put the beer before me, inquired after my health and the length of my stay, and told me I was the first American tourist of the season. I was surprised to find that they had a season, but I thought better of remarking on the phenomenon. Maybe my arrival made it the season.

I contented myself with the thought that, if I did comprise the tourist season, I wouldn't have to put up with any Americans. Maybe I'd stay a month and get some *real* work done; surprise the hell out of my agent with a couple of stories, and maybe the beginning of a good novel, for a change. It had been a long time since I'd done a novel. To hear *him* tell it, my public was holding its collective breath, waiting.

It was a disagreeable surprise, therefore, to see an American enter the cantina. He stopped in the doorway, gazing directly toward me. Somebody must have told him a stranger had hit town. Maybe it was the beginning of his tourist season, too.

From his appearance, he could use one. He was very tall, very thin, and he shambled when he walked. His stained white pants wrinkled in folds about his buttocks, and his shirt was ripped in two or three revealing places. He hadn't shaved yet this week, and his hat looked as if the dogs had played with it in the road before it had got to him.

He took a sight on me, so to speak, and lurched in my direction. "Thank God, an American," he blurted. "Buy me a drink, good man. For God's *sake*, buy me a drink."

He was nothing if not direct.

I surveyed him with considerable revulsion. Close up, his hair was red, turning dirty gray. His stubble of beard was redder still. He had muscular hands and through the torn shirt I could see the string ropes of half-starved muscle.

He had been a man once. Not much left now. A beachcomber, for heaven's sake, I thought. Right out of Joseph Conrad and Somerset Maugham. Except this wasn't a South Sea island. It was a crummy little Mexican fishing village.

"Sure, fellow, if you need it that bad," I said, motioning to the bartender.

The bartender knew what was wanted. He brought a bottle of

cheap sotol and held it behind the beachcomber's head, asking my consent.

"Might as well," I said, motioning him to put it down with the single dirty glass. "Otherwise we'll be running your feet off, bringing it shot by shot."

The bartender set down the bottle, deposited the glass beside it. He spoke to the beachcomber with familiar contempt. The beachcomber, avid eye on full bottle, paid no attention to the insults.

His hands trembled as he filled the thick-walled water glass. He held it with both hands, bringing his mouth down to meet the rim even as he lifted—the classic shaky-drunk gesture. He took a hearty gulp, shuddered to his toenails, took another.

"Good, huh?" I said encouragingly.

He stared at me across the glass of salvation. He set it down, added a few drops of sotol with a finicky touch, as though concocting a very precise and necessary drink.

"My name is Harry Munn," he said in a formal voice. "I welcome you to Venta Prieta."

"Thank you," I said, marveling at the transformation, and wondering how he managed to get over the hump when the tourist season didn't arrive.

He drank again, practically rolling the sotol in his mouth to savor the bouquet. I almost expected him to call for a better year.

"I make it my custom to greet all arriving Americans," he said with dignity. "After all, two countrymen in a strange land—"

"—should look out after each other," I finished for him. "Yes. You're quite right."

He was younger than you'd think at first glance, not over 45 at most.

He peered at me intently. "Say, don't I know you?"

I didn't let my dismay show. "I don't know," I said. "A lot of people seem to."

"Aren't you—?"

I sighed. "Yes," I said. "Just don't spread it around." I leaned forward to impress him. "I'm here to get some work done. A new book. If people start flocking around—"

"You don't have to worry," he said with a magnanimous wave of the hand. He was leaning back now, an arm slung over a chair post. I expected him to put his foot on the table, next. "There's only one other American in town, and we don't speak to each other. In fact, here he comes now. Right on time."

We watched a plump, stubby little man enter the cantina. He had obviously just come from a shave and a haircut, his cheeks glowing with talcum powder and his shoes freshly shined. He wore a white suit, a discreet tie, and looked altogether prosperous and preposterous.

Ignoring us, he went directly to a table, obviously his by long-established right, and waited for the bartender to mix him something that looked as elaborate as a planter's punch.

"Yes, for God's sake don't tell *him*," I said.

The cantina was filling slowly now with the evening trade. A knot of fishermen had taken up positions at the bar. A man with a doctor's bag dangling from one hand as though it had grown there like an appendage had taken a table alone. A table-slapping game of dominoes was going on at another. A dark small girl with enormous eyes had come out through a curtained doorway in the rear to help the bartender.

I noticed, suddenly, that Harry Munn's eyes were following her hungrily as she moved about the room. Once, as she brushed by the table, he spoke in a rush of bad Spanish. She pushed away the hand reaching for her arm. He did not seem crushed, only dogged her with his gaze as she hurried on.

"A lovely child," he said. "She is Rosita. There are a million girls in Mexico named Rosita, but there's only the one, really."

I glanced at him in surprise. The cheap liquor had granted him a return of humanity that, in his natural state, he had seemed incapable of ever again attaining.

He sampled his bottle anew, measuring out a modest amount and quaffing it in quite a civilized manner. He turned to me so suddenly I was startled.

"I guess you're wondering how a man like me could end up in this tail-end of the universe in this condition," he said. "You'd have to be wondering. Because you're a writer."

"I hadn't really thought about it," I said warily.

There are a million stories like his story, all singularly unedifying. He leaned over the table. His voice sharpened, hardened.

"I know you don't want to hear it, but I've got to tell you. You understand? A person lives a whole life and never gets to tell his story. Who in Venta Prieta would listen to the likes of me?"

He jerked a contemptuous thumb toward the spick-and-span American. "Not these Mexicans. Not that American sitting over there."

"You're obviously going to tell it," I said. "So why don't you get on with it?" The air in the small room was curling now with cigarette and cigar smoke, taking on the dampish odors of beer and pulque.

He poured, measured with his eye of the remaining quantity. He seemed to think the bottle had to last the rest of his unnatural life. He sipped daintily, breathed gustily.

"You're a man and a gentleman," he said. "I always liked your stuff—when I used to read. I want you to know that. I *always* liked your stuff."

"I won't write about you," I said in a last forlorn attempt to forestall Mr. Harry Munn. "That's a promise. I *never* write about people who tell me the stories of their lives."

"I don't care about that." He waved his hand. "I just want to tell it to somebody while I still remember. You understand?"

"Yes," I said, touched in spite of myself by such transparent desperation. I looked across the room at the other American. He was watching us. When he saw my head turn, he took a Spanish-language newspaper from his pocket and pretended to read in the dim light.

"Take a good look at a guy, then," Harry Munn said. "He's got a good job, see, fine wife and kids, nice house in the suburbs. Got it made, you understand? He's worked a long time in a trusted position, and he'll retire with a pension that'll put him in Florida at sixty-five with nothing to do for the rest of his life but play shuffleboard and fish from a bridge. Get the picture?"

"I get the picture," I said. I motioned for another beer. The bartender brought it, shook his head sympathetically, went away.

"So what takes hold of a guy like that, that he decides to steal? Can you tell me?"

"Maybe you just had larceny in your soul," I said. "How much did you get? Not enough, apparently."

Ignoring my obvious desire to put a quick end to it, he went on. "He puts his heart and his soul into the art of embezzlement. He juggles books and accounts, he covers up, he shifts and turns. He sweats out the auditors, and he doesn't dare take a vacation because if somebody gets a look at his books on a bad day, he's done for."

He stared blindly. Deep now into the sotol, his tongue was beginning to stutter. He made an effort.

"It's a pattern, you know. Get a guy in your organization with access to money; if that guy is the first in to work and the last to leave, if he's never sick, never takes a vacation—you can just bet he's stealing you blind. Understand?"

"Yes," I said, with what patience I could muster. "I understand."

Harry Munn shook his head. "They never learn," he said sadly. "You can go to the bosses and talk yourself blue in the face. *Why, that's old Joe,* they'll say. *Good Old Joe has been with us forever. He wouldn't take a paper clip home without accounting for it. We've always depended on Good Old Joe.*"

He paused to lubricate his throat. His thirst fighting a losing battle with prudence, he took a pretty good slug this time. He was running through his day pretty fast. With any luck I wouldn't have to hear the story all the tedious way to the end.

He turned his face again toward me.

"But tell me. What takes hold of that guy? That's what I've been trying to figure out now for a long time."

He brooded.

"Something just reaches up and grabs him right out of that nice comfortable middle-class life and makes a criminal out of him. A day-in, day-out, forethoughtful criminal who is systematically stealing hundreds of thousands of dollars, all the time so careful not to spend a dime over his legitimate income that he lives poorer than he needs to."

"You ought to know," I said.

"Yes," he said broodingly. "I ought to, oughtn't I? That's the hell of it."

He took a swift drink—a quick cheat on himself so he wouldn't know he had done it.

"So what happens? He begins to get scared. He's run his luck pretty good, he's been careful, he's been smart. But sooner or later, and he knows it, his luck's got to run out. He sees jail staring him in the face—*long-time* jail, because banks get riled up pretty good when you steal from *them.* So he starts to think about cutting and running. You see the pattern?"

"I see the pattern," I said wearily.

He sneaked another quick drink. The bottle was getting low, and he didn't want to know it was close to becoming a dead soldier.

"He figures he's got 'em fooled. If he can only get away with the loot, he can live a life of ease in some foreign country. Maybe by now that American wife, and the brattish kids, and that split-level house are beginning to pall on him, anyway. So he looks at the half-naked girls on the travel folders and allows himself a dream or two."

He turned his head, searching for Rosita. She swung by the table. He reached for her with one hand, almost touching a smooth, black-satin hip.

"Rosita," he said, "I love you, baby"—all of it in barbaric Spanish except for the endearment.

Rosita grimaced at me, twisted away.

"So he plans his escape as carefully as he planned the original crime. It's not all that easy to get out of the country with cash money. But he figures it out—maybe he sews large bills into an overcoat, or he hides it in his car, and once over the border on a tourist card, he abandons the automobile. There's lots of ways, some of them legitimate enough if you can afford the cost. Though it's best to be a loner, because there's something about money in large illegal stacks that tends to make people pretty chancy."

"You can say that again," I said, signaling for another beer and thinking that if ever I'd heard a story I had no use for, this was it. How trite can you get, for God's sake? He had traveled the road as though he had invented it—and it had used him up, too, as though he were the pioneer of pioneers.

"Anyway, he gets it over the border," he said. "He finds an obscure place where nobody will ever come looking—he thinks. He settles down to the tropical life he's dreamed about, all those years back and forth between drab wife and drab job." He gazed on me anxiously. "You understand how it goes?"

"Sure," I said. "That's quite a story you've got there, Mr. Munn. Fascinating."

He regarded me suspiciously. "Wait till you hear it all," he said, "before you make up your mind. All right?"

"All right," I said as patiently as I could.

He looked at his bottle. Nearly empty. His hand fumbled, toppling it. He lunged, but too late; the remaining portion spilled irrevocably. Balancing the empty bottle on the table, he regarded it mournfully.

"I suppose, by rights, it's my round." He transferred the plaintive look to me. "I'd be honored to treat you to a drink, mister. I just happen to be strapped right now."

I was already motioning. The bartender shook his head reproachfully, but fetched a fresh bottle. The cantina population watched —including our American friend.

Harry Munn's face was smeared with a smirk of satisfied greed. He had gambled a couple of swallows against my sympathetic response to the loss, and he had won. He didn't know that I simply wanted to get him so drunk I could leave him. And I'd make damn sure he didn't sit at my table again during my stay in Venta Prieta.

He drank generously. His tongue was perceptibly thicker when he spoke again, and his eyes would not focus.

"You think that's the end of it," he said. "It's just the starting point. Because, you know what happens then?"

"No," I said.

"They start looking for our friend," he said triumphantly. He stared blearily. "Oh, the bank's not *too* upset—they're insured against that sort of thing. But insurance companies, now; they don't like to pay off a loyal employee's embezzlement. So they're likely to put a man on your trail. You know?"

I looked at the American across the room. He was obviously listening, now that Harry Munn was forgetting to keep his voice low.

Harry Munn, wagging a finger, lowered his voice conspiratorially.

"Don't underestimate that man. He's tracked down a lot of people in his time. His job depends on finding people while they've still got enough of the loot left to make it worthwhile for the insurance company. So it behooves him to work fast."

He was still wagging the finger.

"He's smart, you see. He's been there before. He doesn't want to flush his bird too soon. He's most interested in the money. So he works quietly, and because he knows how to look, he finds his man." He peered at me belligerently. "Can you tell me what happens next?"

"No," I said. "Tell *me*."

"In the capital he provides himself with the necessary legal documents to enlist the arresting power of the local authorities. He comes into Venta Prieta—where our culprit thinks he's safely hidden forever—to look the ground over. You understand?"

"No," I said frankly. "The investigator, with one good look at you, could tell the money's gone—so why doesn't he go on away?" I thought about it. "Or, if you're out to convince him the money *is* gone, if this is all just an act—"

Harry Munn peered for a long minute. Then, surprisingly, he giggled.

"Say now, that would make you a pretty good story, wouldn't it? All an act!" He frowned portentously. "A story. But not real life, mister. Because there's just one fractor you haven't taken into account."

He actually said "fractor." I looked at him closely. The new bottle was half finished, and so was he. Better than half. The rest of his story had better be short.

"What fractor is that?" I said.

"The investigator," he said, waving loose fingers in my face. "He's a human being, too. You haven't given him proper consideration."

He made a pretty good fight out of that last big word.

"You're right," I said. "I haven't."

"*Think* about that man. He knows his bird, inside and out. Understand? But—his bird's not at all like he expected him to be. You understand?"

"No," I said.

"Embezzlers run to a type," he said. "The more *successful* they are, the more *guilt* there is in their souls. And . . ." He nodded wisely. "The American character doesn't fit well with life in the Tropic Zone. It's what they call"—he struggled with it, won—"the Protestant Work Ethic."

He brooded again.

"But *this* bird. He's happy. He's contented. The new life is not just dream stuff; it's *really* all it was cracked up to be. So, don't you think that insurance man has got to stop and think?"

He had bewildered me this time. I wondered if his mind, so awash in the sea of cheap sotol, had cut its moorings.

"Explain it," I said.

"This investigator," he said. "He's got problems of his own, right? All his working life he's been on the go, tracking down thieves and giving them a hard time. No wife, no children, no place to call home. Just his job, and he's good at it, and all the time he sees these other men trying for the perfect thing and never making it—when he hasn't even had the guts to *try*. You understand?"

"No," I said.

He took a long drink this time. Unaccountably, it lifted the fog from his speech.

"Except *this* bird," he said. "This bird brought it off. He's living peaceful, in a peaceful place." He nodded. Slowly. "So our hotdog investigator, he finds a hunger inside himself for a share of it. He finds a decent place to stay. There's a beautiful young woman he can love. So—he stays right here in Venta Prieta, along with his bird-in-the-hand, and all the time he's carrying the documents. But he doesn't use them. You understand now?"

"No," I said again.

He leaned across the table. His voice was a husky whisper.

"See that American over there? Look at him. He's got his happy little pattern of living that just suits him to a T. Every day he sleeps until noon. He goes to the barber shop for a shave and a shine. He dines in style, after which he visits the cantina to read his paper and drink those fancy punches. Then he goes home and sleeps like a baby until it's time to do it all again tomorrow."

"So you're safe," I said. "There's no need to drink yourself to death out of daily fear he'll use those documents."

Harry Munn stared.

"You're crazy stupid," he said flatly. "*He's* the guy with the money. Me, I've got the papers right here"—he touched his breast pocket—"to put him in jail for the rest of his natural life. And I know where the loot is stashed. To pull his string, all I've got to do is take a stroll down to the police station. Any time I want."

He swung his head despairingly.

"So why don't I do it? Why?" He gazed at me. "That American over there—*he doesn't even know who I am*. You understand? He won't speak to me, because I'm the local American drunk. I came in here, *playing* the drunk, just to stake him out. Pretty soon I wasn't playing any more. Why? *Why?*"

"Don't you know?" I said.

His eyes shifted. Rosita was hurrying by. He watched her hungrily. When she came back, he barred her way with an arm.

"Rosita," he said. "There's a moon on the beach tonight, Rosita."

She gave him a tiny smile. I knew, suddenly: Rosita walked secretly on moonlit beaches with this strange, drunken American. She probably fed him, too, and provided the necessary daily minimum of alcohol level in his bloodstream. But, ashamed, she couldn't let the village know.

"I'll be there, baby," he told her. "See if I'm not, drunk as I am. So don't stand me up, Rosita baby."

She sneered, pushing his arm way. At the bar a fisherman laughed. Harry acted as if he were unaware of the derision; maybe he couldn't let himself hear. He drank deeply, directly from the bottle this time. It was the *coup de grâce*. His head went down on his outstretched arm.

"You understand?" he murmured, a strangely peaceful expression on his face.

I felt disturbed, vaguely guilty. I took bills out of my pocket, put them on the table. I scraped my chair back, looked up to see the spick-and-span American standing beside the table.

His tone of voice was censorious. "You bought him too much sotol," he said. "Even a tourist ought to know better." His tone softened. "Of course, you couldn't know how Mr. Munn is. You'll learn . . . I hope."

He put his hands into Mr. Munn's armpits, dragged him upright.

"Come on, Harry," he said. "Home to bed. No beach for you to-night."

Harry Munn sagged helplessly against his dapper protector. The heavyset little man got his weight under the lanky body, started for the door. He stopped, to smile sadly at me.

"I do this many nights," he said. "Sad, but   two Americans alone in a foreign town. It's the least I can do."

"Yes," I said. "It is, isn't it?"

I watched him struggle through the doorway with his compatriot. I noticed that Rosita cast an anxious glance as they left.

I went upstairs to my room. But I lay awake a long, long time in the tropical moonlight.

You understand?

South America

ARGENTINA

Borges

Jorge Luis Borges

The Two Kings and the Two Labyrinths

(translated by Donald A. Yates)

*We are proud that Ellery Queen's Mystery Magazine published
Jorge Luis Borges' first work to appear in the English language.
The story was titled "The Garden of Forking Paths," and it was
included in our issue of August 1948 . . .*

M en whose word may be trusted (but Allah knows more) relate
that in the early days there was a king of the islands of Babylon
who gathered together his architects and magicians and ordered
them to construct a labyrinth so perplexing and so subtle that pru-
dent men would not venture to set foot in it, and those that did
would become lost. This creation was a scandal, for confusion and
marvel are properly operations of God and not of man.

With the passing of time there came to his court a king of the
Arabs, and the king of Babylon, in order to make fun of his guest's
simplicity, had him enter the labyrinth, where he wandered ashamed
and humiliated until the setting of the sun. Then the king of Arabia
begged divine succor and came across the exit. His lips uttered no
complaint, but he said to the king of Babylon that in Arabia he had
a better labyrinth and that, God willing, he would make it known
to him one day.

Then the king returned to Arabia, called together his captains
and his lords, and overran the kingdom of Babylon with such bright
fortune that he destroyed its palaces, defeated its peoples, and cap-
tured the king himself. He tied the king of Babylon on the back of
a swift camel and led him to the desert.

They rode for three days at the end of which he said to the captive,
"Oh, King of Time and Substance and Great Presence of the Century,
in Babylon it was your will to lose me in a labyrinth of bronze with
many stairs and doors and walls; now the Almighty has seen fit that
I should show you mine own labyrinth, in which there are no stairs

for you to climb, nor fatiguing corridors for you to explore, nor walls to block your way."

Then the king of Arabia untied the cords and abandoned the king of Babylon in the middle of the desert, where he died of hunger and thirst.

Europe

ENGLAND

Lovesey
Rendell
Fremlin
Symons

DENMARK

Remar

THE NETHERLANDS

van de Wetering

BELGIUM

Simenon

FRANCE

Catalan

ITALY

Grimaldi

Peter Lovesey

Behind the Locked Door

*Peter Lovesey is well known on the mystery scene as a specialist
in historical detective stories (a division of the genre in which the
late John Dickson Carr was a master). Mr. Lovesey's first book,
WOBBLE TO DEATH (1970), won the Macmillan-Panther First
Crime Novel Competition, and introduced Sergeant Cribb and
his assistant, Constable Thackeray, two authentic police officers
of the Victorian era who have since appeared in seven more novels.*

*Mr. Lovesey's first story in Ellery Queen's Mystery Magazine
is not a tale of historical detection, although the story has its
roots, its beginnings, in 1840. But the action takes place today—a
persistent investigation by Inspector Gent of the C.I.D. Why did
the mysterious tenant want that particular flat and be willing to
wait nearly a year for it to become vacant? Join Inspector Gent
in ferreting out the secret behind the locked door, the unusual
secret of the room above the tobacconist's shop . . .*

Sometimes when the shop was quiet Braid would look up at the
ceiling and give a thought to the locked room overhead. He was
mildly curious, no more. If the police had not taken an interest he
would never have done anything about it.

The Inspector appeared one Wednesday soon after eleven, stepping
in from Leadenhall Street with enough confidence about him to show
he was no tourist. Neither was he in business; it is one of the City's
most solemn conventions that between ten and four nobody is seen
on the streets in a coat. This one was a brown imitation-leather coat,
categorically not City at any hour.

Gaunt and pale, a band of black hair trained across his head to
combat baldness, the Inspector stood back from the counter, not
interested in buying cigarettes, waiting rather, one hand in a pocket
of the coat, the other fingering his woolen tie, while the last genuine
customer named his brand and took his change.

When the door was shut he came a step closer and told Braid, "I

won't take up much of your time. Detective Inspector Gent, C.I.D."
The hand that had been in the pocket now exhibited a card. "Routine
inquiry. You are Frank Russell Braid, the proprietor of this shop?"

Braid nodded, and moistened his lips. He was perturbed at hearing
his name articulated in full like that, as if he were in court. He had
never been in trouble with the police, had never done a thing he was
ashamed of. Twenty-seven years he had served the public loyally
over this counter. He had not received a single complaint he could
recollect, or made one. From the small turnover he achieved he had
always paid whatever taxes the government imposed.

Some of his customers—bankers, brokers, accountants—made fortunes and talked openly of tax dodges. That was not Frank Braid's
way. He believed in fate. If it was decreed that he should one day
be rich, it would happen. Meanwhile he would continue to retail
cigarettes and tobacco honestly and without regret.

"I believe you also own the rooms upstairs, sir?"

"Yes."

"There is a tenant, I understand."

So Messiter had been up to something. Braid clicked his tongue,
thankful that the suspicion was not directed his way, yet irritated
at being taken in. From the beginning Messiter had made a good
impression. The year of his tenancy had seemed to confirm it. An
educated man, decently dressed, interesting to talk to, and completely reliable with the rent. This was a kick in the teeth.

"His name, sir?"

"Messiter." With deliberation Braid added, "Norman Henry Messiter."

"How long has Mr. Messiter been a lodger here?"

" 'Lodger' isn't the word. He uses the rooms as a business address.
He lives in Putney. He started paying rent in September last year.
That would be thirteen months, wouldn't it?"

It was obvious from the Inspector's face that this was familiar
information. "Is he upstairs this morning, sir?"

"No. I don't see a lot of Mr. Messiter. He calls on Tuesdays and
Fridays to collect the mail."

"Business correspondence?"

"I expect so. I don't examine it."

"But you know what line Mr. Messiter is in?" It might have been
drugs from the way the Inspector put the question.

"He deals in postage stamps."

"It's a stamp shop upstairs?"

"No. It's all done by correspondence. This is simply the address he uses when he writes to other dealers."

"Odd," the Inspector commented. "I mean, going to the expense of renting rooms when he could just as easily carry on the business from home."

Braid would not be drawn. He would answer legitimate questions, but he was not going to volunteer opinions. He busied himself tearing open a carton of cigarettes.

"So it's purely for business?" the Inspector resumed. "Nothing happens up there?"

That started Braid's mind racing. Nothing *happens* . . . ? What did they suspect? Orgies? Blue films?

"It's an unfurnished flat," he said. "Kitchen, bathroom, and living room. It isn't used."

At that the Inspector rubbed his hands. "Good. In that case you can show me over the place without intruding on anyone's privacy."

It meant closing for a while, but most of his morning regulars had been in by then.

"Thirteen months ago you first met Mr. Messiter," the Inspector remarked on the stairs.

Strictly it was untrue. As it was not put as a question, Braid made no response.

"Handsome set of banisters, these, Mr. Braid. Individually carved, are they?"

"The building is at least two hundred years old," Braid told him, grateful for the distraction. "You wouldn't think so to look at it from Leadenhall Street. You see, the front has been modernized. I wouldn't mind an old-fashioned front if I were selling silk hats or umbrellas, but cigarettes—"

"Need a more contemporary display," the Inspector cut in as if he had heard enough. "Was it thirteen months ago you first met Mr. Messiter?"

Clearly this had some bearing on the police inquiry. It was no use prevaricating. "In point of fact, no. More like two years." As the Inspector's eyebrows peaked in interest, Braid launched into a rapid explanation. "It was purely in connection with the flat. He came in here one day and asked if it was available. Just like that, without even looking over the place. At the time I had a young French couple as tenants. I liked them and I had no intention of asking them to leave. Besides, I know the law. You can't do that sort of thing. I told Mr. Messiter. He said he liked the location so much that he would wait till they moved out, and to show good faith he was ready to pay the first month's rent as a deposit."

"Without even seeing inside?"

"It must seem difficult to credit, but that was how it was," said Braid. "I didn't take the deposit, of course. Candidly, I didn't expect to see him again. In my line of business you sometimes get people coming in off the street simply to make mischief. Well, the upshot was that he *did* come back—repeatedly. I must have seen the fellow once a fortnight for the next eleven months. I won't say I understood him any better, but at least I knew he was serious. So when the French people eventually went back to Marseilles, Mr. Messiter took over the flat." By now they were standing on the bare boards of the landing. "The accommodation is unfurnished," he said in explanation. "I don't know what you hope to find."

If Inspector Gent knew, he was not saying. He glanced through the open door of the bathroom. The place had the smell of disuse.

He reverted to his theme. "Strange behavior, waiting all that time for a flat he doesn't use." He stepped into the kitchen and tried a tap. Water the color of weak tea spattered out. "No furniture about," he went on. "You must have thought it was odd, his not bringing in furniture."

Braid made no comment. He was waiting by the door of the locked room. This, he knew, was where the interrogation would begin in earnest.

"What's this—the living room?" the Inspector asked. He came to Braid's side and tried the door. "Locked. May I have the key, Mr. Braid?"

"That isn't possible, I'm afraid. Mr. Messiter changed the lock. We—er—came to an agreement."

The Inspector seemed unsurprised. "Paid some more on the rent, did he? I wonder why." He knelt by the door. "Strong lock. Chubb mortice. No good trying to open that with a piece of wire. How did he justify it, Mr. Braid?"

"He said it was for security."

"It's secure, all right." Casually, the Inspector asked, "When did you last see Mr. Messiter?"

"Tuesday." Braid's stomach lurched. "You don't suspect he is—"

"Dead in there? No, sir. Messiter is alive, no doubt of that. Active, I would say." He grinned in a way Braid found disturbing. "But I wouldn't care to force this without a warrant. I'll be arranging that. I'll be back." He started downstairs.

"Wait," said Braid, going after him. "As the landlord, I think I have the right to know what you suspect is locked in that room."

"Nothing dangerous or detrimental to health, sir," the Inspector told him without turning his head. "That's all you need to know. You trusted Messiter enough to let him install his own lock, so with respect you're in no position to complain about rights."

After the Inspector had left, Braid was glad he had not been stung into a response he regretted; but he was angry, and his anger refused to be subdued through the rest of the morning and afternoon. It veered between the Inspector, Messiter, and himself. He recognized now his mistake in agreeing to a new lock, but to be rebuked like a gullible idiot was unjust. Messiter's request had seemed innocent enough at the time.

Well, to be truthful, it had crossed Braid's mind that what was planned could be an occasional afternoon up there with a girl, but he had no objection to that if it was discreet. He was not narrow-minded. In its two centuries of existence the room must have seen some passion. But crime was quite another thing, not to be countenanced.

He had trusted Messiter, been impressed by his sincerity. The man had seemed genuinely enthusiastic about the flat, its old-world charm, the high corniced ceilings, the solid doors. To wait, as he had, nearly a year for the French people to leave had seemed a commitment, an assurance of good faith.

It was mean and despicable. Whatever was locked in that room had attracted the interest of the police. Messiter must have known this was a possibility when he took the rooms. He had cynically and deliberately put at risk the reputation of the shop. Customers were quick to pick up the taint of scandal. When this got into the papers, years of goodwill and painstaking service would go down the drain.

That afternoon, when Braid's eyes turned to the ceiling, he was not merely curious about the locked room. He was asking questions. Angry, urgent questions.

By six, when he closed, the thing had taken a grip on his mind. He had persuaded himself he had a right to know the extent of Messiter's deceit. Dammit, the room belonged to Braid. He would not sleep without knowing what was behind that locked door.

And he had thought of a way of doing it.

In the back was a wooden ladder about nine feet long. Years before, when the shop was a glover's, it had been used to reach the high shelves behind the counter. Modern shop design kept everything in easy reach. Where gloves had once been stacked in white boxes were displays of Marlboro country and the pure gold of Benson and Hedges. One morning in the summer he had taken the ladder outside the shop to investigate the working of the awning, which was jammed. Standing several rungs from the top he had been able to touch the ledge below the window of the locked room.

The evening exodus was over, consigning Leadenhall Street to surrealistic silence, when Braid propped the ladder against the shop-front. The black marble and dark-tinted glass of banks and insurance buildings glinted funereally in the streetlights, only the brighter windows of the Bull's Head at the Aldgate end indicating, as he began to climb, that life was there. If anyone chanced to pass that way and challenge him, he told himself, he would inform them with justification that the premises were his own and he was simply having trouble with a lock.

He stepped onto the ledge and drew himself level with the window, which was of the sash type. By using a screwdriver he succeeded in slipping aside the iron catch. The lower section was difficult to move, but once he had got it started it slid easily upward. He climbed inside and took out a flashlight.

The room was empty.

Literally empty. No furniture, no curtains, no carpet. Bare floorboards, ceiling, and walls with paper peeled away in several places.

Uncomprehending, he beamed the flashlight over the floorboards. They had not been disturbed in months. He examined the skirting board, the plaster cornice, and the window sill. He could not see how anything could be hidden here. The police were probably mistaken about Messiter. And so was he. With a sense of shame he climbed out of the window and drew it down.

On Friday, Messiter came in about eleven as usual, relaxed, indistinguishable in dress from the stockbrokers and bankers: dark suit, old boys' tie, shoes gleaming. With a smile he peeled a note from his wallet and bought his box of five Imperial Panatellas, a ritual that from the beginning had signaled goodwill toward his landlord. Braid sometimes wondered if he actually smoked them. He did not carry conviction as a smoker of cigars. He was a quiet man, functioning best in private conversations. Forty-seven by his own admission, he looked ten years younger, dark-haired with brown eyes that moistened when he spoke of things that moved him.

"Any letters for me, Mr. Braid?"

"Five or six." Braid took them from the shelf behind him.

"How is business?"

"No reason to complain," Messiter said, smiling. "My work is my hobby, and there aren't many lucky enough to say that. And how is the world of tobacco? Don't tell me. You'll always do a good trade here, Mr. Braid. All the pressures—you can see it in their faces. They need the weed and always will." Mildly he inquired, "Nobody called this week asking for me, I suppose?"

Braid had not intended saying anything, but Messiter's manner disarmed him. That and the shame he felt at the suspicions he had harbored impelled him to say, "Actually there *was* a caller. I had a detective in here—when was it?—Wednesday—asking about you. It was obviously a ridiculous mistake."

He described Inspector Gent's visit without mentioning his own investigation afterward with the ladder. "Makes you wonder what the police are up to these days," he concluded. "I believe we're all on the computer at Scotland Yard now. This sort of thing is bound to happen."

"You trust me, Mr. Braid. I appreciate that," Messiter said, his eyes starting to glisten. "You took me on trust from the beginning."

"I'm sure you aren't stacking stolen goods upstairs, if that's what you mean," Braid told him with sincerity.

"But the Inspector was not so sure?"

"He said something about a search warrant. Probably by now he has realized his mistake. I don't expect to see him again."

"I wonder what brought him here," Messiter said, almost to himself.

"I wouldn't bother about it. It's a computer error."

"I don't believe so. What did he say about the lock I fitted on the door, Mr. Braid?"

"Oh, at the time he seemed to think it was quite sinister." He grinned. "Don't worry—it doesn't bother me at all. You consulted me about it and you pay a pound extra a week for it, so who am I to complain? What you keep in there—if anything—is your business." He chuckled in a way intended to reassure. "That detective carried on as if you had a fortune hidden away in there."

"Oh, but I have."

Braid felt a pulse throb in his temple.

"It's high time I told you," said Messiter serenely. "I suppose I should apologize for not saying anything before. Not that there's anything criminal, believe me. Actually it's a rather remarkable story. I'm a philatelist, as you know. People smile at that and I don't blame them. Whatever name you give it, stamp collecting is a hobby for kids. In the business we're a little sensitive on the matter. We dignify it with its own technology—dies and watermarks and so forth—but I've always suspected this is partly to convince ourselves that the whole thing is serious and important.

"Well, it occurred to me four or five years ago that there was a marvelous way of justifying stamp collecting to myself and that was by writing a book about stamps. You must have heard of Rowland Hill, the fellow who started the whole thing off?"

"The Penny Post?"

Messiter nodded. "1840—the world's first postage stamps, the One-Penny Black and the Twopence Blue. My idea was not to write a biography of Hill—that's been done several times over by cleverer writers than I am—but to analyze the way his idea caught on. The response of the Victorian public was absolutely phenomenal, you know. It's all in the newspapers of the period. I went to the Newspaper Library at Colindale to do my research. I spent weeks over it."

Messiter's voice conveyed not fatigue at the memory, but excitement. "There was so much to read. Reports of Parliament. Letters to the Editor. Special articles describing the collection and delivery of the mail." He paused, pointing a finger at Braid. "You're wondering what this has to do with the room upstairs. I'll tell you. Whether it was providence or pure good luck I wouldn't care to say, but one afternoon in that Newspaper Library I turned up *The Times* for a day in May 1841, and my eye was caught—riveted, I should say—by an announcement in the Personal Column on the front page."

Messiter's hand went to his pocket and withdrew his wallet. From it he took a folded piece of paper. "This is what I saw."

Braid took it from him, a photostat of what was unquestionably a column of old newspaper type. The significant words had been scored round in ballpoint.

A Young Lady, being desirous of covering her dressing-room with cancelled postage stamps, has been so far encouraged in her wish by private friends as to have succeeded in collecting 16,000. These, however, being insufficient, she will be greatly obliged if any good-natured person who may have these otherwise worthless little articles at their disposal, would assist her in her whimsical project. Address to Miss E. D., Mr. Butt's, Glover, Leadenhall Street.

Braid made the connection instantly.

His throat went dry. He read it again. And again.

"You understand?" said Messiter. "It's a stamp man's dream—a room literally papered with Penny Blacks!"

"But this was—"

"1841. Right. More than a century ago. Have you ever looked through a really old newspaper? It's quite astonishing how easy it is to get caught up in the immediacy of the events. When I read that announcement, I could see that dressing room vividly in my imagination—chintz curtains, gas brackets, brass bedstead, washstand and mirror. I could see Miss E. D. with her paste pot and brush assiduously covering the wall with stamps.

"It was such an exciting idea that it came as a jolt to realize that it all had happened so long ago that Miss E. D. must have died about the turn of the century. And what of her dressing room? That, surely, must have gone, if not in the Blitz, then in the wholesale rebuilding of the City. My impression of Leadenhall Street was that the banks and insurance companies had lined it from end to end with gleaming office buildings five stories high. Even if by some miracle the shop that had been Butt's the Glover's *had* survived, and Miss E. D.'s room *had* been over the shop, common sense told me that those stamps must long since have been stripped from the walls."

He paused and lighted a cigar. Braid waited, his heart pounding.

"Yet there was a possibility, remote but tantalizing and irresistible, that someone years ago redecorated the room by papering *over* the stamps. Any decorator will tell you they sometimes find layer on layer of wallpaper. Imagine peeling back the layers to find thousands of Penny Blacks and Twopence Blues unknown to the world of philately! These days the commonest ones are catalogued at ten pounds or so, but find some rarities—inverted watermarks, special cancellations—and you could be up to five hundred pounds a stamp. Maybe a thousand pounds. Mr. Braid, I don't exaggerate when I tell you the value of such a room could run to half a million pounds. Half a million for what that young lady in her innocence called 'worthless little articles'!"

As if he read the thought, Messiter said, "It was my discovery. I went to a lot of trouble. Eventually I found the *Post Office Directory* for 1845 in the British Library. The list of residents in Leadenhall Street included a glover by the name of Butt."

"So you got the number of this shop?" Messiter nodded. "And when you came to Leadenhall Street, here it was, practically the last pre-Victorian building this side of Lloyd's?"

Messiter drew on his cigar, scrutinizing Braid.

"All those stamps," Braid whispered. "Twenty-seven years I've owned this shop and the flat without knowing that in the room upstairs was a fortune. It took you to tell me that."

"Don't get the idea it was easy for me," Messiter pointed out. "Remember I waited practically a year for those French people to move out. That was a test of character, believe me, not knowing what I would find when I took possession."

Strangely, Braid felt less resentment toward Messiter than the young Victorian woman who had lived in this building, *his* building, and devised a pastime so sensational in its consequence that his own walls mocked him.

Messiter leaned companionably across the counter. "Don't look so shattered, chum. I'm not the rat you take me for. Why do you think I'm telling you this?"

Braid shrugged. "I really couldn't say."

"Think about it. As your tenant, I did nothing underhanded. When I took the flat, didn't I raise the matter of redecoration? You said I was free to go ahead whenever I wished. I admit you didn't know then that the walls were covered with Penny Blacks, but I wasn't certain myself till I peeled back the old layers of paper. What a moment that was!"

He paused, savoring the recollection. "I've had a great year thanks to those stamps. In fact, I've set myself up for some time to come. Best of all, I had the unique experience of finding that room." He flicked ash from the cigar. "I estimate there are still upwards of twenty thousand stamps up there, Mr. Braid. In all justice, they belong to you."

Braid stared in amazement.

"I'm serious," Messiter went on. "I've made enough to buy a place in the country and write my book. The research is finished. That's been my plan for years, to earn some time, and I've done it. I want no more."

Frowning, Braid said, "I don't understand why you're doing this. Is it because of the police? You said there was nothing dishonest."

"And I meant it, but you are right, Mr. Braid. I am a little shaken to hear of your visit from the Inspector."

"What do you mean?"

Messiter asked obliquely, "When you read your newspaper, do you ever bother with the financial pages?"

Braid gave him a long look. Messiter held his stare.

"If it really has any bearing on this, the answer is no. I don't have much interest in the stock market. Nor any capital to invest," he added.

"Just as well in these uncertain times," Messiter commented. "Blue-chip investments have been hard to find these last few years. That's why people have been putting their money into other things. Art, for instance. A fine work of art holds its value in real terms even in a fluctuating economy. So do jewelry and antiques. And old postage stamps, Mr. Braid. Lately a lot of money has been invested in old stamps."

"That I can understand."

"Then you must also understand that information such as this"—he put his hand on the photostat between them—"is capable of causing flutters of alarm. Over the last year or so I have sold to dealers a number of early English stamps unknown to the market. These people are not fools. Before they buy a valuable stamp, they like to know the history of its ownership. I have had to tell them my story and show them the story in *The Times*. That's all right. Generally they need no more convincing. But do you understand the difficulty? It's the prospect of twenty thousand Penny Blacks and Twopence Blues unknown to the stamp world shortly coming onto the market. Can you imagine the effect?"

"I suppose it will reduce the value of those stamps people already own."

"Precisely. The rarities will not be so rare. Rumors begin, and it isn't long before there is a panic and stamp prices tumble."

"Which is when the sharks move in," said Braid. "I see it now. The police probably suspect the whole thing is a fraud."

Messiter gave a nod.

"But you and I know it isn't a fraud," Braid went on. "We can show them the room. I still don't understand why you are giving it up."

"I told you the reason. I always planned to write my book. And there is something else. It's right to warn you that there is sure to be publicity over this. Newspapers, television—this is the kind of story they relish, the unknown Victorian girl, the stamps undiscovered for over a century. Mr. Braid, I value my privacy. I don't care for my name being printed in the newspapers. It will happen, I'm sure, but I don't intend to be around when it does. That's why I am telling nobody where I am going. After the whole thing has blown over, I'll send you a forwarding address, if you would be so kind—"

"Of course, but—"

A customer came in, one of the regulars. Braid gave him a nod and wished he had gone to the kiosk up the street.

Messiter picked up the conversation. "Was it a month's notice we agreed? I'll see that my bank settles the rent." He took the keys of the flat from his pocket and put them on the counter with the photostat. "For you. I won't need these again." Putting a hand on Braid's arm, he added, "Some time we must meet and have a drink to Miss E. D.'s memory."

He turned and left the shop and the customer asked for 20 Rothmans. Braid lifted his hand in a belated salute through the shop window and returned to his business. More customers came in. Fridays were always busy with people collecting their cigarettes for the weekend. He was thankful for the activity. It compelled him to adjust by degrees and accept that he was now a rich man. Unlike Messiter, he would not object to the story getting into the press. Some of these customers who had used the shop for years and scarcely acknowledged him as a human being would choke on their toast and marmalade when they saw his name one morning in *The Times*.

It satisfied him most to recover what he owned. When Messiter had disclosed the secret of the building, it was as if the 27 years of Braid's tenure were obliterated. The place was full of Miss E. D. That young lady—she would always be young—had in effect asserted her prior claim. He had doubted if he would ever again believe the building was truly his own. But now that her "whimsical project" had been ceded to him, he was going to take pleasure in dismantling the design, stamp by stamp, steadily accumulating a fortune Miss E. D. had never supposed would accrue. Vengeful it might be, but it would exorcise her from the building that belonged to him.

Ten minutes before closing time Inspector Gent entered the shop. As before, he waited for the last customer to leave.

"Sorry to disturb you again, sir. I have that warrant now."

"You won't need it," Braid cheerfully told him. "I have the key. Mr. Messiter was here this morning." He started to recount the conversation.

"Then I suppose he took out his cutting from *The Times*," put in the Inspector.

"You *know* about that?"

"Do I?" he said caustically. "The man has been round just about every stamp shop north of Birmingham telling the tale of that young woman and the Penny Blacks on her dressing-room wall."

Braid frowned. "There's nothing dishonest in that. The story really did appear in *The Times,* didn't it?"

"It did, sir. We checked. And this *is* the address mentioned." The Inspector eyed him expressionlessly. "The trouble is that the Penny Blacks our friend Messiter has been selling in the north aren't off any dressing-room wall. He buys them from a dealer in London, common specimens, about ten pounds each one. Then he works on them."

"Works on them? What do you mean?"

"Penny Blacks are valued according to the plates they were printed from, sir. There are distinctive markings on each of the plates, most particularly in the shape of the guide letters that appear in the corners. The stamps Messiter has been selling are doctored to make them appear rare. He buys a common Plate 6 stamp in London, touches up the guide letters, and sells it to a Manchester dealer as a Plate 11 stamp for seventy-five pounds. As it's catalogued at more than twice that, the dealer thinks he has a bargain. Messiter picks his victims carefully: generally they aren't specialists in early English stamps, but almost any dealer is ready to look at a Penny Black in case it's a rare one."

Braid shook his head. "I don't understand this at all. Why should Messiter have needed to resort to forgery? There are twenty thousand stamps upstairs."

"Have you seen them?"

"No, but the newspaper story—"

"That fools everyone, sir."

"You said it was genuine."

"It is. And the idea of a roomful of Penny Blacks excites people's imagination. They *want* to believe it. That's the secret of all the best confidence tricks. Now why do you suppose Messiter had a mortice lock fitted on that room? You thought it was because the contents were worth a fortune? Has it occurred to you as a possibility that he didn't want anyone to know there was nothing there?"

Braid's dream disintegrated.

"It stands to reason, doesn't it," the Inspector went on, "that the stamps were ripped off the wall generations ago? When Messiter found empty walls, he couldn't abandon the idea. It had taken a grip on him. That young woman who thought of papering her wall with stamps could never have supposed she would be responsible over a century later for turning a man to crime."

The Inspector held out his hand. "If I could have that key, sir, I'd like to see the room for myself." Braid followed the Inspector upstairs and watched him unlock the door. They entered the room.

"I don't mind admitting I have a sneaking admiration for Messiter," the Inspector said. "Imagine the poor beggar coming in here at last after going to all the trouble he did to find the place. Look, you can see where he peeled back the wallpaper layer by layer"—gripping a furl of paper, he drew it casually aside—"to find absolutely—" He stopped. "My God!"

The stamps were there, neatly pasted in rows.

Braid said nothing, but the blood slowly drained from his face.

Miss E. D.'s scheme of interior decoration had been more ambitious than anyone expected. She had diligently inked over every stamp with red, purple, or green ink—to form an intricate mosaic of colors. Originally Penny Blacks or Twopence Blues, Plate 6 or Plate 11, they were now as she had described them in *The Times*—"worthless little articles."

Ruth Rendell

On the Path

Six victims so far—and there hadn't been a killing for a week . . . something unusual from one of England's finest crime writers . . .

There hadn't been a killing now for a week. The evening paper's front page was devoted instead to the economic situation and an earthquake in Turkey. But page three kept up the interest in this series of murders. On it were photographs of the six victims, all recognizably belonging to the same type. There, in every case, although details of feature naturally varied, were the same large liquid eyes, full soft mouth, and long dark hair.

Barry's mother looked up from the paper.

"I don't like you going out at night."

"What, me?" said Barry.

"Yes, you. All these murders happened round here. I don't like you going out after dark. It's not as if you had to, it's not as if it was for work." She got up and began to clear the table, but continued to speak in a low whining tone. "I wouldn't say a word if you were a big chap. If you were the size of your cousin Ronnie I wouldn't say a word. A fellow your size doesn't stand a chance against that maniac."

"I see," said Barry. "And whose fault is it I'm only five feet two? I might just point out that a woman of five feet that marries a bloke only two inches more can't expect to have giants for kids. Right?"

"I sometimes think you only go roving about at night, doing what you want, to *prove* you're as big a man as your cousin Ronnie."

Barry thrust his face close up to her. "Look, leave off, will you?" He waved the paper at her. "I may not have the height but I'm not in the right category. Has that occurred to you? Has it?"

"All right, all right. I wish you wouldn't be always shouting."

In his bedroom Barry put on his new velvet jacket and dabbed cologne on his wrists and neck. He looked spruce and dapper. His mother gave him an apprehensive glance as he passed her on his

101

way to the back door, and returned to her contemplation of the pictures in the newspaper. Six of them in two months. The girlish faces, doe-eyed, diffident, looked back at her or looked aside or stared at distant unknown objects. After a while she folded the paper and switched on the television. Barry, after all, was not in the right category, and that must be her comfort.

He liked to go and look at the places where the bodies of the victims had been found. It brought him a thrill of danger and a sense of satisfaction. The first of them had been strangled very near his home on a path which first passed between draggled allotments, then became an alley plunging between the high brown wall of a convent and the lower red brick wall of a school.

Barry took this route to the livelier part of the town, walking rapidly but without fear and pausing at the point—a puddle of darkness between lamps—where the one they called Pat Leston had died. It seemed to him, as he stood there, that the very atmosphere, damp, dismal, and silent, breathed evil and the horror of the act. He appreciated it, inhaled it, and then passed on to seek, on the waste ground, the common, in a deserted back street of condemned houses, those other murder scenes. After the last killing they had closed the underpass, and Barry found to his disappointment that it was still closed.

He had walked a couple of miles and had hardly seen a soul. People stayed at home. There was even some kind of panic, he had noticed, when it got to six and the light was fading and the buses and tube trains were emptying themselves of the last commuters. In pairs they walked, and sometimes they scurried. They left the town as depopulated as if a plague had scoured it.

Entering the high street, walking its length, Barry saw no one, apart from those protected by the metal and glass of motor vehicles, but an old woman hunched on a step. Bundled in dirty clothes, a scarf over her head and a bottle in her hand, she was as safe as he—as far, or farther, from the right category.

But he was still on the watch. Next to viewing the spots where the six had died, he best enjoyed singling out the next victim. No one, for all the boasts of the newspapers and the policemen, knew the type as well as he did. Slight and small-boned, long-legged, sway-backed, with huge eyes, pointed features, and long dark hair. He was almost sure he had selected the Italian one as a potential victim some two weeks before the event, though he could never be certain.

So far today he had seen no one likely, in spite of watching with fascination the exit from the tube on his own way home. But now, as he entered the Red Lion and approached the bar, his eye fell on a candidate who corresponded to the type more completely than anyone he had yet singled out. Excitement stirred in him. But it was unwise, with everyone so alert and nervous, to be caught staring. The barman's eyes were on him. He asked for a half of lager, paid for it, tasted it, and, as the barman returned to rinsing glasses, turned slowly to appreciate to the full that slenderness, that soulful timid look, those big expressive eyes, and that mane of black hair.

But things had changed during the few seconds his back had been turned. Previously he hadn't noticed that there were two people in the room, another as well as the candidate, and now they were sitting together. From intuition, at which Barry fancied himself as adept, he was sure the girl had picked the man up. There was something in the way she spoke as she lifted her full glass which convinced him, something in her look, shy yet provocative.

He heard her say, "Well, thank you, but I didn't mean to . . . " and her voice trailed away, drowned by the other's brashness.

"Catch my eye? Think nothing of it, love. My pleasure. Your fella one of the unpunctual sort, is he?"

She made no reply. Barry was fascinated, compelled to stare, by the resemblance to Pat Leston, by more than that, by seeing in this face what seemed a quintessence, a gathering together and a concentrating here of every quality variously apparent in each of the six. And what gave it a particular piquancy was to see it side by side with such brutal ugliness. He wondered at the girl's nerve, her daring to make overtures. And now she was making them afresh, actually laying a hand on his sleeve.

"I suppose you've got a date yourself?" she said.

The man laughed. "Afraid I have, love. I was just whiling away ten minutes." He started to get up.

"Let me buy you a drink."

His answer was only another harsh laugh. Without looking at the girl again, he walked away and through the swing doors out into the street. That people could expose themselves to such danger in the present climate of feeling intrigued Barry, his eyes now on the girl who was also leaving the pub. In a few seconds it was deserted, the only clients likely to visit it during that evening all gone.

A strange idea, with all its amazing possibilities, crossed his mind and he stood on the pavement, gazing the length of the High Street. But the girl had crossed the road and was waiting at the bus stop, while the man was only just visible in the distance, turning into the entrance of the underground car park.

Barry banished his idea, ridiculous perhaps and, to him, rather upsetting, and he crossed the road behind the oncoming bus, wondering how to pass the rest of the evening. Review once more those murder scenes, was all that suggested itself to him, and then go home.

It must have been the wrong bus for her. She was still waiting. And as Barry approached, she spoke to him.

"I saw you in the pub."

"Yes," he said. He never knew how to talk to girls. They intimidated and irritated him, especially when they were taller than he, and most of them were. The little thin ones he despised.

"I thought," she said hesitantly, "I thought I was going to have someone to see me home."

Barry made no reply. She came out of the bus shelter, quite close up to him, and he saw that she was much bigger and taller than he had thought at first.

"I must have just missed my bus. There won't be another for ten minutes." She looked, and then he looked, at the shiny desert of this shopping center, lighted and glittering and empty, pitted with the dark holes of doorways and passages. "If you're going my way," she said, "I thought maybe . . . "

"I'm going through the path," he said. Round there that was what everyone called it, the path.

"That'll do me." She sounded eager and pleading. "It's a short cut to my place. Is it all right if I walk along with you?"

"Suit yourself," he said. "One of them got killed down there. Doesn't that bother you?"

She only shrugged. They began to walk along together up the yellow and white glazed street, not talking, at least a yard apart. It was a chilly damp night and a gust of wind caught them as, past the shops, they entered the path. The wind blew out the long red silk scarf she wore and she tucked it back inside her coat. Barry never wore a scarf, though most people did at this time of the year. It amused him to notice just how many did, as if they had never taken in the fact that all those six had been strangled with their own scarves.

There were lamps in this part of the path, attached by iron brackets to the red wall and the brown. Her sharp-featured face looked greenish in the light, and gaunt and scared. Suddenly he wasn't intimidated by her any more or afraid to talk to her.

"Most people," he said, "wouldn't walk down here at night for a million pounds."

"You do," she said. "You were coming down here alone."

"And no one gave me a million," he said cockily. "Look, that's where the first one died, just round this corner."

She glanced at the spot expressionlessly and walked on ahead of Barry. He caught up to her. If she hadn't been wearing high heels she wouldn't have been that much taller than he. He pulled himself up to his full height, stretching his spine, as if effort and desire could make him as big as his cousin Ronnie.

"I'm stronger than I look," he said. "A man's always stronger than a woman. It's the muscles."

He might not have spoken for all the notice she took. The walls ended and gave place to low railings behind which the allotments, scrubby plots of cabbage stumps and waterlogged weeds, stretched away. Beyond them, but a long way off, rose the backs of tall houses hung with wooden balconies and iron staircases. A pale moon had come out and cast over this dismal prospect a thin cold radiance.

"There'll be someone killed here next," he said. "It's just the place. No one to see. The killer could get away over the allotments."

She stopped and faced him. "Don't you ever think about anything but those murders?"

"Crime interests me. I'd like to know why he does it." He spoke insinuatingly, his resentment of her driven away by the attention she was at last giving him. "Why d'you think he does it? It's not for money or sex. What's he got against them?"

"Maybe he hates them." Her own words seemed to frighten her and, strangely, she pulled off the scarf which the wind had again been flapping, and thrust it into her coat pocket. "I can understand that." She looked at him with a mixture of dislike and fear. "I hate men, so I can understand it," she said, her voice trembling and shrill.

"Come on, let's walk."

"No." Barry put out his hand and touched her arm. His fingers clutched her coat sleeve. "No, you can't just leave it there. If he hates them, why does he?"

"Perhaps he's been turned down too often," she said, backing away from him. "Perhaps a long time ago one of them hurt him. He doesn't want to kill them but he can't help himself." As she flung his hand off her arm, the words came spitting out. "Or he's just ugly. A little like you."

Barry stood on tiptoe to bring himself to her height. He took a step toward her, his fists up. She backed against the railings and a longer shudder went through her. Then she wheeled away and began to run, stumbling because her heels were high. It was those heels or the roughness of the ground or the new darkness as clouds dimmed the moon that brought her down.

Collapsed in a heap, one shoe kicked off, she slowly raised her head and looked up into Barry's eyes. He made no attempt to touch her. She struggled to her feet, wiping her grazed and bleeding hands on the scarf, and immediately, without a word, they were locked together in the dark.

Several remarkable features distinguished this murder from the others. There was blood on the victim who had fair hair instead of dark, though otherwise strongly resembling Patrick Leston and Dino Facci. Apparently, since Barry Halford hadn't been wearing a scarf, the murderer's own had been used. But it was the evidence of a slim dark-haired customer of the Red Lion which led the police to the conclusion that the killer of these seven young men was a woman.

Celia Fremlin

A   Lovely   Morning   to   Die

*A horrifying story, told with Celia Fremlin's "special touch"—one
that will touch us all . . .*

If only she'd known it would be as easy as this, she'd have done
it long ago. Still holding the pillow firmly over the old woman's
face, Millicent allowed her eyes to travel warily down the length of
the wide old-fashioned bed. Beneath the blankets and the worn limp
eiderdown the emaciated body raised scarcely a hump; a long thin
irregularity was all it was, not as high as even the shallowest of the
graves in the nearby churchyard.

She had been afraid there would be some sort of struggle, that at
the approach of death the feeble, almost useless old limbs would be
infused with demonic strength, that the old worn-out body would
thresh about like a great fish beneath the blankets, refusing to die.
Most of all, she had feared there might be gasps and chokings and
moans of protest from under the pillow. If this had happened, would
she have been able to go on with it? Or would her nerve have cracked,
forcing her to abandon the resolution that had cost her so many
heart-searchings, so many self-questionings, over so many weeks?

If only she'd known it was going to be like this—the victim so
peaceful, so cooperative almost, the bedroom so quiet! Had she only
known this was how it would be, she'd have done it months—no,
years—ago.

But how long did she have to stay like this, clutching and pressing
down on the pillow? How long *do* you have to hold a pillow over a
person's face before you can be sure—quite, quite sure—that the last
breath is gone? For the first time she comprehended the awful loneliness of the task she had undertaken, with no precedents to go by,
no one in all the world to give advice or guidance.

She bent low, pressing her ear against the pillow, as though trying
to catch some whispered last words, some final message from her
once-beloved mother.

It was breathing she was listening for, of course; and there was none. No sound; no stir of movement; and yet still she dared not release the pressure, not just yet. Edging the weight of her body farther over the pillow, to make sure that it stayed in place, she slid her hand beneath the blankets and felt for the old woman's heart. The ribs stuck out like the slats of a plate rack, the pouches of wrinkled skin lay still and flaccid beneath her touch.

No heartbeat. No flutter of breath. Nothing. It was over! So quietly, so decently! It was beyond belief!

And then, suddenly, like a great yellow sea monster rising from the deep, her mother's face lurched upward, grimacing, contorted, and a howl like a wolf's burst from the parched lips as with hands like claws the creature wrenched the pillow from her daughter's grasp, and flung it to the ground—

Millicent woke, sweating with terror, to find herself safe in bed, in her own neat, austere little bedroom just across the landing from her mother's; and for a moment she lay still, breathing deeply, recovering from the nightmare: reorientating herself, reassuring herself that she *was* awake, and that none of those awful things had actually happened.

Yes, it was all right. It had only been a dream—one of those unnerving nightmares that had been troubling her increasingly of late.

She really ought to consult Dr. Ferguson about these bad nights she was having, get him to prescribe something. He was a kind man, and, so far as his busy schedule permitted, concerned for Millicent's plight. Always, after his routine visit to her mother every Wednesday, he would make a point of asking Millicent how she felt. Eating all right, was she? Not overdoing it? She must remember that she wasn't getting any younger—62, wasn't it, this year?

More than once he had insisted on taking her blood pressure, had tut-tutted, with slightly raised eyebrows, at the result, and had urged her to take things easy for a while, to try not to do too much. He had known as well as she had that with a senile, bedridden old mother of 92 in her sole charge, there was no way Millicent could take things easy, no way she could not do too much but since there was nothing that either of them could do about it, they had smiled appropriate politenesses at one another, and he had gone on his way. At least it was nice to know that he cared.

It was useless to hope for any more sleep that night. Already the light was beginning to show round the edges of the curtains, and outside the twittering of the first birds had begun. Through the open door across the landing (both doors were kept wide-open at night now, lest Mother's low moans of distress should fail to rouse her) Millicent could see the outlines of Mother's vast mahogany wardrobe, glimmering grayly in the half light of early dawn; and beyond it, deep in the shadowed heart of the sickroom, she could hear the harsh, rasping snores that for so long had been the backdrop of all her days and nights.

Only occasionally, now, did the old woman rouse herself from this ugly, uneasy sleep; to moan, or babble, or sometimes to plead wordlessly, unavailingly, staring desperately into her daughter's eyes, begging urgently for Millicent knew not what. A bedpan? A loving kiss on her cracked lips? Or merely a nice cup of tea, to be fed, trickles of it dribbling down the wrinkled, flabby jowls onto the pillow, whose cases Millicent often had to change four or five times a day.

There was no knowing what Mother wanted: and often Millicent, who had once loved her mother so much, had drawn from her such strength and love and comfort through the long years of family crises, family rejoicings—often, Millicent would eagerly proffer all three—the bedpan, the kiss, and the cool tea—almost simultaneously; and when, afterward, the old woman sank once more into noisy, unrefreshing sleep, it was hard to tell which, if any of them, had done the trick.

Perhaps none of them had. Perhaps the invalid had fallen asleep from sheer weariness, exhausted by the futile effort of asking ... asking ... asking for the one relief her daughter would not, could not give.

Or could she? More and more often lately, through the long wearying days of nursing, and housework, and more nursing, and through the even longer anxious, insomniac nights, forever on the alert, forever half listening through the two wide-open doors for sounds of distress—more and more, during these past weeks, Millicent had found herself turning over and over in her mind the ethics of her impending decision.

There was no doubt at all about what her mother would have wanted—her *real* mother, that is, the loving, energetic, courageous woman who even at 80 had tended her home single-handed, and her half acre of garden; had invited grandchildren and great-grandchildren on long visits, and had even found time to do volunteer work at the local hospital as well; about the views of this vigorous, life-loving person there could be no question at all:

"You won't let me get like that ever, will you, darling?" she'd said more than once to her daughter after a particularly harrowing session at the geriatric ward. "It's wicked, it's obscene, to let a person linger on like that—just a hulk of flesh, all meaning, all dignity gone! It's a wicked thing, it's the one and only fear I have about getting old—that I might end up like that! You won't let it happen to me, will you, darling? You'll make sure, won't you, if I'm past doing for myself, that they bump me off good and early?"

Such an easy promise to make, with the August sun streaming in through the kitchen window, and the putative victim up to her elbows in flour, preparing a batch of jam tarts for the impending visit of her two great-grandsons, aged nine and eleven, and with appetites like wolves.

"Of course I promise," she'd answered, and meant it; for in fact she agreed entirely with her mother's attitude, admired and respected her for it. Besides, it all seemed so incredibly unlikely. Mother was the kind of person who would die in harness when the time came—drop dead wheeling the library cart along some polished corridor, or while sawing too vigorously at a dead branch overhanging her beloved garden.

But it hadn't happened like that; and how could you be sure, now, that this mumbling, senile old wreck was still of the same mind?

Once, several years ago, while Mother had still been her sane and sharp-witted self, Millicent had posed this very question to her; and her reply had been immediate and unhesitating:

"You must do what *I've* asked you to do, darling—*I, myself*—the real *me*. This person talking to you now—the one you see in front of you, *she's* the *real* me, the one you must listen to. Pay no attention to the views—if any—of the mindless, dribbling old loony I may one day turn into, because she won't be *me* any more, not in any real sense. Do you think I'd allow *that* senile old hag to decide how *I* am going to die?"

Proud words, and unanswerable. Quietly Millicent had resolved that, should the occasion ever arise, she would do exactly as her mother had asked. For so brave, so indomitable a person, how could a loving daughter do less?

"Aah . . . aah. . . !"

The snoring had ceased, and at the familiar, urgent summons, Millicent scrambled hurriedly out of bed, her night's rest at an end, and hastened to her mother's bedside.

Too late; but of course the poor old creature couldn't help it. Wrinkling her nose as she edged the soiled sheet, inch by inch, from under the inert, unhelpful length of flesh, it came to her, with sudden, piercing intensity, that if only she had the courage of her convictions, she would never have to do this again.

Never. Ever. By tonight she could be free. Free to go to bed, and sleep and sleep and sleep the whole night through, for the first time in years. And her mother, her beloved mother, could be lying clean and dignified at last, in a nice clean coffin, all the humiliations at an end.

Clean. Clean. That, somehow, seemed the most important thing of all for someone like Mother, so proud, so capable, bustling around her shining, well kept home, full of flowers, and with windows thrown wide to the sweet morning air.

And later Millicent said to herself, I will do it. I will do as she asked. I promised her I would, and I will.

But not today. Not with my nerves all to pieces from that awful dream. Not with my hands trembling like this and my throat closing up with fear at the very idea—

No, not today. Tomorrow.

But that night she had the same dream all over again. Well, not exactly the same, though it started off in just the same way—with the pillow held quietly but firmly over the sleeping face, and the thin acquiescent figure lying so still and unprotesting beneath the bedclothes; and there was, too, that same sense of vague surprise, of uneasy relief, that it was all so simple.

But after that the dream changed. This time there was no yellow, accusing face lunging upward. Instead, just as Millicent was beginning to feel sure that the thing was finished, that breath and heartbeat were at an end—at just this moment there came suddenly from beneath the bedclothes an ominous gurgling sound, louder and louder.

So, even after death, this was going to go on—and on and on and on—to all eternity? To Millicent's dreaming brain there seemed no absurdity in the idea, and she stared, numb with horror, at the silent, murdered figure . . .

Again Millicent woke in a sweat of terror; again she had to lie for a few minutes, recovering, getting her breath back, reassuring herself that it had only been a dream.

And even after this, and even though the familiar, rasping snores could be clearly heard from across the landing, she still did not feel wholly at ease. The dream itself was nonsense, obviously, but what more likely than that some sound, some disturbance from the next room had triggered it off? The most probable thing was that the old woman, failing to rouse her daughter with her feeble moans, had had another accident; and that Millicent, subliminally aware of this, and subliminally guilty about sleeping on when she should have wakened, had converted the whole thing into a hideous dream.

Yes, that's what must have happened. And so, tired though she was, her eyes drooping with sleep, there seemed no alternative but to tiptoe across the landing and investigate.

It was all right. There was no accident—only the unchanging, all-pervading odor of sickness and old age, and this would go only when the old woman, too, was gone. Strange that it is death alone that has the power, like a mighty sea wind, to sweep away the smell of death.

The old woman was deeply snoring, and did not stir as Millicent leaned over her. The sunken yellow face looked as peaceful as it would ever look this side of the grave, but even so it was not entirely at rest. Every so often, while Millicent watched, it would twitch a little, as if at some small irritation—the gnats and midges, perhaps, of some long-past summer evening in a more leisured world than this: friends gathered for after-dinner conversation on the terrace: the tinkle of coffee spoons, the easy rise and fall of long-dead talk and laughter, far into the summer night . . .

I ought to do it now—*now*—so that these tranquil thoughts will be the last she will ever have; so that a sort of dim peace, at least, and the absence of discomfort, may be her last experiences on this earth.

Slowly, carefully, and making every effort not to rouse the sleeping figure, Millicent reached for the spare pillow and laid it softly across the dreaming face. Then, leaning forward with all her weight, she pressed down . . . down . . .

Not even the most frightful of the recent nightmares, not even the most exaggerated of all her fevered imaginings, had prepared Millicent for anything like *this*. Instantly, and as if galvanized into hideous life by some sort of monstrous shock treatment out of science fiction, the body leaped and plunged beneath her, with a strength that was beyond belief.

The old withered arms, like sticks, flailed and fought their way out from under the blankets and battered at the empty air. The knees, immobile for years, jackknifed beneath the bedclothes, pitching blankets and eiderdown to left and right; the legs, weak as string, kicked out in all directions, pounding against the mattress. The whole moribund body, which had scarcely stirred in years, lashed this way and that beneath the covers, arching, heaving—even with all her strength, all the weight of her body, Millicent could barely hold the creature down.

Promises, promises! How could either of them, making their humane and civilized pact all those years ago, have guessed that *this* was what they were undertaking? That Life, even at its last gasp, even with all its faculties rotted beyond repair and all its muscles wasted away to nothing, is like a tiger, mad with purpose, glittering with awful power; with teeth bared, claws outstretched, hurling into the face of the universe its surging, unquenchable determination to go on and on and on.

Half sobbing with the effort to hold the creature down, Millicent cried aloud, "I can't . . . I can't!"—or rather, fancied she was crying it aloud; but somehow no sound came. It was in her head that the words were pounding, "I can't . . . I can't!" and the sobbing was deep in her heart, and it only felt as if her cheeks were wet with tears . . .

This time when she woke, it was bright morning, and she started up in dismay, knowing at once, from the bright bands of sunlight across the carpet, that it was late, very late. And on a Wednesday, too, just when there was such a lot to do, with the doctor coming, and everything! How dreadfully unfortunate—though of course it was obvious how it had happened. Lying in bed recovering from that first nightmare, she must have dropped off again and gone straight into a second nightmare, almost like a continuation of the first.

Two nightmares in a single night! It was getting past a joking matter. Something would really have to be done.

And that afternoon, when Dr. Ferguson paid his routine visit to Mother, Millicent braced herself to tell him about the bad nights she'd been having lately, and how she'd been suffering from nightmares. At once he was full of sympathy, as she'd known he would be. He readily prescribed sleeping tablets for the next few nights, quite strong ones, guaranteed to eliminate dreaming of any kind.

"You've been overdoing it, my dear," he said, as he'd said so often. "Are you sure you wouldn't like me to get onto the Social Services and arrange for—"

But Millicent was adamant.

"I'll be fine," she assured him. "All I need is to catch up on my sleep, and then I'll be as right as rain."

He did not press the matter. He knew how proud they could be, these single women of Millicent's generation, how self-sufficient, how determined never to show any weakness. You couldn't help admiring it, in a way; and perhaps it was a fortunate thing that such people did still exist, what with nursing help being in such short supply, and most of his other patients, untroubled by pride, clamoring and badgering for every kind of help that was available.

And of course he couldn't guess—or if he did guess—he was certainly going to keep his own counsel about it—that Millicent's main reason for not wanting a nurse or a home-help around was that once such a professional was installed, it would at once become enormously more difficult to carry out her plan.

For carry it out she would, despite the nightmares, despite all the doubts and terrors in her heart. A promise was a promise. Mother had trusted her, and she would not, must not, betray that trust.

That night she took one of the new sleeping pills, and it was marvelous. She felt herself sinking, within minutes, into a deep dreamless sleep such as she hadn't enjoyed in years. And when morning came, she couldn't remember when she'd felt so refreshed, so strong, so rested; so *right,* somehow, and ready for anything. And at once it came to her, with quiet, overwhelming certainty, and even with a strange sense of exhilaration, that *now* was the time.

Now, in the first bright freshness of the morning, with the early sunshine glinting through the trees, and herself feeling so well, so vigorous. And there had been no nightmares, either, this was the biggest blessing. For months now it had been the nightmares that had stood between the decision and the execution.

The sun was brightening every moment, and the soft air was filled with birdsong. A lovely morning to die. And to die in one's sleep, too, without—in all probability—a single pang.

It must be nearly seven now, but the snores from across the landing were still deep and regular. With any luck the poor creature would know nothing, her dark, comatose world growing merely a little darker, a little more bewildering, before it blacked out forever. Her last sensation—if indeed there would be any sensation—would surely be a sensation of peace, like sweet rain pattering down on her parched soul, and filling to the brim the dried-up hollows and spaces of her ruined mind.

Yes, that's how it would be. A small quiver, perhaps, as the snores rasped to an unaccustomed halt, and then the laboring lungs would be at rest, the flaccid, long-useless muscles would sink, almost imperceptibly, into a deeper stillness.

That was all. Those fevered nightmares, which had transformed a helpless, harmless old woman on her deathbed into a monstrous effigy of malignancy and power—these had been nothing but the sick fantasies of Millicent's own mind—a mind strained almost beyond endurance, and racked by anxiety, guilt, and indecision. Nothing to do with the reality at all. The reality was merely sad, and almost ordinary—just one more ancient, helpless body which had outlived its mind—outlived its owner, in a manner of speaking. A body already dead, to all intents and purposes, and laid out ready for the small final formality of "Clinical Death," entitling it, at last, to a funeral and a proper death certificate.

Nothing alarming, then, in what Millicent was about to do. Nothing even very important. Just a small formality.

Tiptoeing round the wide bed, as she had done so often in her dreams, Millicent paused for a moment, clutching the fat feather pillow to her breast, and holding her breath, fearful lest the old woman was about to wake. The snoring, though still loud, seemed not quite so regular as it had been a minute earlier; and when she ventured to creep nearer, Millicent observed that the invalid's crumpled yellow face was no longer wholly at rest. A small grimace twisted her mouth, as though at some twinge of pain pushing up through the dim medley of her dreams; and the eyelids, too, were twitching uneasily, as though the old eyes beneath, restless from too much darkness, were fumbling inexpertly for the light.

This was *Mother!* It was incredible, it was beyond the power of the human imagination to encompass, but this creature really, actually, was her! *Mother,* who had once laughed and chatted and run a home and bounced children on her knee and cooked meals for everybody. Somewhere, hidden deep, deep behind that withered mask, in a darkness and a silence that no voice could any longer penetrate, she was still there.

It was *Mother* whom Millicent was about to kill—and how could she be sure, absolutely sure, that this was still what Mother wanted? Locked away in there, beyond the range of communication—how could one *know?*

And instantly, it seemed to Millicent, the answer came, loudly and clearly across the years, in Mother's own dear, familiar voice: "Do what *I* ask you, darling! Don't allow that old hag to decide how *I* am going to die!"

"She won't, Mum! She won't!" Millicent whispered, low and urgent, "I won't let her!"—and with tears pouring down her cheeks, and her heart overflowing with tenderness and love, she laid the pillow gently over the twitching, wizened face, and pressed down . . . down . . . down . . . Leaning close, as though gathering her mother up in a final, loving embrace . . .

Perfect love casteth out fear. Why, then, this chill of terror creeping through every limb? Why this sense of awful foreboding, this pounding of the heart, louder, louder, like the very tramp of doom?

When she woke this time, it was to the sound of voices; low voices, not much above whispers:

"A stroke . . . Yes. Yes, completely, I'm afraid—right down both sides." And then another voice, strangely familiar this time, though for some reason Millicent could not put a name to it.

"I've been afraid that something like this would happen. High blood pressure. All that heavy nursing, and adamant about refusing any outside help—always so proud. Yes, rather odd, that; she must have collapsed while making the bed, because they found her on the floor in a great tangle of bedclothes, and the pillows all everywhere, and the poor old woman shivering and groaning on not much more than the mattress. Quite a problem she'll be, now that there'll be no one at home to look after her. They've brought her here for the time being, but—"

Here? Where was "here"? And who *were* all these people, anyway? What was going on? Millicent tried to open her eyes, but somehow it was too difficult. What had happened? Where was she? Was she still asleep, perhaps, still dreaming?

"Where am I?" she tried to say, and now she was sure she was still dreaming, for her voice made no sound, as is the way of dreams; and when she tried to sit up she found that her limbs, too, were paralyzed as so often happens in a nightmare.

As anyone who has ever suffered from nightmares well knows, it is no use struggling to wake up. All you can do is lie there quietly and wait, in the certain knowledge that you are bound to wake up in the end.

And so it was that Millicent lay there quietly and waited. And waited . . .

Julian Symons

The Boiler

One of Julian Symons' finest short stories, destined to become a favorite choice of anthologists on both sides of the Atlantic. The story of Harold Boyle, who lived under the curse of being a boiler—"a boiler fails in everything he tries." The story will grip your attention from first word to last, and then hang on ...

Harold Boyle was on his way out to lunch when the encounter took place that changed his life. He was bound for a vegetarian restaurant deliberately chosen because to reach it he had to walk across the park. A walk during the day did you good, just as eating a nut, raisin, and cheese salad was better for you than consuming chunks of meat that lay like lead in the stomach. He always returned feeling positively healthier, ready and even eager for the columns of figures that awaited him.

On this day he was walking along by the pond, stepping it out to reach the restaurant, when a man coming toward him said, "Hallo." Harold gave a half smile, half grimace, intended as acknowledgement while suggesting that in fact they didn't know each other. The man stopped. He was a fleshy fellow, with a large aggressive face. When he smiled, as he did now, he revealed a mouthful of beautiful white teeth. His appearance struck some disagreeable chord in Harold's memory. Then the man spoke, and the past came back.

"If it isn't the boiler," the man said. "Jack Cutler, remember me?"

Harold's smallish white hand was gripped in a large red one.

From that moment onward things seemed to happen of their own volition. He was carried along on the tide of Cutler's boundless energy. The feeble suggestion that he already had a lunch engagement was swept aside, they were in a taxi and then at Cutler's club, and he was having a drink at the bar although he never took liquor at lunchtime.

Then lunch, and it turned out that Cutler had ordered already, great steaks that must have cost a fortune, and a bottle of wine. During the meal Cutler talked about the firm of building contractors he ran and of its success, the way business was waiting for you if you had the nerve to go out and get it. While he talked, the large teeth bit into the steak as though they were shears. Then his plate was empty.

"Talking about myself too much, always do when I eat. Can't tell you how good it is to see you, my old boiler. What are you doing with yourself?"

"I am a contract estimator for a firm of paint manufacturers."

"Work out price details, keep an eye open to make sure nobody's cheating? Everybody cheats nowadays, you know that. I reckon some of my boys are robbing me blind, fiddling estimates, taking a cut themselves. You reckon something can be done about that sort of thing?"

"If the estimates are properly checked in advance, certainly."

Cutler chewed a toothpick. "What do they pay you at the paint shop?"

It was at this point, he knew afterward, that he should have said no, he was not interested, he would be late back at the office. Perhaps he should even have been bold enough to tell the truth, and say that he did not want to see Cutler again. Instead he meekly gave the figure.

"Skinflints, aren't they? Come and work for me and I'll double it."

Again he knew he should have said no, I don't want to work for you. Instead, he murmured something about thinking it over.

"That's my good old careful boiler," Cutler said, and laughed.

"I must get back to the office. Thank you for lunch."

"You'll be in touch?"

Harold said yes, intending to write a note turning down the offer. When he got home, however, he was foolish enough to mention the offer to his wife, in response to a question about what kind of day he had had. He could have bitten out his tongue the moment after. Of course she immediately said that he must take it.

"But Phyl, I can't. I don't like Cutler."

"He seems to like you, taking you to lunch and making this offer. Where did you know him?"

"We were at school together. He likes power over people, that's all he thinks of. He was an awful bully. When we were at school he called me a boiler."

"A *what?* Oh, I see, a joke on your name. I don't see there's much harm in that."

"It wasn't a joke. It was to show his—his contempt. He made other people be contemptuous too. And he still says it—when we met he said it's the boiler."

"It sounds a bit childish to me. You're not a child now, Harold."

"You don't understand," he cried out in despair. "You just don't understand."

"I'll tell you what I do understand," she said. Her small pretty face was distorted with anger. "We've been married eight years, and you've been in the same firm all the time. Same firm, same job, no promotion. Now you're offered double the money. Do you know what that would mean? I could get some new clothes, we could have a washing machine, we might even be able to move out of this neighbourhood to somewhere really nice. And you just say no to it, like that. If you want me to stay you'd better change your mind."

She went out, slamming the door. When he went upstairs later he found the bedroom door locked. He slept in the spare room.

Or at least he lay in bed there. He thought about Cutler, who had been a senior when he was a junior. Cutler was the leader of a group who called themselves The Razors, and one day Harold found himself surrounded by them while on his way home. They pushed and pulled him along to the house of one boy whose parents were away. In the garden shed there they held a kind of trial in which they accused him of having squealed on a gang member who had asked Harold for the answers to some exam questions. Harold had given the answers, some of them had been wrong, and the master had spotted these identical wrong answers. Under questioning, Harold told the master what had happened.

He tried to explain that this was not squealing, but the gang remained unimpressed. Suggestions about what should be done to him varied from cutting off all his hair to holding him face down in a lavatory bowl. Somebody said that Boyle should be put in a big saucepan and boiled, which raised a laugh. Then Cutler intervened. He was big even then, a big red-faced boy, very sarcastic.

"We don't want to *do* anything. He'll only go sniveling back to teacher. Let's call him something. Call him the boiler."

Silence. Somebody said, "Don't see he'll mind."

"Oh, yes, he will." Cutler came close to Harold, his big face sneering. "Because I'll tell him what it means, and then he'll remember every time he hears it. Now, you just repeat this after me, boiler." Then Cutler recited the ritual of the boiler and Harold, after his hair had been pulled and his arm twisted until he thought it would break, repeated it.

He remembered the ritual. It began: *I am a boiler. A boiler is a mean little sneak. He can't tie his own shoelaces. A boiler fails in everything he tries. A boiler stinks. I am a boiler.*

Then they let him go, and he ran home. But that was the beginning of it, not the end. Cutler and his gang never called him anything else. They clamped their fingers to their noses when he drew near and said, "Watch out, here's the boiler, pooh, what a stink."

Other boys caught on and did the same. He became a joke, an outcast. His work suffered, he got a bad end-of-term report. His father had died when he was five, so it was his beloved mother who asked him whether something was wrong. He burst into tears. She said that he must try harder next term, and he shook his head.

"It's no good, I can't. I can't do it, I'm a boiler."

"A boiler? What do you mean?"

"A boiler, it means I'm no good, can't do anything right. It's what they call me."

"Who calls you that?"

He told her. She insisted on going up to school and seeing the headmaster, although he implored her not to, and afterward of course things were worse than ever. The head had said that he would see what could be done, but that boys would be boys and Harold was perhaps oversensitive. Now the gang pretended to burst into tears whenever they saw him, and said poor little boiler should run home to mummy.

And he often did run home from school to mummy. He was not ashamed to remember that he had loved his mother more than anybody else in the world, and that his love had been returned. She was a highly emotional woman, and so nervous that she kept a tiny pearl-handled revolver beside her bed. Harold had lived with her until she died. She left him all she had, which was a little money in gilt-edged stocks, some old fashioned jewelry, and the revolver. He sold the stocks and the jewelry, and kept the revolver in a bureau which he used as a writing desk.

It was more than 20 years ago that Cutler had christened him boiler, but the memory remained painful. And now Phyllis wanted him to work with the man. Of course she couldn't know what the word meant, how could anybody know? He saw that in a way Phyllis was right. She had been only 22, ten years younger than Harold, when they married after his mother's death. It was true that he had expected promotion, he should have changed jobs, it would be wonderful to have more money. You mustn't be a boiler all your life, he said to himself. Cutler was being friendly when he offered him the job.

And he couldn't bear to be on bad terms with Phyl, or to think that she might leave him. There had been an awful time, four years ago, when he had discovered that she was carrying on an affair with another man, some salesman who had called at the door to sell a line of household brooms and brushes. He had come home early one day and found them together. Phyl was shamefaced but defiant, saying that if he only took her out a bit more it wouldn't have happened. Was it the fact that the salesman was a man of her own age, he asked. She shook her head, but said that it might help if Harold didn't behave like an old man of 60.

In the morning he told Phyl that he had thought it over, and changed his mind. She said that he would have been crazy not to take the job. Later that day he telephoned Cutler.

To his surprise he did not find the new job disagreeable. It was more varied than his old work, and more interesting. He checked everything carefully, as he had always done, and soon unearthed evidence showing that one of the foremen was working with a sales manager to inflate the cost of jobs by putting in false invoices billed to a non-existent firm. Both men were sacked immediately.

He saw Cutler on most days. Harold's office overlooked the entrance courtyard, so that if he looked out of the window he could see Cutler's distinctive gold-and-silver-colored Rolls-Royce draw up. A smart young chauffeur opened the door and the great man stepped out, often with a cigar in his mouth, and nodded to the chauffeur who then took the car round to the parking lot. Cutler came in around ten thirty, and often invaded Harold's office after lunch, smelling of drink, his face very red. He was delighted by the discovery of the invoice fraud, and clapped Harold on the back.

"Well done, my old boiler. It was a stroke of inspiration asking you to come here. Hasn't worked out too badly for you either, has it?" Harold agreed. He talked as little as possible to his employer. One day Cutler complained of this.

"Damn it, man, anybody would think we didn't know each other. Just because I use a Rolls and have young Billy Meech drive me in here every morning doesn't mean I'm stand-offish. You know why I do it? The Rolls is good publicity, the best you can have, and I get driven in every morning because it saves time. I work in the car dictating letters and so forth. I drive myself most of the time though—Meech has got a cushy job and he knows it. But don't think

I forget old friends. I tell you what, you and your wife must come out and have dinner one night. And we'll use the Rolls."

Harold protested, but a few days later a letter came, signed "Blanche Cutler," saying that Jack was delighted that an old friendship had been renewed, and suggesting a dinner date. Phyllis could hardly contain her pleasure, and was both astonished and furious when Harold said they shouldn't go, they would be like poor relations.

"What are you talking about? He's your old friend, isn't he? And he's been decent to you, giving you a job. If *he's* not snobby, I don't see why you should be."

"I told you I don't like him. We're not friends."

She glared at him. "You're jealous, that's all. You're a failure yourself, and you can't bear anybody else to be a success."

In the end, of course, they went.

Cutler and Harold left the office in the Rolls, driven by Meech, who was in his middle twenties, and they collected Phyllis on the way. She had bought a dress for the occasion, and Harold could see that she was taking everything in greedily—the way Meech sprang out to open the door, the luxurious interior of the Rolls, the cocktail cabinet from which Cutler poured drinks, the silent smoothness with which they traveled. Cutler paid what Harold thought were ridiculous compliments on Phyllis' dress and appearance, saying that Harold had kept his beautiful young wife a secret.

"You're a lucky man, my old boiler."

"Harold said that was what you called him. It seems a silly name."

"Just a reminder of schooldays," Cutler said easily, and Harold hated him.

The Cutlers lived in a big red-brick house in the outer suburbs, with a garden of more than an acre and a swimming pool. Blanche was a fine imposing woman, with a nose that seemed permanently raised in the air. Another couple came to dinner, the man big and loud-voiced like Cutler, his wife a small woman loaded down with what were presumably real pearls and diamonds. The man was some sort of stockbroker, and there was a good deal of conversation about the state of the market.

Dinner was served by a maid in cap and apron, and was full of foods covered with rich sauces which Harold knew would play havoc with his digestion. There was a lot of wine, and he saw with dismay that Phyllis' glass was being refilled frequently.

"You and Jack were great friends at school, he tells me," Blanche

Cutler said, nose in air. What could Harold do but agree? "He says
that now you are his right-hand man. I do think it is so nice when
old friendships are continued in later life."

He muttered something, and then was horrified to hear the word
boiler spoken by Phyllis.

"What's that?" the stockbroker asked, cupping hand to ear. Phyllis
giggled. She was a little drunk.

"Do you know what they used to call Harold at school? A boiler.
What does it mean, Jack, you must tell us what it means."

"It was just a nickname." Cutler seemed embarrassed. "Because
his name was Boyle, you see."

"I know you're hiding something from me." Phyllis tapped Cutler
flirtatiously on the arm. "Was it because he looks like a tough old
boiling fowl, very tasteless? Because he does. I think it's a very good
name for him, a boiler."

Blanche elevated her nose a little higher and said that they would
have coffee in the drawing room.

Meech drove them home in the Rolls, and gave Phyllis his arm
when they got out. She clung to it, swaying a little as they moved
toward the front door. Indoors, she collapsed on the sofa and said,
"What a lovely lovely evening."

"I'm glad you enjoyed it."

"I liked Jack. Your friend Jack. He's such good company. *Such*
good company."

"He's not my friend, he's my employer."

"Such an attractive man, very sexy."

He remembered the salesman. "I thought you only liked younger
men. Cutler's older than I am."

She looked at him with a slightly glazed eye. "Dance with me."

"We haven't got any music."

"Come *on,* doesn't matter." She pulled him to his feet and they
stumbled through a few steps.

"You're drunk." He half pushed her away and she fell to the floor.
She lay there staring up at him.

"You damn—you pushed me over."

"I'm sorry, Phyl. Come to bed."

"You know what you are? You're a boiler. It's a good name for
you."

"Phyl. Please."

"I married a boiler," she said, and passed out. He had to carry her
up to bed.

In the morning she did not get up as usual to make his breakfast; in the evening she said sullenly that there was no point in talking anymore. Harold was just a clerk and would never be anything else, didn't want to be anything else.

After lunch on the next day Cutler came into Harold's office and said he hoped they had both enjoyed the evening. For once he was not at ease, and at last came out with what seemed to be on his mind.

"I'm glad we got together again, for old times' sake. But look here, I'm afraid Phyl got hold of the wrong end of the stick. About that nickname."

"Boiler."

"Yes. Of course it was only meant affectionately. Just a play on your name." Did Cutler really believe that, could he possibly believe it? His red shining face looked earnest enough. "But people can get the wrong impression as Phyl did. Better drop it. So, no more boiler. From now on it's Jack and Harold, agreed?"

He said that he agreed. Cutler clapped him on the shoulder, and said that he was late for an appointment on the golf course. He winked as he said that you could do a lot of business between the first and the eighteenth holes. Five minutes later Harold saw him driving away at the wheel of the Rolls-Royce, a big cigar in his mouth.

In the next days Cutler was away from the office a good deal, and came into Harold's room rarely. At home Phyllis spoke to him only when she could not avoid it. At night they lay like statues side by side. He reflected that, although they had more money, it had not made them happier.

Ten days after the dinner party it happened.

Harold went that day to the vegetarian restaurant across the park. Something in his nut steak must have disagreed with him, however, because by mid-afternoon he was racked by violent stomach pains. He bore them for half an hour and then decided to go home.

The bus took him to the High Road, near his street. He turned the corner into it, walked a few steps, and then stopped, unbelieving.

His house was a hundred yards down the street. And there, drawn up outside it, was Cutler's gold-and-silver Rolls.

He could not have said how long he stood there staring, as though by looking he might make the car disappear. Then he turned away, walked to the Post Office in the High Road, entered a telephone box and dialed his own number.

The telephone rang and rang. On the wooden framework of the box somebody had written "Peter loves Vi." He rubbed a finger over the words, trying to erase them.

At last Phyllis answered. She sounded breathless.

"You've been a long time."

"I was in the garden hanging out washing, didn't hear you. You sound funny. What's the matter?"

He said that he felt ill and was coming home, was leaving the office now.

She said sharply, "But you're in a call box, I distinctly heard the pips."

He explained that he had suddenly felt faint and had been near a pay telephone in the entrance hall.

"So you'll be back in half an hour." He detected relief in her voice.

During that half hour he walked about; he could not afterward have said in what streets, except that he could not bear to approach his own. He could not have borne to see Cutler driving away, a satisfied leer on his face at having once again shown the boiler who was master. Through his head there rang, over and over, Phyllis' words *such an attractive man, very sexy,* words that now seemed repeated in the sound of his own footsteps.

When he got home Phyllis exclaimed at sight of him, and said that he did look ill. She asked what he had eaten at lunch, and said that he had better lie down.

In the bedroom he caught the lingering aroma of cigar smoke, even though the window was open. He threw up in the lavatory and then said to Phyllis that he would stay in the spare room. She made no objection. During the evening she was unusually solicitous, coming up three times to ask whether there was something he would like, taking his temperature, and putting a hand on his forehead. The touch was loathsome to him.

He stayed in the spare room. In the morning he dressed and shaved, but ate no breakfast. She expressed concern.

"You look pale. If you feel ill come home, but don't forget to call first just in case I might be out."

So, he thought, Cutler was coming again that day. The pearl-handled revolver, small as a toy, nestled in his pocket when he left. He had never fired it.

He spent the morning looking out of his window, but Cutler did not appear. He arrived soon after lunch, brought by Meech. He did not come to Harold's office.

Half an hour passed. Harold took out the revolver and balanced it in his hand. Would it fire properly, would he be able to shoot straight?

He felt calm, but his hand trembled.

He took the lift up to the top floor and opened the door of Cutler's office without knocking. Cutler was talking to a recording machine, which he switched off.

"Why the hell don't you knock?" Then he said more genially, "Oh, it's you, my old—Harold. What can I do for you?"

Harold took out the little revolver. Cutler looked astonished, but not frightened. He asked what Harold thought he was doing.

Harold did not reply. Across the desk the boiler faced the man who had ruined his life. The revolver went *crack crack*. Blue smoke curled up from it. Cutler continued to stare at him in astonishment, and Harold thought that he had failed in this as he had failed in so many things, that even from a few feet he had missed. Then he saw the red spot in the middle of Cutler's forehead, and the big man collapsed face down on his desk.

Harold walked out of the room, took the lift, and left the building. He did not reply to the doorman, who asked whether he was feeling all right, he looked rather queer. He was going to give himself up to the police, but before doing so he must speak to Phyllis. He did not know just what he wanted to say, but it was necessary to show her that he was not a boiler, that Cutler had not triumphed in the end.

The bus dropped him in the High Road. He reached the corner of his street.

The gold-and-silver Rolls was there, standing in front of his house.

He walked down the street toward it, feeling the terror of a man in a nightmare. Was Cutler immortal, that he should be able to get up from the desk and drive down here? Had he imagined the red spot, had his shots gone astray? He knew only that he must find out the truth.

When he reached the car it was locked and empty. He opened his front door. The house was silent.

The house was silent and he was silent, as he moved up the stairs delicately on tiptoe. He opened the door of the bedroom.

Phyllis was in bed. With her was the young chauffeur Meech. A cigar, one of his master's cigars, was stubbed out in an ashtray.

Harold stared at them for a long moment of agony. Then, as they started up, he said words incomprehensible to them, words from the ritual of school. "A boiler fails in everything he tries . . . I am a boiler."

He shut the door, went into the bathroom, took out the revolver, and placed the tiny muzzle in his mouth. Then he pulled the trigger.

In this final action the boiler succeeded at last.

EDITORIAL POSTSCRIPT

The story you have just read was nominated by MWA (Mystery Writers of America) as one of the five best new mystery short stories published in American magazines and books during 1979.

Frits Remar

The Photo

This story, written by a Danish author new to Ellery Queen's Mystery Magazine and probably new to the American public, won second prize in a crime short-story contest run by a Norwegian weekly called "A—Magazine," and sponsored by The Riverton Club of Norway, the Swedish Crime Novel Academy, and the Poe Club of Denmark.

The author, Frits Remar, is a former advertising man, in his early forties, blond, married, has two children, is "recently a teetotaler," and lives in a small community north of Copenhagen. In 1972 one of his books won the prize as the best Danish crime novel of that year.

Mr. Remar's prizewinning short story tells of two young men of the Danish navy who have been assigned to patrol-guard duty on the eastern shore of Greenland. The area is so sparsely populated that they rarely meet another person on their 2,000-mile trip, which takes about three months from the base to almost the North Pole and back. Patrol-guarding can be a lonely and dangerous business . . .

Kurt has behaved strangely this last fortnight. That is, in the daytime there hasn't been any trouble. As usual we have been working by turns, making the usual observations, keeping the log, and so on. But in the night when we had camped and eaten, he would crawl into his sleeping bag, slip a photo out of his pocket, and stare at it, sighing and groaning.

Generally we would chat for a couple of hours, have a game of cards or chess, or try and tune in on some music station on our short-wave radio before going to sleep. But there hasn't been anything like that these past two weeks.

He thinks I haven't noticed. He mumbles something about being dead-tired and wanting to turn in early. And then, when I have picked up a book and pretend to be reading it, he will take the photo out of the pocket of his shirt and start his adoration.

It's the photograph of a girl, of course. There's nothing unnatural about that. I too have a girl waiting for me at home. But I didn't know that Kurt had a girl. At any rate, he never spoke about one, and now that we have been here for almost one year, there isn't much we don't know about each other.

I have started fearing that he has what we call "the polar tantrum." As far as I know, there have only been a few cases of that up here. And light attacks have been cured by a sensible talk and 12 or 14 hours of sleep after an injection.

I have tried to talk sense to Kurt, but each time it has come to nothing. He has just been grunting or nodding yes or no. I have begun wondering if we should stay over for a couple of days and nights in our next camp, after tomorrow's march.

But how I shall persuade Kurt to accept an injection voluntarily, I don't know. And I don't think I shall be able to give him one forcibly. We are of the same size and strength and have been through the same training of hand-to-hand fighting. So if I start struggling with him inside the tent, it will only take a couple of minutes before everything is broken.

And that won't do. It will be at least two months before we get back to the base, so in order to survive we need every bit of our equipment.

And outside the tent it's no good, either. If I can't get behind him and take him by surprise, I may as well forget it, and the chances of catching him off guard are very small. During such a long trip as ours everything becomes routine, so if I do anything unexpected he will grow suspicious immediately.

The only possibility is to try while he is asleep, for I don't think I alone can persuade him. It would be something quite different, of course, if we were at the base. In the first place, the others would be there to hold him, and then there's the boss who far better than I would be able to bring him to his senses.

Until tomorrow I shall consider it thoroughly, and if he then turns in right after we eat our meal and feed the dogs, I'll stay awake till I'm sure he's asleep. Then I'll knock him out with a blow on the head so that he'll be unconscious when I insert the needle.

For, even if I give him a double dose, it will take about 15 minutes for the drug to work, and in that quarter of an hour we would have enough time to tear the tent apart.

I cast a sidelong glance at him over the book, which I had in my hands. He lay with his back to me and had stopped sighing. He drew a deep and regular breath. Apparently he was asleep. Should I try it tonight instead? No, this camp isn't good for more than one night's stay. We are too exposed if a storm should arise, and that is something you can never be sure about in these latitudes.

The place we are to reach by tomorrow is a much better site. There we can pitch the tent properly, sheltered by rocks protruding above the ice cap. So we would manage even if it should blow great guns from the north.

Yes, it'll have to wait till tomorrow.

I laid the book aside, then said good night to my girl. She smiled back at me, her red lips slightly apart, the expression in her eyes at once loving and seductive, her black hair showering about her head and shoulders.

The photo of my girl had become badly creased after having been so long in my breast pocket and having been taken out and put back so many times.

When we return to the base I am going to write and ask her to send me a new one. After all, I will be staying up here for another six months. But it will have to be a print exactly like this one, for it is in this pose that I always see her when closing my eyes.

I put the photograph back in my pocket, checked the stove, and turned the kerosene lamp down to low flame before crawling into my bag and falling asleep.

Kurt behaved normally next morning. We had breakfast, fed the dogs, took down the tent, and packed our sled. There was the usual shouting while we hitched up the dogs and got going.

But he didn't fool me. He had the tantrum—of that I was fully convinced—and I was going to give him the injection tonight so that he could become his old self again. Not only for his sake, for mine too.

Once the tantrum was ablaze, he would be completely unbearable and it would be impracticable to be together for another two months. It had to be nipped in the bud—I could not wait any longer.

We worked our way swiftly across the ice one kilometer offshore. The ice lay unbroken for miles in front of us, and by noon we could dimly see the inland formation of rocks, where we had planned to camp that night.

The afternoon went by uneventfully, but at about four o'clock, when we had started pulling in toward land, something went wrong.

An arctic fox suddenly jumped up about 50 yards in front of our sled. The *baas* started howling and went for it. The other dogs were yelping as well, and in a very few seconds the sled raced off across the ice toward the rocks, and we had totally lost control of the dogs and the sled.

In order to regain warmth I had been running slowly beside the sled after my rest interval, and very soon I was hundreds of yards behind it. Kurt lay clinging to the equipment in order not to fall off the sled, as it swayed from side to side or jumped high up into the air, jolting against outcroppings and out of holes in the far more uneven ground here along the coast.

The hue and cry ended abruptly. The arctic fox disappeared among the rocks, and the sled turned round after colliding with a big boulder. Kurt was hurled into the air and landed heavily on a granite knoll. The lines of the dogs were hopelessly tangled, and the dogs were howling at the top of their lungs, both from disappointment in the interrupted hunt and from the pain of the jerk that had stopped them.

But the dogs would have to wait. So would all the equipment lying scattered about. First I had to attend to Kurt.

He lay unconscious. I took off his fur hood. He was bleeding from a large wound in the back of his head, but as far as I could see, he hadn't fractured his skull. He must have had a tremendous concussion, however. He was breathing faintly, his pulse slow and irregular.

I groped with my hands along his body on the outside of his clothes to find out if he had broken any bones. When I touched his right thigh just above the knee, he whimpered though still unconscious.

A femoral fracture! Damn!

I cut along the trouser leg to see if it was a compound fracture. It wasn't, but there was no doubt about it being a fracture. The big dark swollen bump on the inside of his leg just above the knee spoke its own silent but distinct language.

I put him as comfortably as possible in the snow by the side of the boulder and started rummaging for our medicine chest in the mess around the sled. Finding it, I stuck a couple of blankets under my arm and hurried back to him.

First of all I had to secure him against shock or treat him if he'd already had one. When I examined him again, he was breathing more faintly than before, his pulse almost imperceptible and extremely irregular, his face pale and covered with cold sweat, and no doubt his body temperature had lowered.

I wrapped him up in the blankets, so that he wouldn't cool too much before I could get the tent pitched and the stove lit. Then I gave him half a liter of blood plasma, and presently his breathing became deeper and his pulse more rapid and regular.

Next I attended to the wound in the back of his head. It was large, but not too deep. Carefully I dabbed away the dried-up blood, considered for a moment if I should shave off his hair, but gave up the thought, sprinkled on sulfa powder, and affixed a large piece of adhesive plaster.

Now that he wasn't going to die, I could begin pitching the tent. It took more time than usual. First, I was alone, and second, all the equipment was scattered. But at last I had the tent pitched and got the stove going, so that I could get Kurt inside. It was hard dragging him through the snow, and I was glad he was unconscious, for it must have hurt him like hell. In fact, he groaned constantly even though he didn't wake up.

During the next hour I was very busy. I put splints on his leg. I was very careful to make the fracture surfaces fit together, but I didn't know if I had succeeded. Then I gathered the rest of our equipment. I cursed when I discovered that our radio had been smashed. Now we couldn't get in touch with the base. Then I packed the sled with those things we didn't need immediately. And finally I took care of the dogs before re-entering the tent.

It had become tolerably warm in there, and Kurt had got some color back in his cheeks and was now breathing quite normally. And his pulse was stronger.

I didn't care that he was still unconscious, for I had given him an injection before starting to work on his leg. I couldn't help thinking of yesterday's plan to catch him off guard during his sleep to give him an injection to rid him of his tantrum. Now destiny had interfered and done my job. In fact, it had forced me to give him the injection that was to ease his overtaxed mind for those ten or twelve hours necessary to bring him out of his polar tantrum.

I prepared some food and wondered if I should have waited to give him the injection till I had squeezed some beef tea into him, but it was too late for that now. It wouldn't harm him not having anything to eat during the next twenty hours, which it was going to take at the most. We had had a solid lunch, and I figured he would wake up around four or five in the morning.

After dinner I started playing solitaire. I examined him every once in a while, felt his pulse, but he was sound asleep, and there was no further danger. And then curiosity began pulling at me.

The last time I had examined him, one of my hands happened to rest on his breast pocket, and I had felt the photograph rustling under my palm.

For a long time I sat staring out into the air, but curiosity won.

I unbuttoned his breast pocket, took out the photo, and had the shock of my life.

The girl smiled back at me, her red lips slightly apart, the expression in her eyes at once loving and seductive, her black hair showering about her head and shoulders.

It was *my* girl.

Rage and jealousy gushed through me, and for a moment I could see nothing. I fell heavily on my bed, crumpling the photo into a small hard pellet.

My girl and Kurt. A photo exactly like the one I had. How could that possibly have come about? She had never betrayed anything. I hadn't had the slightest suspicion she was in love with anyone but me. And, as I told you, Kurt had never talked about any girl.

No, this had not happened.

If Kurt disappeared, if Kurt died, she would quickly forget all about him. And I would never mention a single word about my knowing that he, too, had had a print of her picture.

For this had not happened at all.

I went outside the tent and found a big stone. I tested its weight in my hand. Yes, it would do.

Then I re-entered the tent, tore the adhesive plaster off the wound, and hammered the stone against his head. He died without regaining consciousness.

I stood for a long time breathing heavily before going outside to throw the stone far away into the darkness.

There, now it had not happened.

I bandaged the wound in his head, covered him with the blanket, and quietly lay down to sleep after saying good night to my girl.

Now she was mine again.

All mine.

Next morning I strapped him firmly to the sled and started on the trip home.

About 500 kilometers of patrolling remained to be done, but I was sure that the boss of the Sirius Sled Patrol here in Greenland and of the Naval Command at home in Denmark was not going to wink at that under these circumstances.

One month and a thousand kilometers later I was back at the base.

I made my report calmly, and the boss approved of my line of action. In fact, he commended me for having accomplished the return safely and making all the necessary observations on my way.

Mumbling words of sympathy, my buddies patted my shoulders.

There was a lot of mail waiting for me—among other things, a letter from my girl. So as soon as I could get away, I went to my room.

First I opened the letter from my girl. There was another photograph in it—the same pose. So, in my last letter, I must apparently have asked her for a new one.

She smiled at me. Her red lips were slightly apart, the expression in her eyes loving and seductive, her black hair showering about her head and shoulders.

Only obliquely did my eye catch what was printed in large black type below the photograph.

Nine out of ten movie stars use STAR.

Ruby Delany, too, uses STAR in her daily facial treatment, because STAR contains . . .

Now she was mine again.

All mine.

Janwillem van de Wetering

The Deadly Egg

*As of the time of this writing Janwillem van de Wetering has
written eight novels about the Amsterdam police, featuring Detective Adjutant Grijpstra and Detective Sergeant de Gier. The
novels have been highly praised by critics, have sold to eleven
foreign publishers, and have been serialized and selected by book
clubs.*

*Mr. van de Wetering was born in The Netherlands in 1931.
The German bombing of Rotterdam and the subsequent five years
of military occupation strongly influenced his early thinking.
After graduation from a business college he traveled exten-
sively—Africa, South America, Australia, Japan. He studied phi-
losophy in London and became a disciple of a Zen master in
Kyoto, Japan, later writing two books on Zen.*

*In 1965 he returned to The Netherlands where he became an
active member of the Special Constabulary of the Amsterdam
Municipal Police (so he knows at first-hand what he's writing
about). He and his family live at present in the United States.*

*Now, meet for the first time in a short story the most famous
pair of detectives in the Criminal Investigation Department (also
called the Murder Brigade) of the Municipal Police of Amsterdam—Adjutant Grijpstra and Sergeant de Gier, two of the most
human sleuths you have ever encountered in print. The crime
they investigate on Easter Day is a fascinating double mystery—"a
dead man dangling from a branch in the forest" and "a lady
poisoned, presumably by a chocolate Easter egg" . . .*

The siren of the tiny dented Volkswagen shrieked forlornly between the naked trees of the Amsterdam Forest, the city's largest park, set on its southern edge: several square miles of willows,
poplars, and wild growing alders, surrounding ponds and lining
paths. The paths were restricted to pedestrians and cyclists, but the

Volkswagen had ignored the many No Entry signs, quite legally, for the vehicle belonged to the Municipal Police and more especially to its Criminal Investigation Department, or the Murder Brigade. Even so it looked lost and its howl seemed defensive.

It was Easter Sunday and it rained, and the car's two occupants, Detective Adjutant Grijpstra and Detective Sergeant de Gier, sat hunched in their overcoats, watching the squeaky rusted wipers trying to deal with the steady drizzle. The car should have been junked some years before, but the adjutant had lost the form that would have done away with his aging transport, lost it on purpose and with the sergeant's consent. They had grown fond of the Volkswagen, of its shabbiness and its ability to melt away in traffic.

But they weren't fond of the car now. The heater didn't work, it was cold, and it was early. Not yet nine o'clock on a Sunday is early, especially when the Sunday is Easter. Technically they were both off duty, but they had been telephoned out of warm beds by Headquarters' radio room. A dead man dangling from a branch in the forest; please, would they care to have a look at the dead man?

Grijpstra's stubby index finger silenced the siren. They had followed several miles of winding paths so far and hadn't come across anything alive except tall blue herons, fishing in the ponds and moats and flapping away slowly when the car came too close for their comfort.

"You know who reported the corpse? I wasn't awake when the radio room talked to me." De Gier had been smoking silently. His handsome head with the perfect curls turned obediently to face his superior. "Yes, a gentleman jogger. He said he jogged right into the body's feet. Gave him a start. He ran all the way to the nearest telephone booth, phoned headquarters, then headquarters phoned us, and that's why we are here, I suppose. I am a little asleep myself—we are here, aren't we?"

They could hear another siren, and another. Two limousines came roaring toward the Volkswagen, and Grijpstra cursed and made the little car turn off the path and slide into a soggy lawn; they could feel its wheel sink into the mud.

The limousines stopped and men poured out of them; the men pushed the Volkswagen back on the path.

"Morning, Adjutant, morning, Sergeant. Where is the corpse?"

"Shouldn't you know too?"

"No, Adjutant," several men said simultaneously, "but we thought maybe you knew. All we know is that the corpse is in the Amsterdam Forest and that this is the Amsterdam Forest."

Grijpstra addressed the sergeant. "You know?"

De Gier's well modulated baritone chanted the instructions. "Turn right after the big pond, right again, then left. Or the other way round. I think I have it right, we should be close."

The three cars drove about for a few minutes more until they were waved down by a man dressed in what seemed to be long blue underwear. The jogger ran ahead, bouncing energetically, and led them to their destination. The men from the limousines brought out their boxes and suitcases, then cameras clicked and a videorecorder hummed. The corpse hung on and the two detectives watched it hang.

"Neat," Grijpstra said, "very neat. Don't you think it is neat?"

The sergeant grunted.

"Here. Brought a folding campstool and some nice new rope, made a perfect noose, slipped it around his neck, kicked the stool. Anything suspicious, gentlemen?"

The men from the limousines said there was not. They had found footprints—the prints of the corpse's boots. There were no other prints, except the jogger's. The jogger's statement was taken, he was thanked and sent on his sporting way. A police ambulance arrived and the corpse was cut loose, examined by doctor and detectives, and carried off. The detectives saluted the corpse quietly by inclining their heads.

"In his sixties," the sergeant said, "well dressed in old but expensive clothes. Clean shirt. Tie. Short gray beard, clipped. Man who took care of himself. A faint smell of liquor—he must have had a few to give him courage. Absolutely nothing in his pockets. I looked in the collar of his shirt—no laundry mark. He went to some trouble to be nameless. Maybe something will turn up when they strip him at the mortuary; we should phone in an hour's time."

Grijpstra looked hopeful. "Suicide?"

"I would think so. Came here by himself, no traces of anybody else. No signs of a struggle. The man knew what he wanted to do, and did it, all by himself. But he didn't leave a note; that wasn't very thoughtful."

"Right," Grijpstra said, "time for breakfast, Sergeant! We'll have it at the airport—that's close and convenient. We can show our police cards and get through the customs barrier; the restaurant on the far side is better than the coffee shop on the near side."

De Gier activated the radio when they got back to the car.

"Male corpse, balding but with short gray beard. Dentures. Blue eyes. Sixty-odd years old. Three-piece blue suit, elegant dark gray overcoat, no hat. No identification."

"Thank you," the radio said.

"Looks very much like suicide. Do you have any missing persons of that description in your files?"

"No, not so far."

"We'll be off for breakfast and will call in again on our way back."

"Echrem," the radio said sadly, "there's something else. Sorry."

De Gier stared at a duck waddling across the path and trailing seven furry ducklings. He began to mumble. Adjutant Grijpstra mumbled with him. The mumbled four-letter words interspersed with mild curses formed a background for the radio's well articulated message. They were given an address on the other side of the city. "The lady was poisoned, presumably by a chocolate Easter egg. The ambulance that answered the distress call just radioed in. They are taking her to hospital. The ambulance driver thought the poison was either parathion, something used in agriculture, or arsenic. His assistant is pumping out the patient's stomach. She is in a bad way but not dead yet."

Grijpstra grabbed the microphone from de Gier's limp hand. "So if the lady is on her way to hospital who is left in the house you want us to go to?"

"Her husband, man by the name of Moozen, a lawyer, I believe."

"What hospital is Mrs. Moozen being taken to?"

"The Wilhelmina."

"And you have no one else on call? Sergeant de Gier and I are supposed to be off-duty for Easter, you know!"

"No," the radio's female voice said, "no, Adjutant. We never have much crime on Easter day, especially not in the morning. There are only two detectives on duty and they are out on a case too—some boys have derailed a streetcar with matches."

"Right," Grijpstra said coldly, "we are on our way."

The old Volkswagen made an effort to jump away, protesting feebly. De Gier was still muttering but had stopped cursing. "Streetcar? Matches?"

"Yes. They take an empty cartridge, fill it with matchheads, then close the open end with a hammer. Very simple. All you have to do is insert the cartridge into the streetcar's rail and when the old tram comes clanging along, the sudden impact makes the cartridge explode. If you use two or three cartridges the explosion may be strong enough to lift the wheel out of the rail. Didn't you ever try that? I used to do it as a boy. The only problem was to get the cartridges. We had to sneak around on the rifle range with the chance of getting shot at."

"No," de Gier said. "Pity. Never thought of it, and it sounds like a good game."

He looked out of the window. The car had left the park and was racing toward the city's center through long empty avenues. There was no life in the huge apartment buildings lining the old city—nobody had bothered to get up yet. Ten o'clock and the citizenry wasn't even considering the possibility of slouching into the kitchen for a first cup of coffee.

But one man had bothered to get up early and had strolled into the park, carrying his folding chair and a piece of rope to break off the painful course of his life, once and for all. An elderly man in good but old clothes. De Gier saw the man's beard again, a nicely cared-for growth. The police doctor had said that he hadn't been dead long. A man alone in the night that would have led him to Easter, a man by himself in a deserted park, testing the strength of his rope, fitting his head into the noose, kicking the campstool.

"Bah!" he said aloud.

Grijpstra had steered the car through a red light and was turning the wheel.

"What's that?"

"Nothing. Just bah."

"Bah is right," Grijpstra said.

They found the house, a bungalow, on the luxurious extreme north side of the city. Spring was trying to revive the small lawn and a magnolia tree was in hesitant bloom. Bright yellow crocuses set off the path. Grijpstra looked at the crocuses. He didn't seem pleased.

"Crocuses," de Gier said, "very nice. Jolly little flowers."

"No. Unimaginative plants, manufactured, not grown. Computer plants. They make the bulbs in a machine and program them to look stupid. Go ahead, Sergeant, press the bell."

"Really?" the sergeant asked.

Grijpstra's jowls sagged. "Yes. They are like mass-manufactured cheese, tasteless; cheese is probably made with the same machines."

"Cheese," de Gier said moistly, "there's nothing wrong with cheese either, apart from not having any right now. Breakfast has slipped by, you know." He glanced at his watch.

They read the nameplate while the bell rang. *H. F. Moozen, Attorney at Law.* The door opened. A man in a housecoat made out of brightly striped towel material said good morning. The detectives showed their identifications. The man nodded and stepped back. A pleasant man, still young, 30 years or a bit more. The ideal model for an ad in a ladies' magazine. A background man, showing off a modern house, or a mini-car, or expensive furniture. The sort of man ladies would like to have around. Quiet, secure, mildly good-looking. Not a passionate man, but lawyers seldom are. Lawyers practice detachment; they identify with their clients, but only up to a point.

"You won't take long, I hope," Mr. Moozen said. "I wanted to go with the ambulance, but the driver said you were on the way, and that I wouldn't be of any help if I stayed with my wife."

"Was your wife conscious when she left here, sir?"

"Barely. She couldn't speak."

"She ate an egg, a chocolate egg?"

"Yes. I don't care for chocolate myself. It was a gift, we thought, from friends. I had to let the dog out early this morning, an hour ago, and there was an Easter bunny sitting on the path. He held an egg wrapped up in silver paper. I took him in, woke up my wife, and showed the bunny to her, and she took the egg and ate it, then became ill. I telephoned for the ambulance and they came almost immediately. I would like to go to the hospital now."

"Come in our car, sir. Can I see the bunny?"

Mr. Moozen took off the housecoat and put on a jacket. He opened the door leading to the kitchen and a small dog jumped around the detectives, yapping greetings. The bunny stood on the kitchen counter; it was almost a foot high. Grijpstra tapped its back with his knuckles; it sounded solid.

"Hey," de Gier said. He turned the bunny and showed it to Grijpstra.

"Brwah!" Grijpstra said.

The rabbit's toothless mouth gaped. The beast's eyes were close together and deeply sunk into the skull. Its ears stood up aggressively. The bunny leered at them, its torso crouched; the paws that had held the deadly egg seemed ready to punch.

"It's roaring," de Gier said. "See? A roaring rabbit. Easter bunnies are supposed to smile."

"Shall we go?" Mr. Moozen asked.

They used the siren and the trip to the hospital didn't take ten minutes. The city was still quiet. But there proved to be no hurry.

An energetic bright young nurse led them to a waiting room. Mrs. Moozen was being worked on; her condition was still critical. The nurse would let them know if there was any change.

"Can we smoke?" Grijpstra asked.

"If you must." The nurse smiled coldly, appraised de Gier's tall wide-shouldered body with a possessive feminist glance, swung her hips, and turned to the door.

"Any coffee?"

"There's a machine in the hall. Don't smoke in the hall, please."

There were several posters in the waiting room. A picture of a cigarette pointing to a skull with crossed bones. A picture of a happy child biting into an apple. A picture of a drunken driver (bubbles surrounding his head proved he was drunk) followed by an ambulance. The caption read: "Not *if* you have an accident, but *when* you have an accident."

De Gier fetched coffee and Grijpstra offered cigars. Mr. Moozen said he didn't smoke.

"Well," Grijpstra said patiently and puffed out a ragged dark cloud, "now who would want to poison your wife, sir? Has there been any recent trouble in her life?"

The question hung in the small white room while Moozen thought. The detectives waited. De Gier stared at the floor, Grijpstra observed the ceiling. A full minute passed.

"Yes," Mr. Moozen said, "some trouble. With me. We contemplated a divorce."

"I see."

"But then we decided to stay together. The trouble passed."

"Any particular reason why you considered a divorce, sir?"

"My wife had a lover." Mr. Moozen's words were clipped and precise.

"Had," de Gier said. "The affair came to an end?"

"Yes. We had some problems with our central heating, something the mechanics couldn't fix. An engineer came out and my wife fell in love with him. She told me—she doesn't like to be secretive. They met each other in motels for a while."

"You were upset?"

"Yes. It was a serious affair. The engineer's wife is a mental patient; he divorced her and was awarded custody of his two children. I thought he was looking for a new wife.

My wife has no children of her own—we have been married some six years and would like to have children. My wife and the engineer seemed well matched. I waited a month and then told her to make up her mind—either him or me, not both, I couldn't stand it."

"And she chose you?"

"Yes."

"Do you know the engineer?"

A vague pained smile floated briefly on Moozen's face. "Not personally. We did meet once and discussed central heating systems. Any further contact with him was through my wife."

"And when did all this happen, sir?"

"Recently. She only made her decision a week ago. I don't think she has met him since. She told me it was all over."

"His name and address, please, sir."

De Gier closed his notebook and got up. "Shall we go, Adjutant?"

Grijpstra sighed and got up too. They shook hands with Moozen and wished him luck. Grijpstra stopped at the desk. The nurse wasn't helpful, but Grijpstra insisted and de Gier smiled and eventually they were taken to a doctor who accompanied them to the next floor. Mrs. Moozen seemed comfortable. Her arms were stretched out on the blanket. The face was calm. The detectives were led out of the room again.

"Bad," the doctor said, "parathion is a strong poison. Her stomach is ripped to shreds. We'll have to operate and remove part of it, but I think she will live. The silly woman ate the whole egg, a normal-sized egg. Perhaps she was still too sleepy to notice the taste."

"Her husband is downstairs. Perhaps you should call him up, especially if you think she will live." Grijpstra sounded concerned. He probably was, de Gier thought. He felt concerned himself. The woman was beautiful, with a finely curved nose, very thin in the bridge, and large eyes and a soft and sensitive mouth. He looked at her long delicate hands.

"Husbands," the doctor said. "Prime suspects in my experience. Husbands are supposed to love their wives, but usually they don't. It's the same the other way round. Marriage seems to breed violence—it's one of the impossible situations we humans have to put up with."

Grijpstra's pale blue eyes twinkled. "Are you married, Doctor?"

The doctor grinned back. "Very. Oh, yes."

"A long time?"

"Long enough."

Grijpstra's grin faded. "So am I. Too long. But poison is nasty. Thank you, Doctor."

There wasn't much conversation in the car when they drove to the engineer's address. The city's streets had filled up. People were stirring about on the sidewalks and cars crowded each other, honking occasionally. The engineer lived in a block of apartments, and Grijpstra switched off the engine and lit another small black cigar.

"A family drama. What do you think, Sergeant?"

"I don't think. But that rabbit was most extraordinary. Not bought in a shop. A specially made rabbit, and well made, not by an amateur."

"Are we looking for a sculptor? Some arty person? Would Mr. Moozen or the engineer be an artist in his spare time? How does one make a chocolate rabbit, anyway?"

De Gier tried to stretch, but didn't succeed in his cramped quarters. He yawned instead. "You make a mold, I suppose, out of plaster of Paris or something, and then you pour hot chocolate into the mold and wait for it to harden. That rabbit was solid chocolate, several kilos of it. Our artistic friend went to a lot of trouble."

"A baker? A pastry man?"

"Or an engineer—engineers design forms sometimes, I believe. Let's meet this lover man."

The engineer was a small nimble man with a shock of black hair and dark lively eyes, a nervous man, nervous in a pleasant childlike manner. De Gier remembered that Mrs. Moozen was a small woman too. They were ushered into a four-room apartment. They had to be careful not to step on a large number of toys, spread about evenly. Two little boys played on the floor; the eldest ran out of the room to fetch his Easter present to show it to the uncles. It was a basketful of eggs, homemade, out of chocolate. The other boy came to show his basket, identical but a size smaller.

"My sister and I made them last night," the engineer said. "She came to live here after my wife left and she looks after the kids, but she is spending the Easter weekend with my parents in the country. We couldn't go because Tom here had measles, hadn't you, Tom?"

"Yes," Tom said. "Big measles. Little Klaas here hasn't had them yet."

Klaas looked sorry. Grijpstra took a plastic truck off a chair and sat down heavily after having looked at the engineer who waved him on. "Please, make yourself at home." De Gier had found himself a chair too and was rolling a cigarette. The engineer provided coffee and shooed the children into another room.

"Any trouble?"

"Yes," Grijpstra said. "I am afraid we usually bring trouble. A Mrs. Moozen has been taken to hospital. An attempt was made on her life. I believe you are acquainted with Mrs. Moozen?"

"Ann," the engineer said. "My God! Is she all right?"

De Gier had stopped rolling his cigarette. He was watching the man carefully; his large brown eyes gleamed, but not with pleasure or anticipation. The sergeant felt sorrow, a feeling that often accompanied his intrusions into the private lives of his fellow citizens. He shifted and the automatic pistol in his shoulder holster nuzzled into his armpit.

He impatiently pushed the weapon back. This was no time to be reminded that he carried death with him, legal death.

"What happened?" the engineer was asking. "Did anybody hurt her?"

"A question," Grijpstra said gently. "A question first, sir. You said your sister and you were making chocolate Easter eggs last night. Did you happen to make any bunnies too?"

The engineer sucked noisily on his cigarette. Grijpstra repeated his question.

"Bunnies? Yes, or no. We tried, but it was too much for us. The eggs were easy—my sister is good at that. We have a pudding form for a bunny, but all we could manage was a pudding. It is still in the kitchen, a surprise for the kids later on today. Chocolate pudding—they like it."

"Can we see the kitchen, please?"

The engineer didn't get up. "My God," he said again, "so she was poisoned, was she? How horrible! Where is she now?"

"In the hospital, sir."

"Bad?"

Grijpstra nodded. "The doctor said she will live. Some sort of pesticide was mixed into chocolate, which she ate."

The engineer got up; he seemed dazed. They found the kitchen. Leftover chocolate mix was still on the counter. Grijpstra brought out an envelope and scooped some of the hardened chips into it.

"Do you know that Ann and I had an affair?"

"Yes, sir."

"Were you told that she finished the affair, that she decided to stay with her husband?"

"Yes, sir."

The engineer was tidying up the counter mechanically. "I see. So I could be a suspect. Tried to get at her out of spite or something.

But I am not a spiteful man. You wouldn't know that. I don't mind being a suspect, but I would like to see Ann. She is in the hospital, you said. What hospital?"

"The Wilhelmina, sir."

"Can't leave the kids here, can I? Maybe the neighbors will take them for an hour or so . . . yes. I'll go and see Ann. This is terrible."

Grijpstra marched to the front door with de Gier trailing behind him. "Don't move from the house today, if you please, sir, not until we telephone or come again. We'll try and be as quick as we can."

"Nice chap," de Gier said when the car found its parking place in the vast courtyard of headquarters. "That engineer, I mean. I rather liked Mr. Moozen too, and Mrs. Moozen is a lovely lady. Now what?"

"Go back to the Moozen house, Sergeant, and get a sample of the roaring bunny. Bring it to the laboratory together with this envelope. If they check we have a heavy point against the engineer."

De Gier restarted the engine. "Maybe he is not so nice, eh? He could have driven his wife crazy and now he tries to murder his girlfriend, his ex-girlfriend. Lovely Ann Moozen who dared to stand him up. Could be, do you think so?"

Grijpstra leaned his bulk against the car and addressed his words to the emptiness of the yard. "No. But that could be the obvious solution. He was distressed, genuinely distressed, I would say. If he hadn't been and if he hadn't had those kids in the house, I might have brought him in for further questioning."

"And Mr. Moozen?"

"Could be. Maybe he didn't find the bunny on the garden path; maybe he put it there, or maybe he had it ready in the cupboard and brought it to his wandering wife. He is a lawyer—lawyers can be devious at times. True?"

De Gier said, "Yes, yes, yes . . . " and kept on saying so until Grijpstra squeezed the elbow sticking out of the car's window. "You are saying *yes,* but you don't sound convinced."

"I thought Moozen was suffering too."

"Murderers usually suffer, don't they?"

De Gier started his "Yes, yes," and Grijpstra marched off.

They met an hour later, in the canteen in headquarters. They munched rolls stuffed with sliced liver and roast beef and muttered diligently at each other. "So it is the same chocolate?"

"Yes, but that doesn't mean much. One of the lab's assistants has a father who owns a pastry shop. He said that there are only three mixes on the market and our stuff is the most popular make. No, not much of a clue there."

"So?"

"We may have a full case on our hands. We should go back to Mr. Moozen, I think, and find out about friends and relatives. Perhaps his wife had other lovers, or jealous lady friends."

"Why her?"

Grijpstra munched on. "Hmm?"

"Why *her?*" de Gier repeated. "Why not him?"

Grijpstra swallowed. "Him? What about him?"

De Gier reached for the plate, but Grijpstra restrained the sergeant's hand. "Wait, you are hard to understand when you have your mouth full. What about him?"

De Gier looked at the roll. Grijpstra picked it up and ate it.

"Him," de Gier said unhappily. "He found the bunny on the garden path, the ferocious bunny holding the pernicious egg. A gift, how nice. But he doesn't eat chocolate, so he runs inside and shows the gift to his wife and his wife grabs the egg and eats it. She may have thought *he* was giving it to her, she was still half asleep. Maybe she noticed the taste, but she ate on to please her husband. She became ill at once and he telephoned for an ambulance. Now, if he had wanted to kill her he might have waited an hour or so, to give the poison a chance to do its job. But he grabbed his phone, fortunately. What I am trying to say is, the egg may have been intended for him, from an enemy who didn't even know Moozen had a wife, who didn't care about killing the wife."

"Ah," Grijpstra said, and swallowed the last of the roll. "Could be. We'll ask Mr. Moozen about his enemies. But not just now. There is the dead man we found in the park—a message came in while you were away. A missing person has been reported and the description fits our corpse. According to the radio room a woman phoned to say that a man who is renting a room in her house has been behaving strangely lately and has now disappeared. She traced him to the corner bar where he spent last evening, until two a.m. when they closed.

"He was a little drunk according to the barkeeper, but not blind drunk. She always takes him tea in the morning, but this morning he wasn't there and the bed was still made. But she does think he's been home, for she heard the front door at a little after two a.m., opening and closing twice. He probably fetched the rope and his campstool then."

"And the man was fairly old and has a short gray beard?"

"Right."

"So we go and see the landlady. I'll get a photograph—they took dozens this morning and they should be developed by now. Was anything found in his clothes?"

"Nothing." Grijpstra looked guiltily at the empty plate. "Want another roll?"

"You ate it."

"That's true, and the canteen is out of rolls; we got the last batch. Never mind, Sergeant. Let's go out and do some work. Work will take your mind off food."

"That's him," the landlady with the plastic curlers said. Her glasses had slipped to the tip of her blunt nose while she studied the photograph. "Oh, how horrible! His tongue is sticking out. Poor Mr. Marchant, is he dead?"

"Yes, ma'am."

"For shame, and such a nice gentleman. He has been staying here for nearly five years now and he was always so polite."

Grijpstra tried to look away from the glaring pink curlers, pointing at his forehead from the woman's thinning hair.

"Did he have any troubles, ma'am? Anything that may have led him to take his own life?"

The curlers bobbed frantically. "Yes. Money troubles. Nothing to pay the taxman with. He always paid the rent, but he hadn't been paying his taxes. And his business wasn't doing well. He has a shop in the next street; he makes things—ornaments he calls them, out of brass. But there was some trouble with the neighbors. Too much noise, and something about the zoning too; this is a residential area now, they say. The neighbors wanted him to move, but he had nowhere to move to, and he was getting nasty letters, lawyers' letters. He would have had to close down, and he had to make money to pay the taxman. It was driving him crazy. I could hear him walk around in his room at night, round and round until I had to switch off my hearing aid."

"Thank you, ma'am."

"He was alone," the woman said and shuffled with them to the door. "All alone, like me. And he was always so nice." She was crying.

"Happy Easter," de Gier said, and opened the Volkswagen's door for the adjutant.

"The same to you. Back to Mr. Moozen again—we *are* driving

about this morning. I could use some coffee again. Maybe Mr. Moozen will oblige."

"He won't be so happy either. We aren't making anybody happy today," the sergeant said and tried to put the Volkswagen into first gear. The gear slipped and the car took off in second.

They found Mr. Moozen in his garden. It had begun to rain again, but the lawyer didn't seem to notice that he was getting wet. He was staring at the bright yellow crocuses, touching them with his foot. He had trampled a few of them into the grass.

"How is your wife, sir?"

"Conscious and in pain. The doctors think they can save her, but she will have to be on a stringent diet for years and she'll be very weak for months. I won't have her back for a while."

Grijpstra coughed. "We visited your wife's, ah, previous lover, sir." The word "previous" came out awkwardly and he coughed again to take away the bad taste.

"Did you arrest him?"

"No, sir."

"Any strong reasons to suspect the man?"

"Are you a criminal lawyer, sir?"

Moozen kicked the last surviving crocus, turned on his heels, and led his visitors into the house. "No, I specialize in civil cases. Sometimes I do divorces, but I don't have enough experience to point a finger in this personal case. Divorce is a messy business, but with a little tact and patience reason usually prevails. To try and poison somebody is unreasonable behavior. I can't visualize Ann provoking that type of action—she is a gentle woman, sensuous but gentle. If she did break her relationship with the engineer she would have done it diplomatically."

"He seemed upset, sir, genuinely upset."

"Quite. I had hoped as much. So where are we now?"

"With you, sir. Do *you* have any enemies? Anybody who hated you so badly that he wanted you to die a grotesque death, handed to you by a roaring rabbit? You did find the rabbit on the garden path this morning, didn't you, sir?"

Moozen pointed. "Yes, out there, sitting in between the crocuses, leering, and as you say, roaring. Giving me the egg."

"Now, which demented mind might have thought of shaping that apparition, sir? Are you dealing with any particularly unpleasant cases at this moment? Any cases that have a badly twisted undercurrent? Is anyone blaming you for something bad that is happening to them?"

Moozen brushed his hair with both hands. "No. I am working on a bad case having to do with a truckdriver who got involved in a complicated accident; his truck caught fire and it was loaded with expensive cargo. Both his legs were crushed. His firm is suing the firm that owned the other truck. A lot of money in claims is involved and the parties are becoming impatient, with me mostly. The case is dragging on and on. But if they kill me the case will become even more complicated, with no hope of settlement in sight."

"Anything else, sir?"

"The usual. I collect bad debts, so sometimes I have to get nasty. I write threatening letters, sometimes I telephone people or even visit them. I act tough—it's got to be done in my profession. Usually they pay but they don't like me for bothering them."

"Any pastry shops?"

"I beg your pardon?"

"Pastry shops," Grijpstra said, "people who make and sell confectionery. That rabbit was a work of art in a way, made by a professional. Are you suing anybody who would have the ability to create the roaring rabbit?"

"Ornaments!" de Gier shouted. His shout tore at the quiet room. Moozen and Grijpstra looked up, startled.

"Ornaments! Brass ornaments. Ornaments are made from molds. We've got to check his shop."

"Whose shop?" Grijpstra frowned irritably. "Keep your voice down, Sergeant. What shop? What ornaments?"

"Marchant!" de Gier shouted. "Marchant's shop."

"Marchant?" Moozen was shouting too. "Where did you get that name? *Emil* Marchant?"

Grijpstra's cigar fell on the carpet. He tried to pick it up and it burned his hand, sparks finding their way into the carpet's strands. He stamped them out roughly.

"You know a Mr. Marchant, sir?" de Gier asked quietly.

"No, I haven't met him. But I have written several letters to a man named Emil Marchant. On behalf of clients who are hindered by the noise he makes in his shop. He works with brass, and it isn't only the noise but there seems to be a stink as well. My clients want him to move out and are prepared to take him to court if necessary. Mr. Marchant telephoned me a few times, pleading for mercy. He said he owed money to the tax department and wanted time to make the money, that he would move out later; but my clients have lost patience. I didn't give in to him—in fact, I just pushed harder. He will have to go to court next week and he is sure to lose out."

"Do you know what line of business he is in, sir?"

"Doorknobs, I believe, and knockers for doors, in the shape of lions' heads—that sort of thing. And weathervanes. He told me on the phone. All handmade. He is a craftsman."

Grijpstra got up. "We'll be on our way, sir. We found Mr. Marchant this morning, dead, hanging from a tree in the Amsterdam Forest. He probably hanged himself around seven a.m., and at some time before he must have delivered the rabbit and its egg. According to his landlady he has been behaving strangely lately. He must have blamed you for his troubles and tried to take his revenge. He didn't mean to kill your wife, he meant to kill you. He didn't know that you don't eat chocolate and he probably didn't even know you were married. We'll check further and make a report. The rabbit's mold is probably still in his shop, and if not we'll find traces of the chocolate. We'll have the rabbit checked for fingerprints. It won't be difficult to come up with irrefutable proof. If we do, we'll let you know, sir, a little later today. I am very sorry all this has happened."

"Nothing ever happens in Amsterdam," de Gier said as he yanked the door of the Volkswagen open, "and when it does it all fits in immediately."

But Grijpstra didn't agree.

"We would never have solved the case, or rather *I* wouldn't have if you hadn't thought of the rabbit as an ornament."

"No, Grijpstra, we would have found Marchant's name in Moozen's files."

The adjutant shook his heavy grizzled head. "No, we wouldn't have checked the files. If he had kept on saying that he wasn't working on any bad cases I wouldn't have pursued that line of thought. I'd have reverted to trying to find an enemy of his wife. We might have worked for weeks and called in all sorts of help and wasted everybody's time. You are clever, Sergeant."

De Gier was studying a redheaded girl waiting for a streetcar.

"Am I?"

"Yes. But not as clever as I am," Grijpstra said and grinned. "You work for me. I personally selected you as my assistant. You are a tool in my expert hands."

De Gier winked at the redheaded girl and the girl smiled back.

The traffic had jammed up ahead and the car was blocked. De Gier opened his door.

"Hey! Where are you going?"

"It's a holiday, Adjutant, and you can drive this wreck for a change. I am going home. That girl is waiting for a streetcar that goes to my side of the city. Maybe she hasn't had lunch yet. I am going to invite her to go to a Chinese restaurant."

"But we have reports to make, and we've got to check our Marchant's shop; it'll be locked, we have to find the key in his room, and we have to telephone the engineer to let him off the hook."

"I am taking the streetcar," de Gier said. "You do all that. You ate my roll."

Georges Simenon

The Man from Out There

(translated by Suzie deSurvilliers and Bolton Melliss)

Something different from Georges Simenon, creator of Inspector Maigret . . . not a bulldoggish manhunt in the streets and bistros of Paris—rather what might be termed a "moody murder." Was it a dream or a nightmare come true? For years Boussus had dreaded a possible confrontation with the man he had doubly wronged. And now—was it happening? . . .

If you ever land in this paradise that is the island of Porquerolles, a few miles south of the sleeping Hyères, it is possible they may tell you different stories about the sinking of *The Mirrored Armoire*. It is even possible, depending on whether you speak to Chief Skipper Grimaud, to Pirate's-Head-Tadot, to the Nerve, to Maurice-the-Bouillabaisse, or to others you will find playing cards in the shade of the meager eucalyptus in the square, that you will hear still other accounts.

I would have you know that none of them is lying. But, lacking knowledge of the *only* truth, they imagine various "truths." And as time goes on there will be still more . . .

As to the exact time it happened, there is no evidence at all. The church clock which, among other things, tells its own whimsical hours, is several kilometers from the headland of Mèdes. This promontory is itself a good distance from the Notre Dame farm; and the people of the farm—that day, as on any other—were bent over in the burning light of the vineyards. Might one perhaps have been able, with binoculars, to witness the tragedy from the deck of a warship anchored in the bay of the Salines?

The fact remains that Boussus—the big Boussus, as he was called—had left his flowering home on the square and arrived at the harbor about six in the morning, dressed in pajamas, his dirty feet in espadrilles, and a straw hat like a helmet on his head. He hadn't shaved or washed. In a basket he was carrying a bottle of the rosé

152

wine of the island, a two-pound loaf of bread, a can of anchovies in piquant sauce, and a thick slice of roquefort cheese.

Casimir, who had drawn up his nets at dawn, saw him board his ship, the *Royal Girella,* better known as *The Mirrored Armoire.* As on every night, the motor made a fuss before starting. While it was warming up, Boussus settled himself astern, under a striped red-and-yellow awning, opened his folding chair, made sure his boulter fishing lines were in order, and took out of the water the container of hermit crabs he was going to use for bait.

A short time later the *Royal Girella,* not over six meters long (in the country they said twenty-eight shirt tails long), was cutting the silken water in the direction of Mèdes, at the extreme tip of the island.

Boussus had his place to fish and he never changed it. The headland of Mèdes is a sheer rock, out of sight of all habitation. Barely twenty meters farther out a rocky peak emerges from the deep water.

"My beach umbrella," Boussus liked to say of this peak which provided his shade.

Once there, exploring the sea floor through the transparent water, he let go the stone tied to a rope which he used as an anchor. He broke open the hermit crab shells, settled himself in his folding chair, and paying out his lines, started to fish.

One thing is certain: at nine o'clock there were in his basket, which he kept covered with a wet cloth, about forty girellas, twenty orange sérans, five hogfish (more brown than red with their bristling spines), and three blue-and-green iridescent serres.

The Porquerolles bottle of wine, always within Boussus' reach, had been sampled often. The can of anchovies in piquant sauce was empty. The sun was already high. And the sea, without a ripple under the breezeless sky, rose in a swell that was smooth and slow, like the breast of a young woman sighing.

Some residents of Porquerolles have mentioned two bottles of wine, others three. The fact remains that they found only one. Boussus had just pulled in one of his boulter lines on which two sérans were hooked. Bending over, he could see, at the bottom of the clear water, the rocks he recognized as clearly as a peasant who recognized the smallest details of his field—the shady holes, the algae, the schools of girellas as agile and silly as young goats.

Not a soul was in sight. Not the faintest hum of a motor. No one on land or sea.

And yet a voice suddenly called out, "Mimile!"

Now, Boussus was not startled. He only said to himself, I knew it!

No one, for 25 years, had called him Mimile. No one in Porquerolles knew that long ago it had been his nickname. And no one now was anywhere in his field of vision.

Nevertheless, he slowly raised his head. His eyes, still shielded by sunglasses, scanned the landscape. And, like Cain in the past, he thought of nothing better than to stammer, "Where are you?"

"Mimile."

One of the sérans slipped from his fingers. It was already lost because, pulled up from a depth of twenty meters, it would soon die and be found floating belly up.

"Mimile."

At that moment there was a sound of lapping waves. From behind the rock that sheltered the *Royal Girella,* a flat-bottomed fishing boat—a *bette,* as they say in the south—appeared silently, with a man sitting alone in the middle.

"It's you," declared Boussus.

Did he, or didn't he, say it? The fact remains that his lips moved and he had the illusion of speaking. Just as he had the illusion of leaning over and taking from a handy drawer a loaded gun that he always kept there.

At this, the other one in his flat boat, who had rested on his oars and was drifting within a few meters of the *Royal Girella,* appeared to murmur in a hurt tone, "What are you afraid of?"

"I knew you were going to come back."

"Because the newspapers said so? I still could have gone anywhere else."

"I knew you would come here. I knew you would find my address."

"Don't shoot, Mimile."

"What do you want of me?"

"I've come to say hi—to an old pal. Isn't it natural, after all this time, to say hi to a buddy?"

The sky was turquoise, the sea opaline, with its slow and tranquil breathing, like the very rhythm of nature. The boats were now riding idly. The water rose and fell along the rocks, showing wet areas of green moss and shells.

But it was the man in the flat-bottomed boat who showed the greatest tranquillity, even beatitude. For months, for years, Boussus had been wondering: "Will I recognize him when he comes?"

A man 22 years old at their last encounter and lean as a stray cat. How long since then? Twenty-five years. Twenty-five years of penal servitude out there in Guyana.

For months he had been checking all strangers who landed on the island and had asked himself, Does he look like Mauvoisin?

Perhaps he now had only one eye. Or a broken nose, or cauliflower ears, or a gruff voice, or a crippled body.

How would Mauvoisin act? As someone hateful, savage, impatient for revenge?

But there was the man in the flat-bottomed boat saying simply, in a soft, half-shy voice, "Hi, friend."

With Boussus, trying to force a grin, mumbling, "Hi."

"You see? I came only to say hello."

There was no irony, no hint of menace. It was peace on earth or, rather, on sea.

"You have a very pretty boat, Mimile."

Mimile was embarrassed, as he was when a pretty woman paid him a compliment. Did Mauvoisin know that, in the country, his boat was nicknamed *The Mirrored Armoire?* Did he know that only Boussus defended it against the jibes of people like Chief Skipper Grimaud, Pirate's-Head-Tadot, and all the others at Maurice's Golden Isles Café?

"I fixed it up by myself," he murmured.

Boussus was large, fat, and soft, and his huge thighs forced him to walk in a straddle. He liked his comfort and his conveniences—which was why he had a striped awning over his boat's stern, why he had rigged up a diminutive cabin with an armoire, some drawers, a mini-icebox, and some cushions.

As they were saying on the island: "Weighted with all that heavy superstructure, the boat will sink like a stone. Besides, it's no longer a boat. It's a mirrored armoire."

Mauvoisin was the only one to admire it.

"A very beautiful boat, Mimile. If we had only had it in the Mediterranean, in San Quentin."

Boussus was still distrustful. But no, it wasn't the former Mauvoisin he saw before him, or the Mauvoisin he had feared.

"Twelve of the most dangerous convicts have just escaped from Guyana and have tried to reach Venezuela in a rowboat," the newspapers had printed.

And then: "Seven of them have been eaten by sharks."

Finally: "Among those reported as having succeeded in reaching San Marguerite, exhausted, starved, without water for eight days, is Jules Mavoisin, the killer of the cashier of the San Quentin Wire Works."

It was that very Mauvoisin who was now showing himself as gentle as a lamb. He was speaking without hate, almost with the sentimentality of a drunk. His hair had turned white as snow. His complexion, too, was white and his eyes were pallid—he looked very small and very thin in the middle of his baby-blue *bette*.

"I am very happy, Mimile, that you ran off. I was always saying to myself out there, 'I hope Mimile got away!' You have a beautiful boat. They say you own a pretty house on the square."

Boussus, himself like a sentimental drunk, felt his heart melting.

"It's true. It's the prettiest one, Mauvoisin."

"Call me Jules."

"It's the prettiest one, Jules. Last year I lined the kitchen walls with faience tiles. This year I put flowers around the terrace. I've even fitted up a bathroom which I don't use."

"You've done well, Mimile."

"You can't imagine. . . I'm so lonely! I have to make my own diversions."

"Your garden has the best peach trees on the island."

"Yet I don't like peaches! . . . You remember, Jules? The guy Mr. Michel? Well, no matter what I do, I can't forget. I still feel his limp body in the sack."

"That was so long ago, Mimile."

"Well . . . and then, you see, there's you. There's you who I knew was breaking stones, out there on the road."

"That did my lungs good. I had weak lungs, you know. The doctors had x-rayed me and wanted to send me to the mountains. So you see the outdoor work did me good."

Mauvoisin's smile was as cold as the bottom of the sea.

"You don't resent me, Jules?"

"What for?"

He was so gentle, so full of magnanimity, that Boussus could not stop talking.

"I'm going to confess the truth to you, Jules. I have a beautiful house, hundreds of thousands of francs in the bank, a beautiful boat, no matter what they say. Anyway, it suits me. And yet, Jules, I've never been happy."

"Why?"

"Because of you."

"Have I ever made you any reproaches?"

"You never wrote to me."

"I could have. We have ways, through buddies. Why would I have made you any reproaches?"

"You don't know, Jules?"

"I know everything."

"Everything?"

In the face of such understanding, such kindness, the big Boussus felt like bursting into tears.

"You see, when you come back from out there it's like coming back from hell. You see things differently. You can't imagine . . . " Jules's voice diminished.

He still had the gentleness of a saint out of a stained-glass window. And all this time, for years and years, Boussus had been haunted by the image of a grim avenger.

"You remember *everything,* Jules?"

"Everything."

"It was a Saturday—"

"In November, yes. It was raining, windy. I was managing a small roadside garage about five kilometers from San Quentin. Because I couldn't make both ends meet, I had opened a tavern next door, but in spite of it I was threatened with eviction. My wife, who was pretty, had gone to visit her sick aunt in Paris, remember? I wonder now if it really was her aunt—"

"Well, Jules, since we are now like brothers, I can tell you—"

"I suspected—but it doesn't matter. Besides, afterwards she asked me for a divorce."

"I arrived at your home around six in the evening," Boussus recalled. "I lived about two hundred meters away from you and I was doing handy work in the neighborhood."

It was unheard of! Boussus would never have imagined that the conversation would go this way. It was as if they were in heaven, where souls can evoke their earthly concerns with the utmost serenity.

"When I came into your house, there were feet sticking out from a closet," Boussus continued.

"I'd just killed him," Jules explained.

"Beaten him with a monkey wrench."

"I used what I had at hand."

Thanks to this disembodied mood of Jules Mauvoisin, the most sordid details seemed to lose their vilest qualities.

And yet—the wet road—the garage and the tavern—this poor

Michel, the cashier of the San Quentin Wire Works, who had a wooden leg and was going about on his auxiliary motor-bicycle . . . It was not only Saturday, it was the thirtieth of the month. He had gone to the bank to bring back the pay of the thousands of factory workers.

"Hi! Jules, could you see if there's any water in my carburetor?" Michel had said.

His motor-bicycle was coughing and he was afraid of a breakdown halfway up the hill.

"Why don't you go and have a drop of gin while I fix it, Mr. Michel?"

Mauvoisin knew there were hundreds of thousands of francs, in bills, in the toolbox. Boussus had not yet arrived.

Boussus didn't actually see the tragedy—the blow with the monkey wrench on the cashier's head, the further blows, the gesture of pushing the inert body into a closet . . .

With as much serenity as his visitor, Boussus was now saying, "I saw the feet showing and you told me, 'If you help me get rid of the body, it'll be fifty-fifty between us.' "

"We were young then," Jules said softly.

"We took the light truck and went over to the canal, after tying the body in a coal sack. It was limp. I could never forget that limp bundle."

"We were young then."

"Since then, each day while I fish with boulters, or spade my garden, or play cards at Maurice's, I—"

"It only shows you have not been out there."

"Maybe you don't know the whole story, Jules."

"Out there we know everything."

"Including what I did afterwards? You see, I'm a blackguard, Jules, a scoundrel. Worse still, nobody knows that I'm one. I was waiting to tell you . . . your wife . . . "

"Fernande?"

"Well, yes. You see, even before—"

"It matters so little."

"I still wonder why she preferred me to you. I surely wasn't handsome."

"Neither was I."

"I wasn't rich."

"I wasn't either. Maybe she just wanted a change."

"But afterwards, when you were arrested—"

"It doesn't matter any more."

"I swear it does, Jules! I acted like a swine, like a—I don't know what. We had shared the seven hundred thousand francs from the toolbox—"

"That was only fair."

"Not quite, since you killed Michel all by yourself. I only helped you put him in the sack."

"It's the same thing."

"Except that, eight days later, when the cops began to look hard at you—"

"I brought you my share and asked you to keep it for me during the inquiry."

"That's when I began to be a real bad one, Jules. I had the seven hundred thousand francs. I wanted to keep Fernande for myself alone. I wrote the anonymous letter—it must have occurred to you that I was the one who had written it."

"Yes."

"And you didn't mind?"

"It's all so long ago."

"Just the same, it was I who wrote the Commissioner that you killed Michel with blows from a monkey wrench, that the towel you used to clean your hands with was buried in your garden, near a well, and that the wooden toolbox was burned in your garage where they found the ashes. I'm a blackguard, Jules, but I swear to you that since then I've not been any happier than you. Fernande walked out on me. They say she died two years ago in a hospital."

"Good for her!"

"And myself . . . I live, of course. I get up in the morning, I go fishing, I eat bouillabaisse, I play cards, but all day and all night I'm thinking: 'This poor Jules, all that time out there.' "

Is a prison really capable of changing a man that much? Jules was falling, if not into a trap, at any rate into acquiescence. He was nodding.

"You're a chum," he asserted.

"I'm a bad one, Jules."

"Bah! You see, I came only to say a short hello. But I'll come back from time to time."

"Where are you living? You're not afraid they'll take you back?"

Jules pointed vaguely to the coast mountains and said, "Over there."

With this turn in the conversation, Boussus found himself thinking of a hammer he kept in the mirrored armoire for breaking the hard shells of the hermit crabs. If the flat boat came nearer—

"It's all so long ago," Jules Mauvoisin was repeating philosophically.

He was gentle. So gentle that—

Having for years read the newspapers in fear of learning that Mauvoisin, the convict, had escaped, having for months checked all strangers who landed at Porquerolles, having for so long—

And now it was so simple, so pleasant, so easy!

They say that our dreams, even the longest ones, last only a few seconds.

Is the following, perhaps, a proof?

Boussus opened his eyes and was amazed to find no flat boat around—nothing on the water as far as he could see, except a large, gray, light cruiser anchored in the bay of the Salines.

The bottle of Porquerolles wine was almost empty. The can that had contained anchovies in piquant sauce was covered with flies. The cheese was gone. The last chunk of bread was drying in the sun.

Now, for the first time, Boussus' face fell, as when he was worried about his liver, and his eyes had the look of marbles that have rolled in the wet.

Could it not have been a dream? Or was it true? That Jules had really returned in this—how to say it—this unearthly frame of mind?

Boussus pulled a large red handkerchief from his pocket to clean his blurred sunglasses.

He wondered.

But no! There was no one. No boat. No *bette!*

He leaned over to look back at the Mèdes rock and was about to feel reassured.

It was, however, the right date. He had figured it out. Starting with the day of Jules Mauvoisin's escape, he had had time, allowing for difficulties, to take a boat to France, to go to the north, and from there to track down Boussus and reach Porquerolles.

He had figured this for so many years! Over and over again!

All the rest was true—the feet sticking out from the closet, the limp body in the sack, the light truck, the canal.

And, above all, the anonymous letter!

Why had Boussus behaved that way? Frankly, he was beginning to have doubts about it now. Was it to have Fernande only for himself? Or to avoid sharing the 700,000 francs?

He had been living ever since in anguish, in fear. Could it be that out there *they were that well guarded?*

He fished, he fitted out his boat and his house. He played cards. Each time anyone, in the eucalyptus shade of the square, called out to him, "Hi, Boussus," he thought he recognized Jules's voice.

He half stood up to draw in one of the boulter lines that he had not payed out in his sleep.

"Mimile!"

The voice was not coming from the sea, but from the land, from the Mèdes headland that was only a bare rock in the sun.

"It's your turn now, Mimile, you son of a—"

That was all. He heard a shot. He toppled over. His body felt both cool and warm and for an instant, coming nearer, he saw the bluish sea floor where the girellas were swimming ...

"I always said his mirrored armoire would end like that!" declared Grimaud, while they were raising the boat, keel-up.

"He must have become dizzy—staring at the sea."

A fisher of sea urchins found the body at mid-depth.

It was not until evening that the doctor found a small round hole in Boussus' temple.

"This man has been killed by a bullet from a revolver."

There was an inquiry by the police from Hyères and Toulon. It was learned that a stranger had disembarked from the *Cormorant*—a nasty-looking stranger with a squint, the ship's captain asserted.

The stranger set out again by boat in three hours and seemed to be laughing to himself.

He had been seen passing the Notre Dame farm.

He had, in fact, asked a boy where Mr. Boussus lived.

"He's fishing," the answer had been.

"Where?"

"At his place."

"And where is his place?"

"Near Mèdes point—right at the foot of the rock. You'll recognize his boat for sure. They call it *The Mirrored Armoire.*"

The squint-eyed stranger had recognized it.

That matters little. What is important is that, from the shore, he must have shouted to Boussus in his sleep: "Mimile!"

And did that "Mimile" reach the fisherman at the bottom of his sleep and release a dream that lasted a few seconds, perhaps only a few tenths of a second?

When the eyes of the sleeper opened, still full of the vision of a Jules all sugar and honey who evoked the past without rancor, he found before him a man who hurled at him, bursting with the bitterness of 25 years of Guyana:

"It's your turn now, Mimile, you son of a—"

A small sharp report in the calm of a Mediterranean morning, a fat body toppling over. The girellas, the hogfish, the sérans, the hermit crabs, and all the gear of abandoned fishing . . .

The *Royal Girella* had sunk like a stone and turned over.

So much the worse, if anyone tells you differently at Maurice's.

Jacques Catalan

The Prisoners

(translated by Suzie deSurvilliers and Bolton Melliss)

The May 1975 French edition of Ellery Queen's Mystery Magazine, called Mystère Magazine, *ran a short-story contest* (le jeu des nouvelles de l'été) *for new writers. First prize was awarded to Jacques Catalan's "Les Prisonniers," which appeared in the February 1976 issue of* Mystère. *This prizewinning story is an unusual* nouvelle—*not a police procedural, rather a police psychological. It raises an interesting and thought-provoking question: Who are the real victims in the world of crime and punishment? . . .*

For an instant the motorcycle cop remains at my eye level as his peremptory hand waves me to slow down. He passes me in a short burst, stops in front of me, and points to the grassy side of the road. I obey, pull over, jolting, and stop my car.

The cop has stopped his machine at the road edge and comes toward me, taking off his white gloves. In the rear-view mirror I see the second cop, still straddling his machine in a slow-motion swagger. The first one, approaching, mechanically slaps his dark trousers with his gloves. He leans over the door and salutes me correctly.

"Yes?" I ask.

"Your papers, please."

Without a word I hand over the car papers and my license which, for occupation, states only "Civil Servant." He examines everything, and it is when he seems to lean toward my companion that I hand him my card.

"Ah!"

He straightens up and gives me a formal salute.

"Excuse me, Mr. Commissioner."

"It's all right. But I don't think I was exceeding the speed limit. Was I?"

163

"No. Just a routine inspection. A prisoner has escaped from Gradignan and—"

"A recent one? I have been on vacation for two days and am avoiding all contact with the Department."

He smiles and nods understandingly.

"This morning, Antoine Milan, the murderer of Neuve Street."

"Really! Well, good luck to you. You will excuse my not staying longer. I am on my way to my summer home and want to get there as soon as possible."

The cop salutes me again and moves off toward his machine. He casts a glance at the low November sky and calls out to me, "Nasty weather for Arcachon. Happy vacation just the same, Mr. Commissioner."

I incline my head with a vague, restrained smile, as if I shared the policeman's opinion of winter vacations. I turn on my backup lights and let in the clutch gently.

Yet I do like this season, even though it heightens my feeling of loneliness. All these years I have taken no holidays in the sun—ever since. . .

My seniority entitles me to take the whole month of August, as before, if I want it. But I have learned to like the winter. The beach and the forest are mine alone. Mine, that is, with the true inhabitants of the place—the fishermen, the resin tappers, the oystermen, and the shopkeepers just getting over the summer-rush invasion.

The one false note in this holiday, which was again to have been a solitary one, is the presence of the man beside me. Together with the fact that he hasn't ceased to cover me, through his pocket, with a Colt .45.

Antoine Milan, the murderer of Neuve Street. . .

The man lets out a deep breath as if he has been holding it in up to now. I don't so much as turn my head toward him, but continue to stare at the straight road lined with pine trees that are plunged into mourning by the oncoming darkness.

"Why didn't you show your card at once? We risked—"

"*You* risked," I cut in drily.

"I would have fired," growls Milan.

"No, you wouldn't. You didn't shoot me at home, did you? You said you wanted to have it out with me calmly. I chiefly feared the motorcycle cop might make a connection between us. The Milan case is mine, Commissioner Bernier's, right? But the cop is a youngster with little experience. He said 'the murderer of Neuve Street' because that's what they told him. Nothing more. So take it easy. Even if you put your gun away, you'll arrive with me tonight just the same."

"Not a chance," says Milan. "I've promised myself too long to hold you at the end of a gun. The roles are reversed now, that's for sure."

"The roles are exactly as they were. When I arrested you it was you who held the gun. My hands were empty."

"I did a ten-year stretch for that."

I don't answer and continue to watch the road. In the fast fading light I check the road signs. The rain bursts suddenly, shrinking the darkened landscape and changing the horizon to a thin liquid curtain.

I love driving in the rain. For me, the beat of the windshield wipers gives rhythm to a strange symphony and leads an orchestra that includes the elements. Rain drumming on the car, spurting wildly under the aggressive wheels, dancing a little ballet of luminous streaks in the sea-green light of the headlights. And the wind in the wet pines, bowing them down in a slow sway along our road, in a kind of proud salute, a renewed farewell, along the unfolding kilometers. . .

Facture, the little country town drowned in the downpour, heaves lifeless into sight.

With a glance in the rear-view mirror I turn sharp left onto the Mios road.

"Where are you going, Commissioner?"

Milan is thrown against me and I shove him back with my shoulder. I feel the naked gun at the end of his arm pressing savagely against my side. I switch to full headlights at the rail crossing, bumping over the rails.

"Home. To Biscarrosse."

"I thought—well, get this. No tricks."

I shrug and shift gears. Not a car in sight and I know the road like my pocket.

"It was the motorcycle cop who mentioned Arcachon, not I. Because at that time we were on the road to Arcachon."

We don't exchange another word the rest of the way. We pass through Cazaux, Sanguinet. Sunk in his seat, Milan doesn't take his eyes off me, his right hand clamped on the gun that covers me. Entering Biscarrosse, we pass a few stray vehicles and a military convoy.

Then there are curves upward, a straight road, and finally the lights of the filling station. I turn right, in the direction of the lake, veer still more to the right, and here is the little square. Lifeless summer houses with shutters closed on deserted interiors.

The headlights reveal my dripping entrance gate and the low white wall streaked with glistening cracks and stained with green moss, and, beyond, the cream-colored walls of my house, the veranda with its dark wood columns, and the long balcony on the second floor.

"It looks large," says Milan mechanically.

"It is large. Shall I get out and open the gate?"

He nods and in the buffeting rain I open the double gate. I rejoin Milan, getting in beside him, and move the car over sodden pine needles to the front of the garage. I shut off the motor and the frantic windshield wipers.

"We go in by the back. The key is in the glove compartment."

Milan finds the key and throws a quick glance at the jumble inside—cards, sundry papers, rags, a flashlight. No gun and, above all, no gloves. He takes the flashlight.

With me leading the way, we skirt the house in the fitful gleam of the flashlight until, spurred by the storm, we break into a run. I open the door while Milan shoves the gun in my back. I smile thinly. A long time ago I learned how to get rid of anyone who threatened me in this way. It's really so simple.

"The main switch. In the laundry room. Shut the door after you."

He still follows me, lighting the way. I switch on the lights. Milan blinks wildly in the sudden glare and I turn my attention to the boiler. Ignoring my unwelcome guest, I get it started; it begins to whir at once and I become a new man at the welcome sight of the flames roaring out of the burners.

"Shall we go to the living room?"

We pass through the kitchen and enter the large L-shaped room. I again enjoy seeing the great fireplace, which is waiting only for a lighted match, the dark tiling, the bright carpet, the deep armchairs, the African masks, and the Moroccan plates of burnished copper.

Home.

Mine.

Milan heads for the telephone.

Oh, no, not that. My one bridge to the outside world, to others, to the living.

"If you cut the wires— My daughter is going to telephone me as she does every night. Especially tonight," I add quickly. "She always calls to find out if I've arrived safe."

He eyes me sharply, and shrugs.

"*You* have a daughter?"

I take off my overcoat and sit down in one of the armchairs. Milan moves back to me and also sits down.

"I have a daughter, Antoine. Twenty-one. And a grandson. Three."

He throws me a bitter glance and the gun in his hand begins to shake.

"Some things you shouldn't speak of, Commissioner. Especially to me."

I look up in surprise. "I'm not trying to appeal to you or provoke you. I'm answering your question, that's all."

"You know why I'm in prison, don't you?" Antoine asks caustically.

"Yes, I know . . . Do you mind?"

Taking the matchbox from the coffee table, I bend toward the fireplace and light the waiting logs.

"I know, Antoine," I say, watching the crackling wood. "You killed your wife, locked yourself in your apartment with her, badly beat up two cops when they broke in, and wounded three of the security police. An inspiring performance that got you a twenty-year sentence."

"And I was arrested by fearless Chief Inspector Bernier who, bare-handed, prides himself on never carrying a gun when facing an opponent. Do you know why I killed my wife?"

"We're not going to start your trial all over again, Antoine. Your wife was deceiving you."

"I loved Anne!"

"You killed your wife because you loved her. You'd never guess how often you made that statement during your trial."

"You've understood nothing, absolutely nothing! When I realized what I had done—don't laugh!—I would have liked to be left alone with Anne. Just the two of us, alone. Perhaps, then, I would have had the courage—but, instead, that senseless raid when all I wanted—"

"Exactly. Meditation, to be followed by suicide. Or surrender."

"That's what I *would* have done! I'm too much of a coward to kill myself, Bernier. I've thought and thought about it—for years. And I've spent the last ten years of my life reproaching myself about Anne. Have you any idea what prison is like, Commissioner? I don't mean the walls and bars you're locked behind. I mean this one"—he strikes his forehead—"the worst prison of all, where thoughts upon thoughts never stop spinning, and in the end destroy you. . ."

I take my pipe and reach toward the drawer of the table.

"My tobacco," I explain.

He shrugs and I pull out one of my blue packets and carefully fill my pipe. He is staring at me thoughtfully.

"You have sad eyes, Commissioner. I look at you and try to read fear in your face, or find the calm you had ten years ago when—"

I drop the blackened match that has started to burn my fingers and strike another.

"But I see only sad eyes," repeats Antoine.

"We all change in ten years, old man."

"Did your wife die?"

I start, in spite of myself. "Yes, my wife died. Two years ago."

It's true. Mathilde died two years ago. Far from here. Far from me.

"That may be the reason for the sadness in your eyes."

"Perhaps."

He puts the gun back in his pocket and starts playing with a long Arabian dagger he has just picked up near the fireplace.

"Let's not go soft, Antoine," I say quietly. "While you've been looking me over so carefully I've also had a good look at you. It's clear you didn't come here to harm me; you could have done that ten years ago. I've seen you beside yourself with rage and despair, firing at my men—and I've seen you resigned as I came toward you, when you threatened to kill me but didn't fire."

"Don't be so sure. I may have come to regret it."

"Oh, no."

I lean toward him across the table.

"Spain, Antoine—and from there to wherever you wish."

He looks at me dumfounded and bursts into joyless laughter.

"This is too good! Are you so afraid, Commissioner—you, above all—that you offer me escape? Even help, perhaps?"

"I can pass you along and take care of you all the way. Through fear, you think? My poor fool, I could have got rid of you twenty times. Even now, in this drawer you've so considerately let me open. . ."

I turn the table toward him with its open drawer and he barely glances at the weapon lying among my packets of tobacco.

"We change, Antoine. We all change."

"It's too late, Commissioner."

He stands up and in a swift movement rests the sharp blade against my neck. I, too, get to my feet, jumping back. For a moment he remains facing me, the hilt low, the point of the dagger now aimed straight at my belly. He moves a few steps nearer and, in spite of myself, I grab my gun from the table drawer and aim it at him.

"I meant what I said, Antoine. Spain—anywhere in the world you want to go."

He comes closer still, then makes a stupid theatrical gesture—he raises the dagger above my head. Not a born killer, this murderer of Neuve Street.

The telephone rings suddenly and its thin, sharp blast makes me start.

"Your daughter!" he shouts. "You won't have time to speak to her! Ever again!"

He clings, suddenly close, and I see his arm coming down. In slow motion the dagger's point enters my jacket, pierces my flesh. While the obsessive phone keeps ringing, ringing—

I haven't even heard my shot.

Antoine Milan reels back and I see intense triumph in his pale eyes that are now dazed with pain. He opens his mouth wide and a stream of blood spurts out. He slowly sinks down, his eyes fixed on me.

The ringing stops and I hear only the crackle of the flames and Antoine's labored breathing and the light tapping of the closed shutters facing the muffled gusts.

The phone resumes its clamor. . .

"I've dialed your number twice. I thought I'd made a mistake the first time. Milan escaped this morning. I'm warning you because—"

"He's here. I've got him . . . yes, Chief."

I hang up wearily and put my gun by the telephone. Antoine's breathing becomes shorter and a veil has come over his eyes which seem to stare at me with great difficulty.

Antoine, don't go . . . Please don't die.

So many things can happen in ten years. The ten years I've been coming to this empty house where I'll never see Mathilde again. Or Jeannine. Or the grandson who doesn't know me. A few moments more and I'd have spoken to you of my wife who left me ten years ago and of my daughter who hates me and who looks so much like her mother. And of my heart that has turned dry and of my spirit that has drowned in solitude.

Stay with me, Antoine . . . I'll listen to your story and to Anne's, which humiliated you, and I'll tell you Mathilde's, of her leaving with another man near whom she died two years ago and of her blind hatred for me who loved her and Jeannine more than anything else in the world . . . I'll tell you how I spent these last two days watching over my daughter's life from a distance and that of my grandson whom I shall never hold in my arms . . .

Don't go, Antoine, my friend . . .

Laura Grimaldi

Affirmation of Truth; or, Justice Done

(translated by Philip Rigby)

We found this story in an Italian anthology titled ANONIMA CAR-
OGNE, *published in 1973 by Arnoldo Mondadori Editore of Milan
and edited by Laura Grimaldi. The book is a thick handsome
volume, beautifully produced, containing eleven stories; ten are
by American and English writers and of these ten stories five
appeared originally in Ellery Queen's Mystery Magazine—stories
by Cornell Woolrich, Jerrold Phaon, Dana Lyon, Mary Barrett,
and Florence V. Mayberry.*

*The Italian story by Laura Grimaldi is titled "Giustizia è fatta."
It has an unusual conception for a crime story—indeed, it may
be that rara avis of mysteries, a unique plot-idea . . .*

W ith the firm resolution to perform my duty as a man of honor,
being conscious of the supreme moral and civil importance of
the task that the Law has entrusted to me, I swear to listen diligently,
and examine earnestly, proofs and reasons presented in this proceeding by the Prosecution and by the Defense. I swear to make my own
judgment with honesty and impartiality and to keep far from my
mind all feeling of aversion or favor, in order to reach a sentence
equivalent to what society expects: an affirmation of truth and justice.
Jurors' oath (Art. 30).

It had been a mistake to accept presiding over that trial. The
Judge closed the court record, shaking his head. Yes, a big mistake.
To begin with, a trial without legal or judicial precedents, one without procedural antecedents, is a minefield. More than that, it is a
stretch of moving sands. And if that wasn't enough, there was the
ridiculousness of a defendant made of printed paper instead of flesh
and blood.

The Judge had the feeling it would all come to no good. In fact,
at the beginning he had resisted all the objections, all the pressures,

firmly entrenched behind the excuse that it had never been heard of before. But then that impertinent young man for the Defense, insistent and stubborn as a mule, had started to release press interviews, to insist that it was in someone's interest to obstruct the trial, to declare that no judge could be found who could give a fair verdict.

And the Prosecutor? He hadn't been idle either. He had managed to collect 10,000 signatures in the district alone, 10,000 respectable and right-thinking people who were demanding a ban on books with any kind of criminal setting. Thrillers, that's what they were, according to popular definition.

Faced with all this, what could the Judge do except surrender and agree to preside over the trial? And he had surrendered. He had agreed, knowing only too well it was a mistake. But he had done it, too, because in the end he had felt involved, intrigued, stimulated. Slightly at first, then with ever-increasing force.

Oh, well, he had to admit it. He had played his part with the knowledge that such a trial would have national repercussions. World-wide, in fact.

The light sense of guilt that nagged him left him at once. When it came down to it, he had spent all his life in the service of justice, among dusty documents, bringing pint-sized criminals to task for squalid little crimes, with prosecution and defense counsels only interested in making a name for themselves. Oh, yes, even the personalities of the Prosecution and the Defense had had their importance: the former was well-prepared, learned, upright in the extreme; the latter, brilliant, young, aggressive.

The Judge sighed and opened the court record again. What was it that had escaped him? At what point had the works clogged up? Why had the situation—at first so clear, so intriguing, so alive—seemed to peter out, to become dim, to lose its clarity? The Judge told himself he had nothing to reproach himself for. He had guided the proceedings carefully, respecting, as always, the jurors' oath—an oath which from his very first case he had held before him like a shining light, an inspiration, something to cling on to. A pledge of honor. Of justice. All the times, on his insistence, that the jury had sworn it, he had felt pervaded by a kind of fierce pride. And he had made it his own oath.

The Judge got up to put on his woolen jacket. It was cold that evening and he intended to read the court record once again, if need be until dawn, to find that *something* which was bothering him, the thing that had to be the starting point of his discomfort, his discontent.

...*I swear to listen diligently, and examine earnestly, proofs and reasons presented in this proceeding by the Prosecution and by the Defense* ...

The Judge sat down and turned once more to the first page.

JUDGE: I declare the hearing open, the Crown versus the Literary Criminal. Since it is a question of proceedings *sui generis,* without judicial precedents, I will state precisely that in this court an attempt will be made to establish—regardless of the fact that the procedure is less than orthodox—whether or not the Literary Criminal has some responsibility, and what that responsibility is to real life.

Some maintain that there are books of a certain type which influence, inspire, and mold the criminal, furnishing him with sophisticated plans, cunning alibis, devious means. Others, conversely, ask: was perhaps the thriller born when Cain betrayed and killed his brother? And did Lucrezia Borgia need to draw on a writer's imagination in order to put her murderous schemes into practice?

It will be this court's task, after hearing both Prosecution and Defense, to decide if the Literary Criminal is guilty or innocent. Notice that it is not by accident that I have spoken of the "Literary Criminal." I wish to make it clear, in fact, that this court will not tolerate the use of a different term.

Let us now turn our attention to the purpose of this trial. As I have said, we are trying to clarify once and for all, in a public hearing, if a certain type of fiction can be considered guilty of influencing, or having influenced, the mind of man. In other words, it will be the duty of this court to decide whether to acquit or condemn those fictional plots which, by nature of their savagery, their malice, their wickedness, can be held as the source of inspiration for the criminal, and, as a consequence, dangerous to public morality ...

The Judge nodded his head. Apart from some repetition which was not indispensable, his introduction seemed to him essential, and above all, to the point. Undoubtedly the Defense had considered it to be a little too "dusty," but the Defending Counsel was one of those modern-speech types, from time to time downright irreverent. That young man had often stepped beyond the limits. He had become irritating. The Prosecutor, on the other hand, was a different kettle of fish, altogether a different breed.

. . . I swear to make my own judgment with honesty and impartiality and to keep far from my mind all feeling of aversion or favor . . .

Yes, thought the Judge. It wasn't always easy to remain so detached, so objective. He wondered if the small sneaking dislike he had felt for the Defending Counsel as the debate went on could have influenced his final decision. No, he told himself. He had acted according to the letter of the law.

PROSECUTOR: As I have already explained to the Court, I am totally convinced, and this conviction is supported by the solidarity of thousands of citizens who, with unswerving purpose, have made this debate possible, that a certain type of fiction must be considered harmful, dangerous, a form of infection—

DEFENSE COUNSEL: You've left out considerations of ecology.

The public gallery had laughed at that point and the Judge had been compelled to admonish the Defense Counsel and suggest a greater respect for the Court. The Defense Counsel had apologized, but his irony had stained the atmosphere, and for a time the members of the public present in court had been distracted, had taken to whispering comments, turning in their seats, shuffling their feet.

PROSECUTOR: I can state as a fact, having consulted the proceedings of various trials, that many criminals have openly confessed to being inspired by actions described in books which, if the matter rested in my hands, would never have been printed. I recall in particular the case of a certain Robert Butler who, on March 23, 1905, climbed the gallows, having been found guilty of mass murder. Well now, Butler stated at his trial that he was an inveterate reader of the works of the Marquis de Sade—a man who can never be deplored enough. Not only that: Butler publicly admitted to being influenced by the wickedness of Fantomas and Fu Manchu in order to carry out his crimes. I repeat, if the matter had rested in my hands, certain books would never have been printed.

DEFENSE COUNSEL: It is a source of relief to me that my illustrious colleague has chosen a forensic rather than an editorial career. If it had not been so, today we would be deprived of his eloquence while conversely the book business would have been shut down years ago . . .

The Judge scratched the lobe of his ear, once again sensing the same irritation. He couldn't have intervened, he recalled clearly, because officially the Defense Counsel had not done anything wrong, even if for a good five minutes he had imitated in his speech the tone and style of the Prosecutor. And again the gallery had laughed, had been distracted.

The Judge rose and walked up and down for a while, more in an attempt to restore a feeling of calm than to stretch his legs. That irritating young man had even reeled off an unending stream of quotations—it had to be admitted he was thoroughly prepared—to oppose the cultural references made by the Prosecution.

DEFENSE COUNSEL: I maintain that men like Napoleon and Frederick the Great should have been brought to trial, not to mention writers like Shakespeare and Aeschylus.

PROSECUTOR: Perhaps that's why *Mein Kampf,* the most criminal of all books, has already been condemned by history.

DEFENSE COUNSEL: I have presented irrefutable evidence of crimes committed in real life which, by their savagery, have no counterpart on the printed page. Let us not forget, moreover, that whereas in stories the guilty person is almost always brought to justice, unfortunately we cannot say the same of everyday life . . .

. . . *I swear to examine earnestly proofs and reasons presented in this proceeding by the Prosecution and by the Defense* . . .

And he had done so. He had examined in all earnestness the proofs and reasons of the Prosecution and Defense Counsels. The former had presented to the Court many cases in which the defendants had freely confessed to being influenced by the plots of this or that book. The latter, on the other hand, had attached to the exhibits a summary of famous trials in which the criminal's savagery had greatly surpassed the fictional imagination of any author.

PROSECUTOR: I ask for an exemplary conviction. I am sure that the Court will have made its—

DEFENSE COUNSEL: It would be an outrage to the freedom of expression, an unforgivable restriction on human imagination, an offense against culture itself. It is not by accident that in this court the names of great writers have echoed. If I am not mistaken, it was my learned colleague who mentioned the works of Poe and Dostoevsky . . .

The Judge, with complete impartiality, had pronounced a verdict of acquittal on grounds of insufficient evidence. He had not heard arguments sufficient either to sentence or absolve the literary prisoner at the bar. The Prosecutor had seemed pleased enough. Had an unconditional discharge really been expected, in light of the turn the trial had taken in the closing moments?

The gallery had become noisy when the Prosecutor, losing for a moment his sense of proportion, had maintained that the man in the street was incapable of free will, that all that was needed was a particularly savage crime to turn him into a bloodthirsty animal.

The Defending Counsel had been much cleverer, more subtle. How many of those present in court, he asked, could swear they had never read a book portraying violence? And maybe the reading of that book had been engraved on their minds, on their moral choices, on the self-control of the reader?

By his own reckoning the Judge was sure he had given a fair verdict even if for his own comfort a more conclusive sentence could have been passed. "All or nothing," the Defense Counsel would have said, with that rather too free and easy style of speaking—although the Judge had to admit it was somewhat effective. The verdict had, in fact, caused pandemonium. Well, there you are, thought the Judge. Everything had hinged on the verdict.

DEFENSE COUNSEL: I protest! Since these proceedings have been, as the Court itself made clear, a trial *sui generis,* with consequences more flexible, less restrictive from the point of view of procedure, I must take the liberty of rejecting the Court's verdict. I consider it iniquitous, oppressive, and totally unjustified. I have cited irrefutable proofs of the innocence of the accused, and if the Court had been objective, the verdict could only have been one of unconditional discharge. A verdict based on insufficient evidence is, in fact, the equivalent of a conviction. I am compelled to think that the Court has not had the courage to accept its full responsibility. In other words it has sinned in the name of timidity . . .

The Defense Counsel had continued in the same vein for a long time, raising his voice, making the atmosphere tense, profiting from the open admiration of the gallery.

JUDGE: I must ask the Defending Counsel to moderate his tone and language, which I consider to be offensive and unworthy of a Court of Justice. Otherwise I shall be compelled to—

DEFENSE COUNSEL: If there is anything unworthy of a Court of Justice, it is this decision—

JUDGE: I demand that the Defending Counsel be removed from the courtroom!

DEFENSE COUNSEL: Ah, now we see the heavy hand of authority, the insensitivity, the closed mind—

JUDGE: Bailiff, approach the Bench!

DEFENSE COUNSEL: Yes, Bailiff, approach the Bench and take *him* out of the courtroom!

*... in order to reach a sentence equivalent to what society expects:
an affirmation of truth and justice.*

The Judge closed his eyes. He recalled the face of the Bailiff: good-natured, surprised, embarrassed. And he recalled his own indignation, and that of the Prosecutor, at how the proceedings had been turned into a farce, a public brawl. He recalled too the Bailiff's holster within reach of his hand, unfastened, the butt seemingly offering itself to his finger.

He recalled also the shot, not so loud as he would have expected—a kind of *phut*, a little more than a smack. And how the Defending Counsel had fallen, breaking off halfway through a word: corr—What was he on the point of saying? Corruption?

The Judge closed the court record. Someone was opening the door. A rattling noise, the jangle of the guard's keys, a cracking sound, then a hoarse common voice: "Half hour fresh air, then clean out your cell."

Africa

Milán

Victor Milán

The Big Ivory

*"Six males, an indeterminate number of females, about a half-
dozen calves, Muzakere said. In this day and age that was a lot
of elephants"* . . .

T he hunters follow the big ivory. That's where the money is.
It was a big herd—even an outlander like me could tell. The
grass was still flattened from their passage, the yellow mud around
the waterhole churned as though by an artillery barrage. Six males,
an indeterminate number of females, about a half-dozen calves,
Muzakere had said. In this day and age that was a lot of elephants.

I scanned the horizon with my binoculars. The herd had moved
on some time since, off toward the river. I had quite a distance to
go to catch up with them.

It didn't matter. I had plenty of time.

Or so I thought. Then I caught sight of something that told me
otherwise.

Tracks again. They were broad swaths like those left by the lum-
bering elephants, but within them ran twin serrated lines as though
two giant snakes were traveling up them side by side. Tire marks.

I climbed into the Landcruiser and drove to where I'd seen the
tracks. There was no mistake. Land Rovers, two of them. Following
the herd, perhaps a few hours ahead of me.

I didn't have so much time after all.

A bird cried from a lonely, flat-topped acacia that stood shading
the mudhole. I got back into the Toyota and let in the clutch. I set
out following the two disparate sets of tracks, slowly, so that my
engine noise wouldn't spook my quarry.

I remembered the village, two days before. The East African heat
had barely been relieved by the small table fan that blew from one
corner of the room, riffling the papers on Muzakere's desk. He'd
rested a hard black hand on them casually, holding them down.

"There aren't many herds like this one left," he said. "I saw them

179

myself a fortnight ago. The leader is the largest bull I've ever seen. He must be four meters tall at the shoulder."

I nodded, trying to envision such a monster. He'd carry a phenomenal weight of ivory, that always-valuable substance that was becoming daily more precious as the only sources for it died off in the face of progress. Just one such creature would draw the ivory poachers like lions to a fresh zebra carcass.

Muzakere was looking at me. There was no friendliness in his gaze. I waited.

"When we achieved our independence," he said at last, speaking in the perfect clipped tones of an English-educated young African, "we believed we were through with you people. But now you come to slaughter our wild animals and speed them on their way to extinction." He looked as if he wanted to spit.

"Most of your emerging nations don't give a damn for the wildlife," I said. "They look at it as an inconvenience to be gotten rid of. The animals are killed off because they carry diseases that threaten cattle, the preserves become factories, cities, agricultural land. Conservation's considered a vestige of colonialism."

His expression told me what he thought of that. He was a young, intense man, not much older than me, handsome as a statue. In his own turn he was studying me, trying to read me.

I let him look. I was dressed in my own style—southwestern American—which suited this climate quite well. The vee between his brows deepened as he glanced at the heavy Ruger Blackhawk revolver hung butt-forward on my right hip. I could almost hear him think: *damned American cowboy.* Most of the poachers were British or white Africans. The thought of a new nationality coming in to massacre the animals he was charged with protecting didn't make him happy.

"You have your orders," I said quietly.

He nodded. "Yes." With bitterness. "I do."

I knew what he thought: some official high up in the interior ministry had been bought with American dollars so that yet another white-skinned hunter could walk a quick path to riches. And bring the elephant that much nearer oblivion. It caused him pain, this one. He really cared.

Let him, I thought. *Let him think whatever he wants to.* I rose to go.

"One thing," he said. He pushed back from the desk and rose, sucking his lips in pensively

The breeze peeled off the top sheet of paper he'd been anchoring down with his hand. It fluttered across the room. He ignored it.

"I saw your rifle. Out in your vehicle."

He seemed reluctant, so I prodded him. "And?"

"It is a Remington .300 magnum."

"So?"

He paused, then shook his head disgustedly. "You can kill an elephant with one, if you're good. But it's a gun for zebra or eland—or leopard, perhaps. It wouldn't stop a bull like this patriarch in a charge."

"It's a damn sight easier on my shoulder than one of these .577 cannons. I'm a specialist. I use the tools that suit me."

His face tautened. Why had he told me? I wondered. Perhaps he had the peculiarly British notion of exercising fair play even with those one despises. Or maybe he was hoping to goad my American *machismo* into making me face the old and mighty bull close up and get trampled flat.

"Thanks for your concern, anyway," I said.

"Get out of here," he said.

I made camp that night in the midst of an endless rippling of tawny grass. Out of some urge doubtless springing from my own arboreal ancestry I pulled the white Cruiser up into the lee of the single tree in sight. I cooked some tasteless foil-wrapped rations on a Coleman stove, not wanting to send up smoke in case anyone was watching, and afterward made myself some tea.

I sat on the hood of the Toyota, sipping, watching the sun sink and the sky go red. The grassland started to come alive around me as the day faded and myriad animals woke to greet the night. So did the bugs, unfortunately. As soon as the sky had shaded through purple and indigo and was starting in on starshot black, I unrolled my sleeping bag in the back of the Landcruiser—no use in tempting any of those leopards Muzakere had mentioned—and draped mosquito netting over windows half open for ventilation. The local fauna might not have qualified as a flight of angels, but their sounds sang me to my rest well enough.

Morning was early. The other party would be up with the sun, the natives gathering up the camp things and packing them into the Rovers, the white hunters rechecking rifles and ammunition, feeling the pulse-quickening that said there'd be a kill today.

I felt a bit of that myself as I sipped my morning coffee.

The herd was making for a nearby river—stream, rather—that ran through a great shallow depression in the land. The group of hunters was following them at what I judged would be a careful distance. They probably hoped for the elephants to be occupied with drinking and bathing when they came in range.

Luck was with them and me. The wind was right in our faces. Those trunks are acutely sensitive olfactory apparatuses as well as the most versatile manipulatory members evolution has produced on this planet. And no bull ever got as big and old as that patriarch without becoming ever so wary of man scent. If the wind blew wrong the herd would bolt, and that would put a stop to the day's hunting.

Unless, of course, somebody happened to be in charging range of the big bull when the wind went foul. In spite of what Muzakere said, I didn't think even a .600 would be much help then.

The map and the gradual rise of the land told me I was getting near the broad bowl. I stopped the Toyota and sat listening. I couldn't hear the growl of other engines. A good sign? We'd see.

It was afoot from here on. I didn't want either the elephants or the other hunters to hear me. If the animals were at the stream the only thing that had kept them from hearing me already was the fold of ground between us.

Flies strafed me as I got out and unzipped my Remington from its case. Everything seemed in order. Bouncing over the landscape might have thrown the scope off, but I sure as hell was in no position to fire off a few rounds to sight it in. I'd been through this before, though. I felt fairly confident.

I fed the magazine full of cartridges. Then I filled my canteen from the tank behind the driver's seat, closed and locked the Landcruiser, and set out after my prey.

I'd diverged from the tracks of the elephants and those who followed them a few kilometers back. I guessed the others had left their vehicles well around the curve of the circular depression to walk in on the animals. When I crested the rise I found I was right. There was no sign of the bulky, broad-shouldered Land Rovers, but perhaps 2000 meters away was a small clump of figures moving steadily down toward the stream. The hunters.

I looked to the stream. They were there, all right. Almost 20 of them. And the patriarch. Muzakere hadn't been mistaken about him. He was the biggest creature I'd ever seen outside the dinosaur room of the Smithsonian. Four, maybe four and a half meters at the shoulder, and the tusks coming out of his mouth like white and twisted bowsprits from the wreck of an ancient sailing ship. A record breaker. It would be a shame for such magnificence to die.

Still, there was the lure of that ivory. That big ivory.

I started moving down, rifle slung and bumping against my rump. In my rising excitement I didn't give the discomfort much thought. They looked like great, gray children, playing in that brown and greasy water. I've never got over the feeling of sheer power they exude. I felt five and small and taken to the zoo again, watching those monolithic beasts.

I quickened my pace. The other hunters were getting close to what they'd probably consider fair range—long enough for some margin of safety, short enough for the fat slugs from their expresses to stagger the giants. Time pressed on me like deep water. I didn't want to allow them first shot.

I was farther away than I liked when they stopped and started to position themselves. We'd been following gradually converging courses whose nexus was the herd. I was still 500 meters from the elephants, the hunters about 300 from the animals and 400 from me.

I sat, unslinging the Remington, bringing it to shoulder and elbows to knees, forcing myself to breathe with deliberation. No use letting myself get flustered. I couldn't afford to fluff a shot.

I brought my cheek near the gleaming receiver and peered through the Bausch & Lomb. I saw a mother and child playfully splashing water on each other. There was something almost human about their easy affection.

The rifle traversed till I saw him, the bull. God, he was huge. My breath caught in my throat as I watched him. He looked like a mountain about to fall on me.

The crosshairs aligned themselves as if by their own accord on his wrinkle-circled right eye. He seemed to be gazing at me. He was aloof, unafraid, as if aware I was there and disdainful of my power to hurt him.

Time was short. I swung the rifle again, dizzily upslope, till the figures of men appeared.

There were two whites, in typical khaki bush clothes and wide-brimmed hats, and six or seven natives in loose trousers and shirts. I was cutting it fine. The older of the whites had his rifle halfway to the ready, squinting at the elephants as if to fix their location in his mind. Once he opened fire he'd have to fire fast to get more than one before the rest fled out of range. Though his range would be long—my eyes widened as I recognized his weapon.

I'd never actually seen one—a World War II German bolt action antitank rifle, 12.5 mm and rechambered to take a .50 caliber machine-gun cartridge. Heavy artillery. He had three of the enormous shells in the cartridge loops on his left breast.

His every move and gesture was that of a professional, a cold, steady, Hemingwayesque hero in his own eyes and those of the world. The other white hung back; younger, he seemed to defer to the man. His own gun was a standard twin-bore Rigby .577.

The .50 came up to a solid shoulder. The time had come. With something like regret I brought the crosshairs onto my own target, inhaled, let it out slowly, squeezed.

The Remington slammed me and the barrel kicked up. I gave way, then leaned forward and lined up the scope in time to see the bullet hit.

The Hemingway type was doing an oddly balletic spin and fall, the rifle dropping from his hands. My slug had bored under his right arm, through lung and heart and out. As calmly as I could, I ejected the spent shell and chambered another round.

The elephants were alerted, trumpeting their alarm. I had no time for them. I centered the crosshairs on the pallid face of the younger hunter, staring in horror at his fallen idol.

The second report left my ears ringing like a carillon. Red mist exploded behind his head. He dropped like a string-snipped marionette as the bearers fled.

I looked at the stream. The herd was in full flight now, all except for the big aged bull. He stood knee-deep in water, facing me, trunk upraised in challenge. I waved to him, though his squinted old eyes doubtless couldn't make me out. *Go in peace, old one,* I thought. *I've no business with you now.*

You see, not *all* emerging African nations care nothing about their endangered native wildlife. Some of them have been fighting the poachers for a long, long time. And some of them have realized the only way to counter the poachers' greed is to appeal to the greed of others. So they offer bounties. Good ones.

The poachers come from all around. Lots of them. They follow the big ivory.

And me, I follow them.

Asia Minor

ISRAEL

Mayberry

Florence V. Mayberry

When Nothing Matters

The story of Solange Jensen, a woman utterly alone after a year-long honeymoon, who has learned that happiness can be a fragile, fleeting thing . . . a perceptive and compassionate story full of poignant memories and bittersweet thoughts, told with the "Mayberry touch" . . .

It was a long tiring walk from the top of Mount Carmel to the shore of the sea, but Solange had taken it again, as she had for the past week, every day since Thorwald was gone. Gone. No longer her husband.

The tiring was good. She yearned for a fatigue so sodden and compelling that she would sleep, stop thinking.

She crossed the highway, stumbled over rough ground to the railroad tracks, stepped over them down to the sandy beach. She kicked off her loafers, rolled up her slacks, and let the waves lick her feet. She shaded her eyes, gazing at the water. Near the shore, the Mediterranean was a brilliant turquoise. A few meters out it deepened into dark blue, almost cobalt. In the distance a white ship, contrasting sharply against the sea, moved slantwise from the horizon toward Haifa's harbor.

Perhaps she should take a ship, go to Greece, Italy, America. Anywhere but Haifa and Israel.

She faced southward, in the direction of Tel Aviv. No ship to be seen there, only the empty horizon. "Like me. Empty. Alone with itself," Solange said aloud. Vaguely she realized that it was aloud, and vaguely she was troubled because it was. For the past week, and only for the past week, she had been holding conversations with herself. "It's because I'm alone. Alone!" she shouted at the sea. The rush and thud of the waves against the shore blotted up the sound, leaving her even more lonely.

She moved away from the soothing touch of the warm sea, rubbed the sand from her damp feet, slipped on her shoes, and continued on down the beach, past a service station, past the public beach, on and on. When she considered she was sufficiently tired she crossed the highway to a weedy space of ground where an Arab shepherd guarded a straggle of black goats and began the long slow climb up the steep height of Carmel. "Surely you'll sleep tonight," she assured herself.

Short of the mountain top she turned along a narrow slanting lane, went down a flight of stairs past terraced gardens, turned the key in the lock of her ground-floor apartment, shut the door behind her. She hesitated, not wanting to go farther into the empty room. "Empty," she said aloud. "Not even a cat or a dog or a bird. Nothing but you." She looked at herself in the hall mirror, watched her mouth twist in a grimace, its bitterness intensified by contrast with the delicate blossoms of the potted plant beneath the mirror. On impulse she picked up the plant, walked through the living room to the window area, pushed aside the glass of one window, and hurled the pot into the deep wadi below. "Nothing," she repeated.

She went to the kitchen, thinking: *boil the water, put in the filter paper, measure the coffee, pour the water, drink it and you'll feel better. Anything else, Solly—a poached egg? No? Corn flakes? Yes, corn flakes. Eat.*

"Why?" she asked.

She removed the bowl she had filled with brown flakes and the bluish Israeli milk from the table, carried it to the sink, poured its contents into the drain. She returned to the living room and lay down on the sofa, her face pressed against an embroidered Indian pillow. Its little metal mirrors scratched her cheek as though to sharpen memory of when she and Thorwald had bought the pillow covers in India, almost in the shadow of the Taj Mahal.

Almost as if she were taking it again, the long taxi drive from New Delhi to Agra ribboned through her mind. Passing crews of women in dull-colored saris as they scrabbled in dirt to build a highway, male supervisors idly watching. Past painted elephants, monkeys chattering in trees above strange long protuberances that their driver said were birds' nests, dangling from branches to protect their eggs from marauders. At Thorwald's request the taxi stopped and laughingly he pulled her toward a painted elephant, insisted she clamber onto it and have her picture taken. "You looked like a princess riding to meet your lover," he said, once they were back in the taxi.

"I am," she said confidently, snuggling close to him. "And I've met him." How long had they been married then? Six months? No, a year but it was still like a honeymoon, traveling continually to Thorwald's engineering assignments in exotic, wonderful places. That was what he liked, a constant change, and so did she as long as he was with her.

That day they had stopped at village rest stations where men charmed snakes out of baskets, where scraggly Himalayan bears danced pathetically to reedy music, where men wandered casually in and out of open-doored relief sheds. The heat throbbed over the land and crescendoed into a blinding, staggering white blaze as they walked past reflecting pools toward the scalding noon beauty of the Taj Mahal. It was so hot she thought she might faint, and she clung to Thorwald to steady herself against the swirling vertigo in her head. He hurried her forward, fleeing from the heat into the shadowed protection of the exquisite mausoleum that the Shad Jahan had built for the wife he loved so dearly.

She had gazed, fascinated, at the jeweled final token of adoration a king had given his beloved, yearning not for it but for the love that caused it. "Thorwald, if you were king and I had died, would you build me a Taj like this?"

"Of course," he said easily. "Now let's find a restaurant. I'm famished." As they walked back past the pools he added, "Jewels are easy to give when they are only promises. Even a poor man can give them."

And she had answered, "But promises like that *are* jewels."

She sat up and asked the empty room, "Are they?" She walked again to the window to distract the memory, but it would not leave. It kept reeling on, like a film, with the rest of that day's journey as they drove back to New Delhi, traveling the same road, past the same houses, trees with monkeys and birds. But the late golden sun changed the scene, made it into a new road, a new country and people. Now the village women were clean and fresh, dressed in brilliant saris, like butterflies freed from the chrysalis of the dusty morning's work. They walked gracefully beside the highway, copper pots of water balanced on their heads, calling to children, laughing with neighbors, their staccato chatter rising like fragmented music. Happy, serene, gentle.

But then, so soon after, she had become tearful, almost hysterical from the awful proof that happiness is fragile, fleeting. Ahead of them a crowd was gathered on the highway. The taxi slowed, then veered sharply to hasten past the group with its terrible center. A body's crumpled figure was flat on the road, face down, one leg askew, a jagged white bone glistening from mangled flesh and torn trousers, the road beneath him streaked red.

"Don't cry," Thorwald had soothed. "Never waste life by crying over things you can't do anything about. Where shall we have dinner tonight? At the hotel, or go adventuring?"

Her stomach had turned at the thought of food, but she forced down the repugnance. This was their continuing honeymoon, it must be kept happy, not spoiled. She leaned against him, drawing on his cool control. For yes, Thorwald was as controlled as the engineering graphs he produced for his company. She determined to learn from him, to become pragmatic, objective.

She had not learned.

"Solly, you're all emotion, no control. And I might add, that's damned wearing," he had told her a week ago. "No, I will not tell you who she is, I'll not have you messing about with some crazy, useless confrontation. It wouldn't change a thing, only make everything more difficult. I've told you before and I tell you again, don't waste strength on things you can't change. Because frankly, Solly, you haven't got what it takes to change what I'm going to do."

But she couldn't stop trying; she was driven to know about the woman who was taking Thorwald away from her. "Thorwald, what is she that I'm not? Prettier? Poised, controlled the way you want me to be? I'll change, truly I will, but don't leave me, Thorwald."

"Oh, God, not that again," he had answered. Turned his back on her. Zipped up his shaving kit, stuffed it in his travel case, snapped the case shut. Snapped her out of his life.

New York. Thorwald's head office. Sooner or later Thorwald would be intending to go to his New York office. "I'll call Simon, that's the thing to do," she said aloud. She sat again on the sofa, reached for the telephone on the low teak table beside it, slowly dialed a familiar number. A secretary in New York answered. "This is Mrs. Thorwald Jensen, calling from Israel," Solange said. "Please connect me right away with Mr. Simon, it's important."

The voice of Simon, Thorwald's chief, came over the wire as clearly as though he was on a telephone in the next apartment. "Hello, hello? Solange? Good to hear your voice. Where is Thorwald anyway, we've been expecting him every day. We need a briefing on that Negev Desert job. Here in New York? No, no sign of him, I said we're waiting for him."

"But he said New York." Her mouth was dry. "I thought . . . I haven't heard . . . where do you suppose . . ."

"Take it easy, Solange, don't go getting upset," Simon was saying. "You ought to know by now how crazy survey engineers can be. Any place they land is home and they never think anybody should be notified, especially bosses and wives. Thorwald's probably stopped off in London to catch some shows, yeah, I'd bet on London. I'll put in a call to the hotel he usually stays at, or have you called there already? No? Well, leave it to me, I'll track him down. Listen, go out on the town yourself. Where are you? Tel Aviv?"

"Haifa," she said. And for no particular reason she added, "It's a quiet town."

"Go to a movie," Simon said. "And listen, the minute I catch Thorwald I'll have him phone you."

A few more soothing words. A click. And she was alone with herself again. Thorwald call her? Never.

She lay on the sofa until the summer sky changed from afternoon brightness to twilight, to dark, and even after that for a long time. "Why not a movie?" she finally asked herself. She rose, chose a light shawl, and went outdoors. As she walked up the stone stairs, from far behind her came the ecstatic hungering cries of animals in the zoo located at the head of the wadi in Gan Ha'em, the Mothers' Park. She shivered, an unbidden primitive fear tightening the muscles of her back. She moved rapidly up the steep lane, pursued by the sounds, gasped with relief as she reached the sidewalk and saw the piercing headlights of cars speeding by.

A last faint, almost laughing howl came from the animals. Then silence. The silence and the howling told her it was too late for the movie. Each night, for what reason she did not know, the animals cried briefly, at almost ten o'clock. And again in the dark early morning before dawn. Not feeding hours surely. Perhaps a check by caretakers; it didn't matter, did it? Nothing mattered, Thorwald was gone.

Even though she decided against the movie she continued up the steeply sloping street toward Central Carmel, the clustered shopping district on the crest of Mount Carmel. There she moved among laughing, noisy groups of youth clustered in front of restaurants, ice-cream stands, fellafel counters. Although so different, yet it made her think of other crowds of youth on Shaftsbury and Piccadilly in London where she and Thorwald had strolled after the theater, window-gazing at shops she might visit the following day. Standing in front of a china shop choosing table settings she would never have. How could birds of passage possess china, or silver, having no home other than hotels, leased apartments, pensions? A few weeks here, a few months there, never a year, then off on another exciting journey, the adventure of change that Thorwald craved.

"I'll go, I'll leave Haifa, I can't stay here any longer," she told herself. Then clapped her hand over her mouth, fearful to be noticed talking to herself. She walked swiftly back down the mountainside, running the last few steps into her apartment. She turned the key and leaned, panting, against the door.

In the night, near morning, she heard the animals cry again and she moaned as she struggled to recapture sleep. With eyes staring into the dark she tried to imagine how the woman, Thorwald's unknown love, might look. Dark hair and violet eyes, like a movie actress? No, Thorwald liked blondes; that was why she had lightened her own red-brown hair, had become a titian blonde. She fretted with the idea of perhaps getting up, turning on the light to see again how well her titian hair contrasted with sage-green eyes. "You're unreal," Thorwald had said when he first saw the change of color. "Absolutely not real, Solly, I must be imagining you. Eyes of an Egyptian cat and hair of an angel. Come here, give us a kiss."

He had loved her then. What had changed him?

Face it, be realistic: Thorwald was in love with change, always another project, another country, and now another woman. Sameness bored him. On the go, here, there, anywhere, everywhere.

"God, tell me, where is he now?"

She sat up, arms clasping her shoulders in a comforting hug. She rocked to and fro in a terrible wrestling with God, "Tell me, God, tell me!" Then fell back on the pillow, exhausted, smothered by the dark and the loneliness.

In the morning she tried to eat, couldn't, only drank coffee. She opened the utility cupboard, found the key to her storeroom, picked up a flashlight, went into the open foyer and down the basement stairs. In the storeroom she surveyed the travel cases, selected one of medium size, and carried it upstairs.

She went to the telephone and called their travel agent. "This is Mrs. Thorwald Jensen. I want to make a flight reservation."

"Shalom, shalom, Mrs. Jensen. You going to join Mr. Jensen? By the way, was he able to make his connection in Europe?"

Connection? To New York? Or to some other place where the woman would be waiting to greet him? *I never looked at his ticket. I should have looked at his ticket. I could only think that he was leaving me.*

"He hasn't cabled," she said. "But make my ticket just like Mr. Jensen's please." *Perhaps I'll find the woman and when I do I'll—*

"Very good. When will you want to leave? And would you like me to make a hotel reservation in Mexico City? Oh, but of course, your husband will be taking care of that."

"Yes. Yes, of course." Mexico City! Then the woman would be there, otherwise Thorwald would have gone directly to New York. "And I want to leave right away, tomorrow. I'll call for the ticket this afternoon."

The arrangements finished, she went into the bedroom with the travel case. "How can I take everything?" she asked, helpless at the thought. It was a leased furnished apartment but the paintings, the books and ornaments were hers. And all the clothes she had delighted to preen herself in before Thorwald. What good had that been?

She sat on the bed beside the case, dully contemplating its limited size. She rose, took the key and flashlight again.

In the foyer that opened directly onto the terraced garden she halted abruptly, startled to see a small deer run across the flagged walkway. Its hoofs spattered on the graveled path which bordered the flower-strewn terrace. In swift succession behind the deer ran a stocky mustached man and two lean youths in work clothes. Tree branches thrashed against the building as the three vanished around the building, their pounding footsteps crescendoing into heavy thuds as they leaped down the last terrace onto the sharply descending sides of the wadi.

She hurried down the basement stairs, picked her way along the narrow hallway beside the row of storerooms to the door that opened onto the side garden. From there she went to the edge of the embankment above the wadi. Dry brush cracked in the canyonlike depths below. She saw, far down, the deer dodging among trees, leaping ahead of its pursuers.

It has run away from the zoo, she thought, *escaped its prison. Did Thorwald do that?*

She began to tremble.

One of the youths left the group and turned back along the wadi's floor toward the zoo located at its end. She stayed to see how the search progressed, but soon the deer and the other two men vanished, concealed by brush and trees. She sat on the ground, waiting, watching. After a time the youth who had returned to the zoo came back with a second older man who carried a gun, an unusual kind of gun which she recognized from a safari trip in Africa she had taken with Thorwald. A gun to shoot tranquilizing darts.

She felt a momentary pang for the fleeing animal, then hardened against it. "It shouldn't run away, it's safer in the zoo, it's not good to run away."

She rose and went back to the storeroom. There she hesitated beside a large travel case, left it untouched, then chose a smaller one and a duffel bag.

Back upstairs the thought of the deer and the men in the wadi clung and troubled her. She went to the wide living-room window which faced the deep sprawling ravine, pushed aside the glass to let in the air, pulled a chair close, and sat down to see if the searchers would succeed. Shortly before noon one youth, carrying the tranquilizer gun, hurried up the wadi toward the zoo. Behind him, moving slowly with the weight of the sleeping beast, were the man who had brought the gun and the other youth. The first man, the one with the mustache, was not with them.

Solange stood up and went to the bedroom.

In late afternoon she decided she was finished with packing. Too bad about the paintings, the fragile ceramics. But she could return; there were months left on the lease. Only she wouldn't, not ever, never see her charming collections again; too bad, too bad, everything was too bad.

She changed clothes, walked to the shopping district. There she closed out her bank account and picked up her ticket that was made out for Mexico City. Yes, surely the woman would be there. Somehow she would find that woman. And she would kill her.

Back home she remembered that she had not eaten all day. She went to the kitchen, prepared tea and toast, thought vaguely about poaching an egg but gave up the idea. She took her tea and toast into the living room, sat before the window, nibbled and sipped as she stared into the wadi. Not seeing it, seeing only the pictures in her mind, she drifted into sleep.

The excited wailing of the zoo animals awakened her in the night. She switched on the light, looked at her watch. Ten o'clock. Why did the animals cry at this hour? Were they lonely? Was the deer awake too? Or perhaps it was dead, never to join again in the nightly excitement of the animals.

She telephoned a taxi company, made arrangements to be picked up early in the morning. Then she bathed, carefully made up her face, blotting out the dark circles under her eyes, outlining her lips, filling between the lines with provocative color. She assessed the mouth Thorwald had kissed so many times. The vulnerable mouth of a baby, he had said, tantalizing with the cat eyes and the angelic hair. *Thorwald, how could you have left me?*

Briefly the eyes in the mirror flamed, then became shuttered.

When she finished dressing she did not lie down but sat in the chair waiting for morning.

Before dawn she carried the two cases up the steep lane to the sidewalk, tucked them against shrubbery, and returned for the duffel bag. Back again in the open entranceway she hesitated uncertainly, looked down the basement stairs, waited, thinking. Then she returned to the apartment and found the storage-room key.

When she came back up the basement stairs she was carrying the large travel case. She took both it and the duffel bag up to the street to wait for the taxi.

At Lod Airport she joined the passenger queue going through security check. When her turn came she lifted the smaller cases to the checking table. *Did you pack these yourself, did anyone give you anything to carry, did anyone other than yourself have access to these, give you any gifts to transport?* Yes, no, no, no. The girl security officer expertly prodded and lifted clothing, felt inside shoes, tested bottles, finally closed the cases.

"You have another case, Madam. Please lift it to the table."

Solange lifted the large case. "Open it, please." She did. The girl's voice sharpened. "Are you certain you packed this case yourself?"

"Yes."

"But these are men's clothes. Is your husband with you?"

Involuntarily Solange started to look behind her, caught herself. "No. They are my husband's clothes. He left earlier. I'm taking this case to him."

The girl hesitated, then systematically lifted out the clothes, searching pockets, unrolling socks, unzipping the shaving kit, squeezing the shaving-cream tube, turning the razor's handle. Finally she said, "It is all right. Thank you."

Solange went to the ticket check-in station, paid the excess-baggage charge, went upstairs, through customs and the body-and-hand-luggage search. Inside the departure lounge she bought the English-language newspaper, then wandered unseeing past jewelry and souvenir displays to the exit gate. Almost time, almost time to leave Israel, almost time . . .

Her flight was announced and she filed down to the bus, onto the plane, found her seat beside the window. Opened the newspaper. Breath whistled through clenched teeth with her sharp intake of air. Even though the headlines were small, the article sprang at her from the middle of the front page. *Body of American Oil Official Found on Mount Carmel.*

The deer had found him. Staggered by the dart it had floundered into the brush and fallen almost on the body mutilated by wild animals almost beyond recognition. Except for the airline ticket, found in the torn and scattered clothing and finally pieced together, it would have been difficult to identify the man. But when all the ticket fragments were rejoined, there it was: Thorwald Jensen, destination New York via Mexico City.

The plane taxied slowly to the runway. Its engines revved, then quieted as a white car sped toward it. Two men got out of the car, motioned authoritatively at a truck which hurried forward. Workmen leaped from it, rolled mobile stairs against the airliner's side. A stewardess unlocked the exit door.

She waited, hands gripped together, eyes closed as scenes of that last night with Thorwald skimmed through her mind. The frightening, furtive struggle to push and pull Thorwald down the basement stairs, past the storerooms, into the garden. Then along the garden path, rolling him down the wadi's sharp incline, every cracking twig an alarm, every lighted window discovery.

The exit door opened and the two men entered the plane. As they started down the aisle she rehearsed in her mind what she would tell them. The truth, only the truth. *He was straightening his tie before the bathroom mirror. I came behind him, begging him again not to leave me. He smiled and shook his head, not even bothering to answer, as though what I said had no importance, merely a whim to be smiled at. I already had the knife, held behind me. I struck. Hard. It was terrible. Awful. I begged him to come alive. But he couldn't. I knew that, and I was terrified. So I took him into the wadi.*

As the men stopped in the aisle beside her row she stood up, almost in welcome.

Australia

Upfield

Arthur W. Upfield

Wisp of Wool and Disk of Silver

Did you know that Arthur W. Upfield wrote a short story about his famous half-aborigine detective, Inspector Napoleon Bonaparte, usually called Bony? Yes, he did, and there's a baffling mystery about the original manuscript of the story. Here are excerpts from a letter written by Mr. Upfield to your Editor:

Dear Mr. Queen,

Two years ago you invited me to enter a short story in your Detective Short Story Contest. Your letter was received when I was very ill, and subsequently other circumstances obtruded.

Recently, I read an announcement in a New York paper that you are conducting a similar contest for this year, and as I have not now the conditions of the earlier Contest, perhaps you would enter the enclosed story for me.

The detective short is strange work for me, this being the first. In the event of non-success, kindly drop it into your w.p.b. .

Cordially yours,
Arthur W. Upfield

Now this letter was dated 7th June, 1948—thirty-three years ago! And your Editor did not see or read that letter until early in 1979! Surely it must have been received at the EQMM office in 1948, and surely no member of EQMM's editorial staff would have failed to send an Upfield contest submission (especially one about Bony) to your Editor. And yet I swear to you that to the best of my recollection I never saw or read that letter and manuscript until thirty-one years after Mr. Upfield mailed them! What happened? How could they have been mislaid all these years? We just don't know. (Can you imagine how Mr. Upfield must have felt never to have heard a single word about the fate of his story?)

But for readers of EQMM, better later than never—even thirty-three years later. We learn from the author's letter that "The Fool

*and the Perfect Murder" (the original title) was the first Bony
short story, and so far as we have been able to check, it is also
the only Bony short story. Strange that Mr. Upfield chose to flirt
with "the inverted detective story" as his technique, but whatever
the form, an Inspector Napoleon Bonaparte short is a most welcome discovery, particularly for future anthologists. Cheers!*

*Why is Bony so successful as an Australian detective? Here is
how he explains it: "I am peculiarly equipped with gifts be-
queathed to me by my white father and my aboriginal mother.
In me are combined the white man's reasoning powers and the
black man's perceptions and bushcraft . . . Which is why I never
fail."*

I t was Sunday. The heat drove the blowflies to roost under the low
staging that supported the iron tank outside the kitchen door.
The small flies, apparently created solely for the purpose of drowning
themselves in the eyes of man and beast, were not noticed by the
man lying on the rough bunk set up under the veranda roof. He was
reading a mystery story.

The house was of board, and iron-roofed. Nearby were other buildings: a blacksmith's shop, a truck shed, and a junk house. Beyond
them a windmill raised water to a reservoir tank on high stilts,
which in turn fed a long line of troughing. This was the outstation
at the back of Reefer's Find.

Reefer's Find was a cattle ranch. It was not a large station for
Australia—a mere half-million acres within its boundary fence. The
outstation was forty-odd miles from the main homestead, and that
isn't far in Australia.

Only one rider lived at the outstation—Harry Larkin, who was,
this hot Sunday afternoon, reading a mystery story. He had been
quartered there for more than a year, and every night at seven
o'clock, the boss at the homestead telephoned to give orders for the
following day and to be sure he was still alive and kicking. Usually,
Larkin spoke to a man face to face about twice a month.

Larkin might have talked to a man more often had he wished. His
nearest neighbor lived nine miles away in a small stockman's hut
on the next property, and once they had often met at the boundary

by prearrangement. But then Larkin's neighbor, whose name was William Reynolds, was a difficult man, according to Larkin, and the meetings stopped.

On all sides of this small homestead the land stretched flat to the horizon. Had it not been for the scanty, narrow-leafed mulga and the sick-looking sandalwood trees, plus the mirage which turned a salt bush into a Jack's beanstalk and a tree into a telegraph pole stuck on a bald man's head, the horizon would have been as distant as that of the ocean.

A man came stalking through the mirage, the blanket roll on his back making him look like a ship standing on its bowsprit. The lethargic dogs were not aware of the visitor until he was about ten yards from the veranda. So engrossed was Larkin that even the barking of his dogs failed to distract his attention, and the stranger actually reached the edge of the veranda floor and spoke before Larkin was aware of him.

"He, he! Good day, mate! Flamin' hot today, ain't it?"

Larkin swung his legs off the bunk and sat up. What he saw was not usual in this part of Australia—a sundowner, a bush waif who tramps from north to south or from east to west, never working, cadging rations from the far-flung homesteads and having the ability of the camel to do without water, or find it. Sometimes Old Man Sun tricked one of them, and then the vast bushland took him and never gave up the cloth-tattered skeleton.

"Good day," Larkin said, to add with ludicrous inanity, "Traveling?"

"Yes, mate. Makin' down south." The derelict slipped the swag off his shoulder and sat on it. "What place is this?"

Larkin told him.

"Mind me camping here tonight, mate? Wouldn't be in the way. Wouldn't be here in the mornin', either."

"You can camp over in the shed," Larkin said. "And if you pinch anything, I'll track you and belt the guts out of you."

A vacuous grin spread over the dust-grimed, bewhiskered face.

"Me, mate? I wouldn't pinch nothin'. Could do with a pinch of tea, and a bit of flour. He, he! Pinch—I mean a fistful of tea and sugar, mate."

Five minutes of this bird would send a man crazy. Larkin entered the kitchen, found an empty tin, and poured into it an equal quantity of tea and sugar. He scooped flour from a sack into a brown paper bag, and wrapped a chunk of salt meat in an old newspaper. On going out to the sundowner, anger surged in him at the sight of the man standing by the bunk and looking through his mystery story.

"He, he! Detective yarn!" said the sundowner. "I give 'em away years ago. A bloke does a killing and leaves the clues for the detectives to find. They're all the same. Why in 'ell don't a bloke write about a bloke who kills another bloke and gets away with it? I could kill a bloke and leave no clues."

"You could," sneered Larkin.

" 'Course. Easy. You only gotta use your brain—like me."

Larkin handed over the rations and edged the visitor off his veranda.

The fellow was batty, all right, but harmless as they all are.

"How would you kill a man and leave no clues?" he asked.

"Well, I tell you it's easy." The derelict pushed the rations into a dirty gunny sack and again sat down on his swag. "You see, mate, it's this way. In real life the murderer can't do away with the body. Even doctors and things like that make a hell of a mess of doing away with a corpse. In fact, they don't do away with it, mate. They leave parts and bits of it all over the scenery, and then what happens? Why, a detective comes along and he says, 'Cripes, someone's been and done a murder! Ah! Watch me track the bloke what done it.' If you're gonna commit a murder, you must be able to do away with the body. Having done that, well, who's gonna prove anythink? Tell me that, mate."

"You tell me," urged Larkin, and tossed his depleted tobacco plug to the visitor. The sundowner gnawed from the plug, almost hit a dog in the eye with a spit, gulped, and settled to the details of the perfect murder.

"Well, mate, it's like this. Once you done away with the body, complete, there ain't nothing left to say that the body ever was alive to be killed. Now, supposin' I wanted to do you in. I don't, mate, don't think that, but I's plenty of time to work things out. Supposin' I wanted to do you in. Well, me and you is out ridin' and I takes me chance and shoots you stone-dead. I chooses to do the killin' where there's plenty of dead wood. Then I gathers the dead wood and drags your body onto it and fires the wood. Next day, when the ashes are cold, I goes back with a sieve and dolly pot. That's all I wants then.

"I takes out your burned bones and I crushes 'em to dust in the dolly pot. Then I goes through the ashes with the sieve, getting out all the small bones and putting them through the dolly pot. The dust I empties out from the dolly pot for the wind to take. All the metal bits, such as buttons and boot sprigs, I puts in me pocket and carries back to the homestead where I throws 'em down the well or covers 'em with sulphuric acid.

"Almost sure to be a dolly pot here, by the look of the place. Almost sure to be a sieve. Almost sure to be a jar of sulphuric acid for solderin' work. Everythin' on tap, like. And just in case the million-to-one chance comes off that someone might come across the fire site and wonder, sort of, I'd shoot a coupler kangaroos, skin 'em, and burn the carcases on top of the old ashes. You know, to keep the blowies from breeding."

Harry Larkin looked at the sundowner, and through him. A prospector's dolly pot, a sieve, a quantity of sulphuric acid to dissolve the metal parts. Yes, they were all here. Given time a man could commit the perfect murder. Time! Two days would be long enough.

The sundowner stood up. "Good day, mate. Don't mind me. He, he! Flamin' hot, ain't it? Be cool down south. Well, I'll be movin'."

Larkin watched him depart. The bush waif did not stop at the shed to camp for the night. He went on to the windmill and sprawled over the drinking trough to drink. He filled his rusty billy-can, Larkin watching until the mirage to the southward drowned him.

The perfect murder, with aids as common as household remedies. The perfect scene, this land without limits where even a man and his nearest neighbor are separated by nine miles. A prospector's dolly pot, a sieve, and a pint of soldering acid. Simple! It was as simple as being kicked to death in a stockyard jammed with mules.

"William Reynolds vanished three months ago, and repeated searches have failed to find even his body."

Mounted Constable Evans sat stiffly erect in the chair behind the littered desk in the Police Station at Wondong. Opposite him lounged a slight dark-complexioned man having a straight nose, a high forehead, and intensely blue eyes. There was no doubt that Evans was a policeman. None would guess that the dark man with the blue eyes was Detective Inspector Napoleon Bonaparte.

"The man's relatives have been bothering Headquarters about William Reynolds, which is why I am here," explained Bonaparte, faintly apologetic. "I have read your reports, and find them clear and concise. There is no doubt in the Official Mind that, assisted by your black tracker, you have done everything possible to locate Reynolds or his dead body. I may succeed where you and the black tracker failed because I am peculiarly equipped with gifts be-queathed to me by my white father and my aboriginal mother. In me are combined the white man's reasoning powers and the black man's perceptions and bushcraft. Therefore, should I succeed there would be no reflection on your efficiency or the powers of your tracker. Between what a tracker sees and what you have been trained to reason, there is a bridge. There is no such bridge between those divided powers in me. Which is why I never fail."

Having put Constable Evans in a more cooperative frame of mind, Bony rolled a cigarette and relaxed.

"Thank you, sir," Evans said and rose to accompany Bony to the locality map which hung on the wall. "Here's the township of Wondong. Here is the homestead of Morley Downs cattle station. And here, fifteen miles on from the homestead, is the stockman's hut where William Reynolds lived and worked.

"There's no telephonic communication between the hut and the homestead. Once every month the people at the homestead trucked rations to Reynolds. And once every week, every Monday morning, a stockman from the homestead would meet Reynolds midway between homestead and hut to give Reynolds his mail, and orders, and have a yarn with him over a billy of tea."

"And then one Monday, Reynolds didn't turn up," Bony added, as they resumed their chairs at the desk.

"That Monday the homestead man waited four hours for Reynolds," continued Evans. "The following day the station manager ran out in his car to Reynolds' hut. He found the ashes on the open hearth stone-cold, the two chained dogs nearly dead of thirst, and that Reynolds hadn't been at the hut since the day it had rained, three days previously.

"The manager drove back to the homestead and organized all his men in a search party. They found Reynolds' horse running with several others. The horse was still saddled and bridled. They rode the country for two days, and then I went out with my tracker to join in. We kept up the search for a week, and the tracker's opinion was that Reynolds might have been riding the back boundary fence when he was parted from the horse. Beyond that the tracker was vague, and I don't wonder at it for two reasons. One, the rain had wiped out tracks visible to white eyes, and two, there were other horses in the same paddock. Horse tracks swamped with rain are indistinguishable one from another."

"How large is that paddock?" asked Bony.

"Approximately two hundred square miles."

Bony rose and again studied the wall map.

"On the far side of the fence is this place named Reefer's Find," he pointed out. "Assuming that Reynolds had been thrown from his horse and injured, might he not have tried to reach the outstation of Reefer's Find which, I see, is about three miles from the fence whereas Reynolds' hut is six or seven?"

"We thought of that possibility, and we scoured the country on the Reefer's Find side of the boundary fence," Evans replied. "There's a stockman named Larkin at the Reefer's Find outstation. He joined in the search. The tracker, who had memorized Reynolds' footprints, found on the earth floor of the hut's veranda, couldn't spot any of his tracks on Reefer's Find country, and the boundary fence, of course, did not permit Reynolds' horse into that country. The blasted rain beat the tracker. It beat all of us."

"Hm. Did you know this Reynolds?"

"Yes. He came to town twice on a bit of a bender. Good type. Good horseman. Good bushman. The horse he rode that day was not a tricky animal. What do Headquarters know of him, sir?"

"Only that he never failed to write regularly to his mother, and that he had spent four years in the Army from which he was discharged following a head wound."

"Head wound! He might have suffered from amnesia. He could have left his horse and walked away—anywhere—walked until he dropped and died from thirst or starvation."

"It's possible. What is the character of the man Larkin?"

"Average, I think. He told me that he and Reynolds had met when both happened to be riding that boundary fence, the last time being several months before Reynolds vanished."

"How many people besides Larkin at the outstation?"

"No one else excepting when they're mustering for fats."

The conversation waned while Bony rolled another cigarette.

"Could you run me out to Morley Downs homestead?" he asked.

"Yes, of course," assented Evans.

"Then kindly telephone the manager and let me talk to him."

Two hundred square miles is a fairly large tract of country in which to find clues leading to the fate of a lost man, and three months is an appreciable period of time to elapse after a man is reported as lost.

The rider who replaced Reynolds' successor was blue-eyed and dark-skinned, and at the end of two weeks of incessant reading he was familiar with every acre, and had read every word on this large page of the Book of the Bush.

By now Bony was convinced that Reynolds hadn't died in that paddock. Lost or injured men had crept into a hollow log to die, their remains found many years afterward, but in this country there were no trees large enough for a man to crawl into. Men had perished and their bodies had been covered with wind-blown sand, and after many years the wind had removed the sand to reveal the skeleton. In Reynolds' case the search for him had been begun within a week of his disappearance, when eleven men plus a policeman selected for his job because of his bushcraft, and a black tracker selected from among the aborigines who are the best sleuths in the world, had gone over and over the 200 square miles.

Bony knew that, of the searchers, the black tracker would be the most proficient. He knew, too, just how the mind of that aborigine would work when taken to the stockman's hut and put on the job. Firstly, he would see the lost man's bootprints left on the dry earth beneath the veranda roof. Thereafter he would ride crouched forward above his horse's mane and keep his eyes directed to the ground at a point a few feet beyond the animal's nose. He would look for a horse's tracks and a man's tracks, knowing that nothing passes over the ground without leaving evidence, and that even half an inch of rain will not always obliterate the evidence left, perhaps, in the shelter of a tree.

That was all the black tracker could be expected to do. He would not reason that the lost man might have climbed a tree and there cut his own throat, or that he might have wanted to vanish and so had climbed over one of the fences into the adjacent paddock; or had, when suffering from amnesia, or the madness brought about by solitude, walked away beyond the rim of the earth.

The first clue found by Bonaparte was a wisp of wool dyed brown. It was caught by a barb of the top wire of the division fence between the two cattle stations. It was about an inch in length and might well have come from a man's sock when he had climbed over the fence.

It was most unlikely that any one of the searchers for William Reynolds would have climbed the fence. They were all mounted, and when they scoured the neighboring country, they would have passed through the gate about a mile from this tiny piece of flotsam. Whether or not the wisp of wool had been detached from Reynolds' sock at the time of his disappearance, its importance in this case was that it led the investigator to the second clue.

The vital attribute shared by the aboriginal tracker with Napoleon Bonaparte was patience. To both, Time was of no consequence once they set out on the hunt.

On the twenty-ninth day of his investigation Bony came on the site of a large fire. It was approximately a mile distant from the outstation of Reefer's Find, and from a point nearby, the buildings could be seen magnified and distorted by the mirage. The fire had burned after the last rainfall—the one recorded immediately following the disappearance of Reynolds—and the trails made by dead tree branches when dragged together still remained sharp on the ground.

The obvious purpose of the fire had been to consume the carcase of a calf, for amid the mound of white ash protruded the skull and bones of the animal. The wind had played with the ash, scattering it thinly all about the original ash mound.

Question: "Why had Larkin burned the carcase of the calf?" Cattlemen never do such a thing unless a beast dies close to their camp. In parts of the continent, carcases are always burned to keep down the blowfly pest, but out here in the interior, never. There was a possible answer, however, in the mentality of the man who lived nearby, the man who lived alone and could be expected to do anything unusual, even burning all the carcases of animals which perished in his domain. That answer would be proved correct if other fire sites were discovered offering the same evidence.

At daybreak the next morning Bony was perched high in a sandalwood tree. There he watched Larkin ride out on his day's work, and when assured that the man was out of the way, he slid to the ground and examined the ashes and the burned bones, using his hands and his fingers as a sieve.

Other than the bones of the calf, he found nothing but a soft-nosed bullet. Under the ashes, near the edge of the splayed-out mass, he found an indentation on the ground, circular and about six inches in diameter. The bullet and the mark were the second and third clues, the third being the imprint of a prospector's dolly pot.

"Do your men shoot calves in the paddocks for any reason?" Bony asked the manager, who had driven out to his hut with rations. The manager was big and tough, grizzled and shrewd.

"No, of course not, unless a calf has been injured in some way and is helpless. Have you found any of our calves shot?"

"None of yours. How do your stockmen obtain their meat supply?"

"We kill at the homestead and distribute fortnightly a little fresh meat and a quantity of salted beef."

"D'you think the man over on Reefer's Find would be similarly supplied by his employer?"

"Yes, I think so. I could find out from the owner of Reefer's Find."

"Please do. You have been most helpful, and I do appreciate it. In my role of cattleman it wouldn't do to have another rider stationed with me, and I would be grateful if you consented to drive out here in the evening for the next three days. Should I not be here, then wait until eight o'clock before taking from the tea tin over there on the shelf a sealed envelope addressed to you. Act on the enclosed instructions."

"Very well, I'll do that."

"Thanks. Would you care to undertake a little inquiry for me?"

"Certainly."

"Then talk guardedly to those men you sent to meet Reynolds every Monday and ascertain from them the relationship which existed between Reynolds and Harry Larkin. As is often the case with lonely men stationed near the boundary fence of two properties, according to Larkin he and Reynolds used to meet now and then by arrangement. They may have quarreled. Have you ever met Larkin?"

"On several occasions, yes," replied the manager.

"And your impressions of him? As a man?"

"I thought him intelligent. Inclined to be morose, of course, but then men who live alone often are. You are not thinking that—?"

"I'm thinking that Reynolds is not in your country. Had he been still on your property, I would have found him dead or alive. When I set out to find a missing man, I find him. I shall find Reynolds, eventually—if there is anything of him to find."

On the third evening that the manager went out to the little hut, Bony showed him a small and slightly convex disk of silver. It was weathered and in one place cracked. It bore the initials J.M.M.

"I found that in the vicinity of the site of a large fire," Bony said. "It might establish that William Reynolds is no longer alive."

Although Harry Larkin was supremely confident, he was not quite happy. He had not acted without looking at the problem from all angles and without having earnestly sought the answer to the question: "If I shoot him dead, burn the body on a good fire, go through the ashes for the bones which I pound to dust in a dolly pot, and for the metal bits and pieces which I dissolve in sulphuric acid, how can I be caught?" The answer was plain.

He had carried through the sundowner's method of utterly destroying the body of the murder victim, and to avoid the million-to-one chance of anyone coming across the ashes of the fire and being made suspicious, he had shot a calf as kangaroos were scarce.

Yes, he was confident, and confident that he was justified in being confident. Nothing remained of Bill Reynolds, damn him, save a little grayish dust which was floating around somewhere.

The slight unhappiness was caused by a strange visitation, signs of which he had first discovered when returning home from his work one afternoon. On the ground near the blacksmith's shop he found a strange set of boot tracks which were not older than two days. He followed these tracks backward to the house, and then forward until he lost them in the scrub.

Nothing in the house was touched, as far as he could see, and nothing had been taken from the blacksmith's shop, or interfered with. The dolly pot was still in the corner into which he had dropped it after its last employment, and the crowbar was still leaning against the anvil. On the shelf was the acid jar. There was no acid in it. He had used it to dissolve, partially, buttons and the metal band around a pipestem and boot sprigs. The residue of those metal objects he had dropped into a hole in a tree eleven miles away.

It was very strange. A normal visitor, finding the occupier away, would have left a note at the house. Had the visitor been black, he would not have left any tracks, if bent on mischief.

The next day Larkin rode out to the boundary fence and on the way he visited the site of his fire. There he found the plain evidence that someone had moved the bones of the animal and had delved among the ashes still remaining from the action of the wind.

Thus he was not happy, but still supremely confident. They could not tack anything onto him. They couldn't even prove that Reynolds was dead. How could they when there was nothing of him left?

It was again Sunday, and Larkin was washing his clothes at the outside fire when the sound of horses' hoofs led him to see two men approaching. His lips vanished into a mere line, and his mind went over all the answers he would give if the police ever did call on him. One of the men he did not know. The other was Mounted Constable Evans.

They dismounted, anchoring their horses by merely dropping the reins to the ground. Larkin searched their faces and wondered who was the slim half-caste with, for a half-caste, the singularly blue eyes.

"Good day," Larkin greeted them.

"Good day, Larkin," replied Constable Evans, and appeared to give his trousers a hitch. His voice was affable, and Larkin was astonished when, after an abrupt and somewhat violent movement, he found himself handcuffed.

"Going to take you in for the murder of William Reynolds," Evans announced. "This is Detective Inspector Napoleon Bonaparte."

"You must be balmy—or I am," Larkin said.

Evans countered with: "You are. Come on over to the house. A car will be here in about half an hour."

The three men entered the kitchen where Larkin was told to sit down.

"I haven't done anything to Reynolds, or anyone else," asserted Larkin, and for the first time the slight man with the brilliant blue eyes spoke.

"While we are waiting, I'll tell you all about it, Larkin. I'll tell it so clearly that you will believe I was watching you all the time. You used to meet Reynolds at the boundary fence gate, and the two of you would indulge in a spot of gambling—generally at poker. Then one day you cheated and there was a fight in which you were thrashed.

"You knew what day of the week Reynolds would ride that boundary fence and you waited for him on your side. You held him up and made him climb over the fence while you covered him with your .32 high-power Savage rifle. You made him walk to a place within a mile of here, where there was plenty of dry wood, and there you shot him and burned his body.

"The next day you returned with a dolly pot and a sieve. You put all the bones through the dolly pot, and then you sieved all the ashes for metal objects in Reynolds' clothes and burned them up with sulphuric acid. Very neat. The perfect crime, you must agree."

"If I done all that, which I didn't, yes," Larkin did agree.

"Well, assuming that not you but another did all I have outlined, why did the murderer shoot and burn the carcase of a calf on the same fire site?"

"You tell me," said Larkin.

"Good. I'll even do that. You shot Reynolds and you disposed of his body, as I've related. Having killed him, you immediately dragged wood together and burned the body, keeping the fire going for several hours. Now, the next day, or the day after that, it rained, and that rainfall fixed your actions like words printed in a book. You went through the ashes for Reynolds' bones before it rained, and you shot the calf and lit the second fire after it rained. You dropped the calf at least two hundred yards from the scene of the murder, and you carried the carcase on your back over those two hundred yards. The additional weight impressed your boot prints on the ground much deeper than when you walk about normally, and although the rain washed out many of your boot prints, it did not remove your prints made when carrying the dead calf. You didn't shoot the calf, eh?"

"No, of course I didn't," came the sneering reply. "I burned the carcase of a calf that died. I keep my camp clean. Enough blowflies about as it is."

"But you burned the calf's carcase a full mile away from your camp. However, you shot the calf, and you shot it to burn the carcase in order to prevent possible curiosity. You should have gone through the ashes after you burned the carcase of the calf and retrieved the bullet fired from your own rifle."

Bony smiled, and Larkin glared.

Constable Evans said, "Keep your hands on the table, Larkin."

"You know, Larkin, you murderers often make me tired," Bony went on. "You think up a good idea, and then fall down executing it.

"You thought up a good one by dollying the bones and sieving the ashes for the metal objects on a man's clothes and in his boots, and then—why go and spoil it by shooting a calf and burning the carcase on the same fire site? It wasn't necessary. Having pounded Reynolds' bones to ash and scattered the ash to the four corners, and having retrieved from the ashes remaining evidence that a human body had been destroyed, there was no necessity to burn a carcase. It wouldn't have mattered how suspicious anyone became. Your biggest mistake was burning that calf. That act connects you with that fire."

"Yes, well, what of it?" Larkin almost snarled. "I got a bit lonely livin' here alone for months, and one day I sorta got fed up. I seen the calf, and I up with me rifle and took a pot shot at it."

"It won't do," Bony said, shaking his head. "Having taken a pot shot at the calf, accidentally killing it, why take a dolly pot to the place where you burned the carcase? You did carry a dolly pot, the one in the blacksmith's shop, to the scene of the fire, for the imprint of the dolly pot on the ground is still plain in two places."

"Pretty good tale, I must say," said Larkin. "You still can't prove that Bill Reynolds is dead."

"No?" Bony's dark face registered a bland smile, but his eyes were like blue opals. "When I found a wisp of brown wool attached to the boundary fence, I was confident that Reynolds had climbed it, merely because I was sure his body was not on his side of the fence. You made him walk to the place where you shot him, and then you saw the calf and the other cattle in the distance, and you shot the calf and carried it to the fire.

"I have enough to put you in the dock, Larkin—and one other little thing which is going to make certain you'll hang. Reynolds was in the Army during the war. He was discharged following a head wound. The surgeon who operated on Reynolds was a specialist in trepanning. The surgeon always scratched his initials on the silver plate he inserted into the skull of a patient. He has it on record that he operated on William Reynolds, and he will swear that the plate came from the head of William Reynolds, and will also swear that the plate could not have been detached from Reynolds' head without great violence."

"It wasn't in the ashes," gasped Larkin, and then realized his slip.

"No, it wasn't in the ashes, Larkin," Bony agreed. "You see, when you shot him at close quarters, probably through the forehead, the expanding bullet took away a portion of the poor fellow's head—and the trepanning plate. I found the plate lodged in a sandalwood tree growing about thirty feet from where you burned the body."

Larkin glared across the table at Bony, his eyes freezing as he realized that the trap had indeed sprung on him. Bony was again smiling. He said, as though comfortingly, "Don't fret, Larkin. If you had not made all those silly mistakes, you would have made others equally fatal. Strangely enough, the act of homicide always throws a man off balance. If it were not so, I would find life rather boring."

Asia

JAPAN

Matsumoto

HAWAII

Garfield

Seicho Matsumoto

The Woman Who Took the Local Paper

Seicho Matsumoto is recognized and acclaimed in the East as Japan's leading mystery writer and the most important figure on the Japanese detective-story scene today. He ushered in the second period in the history of the modern Japanese detective story. The first period, called the Tantei Era, began with Edogawa Rampo and ended just before World War Two; the second period, called the Suiri Era, shifted technique from "unrealistic" puzzles to "social" detective stories, and in this second period Seicho Matsumoto was the dominant influence, as he continues to be in the current period, called the Neo-Social Era.

Mr. Matsumoto's novels, which epitomize contemporary life in Japan, are consistently among Japan's best sellers. He has published approximately 50 books, with an average sale of 400,000 copies each, 100,000 in hardcover, 300,000 in paperback. His indefatigable curiosity and his enduring passion to learn have led him recently into the world of archeology and history, and his studies of Japanese society and economy have been praised for their depth and insight.

"The Woman Who Took the Local Paper" is shrewdly plotted, its details released slowly to keep the reader in suspense until the very end . . .

Yoshiko Shioda sent in her money to the Koshin newspaper for a subscription. This newspaper company is located in Kofu city, which is about two hours by express train from Tokyo. Although it is a leading paper in that prefecture, it is not sold in Tokyo, and if one wants to read it, one has to become a subscriber.

She sent the money by registered mail on February 21 and enclosed the following letter: "I would like to subscribe to your newspaper. Enclosed is my payment. The serialized novel, *The Brigands,* in your paper looks interesting and I want to read it. I would like my subscription to begin from the issue of February 19th."

Yoshiko Shioda had seen the Koshin newspaper only once before. It had been at a small restaurant located in a corner of a building in front of Kofu station. The waitress had left the paper on the table while Yoshiko was waiting for her order of Chinese noodles. It was a typical local paper, with rather old-fashioned type, very provincial actually. The third page was devoted to local news. A fire had destroyed five homes. An employee in the village office had embezzled six million yen of public funds. The construction of an annex to the primary school had been completed. The mother of a prefectural assemblyman had died. That sort of news.

At the bottom of the second page there was a serialization of an historical novel. The illustration showed two samurai warriors engaged in a sword fight. The author was Ryuji Sugimoto, a name unfamiliar to Yoshiko. She had read about one-half of the serial episode when her noodles were served and she put the paper aside. But first Yoshiko wrote down in her notebook the name and address of the newspaper and publisher. She also remembered that the name of the story she had been reading was *The Brigands*. Under the title there was a notation that it was the 54th installment of the serial. The newspaper was dated the 18th. Yes, that day had been the 18th of February.

It was about seven minutes before three when Yoshiko left the restaurant and walked around the town. The square in the middle was crowded with people. Above their heads fluttered white banners printed with the words: *Welcome Home, Minister Sato*. A new cabinet had been formed the previous month and Yoshiko realized that the name on the banner was that of a local diet member who had been appointed one of the new ministers.

Then suddenly there was a stirring in the crowd and the people became agitated. Some of them cried, "Banzai!" A great clapping arose. People who were walking some distance away ran to join the crowd.

The speech began. A man had mounted a platform and his mouth was moving. The winter sun struck his bald head. A large white rose was pinned to his breast. The crowd became silent but at times the applause was thunderous.

Yoshiko looked around. A man standing near her was also watching the scene and he too was not listening to the speech. He seemed to have his way blocked by the crowd.

Yoshiko stole a look at the man's profile. He had a broad forehead, sharp eyes, and a high-bridged nose. There had been a time when she had thought of them as an intelligent brow, trustworthy eyes, and a handsome nose. But that memory was now an empty one. The spell the man held over her, however, remained the same as it had been before.

The speech ended and the minister descended from the platform. The crowd began to disperse. An open space appeared in the crowd and Yoshiko began to walk. The man also began to walk away—with another person.

The Koshin newspaper arrived five days later. Three days' issues came together. There was a polite note thanking Yoshiko for her subscription.

As she had requested, the subscription began with the issue of the 19th. Yoshiko opened it. She turned to the local news. A robbery had occurred. Someone had died in a landslide. Dishonesty had been exposed in the Farmers Cooperative. Elections for assemblymen had begun. There was a large photo of Minister Sato in front of Kofu station.

Yoshiko opened the issue of the 20th. There was nothing special in it. She looked at the issue of the 21st. Here too there was only the usual news. She threw the papers into the corner of the closet. They could be used later for wrapping paper.

The newspaper arrived by mail daily after that. Her name and address were mimeographed on the brown kraft-paper wrapper. After all, she was now a monthly subscriber.

Every morning she went to the mailbox in the apartment house to get her paper and slowly read it from beginning to end. There was nothing which attracted her special attention. Disappointed, Yoshiko threw the papers in the closet.

This was repeated for ten days. And every day she was disappointed. In spite of this, she was always filled with anticipation before cutting the brown wrapper.

On the fifteenth day a change occurred. It wasn't an article in the paper but an unexpected postcard she received. The card was signed by Ryuji Sugimoto. Yohiko remembered seeing that name somewhere. It wasn't someone close to her, but she had a clear recollection of it. Yoshiko turned the postcard over. The handwriting was almost indecipherable, but managing to read it, she immediately knew who it was.

"I understand you are reading my novel, *The Brigands,* which is being serialized in the Koshin newspaper and I would like to thank you for your interest."

No doubt someone had told the author that she had subscribed to the paper because she wanted to read his story. The author had evidently been touched and had sent a card of thanks.

It was a small change from the daily newspaper routine. It was something different, however, from what she had expected. She hadn't been reading the novel—like the handwriting on the postcard, it was probably poor.

But every day the paper arrived promptly. Of course, this was only natural because it had been paid for in advance.

One morning, nearly a month after she had subscribed to the paper, she glanced over the various items of local news. The head of the Farmers Cooperative had fled. A bus had fallen from a cliff and fifteen people had been injured. A mountain fire had destroyed three acres. The bodies of a man and woman who had committed suicide had been found at Rinunkyo.

Yoshiko read the report about the double suicide. The bodies had been discovered in the forest in Rinunkyo. The person who had found them was an inspector of the Forestry Bureau. Both bodies were partly decomposed. It was about a month since death and the bodies were partially skeletonized. Their identity was still unknown. The valley, with its crags and deep gorge, was famous as a suicide spot.

Yoshiko folded the paper, lay down, and pulled the quilt up to her chin. She gazed at the ceiling. This apartment was old. The boards in the dark ceiling were on the verge of rotting. Vacantly Yoshiko continued to stare.

In the following day's paper there was a report on the identity of the dead couple. The man was a 35-year-old guard at the Toyo Department Store in Tokyo; the woman, aged 22, was a clerk at the same store. The man had a wife and children. It was seemingly an ordinary, run-of-the-mill case of double suicide.

Yoshiko raised her eyes from the paper. Her face was devoid of expression—emotionless and at the same time, peaceful.

Three days later she received a postcard from the circulation department of the Koshin paper.

"Your subscription has ended. We hope you will renew your subscription to our paper."

Yoshiko wrote back: "The novel has lost its interest for me and I do not wish to continue my subscription."

On her way to the club, where she worked as a hostess, she mailed the postcard. As she walked on, it occurred to her that the author of *The Brigands* would probably be disappointed. "I shouldn't have written that," she thought.

Ryuji Sugimoto read the subscriber's postcard which had been forwarded to him by the Koshin newspaper and it displeased him considerably.

This subscriber was the same person who had taken the paper because she had found his novel interesting. At that time too the paper had forwarded her letter to him. He was sure he had sent her a note of thanks. But now she was saying that the novel had lost its interest, so she was discontinuing her subscription.

"These women readers—they're so fickle," Sugimoto said angrily.

Since *The Brigands* was written for a mass market, the primary purpose had been pure entertainment; nevertheless, he had taken considerable time and care in writing it, and was confident it was not hackneyed or dull.

Sugimoto laughed bitterly, but gradually he became angry again. He felt as though he were being made a fool of. As a matter of fact, the story was better now than when she had first expressed a desire to read it because it was "interesting." The plot was now more complicated and the characters were engaged in a series of colorful encounters. Even he was pleased with the way the story had developed. He expected it to be well-received, and that was all the more reason he found this capricious woman so annoying.

"This is really unpleasant," he thought, and for two days he couldn't rid himself of the bad taste in his mouth. On the third day the hurt had faded, but it still remained in his subconscious. Occasionally it would flicker through his mind. Because he had worked so hard on the story, he felt worse than if a professional had criticized him. Besides, even though it might seem exaggerated, he felt he had lost prestige with the paper.

Sugimoto shook his head, stood up from his desk, and went out for a walk.

"That woman began to read my novel in the paper midway. Now, where did she first see it?"

"The Koshin newspaper was sold only in Yamanashi prefecture, not in Tokyo. So she couldn't have seen it in Tokyo. Therefore, that woman named Yoshiko Shioda, of Tokyo, must have been in Yamanashi at one time.

If that was so, there was no reason why a person who had taken the trouble to subscribe to a paper because she had found the serial interesting would have dropped her subscription after one month. Especially since the novel was undeniably more interesting now than before.

The more he thought about it, the odder it appeared. Obviously the real reason for subscribing to the paper was not to read his novel. She must have used that as an excuse; she was really looking for something else. And because she found it, she no longer needed the paper.

Sugimoto rose from the grass and hurried home. Ideas were whirling through his head.

When he got home, he took the original letter from Yoshiko Shioda out of his file.

"I would like to subscribe to your newspaper. Enclosed is my payment. The serialized novel, *The Brigands,* in your paper looks interesting and I want to read it. I would like my subscription to begin from the issue of February 19th."

The handwriting was neat and precise. But that was beside the point. The puzzling thing was why she specified that the subscription should start two days prior to the date of her letter. In quick cases, newspapers carry news of the previous day. The Koshin did not publish an afternoon paper. Therefore,.if she wanted to get the paper from the 19th, it meant she was looking for news of something that had happened from the 18th on.

He had copies of the paper which the company sent him daily. He opened them on his desk. Starting with the one dated February 19, he looked carefully through it. He read the local news and, just to be sure, he also looked at the tourist ads.

He decided to limit his search to something which would connect Yamanashi prefecture with Tokyo. He looked at the various items. During the month of February nothing fitted into this category. He started going through the March papers. Up to the 5th there was still nothing.

The same through the 10th. The 13th, the 14th. Then, on the 16th, he found the following story:

"On March 15, at two o'clock, a member of the Forestry Bureau discovered the bodies of a man and woman who had committed suicide. The bodies were partly decomposed and it has been about one month since the time of death. The man was wearing a gray overcoat and navy suit and was approximately 37 years old. The woman had on an overcoat of large brown checks and a suit of the same color and was about 23. The only thing found was a handbag with women's cosmetics in it. It is assumed that they were from Tokyo because a round-trip ticket from Shinjuku to Kofu was found in the woman's bag."

The identity of the couple appeared in the next day's paper. "The man found at Rinunkyo was a guard at the Toyo Department Store, named Sakitsugu Shoda (35) and the woman was Umeko Fukuda (22), a clerk at the same store. The man was married and had children."

"This is it." Sugimoto uttered the words without thinking. There was nothing else to link Tokyo and Yamanashi. On seeing this paper, the issue of March 17th, Yoshiko Shioda had decided to stop her subscription. There was no doubt in Sugimoto's mind that this was the reason she had started taking the local paper. It was the type of news that would hardly have appeared in the Tokyo metropolitan papers.

"Wait a minute, though," he thought.

Yoshiko Shioda specified that the paper was to start from February 19th. The bodies were discovered on March 15, approximately one month after the deaths. Therefore, the suicides had occurred around February 18. Time-wise, it tallied. *She knew about this double suicide.* She subscribed to the paper so she could learn when the bodies were discovered. But why?

Ryuji Sugimoto suddenly found himself becoming deeply interested in Yoshiko Shioda.

He studied her address on the postcard that had been forwarded to him. . .

Three weeks later Ryuji Sugimoto received an answer to his inquiry from the private detective agency.

Ryuji Sugimoto read the report twice and thought to himself, "When they put their minds to it, they do a remarkable job. They certainly managed to find out a lot, even that Yoshiko Shioda and Sakitsugu Shoda had been having an affair."

There was now no doubt that Yoshiko Shioda was somehow involved in the double suicide of Sakitsugu Shoda and Umeko Fukuda, and that therefore she knew they had committed suicide in the forest at Rinunkyo. One took the Chuo Line to Kofu to get to Rinunkyo. Where had she seen them off? At Shinjuku station in Tokyo or at Kofu station?

He thumbed through the train schedule. He saw that there were about 20 special express and express trains from the Shinjuku Terminus to the Kofu district daily.

According to the private investigator's report, Yoshiko had left her apartment that day at around 11:30, so it was fair to assume that she had got on the one o'clock special express Azusa #3 which reaches Kofu at 2:53. From Kofu station to the scene of the suicide at Rinunkyo, by bus and on foot, would have taken a full hour. Shoda and Umeko, the suicide couple, would have finally reached the fateful spot just as the winter sun was about to set. Before his eyes, Ryuji Sugimoto could visualize the figures of the two in the craggy ravine, surrounded by woods.

Until their decomposed bodies were found approximately a month later, and the news was reported, only Yoshiko had known about them. She had been reading the local papers to learn when the deaths would come to light. Just what was her part in the whole affair?

Once again he went through the February 19th issue of the Koshin paper. Landslide. Dishonesty in the Farmers Cooperative. Election of town officials. There was nothing exceptional. There was a large photo of the local diet member, Minister Sato, in front of Kofu station.

Sugimoto pushed aside the manuscript which was due the next day, and holding his head in his hands, he sat, sinking deeply into thought. He never dreamed that one reader's rejection of his novel could have involved him in detective work like this. . .

Yoshiko was one of several hostesses at the Bar Rubicon, a club in the Shibuya district. She was busy taking care of customers when one of the girls said to her, "Yoshiko, someone is asking for you."

Yoshiko stood up. She went to the booth and there sat a plump man of about 42, with long hair. She had never seen him before and he was not a regular of the club.

"You're Yoshiko Shioda?" he asked with a smile.

Yoshiko had not changed her name on coming to this club, but when the man addressed her by her full name she was surprised. In the dim indirect lighting, even though there was a lamp on the table with a pink shade, she searched his face, but she could not remember having seen it before.

"Yes, I am. And what's your name?" asked Yoshiko, seating herself beside him.

"Let me introduce myself," he said, taking a slightly bent name card from his pocket. When she saw the name, Ryuji Sugimoto, printed there she gasped.

Watching her face closely, he said, with a little laugh, "Yes, I'm the fellow who is writing *The Brigands* which you have been reading. The Koshin paper told me about your subscription and I dropped you a note of thanks. I happened to be in your neighborhood yesterday, so I stopped by your apartment. You were out but I was told you worked here. So tonight I came here—I wanted to thank you in person."

Yoshiko thought, "Is that all? So he was just curious. I never read his story seriously anyway. What a character to be so pleased by one person's interest in his story!"

"Oh, how kind of you to take the trouble, sir. I've enjoyed your novel so much," gushed Yoshiko, moving closer to him.

"Don't mention it," replied Sugimoto good-naturedly; then, looking around him, he remarked, "This is a nice club." Next he looked at Yoshiko sheepishly and mumbled, "You're a beautiful girl."

With a sidelong glance at him Yoshiko poured beer into his glass and smiled. "Really? I'm so happy you came tonight. You can stay a while, can't you?"

So he still believed she was reading his novel. He couldn't be a very popular writer if he made such a fuss about meeting one of his readers. Or maybe he was impressed because she happened to be a woman.

Sugimoto evidently couldn't drink very much because after one bottle of beer he became quite flushed. Of course, Yoshiko was drinking too, and several of the other hostesses had joined them, so by this time there were half a dozen bottles on the table, as well as some snacks.

The girls kept calling him "sir," which evidently pleased him, and he stayed for more than an hour.

Just after he left, Yoshiko noticed a brown envelope on the cushion where he had been sitting. She picked it up, and thinking it was his, went to look for him; but he was nowhere in sight.

"He'll be back. I'll just keep it for him," Yoshiko thought and slipped the envelope into the bosom of her kimono, completely forgetting about it.

She became aware of it again after she returned to her apartment. As she undid her obi, the brown envelope fluttered to the floor. Remembering, she picked it up. There was nothing written on the outside of the envelope. It was unsealed and seemed to contain only a newspaper clipping. She decided to look at it

It was a newspaper clipping about a quarter of a page in size and neatly folded. Yoshiko unfolded it and her eyes widened in surprise. It was the photo of Minister Sato in front of Kofu station, the photo from the Koshin newspaper.

Over the dark crowd were several white banners. The minister could be seen above the heads of the people. It was a scene that Yoshiko had actually witnessed, exactly as it was in the photo.

Yoshiko stared into space. Her hand shook slightly. One of the cords of her kimono still hung loosely from her waist.

Was this just a coincidence? Or had Ryuji Sugimoto intentionally left it in the club for her to see? She became confused. Her feet were tired, so she sat down on the floor. She didn't even bother to put down her sleeping mat. What did Sugimoto know? She began to feel that he had left the envelope for some special purpose. Her intuition told her so. This was no coincidence. No, it certainly was no coincidence.

Ryuji Sugimoto, whom she had taken to be a pleasant popular novelist, suddenly began to appear in an entirely different light.

Two days later Sugimoto showed up at the club again and asked for Yoshiko.

"Why, good evening, sir," she smiled, sitting beside him; but her face felt stiff.

He smiled back and he didn't look at all like a person with an ulterior or sinister motive.

"You forgot this last time you were here." Yoshiko took the brown envelope from her handbag. The smile remained on her lips, but her eyes watched his expression closely.

He took the envelope and put it in his pocket. There was no change in his expression, but for a moment his narrowed eyes seemed to glint as he met her gaze. Then he quickly looked away and raised the foaming glass of beer to his lips.

Yoshiko felt restless, nervous, apprehensive.

The relationship between Yoshiko and Sugimoto deepened quickly after that. On the days when he didn't come to the club, she called to invite him. She also wrote to him, not the usual letters a hostess would write to her customers to solicit their continued patronage, but very personal letters.

Anyone looking at them would assume theirs was an intimate

relationship. Considering the actual number of times he came to the Bar Rubicon, the liaison formed swiftly. Proof of how far it had developed was shown one day when Yoshiko approached Sugimoto, saying, "Couldn't we go away somewhere together? I could take a day off."

Sugimoto looked delighted. "If it's with you, I'd love to. Where would you like to go?"

"Wherever it's nice and quiet. How about some place in Izu? We could leave early in the morning."

"Izu? That sounds better and better."

"Look now, I'm only suggesting a short excursion."

"What do you mean?" he asked in a disappointed tone.

"I don't want to get too deeply involved—not yet. So let's just make this a pleasure trip. To make sure there is no misunderstanding, why don't you invite a girl friend to go with us? I'm sure you have one."

"I won't say that I don't," Sugimoto said.

"I'd like to get to know her. That's all right with you, isn't it?"

Sugimoto frowned.

"You don't seem very happy."

"There's no point in going if I can't be alone with you."

"Oh, please. That can be the next time."

"Do you promise?"

Yoshiko took Sugimoto's hand in hers and drew her fingernail lightly over his palm.

"Okay. If that's the way you want it, that's how it'll be, this time." Then Sugimoto added, "We might as well decide on the date and time now."

"What? Oh, all right. Wait a minute."

Yoshiko went to the office to borrow the train schedule.

Sugimoto arranged for a woman editor he knew to accompany them. He didn't give her any special reason. Because she knew and trusted him, she accepted the invitation promptly.

Ryuji Sugimoto, Yoshiko Shioda, and Fujiko Sakata, the editor, arrived in Ito on the Izu Peninsula just before noon. The plan was to cross the mountains from there, over to Shuzenji, and return by way of Mishima.

Sugimoto wondered what was about to happen. He knew there was danger and his nerves were tense. It was an effort to look as though he suspected nothing.

Yoshiko appeared composed. She held a plastic-covered parcel in one hand. It probably contained a lunch she had packed. The three of them looked for all the world as if they were off on a happy picnic excursion. The two women seemed to be getting along fine.

The bus left Ito and began to climb the mountains. As they climbed, the town of Ito looked sunken and small, and before them spread Sagami Bay, the water purplish in the late fall and blending with the clouds in the distance.

"It's absolutely lovely," commented Fujiko.

Gradually the ocean disappeared from sight as the bus crossed the summit of the Amagi Mountains.

"Let's get off here," suggested Yoshiko.

The bus halted at a bus stop deep in the mountains.

Yoshiko suggested that they explore the area and then take either the next bus or the one on to Shuzenji.

"Wouldn't you like to see where this goes?" asked Yoshiko, pointing to a mountain path leading into the forest. She looked cheerful and her forehead shone with perspiration.

In some places the path was deeply rutted. The shades of green of the different trees were breathtaking. The silence was so intense that it was oppressive.

They came to a thicket of shrubs. Here there was a break in the forest and the sun poured down onto the grass.

"We can take a rest here," said Yoshiko, and Fujiko agreed.

Sugimoto looked around. He realized they had gone deep into the woods. Seldom would anyone come here, he thought. In his imagination he saw the forest in Rinunkyo.

"You can sit here," said Yoshiko to Sugimoto, spreading the plastic wrapper she had undone from her parcel for him to sit on.

The two women sat down on their handkerchiefs and stretched their legs straight out in front of them.

The editor said, "I'm so hungry."

"Then why don't we have our lunch?" asked Yoshiko.

The two women unwrapped the lunches they had brought. Fujiko had made sandwiches. Yoshiko had prepared *Sushi*. These were placed on the ground along with three bottles of fruit juice.

Taking a sandwich, Fujiko said to the others, "Please have some."

"Thank you, I will," said Yoshiko, taking a sandwich, and added, "I made some *Sushi* and was about to eat it."

"Watch out, Fujiko!" shouted Sugimoto, striking the *Sushi* from her fingers. His face had turned white.

"There's poison in it!"

Fujiko looked at him dumfounded.

Sugimoto stared at Yoshiko's pale face. She looked back fiercely and didn't lower her gaze. Her eyes flashed.

"Yoshiko, this is how you killed those two at Rinunkyo, isn't it? You're the one who made it look like suicide."

Yoshiko bit her trembling lip. She looked ghastly.

Stammering in his excitement, Sugimoto continued, "On February 18th you invited Sakitsugu Shoda and Umeko Fukuda to go to Rinunkyo with you. You poisoned them just as you intended to poison us now, then returned alone. No one would have dreamed they had been murdered. That area is famous for suicides, so it was a perfect setup. People would just think, 'What? Another suicide?' and not give it a second thought. That was what you were counting on."

Yoshiko remained silent. Fujiko was staring wide-eyed. It seemed as if the slightest movement would tear the air.

"You accomplished your purpose. But there was just one thing that troubled you," Sugimoto went on. "You were worried about what would happen to the bodies. You left when they collapsed, but you wanted to know the final outcome. Otherwise, you wouldn't have been able to rest, isn't that so? They say a criminal usually returns to the scene of his crime. You chose to do that through a newspaper. Or maybe you were worried whether the police would call it a suicide or suspect murder. But such a trifling incident was unlikely to appear in the Tokyo papers, so you subscribed to a Yamanashi paper, where Rinunkyo is located.

"That was smart, Yoshiko, but you made two mistakes. You thought you had to give a reason for subscribing to the paper. So you said you wanted to read my novel. You shouldn't have done that. That's what made me suspicious. The other mistake you made was in ordering the paper from the 19th. Therefore, I guessed that something had happened on the previous day, on the 18th.

"My inquiries revealed that you hadn't gone to the club that day. Using my imagination along with the facts, I decided that you must have taken the 1:06 express train from Shinjuku. This train arrives in Kofu at 2:53. You would have to go to Rinunkyo from there, but it just so happened that the local diet member, Minister Sato, was making a speech to a throng of people at that very time. This was reported in the paper, with a photo. I was sure you would have seen it. So I decided to test you with that photo.

"I had a private detective investigate you and Sakitsugu Shoda, and it became clear that you and he were involved with each other. And Shoda was also involved with Umeko Fukuda, the other girl. If they were made to look like a double suicide, it wouldn't cause much of a stir. As I became more and more convinced that my reasoning was correct, I purposely left that photo of Sato for you to see. I knew it would make you suspicious of me. In other words, I wanted you to know that I was testing you. It must have made you nervous, and then you probably became afraid of me. Now it was my turn to wait for you to make the next move. You didn't fail me.

"You suddenly became more friendly and finally, this invitation today. You insisted I bring a girl along. That's because if I were found dead by myself, it wouldn't look like a suicide. If Fujiko and I had eaten your *Sushi*, the poison you put in it would have acted immediately. You could have left us here. Three minus one—that would leave another couple in the mountains of Izu who had evidently committed double suicide. People would be shocked to learn that we two had been so intimate. My wife would probably hide my ashes in a closet."

Suddenly a laugh erupted. Yoshiko Shioda threw back her head and laughed. Suddenly the laughter died and Yoshiko spoke sharply.

"I must say, you really are a fiction writer! You couldn't have made up a better story. So you claim that this *Sushi* is poisoned?"

"Yes, I do."

"Then let's see if it will kill me. I'll eat it all myself. Watch me. If there is poison in it, it should take about three or four minutes to kill me. If it's a slower-acting poison, I'll be in agony."

Yoshiko took the box of *Sushi* from the shocked Fujiko and began to stuff the food into her mouth.

Sugimoto watched fascinated. He couldn't utter a sound.

There were seven or eight pieces of *Sushi* in the box. One by one Yoshiko chewed them and swallowed.

"There, I ate them all. Thanks to you, I'm full. Now we'll see if I drop dead."

And so saying, she lay down full length on the grass.

The warm sun played on her face. Her eyes were closed. A nightingale was singing nearby. Time passed. Sugimoto and Fujiko didn't say a word. More time passed.

Yoshiko seemed to be sleeping. She didn't stir. But, from the corner of her eye, tears made a track down her cheek. Sugimoto was tempted to speak to her, but at that moment she jumped up. It was like a spring uncoiling.

"It's been enough," she said, glaring at Sugimoto. "If the *Sushi* had been poisoned, I would be dead now, or in agony. Yet here I am, perfectly normal. Is this proof enough that you've let your imagination run away with you? You should be more careful about making such wild claims!"

So saying, Yoshiko collected the lunch box and bottles and tied them up into a parcel, stood up, and shook the grass from her skirt.

"I'm going back. Goodbye."

Yoshiko strode back down the path. Her step was firm. Soon her figure was lost in the tangle of branches.

Sugimoto received the following letter from Yoshiko Shioda.

"You were completely right. I did do it. It is true. I am the person who killed those two people at Rinunkyo. Why did I do it? Well, there was no other way, was there? It was just the usual story of a man and two women.

"The way he died is just as you deduced. When I invited the two of them to go with me to Rinunkyo, Shoda was delighted at the prospect of such a picnic. No doubt it gave him a perverse sense of pleasure to be accompanied by his two mistresses.

"I reserved seats on the 1:16 express at one o'clock. I didn't want anyone we might know to see the three of us together. I had about thirty minutes before the other two arrived. During that time I went to a little restaurant in front of the station and had some noodles and that's when I saw your novel in the paper. When I met them, Sato was making a speech in the square.

"At Rinunkyo I gave Shoda and Umeko some sweet cakes that I had made, in which I had put potassium cyanide. They died almost immediately. I got rid of the remaining cakes and returned, leaving the bodies there. Everything went perfectly.

"What a relief! The only misgiving I had was whether the police would suspect murder. Therefore, I decided to take the local newspaper, using your novel as the pretext for subscribing to it. Because of that I ended up arousing your suspicions.

"So I decided to kill you. In the same way I had killed Shoda.

"But you saw through my plan. You suspected I had poisoned the *Sushi*, but actually the poison was in the fruit juice. I thought you would drink the juice after eating the *Sushi* to quench your thirst.

"I brought the bottles of fruit juice back with me. They won't be wasted. I will drink one now . . ."

Brian Garfield

Scrimshaw

*Brenda—stranded in Hawaii . . . Brenda—listless, lonely,
wretched, desperate, at the end of her emotional rope and almost
penniless . . . Brenda—"she wasn't ugly; she wasn't even plain,
really . . . perhaps she was too bony, her shoulders too big, flat
in front, not enough flesh on her—but there were men who liked
their women bony" . . .*

She suggested liquid undulation: a lei-draped girl in a grass skirt
under a windblown palm tree, her hands and hips expressive of
the flow of the hula. Behind her, beyond the surf, a whaling ship
was poised to approach the shore, its square-rigged sails bold against
a polished white sky.

The scene was depicted meticulously upon ivory: a white fragment
of tusk the size of a dollar bill. The etched detail was exquisite: the
scrimshaw engraving was carved of thousands of thread-like lines
and the artist's knife hadn't slipped once.

The price tag may have been designed to persuade tourists of the
seriousness of the art form: it was in four figures. But Brenda was
unimpressed. She put the piece back on the display cabinet and left
the shop.

The hot Lahaina sun beat against her face and she went across
Front Street to the Sea Wall, thrust her hands into the pockets of
her dress and brooded upon the anchorage.

Boats were moored around the harbor—catamarans, glass-bottom
tourist boats, marlin fishermen, pleasure sailboats, outrigger ca-
noes, yachts. Playthings. It's the wrong place for me, she thought.

Beyond the wide channel the islands of Lanai and Kahoolawe
made lovely horizons under their umbrellas of delicate cloud, but
Brenda had lost her eye for that sort of thing; she noticed the stag-
nant heat, the shabbiness of the town, and the offensiveness of the
tourists who trudged from shop to shop in their silly hats, their
sunburnt flab, their hapless T-shirts emblazoned with local graffiti:
"Here Today, Gone to Maui."

A leggy young girl went by, drawing Brenda's brief attention: one of those taut tan sunbleached creatures of the surfboards—gorgeous and luscious and vacuous. Filled with youth and hedonism, equipped with all the optional accessories of pleasure. Brenda watched gloomily, her eyes following the girl as far as the end of the Sea Wall, where the girl turned to cross the street. Brenda then noticed two men in conversation there.

One of them was the wino who always seemed to be there: a stringy unshaven tattered character who spent the days huddling in the shade sucking from a bottle in a brown bag and begging coins from tourists. At night he seemed to prowl the alleys behind the seafood restaurants, living off scraps like a stray dog: she had seen him once, from the window of her flyspecked room, scrounging in the can behind the hotel's kitchen; and then two nights ago near a garbage bin she had taken a shortcut home after a dissatisfying lonely dinner and she'd nearly tripped over him.

The man talking with the wino seemed familiar and yet she could not place the man. He had the lean bearded look of one who had gone native; but not really, for he was set apart by his fastidiousness. He wore sandals, yet his feet seemed clean, the toenails glimmering; he wore a sandy beard but it was neatly trimmed and his hair was expensively cut, not at all shaggy; he wore a blue denim short-sleeved shirt, fashionably faded but it had sleeve pockets and epaulets and had come from a designer shop; and his white sailor's trousers fit perfectly.

I know him, Brenda thought, but she couldn't summon the energy to stir from her spot when the bearded man and the wino walked away into the town. Vaguely and without real interest she wondered idly what those two could possibly have to talk about together.

She found shade on the harborfront. Inertia held her there for hours while she recounted the litany of her misfortunes. Finally hunger bestirred her and she slouched back to her miserable little third-class hotel.

The next day, half drunk in the afternoon and wilting in the heat, Brenda noticed vaguely that the wino was no longer in his usual place. In fact, she hadn't seen the wino at all, not last night and not today.

The headache was painful and she boarded the jitney bus to go up-island a few miles. She got off near the Kapalua headland and trudged down to the public beach. It was cooler here because the northwest end of the island was open to the fresh trade winds; she settled under a palm tree, pulled off her ragged sneakers, and dug her toes into the cool sand. The toes weren't very clean. She was going too long between baths these days. The bathroom in the hotel was at the end of the corridor and she went there as infrequently as possible because she couldn't be sure who she might encounter and anyhow, the tub was filthy and there was no shower.

Across the channel loomed the craggy mountains of Molokai, infamous island, leper colony, its dark volcanic mass shadowed by perpetual sinister rain clouds, and Brenda lost herself in gruesome speculations about exile, isolation, loneliness, and wretched despair, none of which seemed at all foreign to her.

The sun moved and took the shade with it and she moved round to the other side of the palm tree, tucking the fabric of the cheap dress under her when she sat down. The dress was gone—frayed, faded, the material ready to disintegrate. She only had two others left. Then it would be jeans and the boatneck. It didn't matter, really. There was no one to dress up for.

It wasn't that she was altogether ugly; she wasn't ugly; she wasn't even plain, really; she had studied photographs of herself over the years and she had gazed in the mirror and tried to understand, but it had eluded her. All right, perhaps she was too bony, her shoulders too big, flat in front, not enough flesh on her—but there were men who liked their women bony; that didn't explain it. She had the proper features in the proper places and, after all, Modigliani hadn't found that sort of face abominable to behold, had he?

But ever since puberty there'd been something about her gangly gracelessness that had isolated her. Invitations to go out had been infrequent. At parties no one ever initiated conversations with her. No one, in any case, until Briggs had appeared in her life.

... She noticed the man again: the well-dressed one with the neatly trimmed beard. A droopy brown Hawaiian youth was picking up litter on the beach and depositing it in a burlap sack he dragged along; the bearded man ambled beside the youth, talking to him. The Hawaiian said something; the bearded man nodded with evident disappointment and turned to leave the beach. His path brought him close by Brenda's palm tree and Brenda sat up abruptly. "Eric?"

The bearded man squinted into the shade, trying to recognize her. Brenda removed her sunglasses. She said, "Eric? Eric Morelius?"

"Brenda?" The man came closer and she contrived a wan smile.

"Brenda Briggs? What the devil are you doing here? You look like a beachcomber gone to seed."

Over a drink in Kimo's she tried to put on a front. "Well, I thought I'd come out here on a sabbatical and, you know, loaf around the islands, recharge my batteries, take stock."

She saw that Eric wasn't buying it. She tried to smile. "And what about you?"

"Well, I live here, you know. Came out to Hawaii nine years ago on vacation and never went back." Eric had an easy relaxed attitude of confident assurance. "Come off it, duckie, you look like hell. What's happened to you?"

She contrived a shrug of indifference. "The world fell down around my ankles. Happens to most everybody sometimes, I suppose. It doesn't matter."

"Just like that? It must have been something terrible. You had more promise than anyone in the department."

"Well, we were kids then, weren't we. We were all promising young scholars. But what happens after you've broken all the promises?"

"Good Lord. The last I saw of you, you and Briggs were off to revitalize the University of what, New Mexico?"

"Arizona." She tipped her head back with the glass to her mouth; ice clicked against her teeth. "And after that a state college in Minnesota. And then a dinky jerkwater diploma mill in California. The world," she said in a quiet voice, "has little further need of second-rate Greek and Roman literature scholars—or for any sort of non-tenured Ph.D.'s in the humanities. I spent last year waiting on tables in Modesto."

"Duckie," Eric said, "there's one thing you haven't mentioned. Where's Briggs?"

She hesitated. Then—what did it matter?—she told him: "He left me. Four years ago. Divorced me and married a buxom life-of-the-party girl fifteen years younger than me. She was writing advertising copy for defective radial tires or carcinogenic deodorants or something like that. We had a kid, you know. Cute little guy, we named him Geoff, with a G—you know how Briggs used to love reading Chaucer. In the original. In retrospect, you know, Briggs was a prig and a snob."

"Where's the kid, then?"

"I managed to get custody and then six months ago he went to visit his father for the weekend and all three of them, Briggs and the copy-writer and my kid Geoff well, there was a six-car pileup on the Santa Monica Freeway and I had to pay for the funerals and it wiped me out."

Eric brought another pair of drinks and there was a properly responsive sympathy in his eyes and it had been so long since she'd talked about it that she covered her face with the table napkin and sobbed.

"God help me, Eric. Briggs was the only man who ever gave me a second look."

He walked her along the Sea Wall. "You'll get over it, duckie. Takes time."

"Sure," she said listlessly. "I know."

"Sure, it can be tough. Especially when you haven't got anybody. You don't have any family left, do you?"

"No. Only child. My parents died young. Why not? The old man was on the assembly line in Dearborn. We're all on the assembly line in Dearborn. What have we got to aim for? A condominium in some anthill and a bag full of golf clubs? Let's change the subject, all right? What about you, then? You look prosperous enough. Did you drop out or were you pushed too?"

"Dropped out. Saw the light and made it to the end of the tunnel. I'm a free man, duckie."

"What do you do?"

"I'm a scrimshander."

"A what?"

"A bone-ivory artist. I do scrimshaw engravings. You've probably seen my work in the shop windows around town."

Eric's studio, high under the eaves in the vintage whaler's house that looked more New Englandish than tropical, revealed its owner's compulsion for orderly neatness.

She had never liked him much. He and Briggs had got along all right, but she'd always found Eric an unpleasant sort. It wasn't that he was boorish; hardly anything like that. But she thought him pretentious and totally insincere. He'd always had that air of arrogant self-assurance. And the polish was all on the surface; he had the right manners but once you got to know him a little you realized he had no real understanding of courtesy or compassion. Those qualities were meaningless to people like Eric. She'd always thought

him self-absorbed and egotistical to the point of solipsism; she'd felt
he had cultivated Briggs's friendship simply because Eric felt Briggs
could help him advance in the department.

Eric had been good at toadying up to anyone who could help him
learn the arts of politics and ambition. Eric had always been very
actorish: he wasn't real—everything was a role, a part, a performance: everything Eric did was done with his audience in mind. If
you couldn't be any help to him he could, without a second thought,
cut you dead.

He wasn't really handsome. He had a small round head and ordinary features. But he'd always kept himself trim and he'd always
been a natty dresser. And the beard sharpened his face, made it
longer, added polish to his appearance. Back on the mainland, she
remembered, he'd tended to favor three-piece suits.

Eric's studio was spartan, dominated by a scrubbed-clean workbench under the dormer window's north light. An array of carving
tools filled a wooden rack, each tool seated in its proper niche, and
there were four tidy wooden bins containing pieces of white bone of
graduated sizes. Antique inkwells and jars were arranged beside a
tray of paintbrushes and other slender implements. In three glass
display cases, each overhung by a museum light, lay examples of
Eric's art. One piece, especially striking, was a large ivory cribbage
board in the shape of a Polynesian outrigger canoe with intricate
black-and-white scenes engraved upon its faceted surfaces.

"That's a sort of frieze," Eric explained. "If you follow those little
scenes around the board, they illustrate the whole mythology of the
Polynesian emigration that led to the original settlement of Hawaii
a thousand years ago. I'm negotiating to sell it to the museum over
in Honolulu."

"It must be pretty lucrative, this stuff."

"It can be. Do you know anything about scrimshaw?"

"No," she said, and she didn't particularly care to; but Eric had
paid for the bottle and was pouring a drink for her, and she was
desperate for company—anyone's, even Eric's—and so she stayed
and pretended interest.

"It's a genuine American folk art. It was originated in the early
1800s by the Yankee whalers who came out to the Pacific with
endless time on their hands on shipboard. They got into the habit
of scrimshanding to pass the time. The early stuff was crude, of
course, but pretty quickly some of them started doing quite sophisticated workmanship. They used sail needles to carve the fine lines

of the engraving and then they'd trace India ink or lampblack into the carvings for contrast. About the only materials they had were whalebone and whales' teeth, so that's what they carved at first.

"The art became very popular for a while, about a century ago, and there was a period when scrimshanding became a profession in its own right. That was when they ran short of whalebone and teeth and started illustrating elephant ivory and other white bone materials. Then it all went out of fashion. But it's been coming back into favor the past few years. We've got several scrimshanders here now. The main problem today, of course, is the scarcity of ivory."

At intervals Brenda sipped his whiskey and vocalized sounds indicative of her attentiveness to his monologue. Mainly she was thinking morosely of the pointlessness of it all. Was Eric going to ask her to stay the night? If he did, would she accept? In either case, did it matter?

Watching her with bemused eyes, Eric went on, "The Endangered Species laws have made it impossible for us to obtain whalebone or elephant ivory in any quantities any more. It's a real problem."

"You seem to have a fair supply in those bins there."

"Well, some of us have been buying mastodon ivory and other fossilized bones from the Eskimos—they dig for it in the tundra up in Alaska. But that stuff's in short supply too, and the price has gone through the ceiling."

Eric took her glass and filled it from the bottle, extracting ice cubes from the half-size fridge under the workbench. She rolled the cold glass against her forehead and returned to the wicker chair, balancing herself with care. Eric smiled with the appearance of sympathy and pushed a little box across the bench. It was the size of a matchbox. The lid fit snugly. Etched into its ivory surface was a drawing of a humpback whale.

"Like it?"

"It's lovely." She tried to summon enthusiasm in her voice.

"It's nearly the real thing," he said. "Not real ivory, of course, but real bone at least. We've been experimenting with chemical processes to bleach and harden it."

She studied the tiny box and suddenly looked away. Something about it had put her in mind of little Geoff's casket.

"The bones of most animals are too rough and porous," Eric was saying. "They tend to decompose, of course, being organic. But we've had some success with chemical hardening agents. Still, there aren't many types of bone that are suitable. Of course, there are some people who're willing to make do with vegetable ivory or hard plastics, but those really aren't acceptable if you care about the artistry of the thing. The phony stuff has no grain, and anybody with a good eye can always tell."

She was thinking she really had to pull herself together. You couldn't get by indefinitely on self-pity and the liquid largess of old acquaintances, met by chance, whom you didn't even like. She'd reached a point-of-no-return: the end of this week her room rent would be due again and she had no money to cover it; the time to make up her mind was now, right now, because either she got a job or she'd end up like that whiskered wino begging for pennies and eating out of refuse bins.

Eric went on prattling about his silly hobby or whatever it was: something about the larger bones of primates—thigh bone, collarbone. "Young enough to be in good health of course—bone grows uselessly brittle as we get older . . ." But she wasn't really listening; she stood beside the workbench looking out through the dormer window at the dozens of boats in the anchorage, wondering if she could face walking into one of the tourist dives and begging for a job waiting on tables.

The drink had made her unsteady. She returned to the chair, resolving to explore the town first thing in the morning in search of employment. She *had* to snap out of it. It was time to come back to life and perhaps these beautiful islands were the place to do it: the proper setting for the resurrection of a jaded soul.

Eric's voice paused interrogatively and it made her look up. "What? Sorry."

"These two here," Eric said. She looked down at the two etched pendants. He said, "Can you tell the difference?"

"They look pretty much the same to me."

"There, see that? That one, on the left, that's a piece of whale's tooth. This other one's ordinary bone, chemically hardened and bleached to the consistency and color of true ivory. It's got the proper grain, everything."

"Fine." She set the glass down and endeavored to smile pleasantly. "That's fine, Eric. Thank you so much for the drinks. I'd better go now—" She aimed herself woozily toward the door.

"No need to rush off, is there? Here, have one more and then we'll get a bite to eat. There's a terrific little place back on the inland side of town."

"Thanks, really, but—"

"I won't take no for an answer, duckie. How often do we see each other, after all? Come on—look, I'm sorry, I've been boring you to tears with all this talk about scrimshaw and dead bones, and we haven't said a word yet about the really important things."

"What important things?"

"Well, what are we going to do about you, duckie? You seem to have a crucial problem with your life right now and I think, if you let me, maybe I can help sort it out. Sometimes all it takes is the counsel of a sympathetic old friend, you know."

By then the drink had been poured and she saw no plausible reason to refuse it. She settled back in the cane chair. Eric's smile was avuncular. "What are friends for, after all? Relax a while, duckie. You know, when I first came out here I felt a lot the way you're feeling. I guess in a way I was lucky not to've been as good a scholar as you and Briggs were. I got through the Ph.D. program by the skin of my teeth but it wasn't enough. I applied for teaching jobs all over the country, you know. Not one nibble."

Then the quick smile flashed behind the neat beard. "I ran away, you see—as far as I could get without a passport. These islands are full of losers like you and me, you know. Scratch any charter-boat skipper in that marina and you'll find a bankrupt or a failed writer who couldn't get his epic novel published."

Then he lifted his glass in a gesture of toast. "But it's possible to find an antidote for our failure, you see. Sometimes it may take a certain ruthlessness, of course—a willingness to suspend the stupid values we were brought up on. So-called civilized principles are the enemies of any true individualist—you have to learn that or you're doomed to be a loser for all time. The kings and robber barons we've honored throughout history—none of them was the kind to let himself be pushed around by the imbecilic bureaucratic whims of college deans or tenure systems.

"Establishments and institutions and laws are designed by winners to keep losers in their place, that's all. You're only free when you learn there's no reason to play the game by their rules. Hell, duckie, the fun of life only comes when you discover how to make your own rules and laugh at the fools around you. Look—consider your own situation. Is there any single living soul right now who truly gives a damn whether you, Brenda Briggs, are alive or dead?"

Put that starkly it made her gape. Eric leaned forward, brandishing his glass as if it were a searchlight aimed at her face. "Well?"

"No. Nobody," she murmured reluctantly.

"There you are, then." He seemed to relax; he leaned back. "There's not a soul you need to please or impress or support, right? If you went right up Front Street here and walked into the Bank of Hawaii and robbed the place of a fortune and got killed making your escape, you'd be hurting no one but yourself. Am I right, duckie?"

"I suppose so."

"Then why not give it a try?"

"Give what a try?"

"Robbing a bank. Kidnaping a rich infant. Hijacking a yacht. Stealing a million in diamonds. Whatever you feel like, duckie—whatever appeals to you. Why not? What have you got to lose?"

She twisted her mouth into an uneven smile. "You remind me of the sophomoric sophistry we used to spout when we were under-graduates. Existentialism and nihilism galore." She put her glass down. "Well, I guess not, Eric. I don't think I'll start robbing banks just yet."

"And why not?"

"Maybe I'm just not gaited that way."

"Morality? Is that it? What's morality ever done for *you?*"

She steadied herself with a hand against the workbench, set her feet with care, and turned toward the door. "It's a drink too late for morbid philosophical dialectics. Thanks for the booze, though. I'll see you . . ."

"You'd better sit down, duckie. You're a little unsteady there."

"No, I—"

"Sit down." The words came out in a harsher voice. "The door's locked anyway, duckie—you're not going anywhere."

She scowled, befuddled. "What?"

He showed her the key; then he put it away in his pocket. She looked blankly at the door, the keyhole, and—again—his face. It had gone hard; the polite mask was gone.

"I wish you'd taken the bait," he said. "Around here all they ever talk about is sunsets and surfing and the size of the marlin some fool caught. At least you've got a bigger vocabulary than that. I really wish you'd jumped at it, duckie. It would have made things easier. But you didn't, so that's that."

"What on earth are you talking about?"

She stumbled to the door then—and heard Eric's quiet laughter when she tried the knob.

She put her back to the door. Her head swam. "I don't understand . . ."

"It's the ivory, duckie. The best material is fresh human bone. The consistency, the hardness—it takes a fine polish if it's young and healthy enough . . ."

She stared at him and the understanding seeped into her slowly and she said, "That's where the wino went."

"Well, I have to pick and choose, don't I? I mean, I can't very well use people whose absence would be noticed."

She flattened herself against the door. She was beginning to pass out; she tried to fight it but she couldn't; in the distance, fading, she heard Eric say, "You'll make fine bones, duckie. Absolutely first-rate scrimshaw."

EDITORIAL POSTSCRIPT

The story you have just read was nominated by MWA (Mystery Writers of America) as one of the five best new mystery short stories published in American magazines and books during 1979.

North America

UNITED STATES

Jordan
Childs
Adams
Suter
Ellin

Clements Jordan

Mr. Sweeney's Day

*This was the 534th "first story" published by Ellery Queen's
Mystery Magazine . . . an exceptional debut in print . . .*
*   The author, Clements Jordan, is a retired English teacher. Her
age? "Plenty plus." She is "an avid walker and adores traveling."
At a moment's notice she will "go anywhere—to Europe, to the
mountains, to the seashore, or to the corner mailbox." From the
age of nine she has been "fascinated by words," but since teaching
days her "creativity has consisted mainly of notes written in the
margins of students' themes" . . .*

I think I was about ten when I found the puzzle in a magazine. It
was a page-size summer landscape. There was a huge tree with
a profusion of leaves and intricately etched bark. At its foot was a
variety of flowers and grass, and close by a rippling brook. Overhead
was a blue sky interspersed with puffy clouds. The caption at the
top of the page asked: "How many faces can you find?"

At first I thought there must be a mistake. How could there be
faces in a picture that had no people or animals? I was about to turn
the page when—I don't know how it happened, whether I turned my
head or shifted the magazine—dozens of faces suddenly popped into
my amazed view. The leaves on the trees outlined faces; the etched
bark limned profiles; on the ground I saw more faces peeping out
from among the flowers; still others could be tracked in the ripples
of the brook and among the clouds. Delighted, I began to look at the
page from every angle. I was absorbed until my mother interrupted
me by calling me to help her.

Meals, chores, and school intervened so that it was the next afternoon before I could get back to the puzzle. I had thought about it a
lot and anticipated the joy of being surprised again. I'd planned to
hold the page up and at first see nothing. Then I would tilt the page
and move it just a little, then a little more, until suddenly again all
those faces would flash out at me.

But this didn't happen. I found that after you saw a thing, it was impossible to turn back time and not see it. There could be only one first time.

I can't turn back Mr. Sweeney. Never again will it be that hot summer day when I was five, standing on the strip at the bottom of the fence with my feet between the palings so that I could better see the people and cars passing on the road. Now and then a neighbor in a car waved or someone walking to the store spoke to me. Then a flivver stopped by our gate and Mr. Sweeney stepped out of it into my daddy-craving heart.

How did he look? Let me see. Remember, I was only five. After knowing him a couple of years, I came to realize he was not tall. He didn't have much hair in front, but I remember his eyes. How many adults *see* children? They pat their heads, or chuck their chins, or even kiss them, but do they really take a good look at them? Mr. Sweeney *looked* at me. He reached out and put his hand on my arm and stepped back the length of his own arm and looked at me from head to toe. His eyes glowed. He reached down and picked me up and carried me up the path to the house, his hand warmly gripping my thigh. And all the time he was saying the dearest things.

"Where did a little sweetheart like you come from?"

"I came to live here."

"How nice. For a long time?"

"All the time."

"How did we get that lucky?"—giving me an extra squeeze.

"My mama works. I'm going to stay here with grandpa and grandma." My father had been dead for six months. My mother had decided to remain in the city and work there.

We were on the porch then and he put me down to knock on the door. But I, feeling I had known him for a long time, took his hand and led him inside, calling my grandmother. He kept hold of my hand while he talked to her. With country hospitality she invited him into the kitchen for coffee and pie. I learned that he was our paper delivery man. He put our paper into the mailbox on the road early each morning and once a month he came into the house to collect money for it.

Mr. Sweeney was not one of those people who only talk to children when there is no adult around. He didn't sit on a chair but on the table bench by me, with one arm around me, and insisted I have some pie too. He squeezed my shoulders at intervals and when he had finished his pie, he put his chin on the top of my head so I could feel its movement when he talked to grandmother. I thought this hugely funny. When he left, we walked to the gate hand in hand. He got into the car and waved as long as he could see me as he drove down the road, leaving me already lonely for him.

Grandmother spoke of it to grandfather when he came in from the tobacco field for lunch.

"He sure made a lot over her. Didn't know he was so crazy about children."

"He ought to get married. He's plenty young to have a whole raft of youngsters of his own."

"Mella Wilson set her cap for him. She's right good-looking too. But she never hit it off with him."

"Some don't take to marrying." I was sitting by grandfather on the bench and slid down to nestle at his side. He patted me on the head and said absently, "Watch out. You'll get this fork in your eye."

They loved me dearly, but they were old. Grandfather was considered vigorous for his age and grandmother's step was brisk as she canned and cooked and cleaned, but they had "slowed down," my mother said. They had sold the animals until there were only a hog and some chickens left. Grandfather had to "work on shares" because the tobacco crop was too much for him alone. They both took afternoon naps. I had the feeling I must walk on tiptoe and whisper when I really wanted to stamp, run screaming down hills, and jump hurdles. Most of all I wanted my father. I wanted his honey-pie, bristly-cheeked, squeeze-me-tight, toss-me-in-the-air, roll-on-the-rug loving. Mr. Sweeney was the nearest I had found to that in all those lonely months.

I had gone to kindergarten in the city, but there was none here in the country and the nearest house with children was considered too far for me to walk. Only occasionally, when grandfather drove the truck into town, would he drop me off to play at a neighbor's and pick me up on the way home. Between times I made do with cousins who visited frequently in the summer—"watermelon company," my grandfather called them. They might grumble about having to draw water from the well to take baths and complain about the heat in the kitchen when grandmother made a fire to cook, but sometimes a cousin would spend a week with us. They were fun, but there were times, especially around suppertime—daddy time—that the loneliness set in. No man's step in the hall, no man's voice calling, "Where's my little girl doll?"—pretending not to see me just inside the living-room door until, suddenly, he swooped in, grabbed

me, and swung me about, shouting, *"Here's* my doll! *Here* she is!"
Even when my mother came to visit me, it was not enough, even
when we could go down to the orchard and cry a little together.

Only Mr. Sweeney was almost right. I began to get up earlier and
go down to the fence to wait for the paper. He would hand it to me
from his car window, asking, "How's my sweetie this morning?" And
oh, the days he came to collect. Always the meeting at the gate,
always the ride on his shoulders, always the squeezing, hugging,
hand holding, the cheek rubbing and kiss goodbye.

Then one winter's day he found me in disgrace. I can't remember
what I had done, but shortly before he arrived, my "sins had found
me out" and I had been spanked. He saw the traces of tears on my
cheeks. He knelt down to my face level and said, "My, my, whatever
is the matter with my sweetheart?" I confessed with shame and he
said, "Oh, my, we'll just have to see about that." He kissed me on
each cheek, lifted me up tenderly, and carried me into the house.

Inside he sat down, still holding me, and said to grandmother,
"I see that our little girl has been naughty. Now, we want her to be
a darling angel, don't we? I guess I'm just going to have to punish
her too." He turned me over, raised my dress, and slapped me lightly
on my pants. Then he put me on the floor, holding me against his
side with his arm around me and kissed my cheek again. "Now you
let me know when she needs another good whipping. We are going
to have us a *good* girl, aren't we?" Grandmother laughed indulgently
and said I usually behaved pretty well. I decided to always tell him
when I had been bad.

Once when he came I didn't meet him in the yard. I had had a
cold with a slight fever and grandmother had forced me to stay in
bed. I had cried, thinking I would not see him, but we had our visit.
He bounded up the steps and into my room saying, "We can't have
my sweetheart feeling sick." He sat down on the bed, raised me up
into his arms, and kissed me on the forehead, then lowered me into
the bed under the quilt. "Now I'm your own doctor," he said. He put
his hand under the quilt and asked, "Where does it feel bad,
mmmmm? *There? There? There?*" He had me giggling and playing
his game. Each time I admitted to feeling bad, he patted the place
and kissed my cheek. For the first time, I remember, I kissed him
too. He looked into my eyes, got up suddenly, and went away. But
he waved at me from the door. And after that, whenever he left, he
would bend down and point with his finger to a place on his cheek
for me to kiss.

Then the next August I met him at the gate with sad news. I would be in school the next time he came and not see him at all. "Oh, my," he said. "Now let's see about that." He pulled from his shirt pocket a miniature calendar. "What do you know about that?" he asked, amazed. "The good fairy has put collection day on a Saturday." For the first time that day I noticed that the sun was shining.

I liked school. It was fun to play at recess, to write on the board with colored chalk, to show the teacher how well I could read, to drink water out of the fountain. But Saturdays were the best days. I saved everything for him—the jack-o'-lantern the teacher taught us to make, the picture of the turkey we each drew for Thanksgiving, the secret of whose name I drew for pollyanna, the disgrace of "staying in" for talking, for which he spanked me, the good report card for which he kissed me three times—once for each A.

It was the summer I was eight that the brightness dimmed. From smaller than average, I became overnight as though I'd eaten the cake in *Alice in Wonderland*. When grandmother made me new dresses, she kept murmuring, "How she has shot up, goodness!" One month when Mr. Sweeney came, he hoisted me up to carry me to the house; the next month we had to walk with our arms around each other. I noticed that he was no longer tall. "My, my! My little girl has become a young lady," he kept remarking in an astonished voice. In vain I tried to scrunch down to the size of his little girl.

Another month I pressed up to his side and half sat, half leaned against his knee. He quickly put his arm around me to keep me from slipping. Aunt Bess, who was visiting us, frowned. Later I heard her say to grandmother, "She's just too big to be all over him like that."

"Nonsense," grandmother said sharply, "he doesn't mind a bit. He likes children. He has always made a fuss over her."

"That's not the point, Mother," my aunt said and closed her lips to a line. "She's just too big," she added lamely.

I hated my height and developed a stoop. I became quieter, shyer. I sometimes quarreled with playmates at school. One day I was sent home in disgrace. A group of us girls, big and little, were in the schoolyard near the fence right before bell time, when it was too late to start another game, and Mr. Sweeney drove by. Maybelle Purdy, who was 13 and wore rouge, snickered and said, "There goes Touch-up Sweeney."

"Who?" asked someone.

"Touch-up Sweeney. He touches you up, get it? Touches you down, too." Maybelle giggled and whispered in the ear of her friend, who giggled and grew red in the face.

A wave of anger swept over me. "You take that back! Take it back!" I screamed at her.

"Can't take back the truth without telling a lie. What's the matter? Somebody step on your toes? He been touching you up and down and round and round?"

Screaming, I lowered my head and rammed it into her middle and she sat down on the ground, breathless. The teacher monitoring the yard rushed over. Maybelle and I were both crying but some of the other children pieced together a story for her—not the words we had said, just that she had made me angry and I had butted her in the stomach. Maybelle would not tell the teacher what she had said, just that she "didn't mean nothing." I would not repeat those awful words, so the teacher sent me home to "cool off." All the way the name kept beating in my head: "Touch-up, Touch-up, Touch-up!" Since the teacher didn't send a note, I told grandmother that I'd come home because I didn't feel too good. By now it was true. I felt miserable. I threw up until I was all dried out. I drank some water and threw up again.

I was home from school for two days. When I returned, everything was seemingly as usual. Maybelle and I were not often in the same part of the yard at recess, so it was not necessary for us to meet. Nobody realized there was any change in me.

The following Saturday was Mr. Sweeney's day, as I knew. Hadn't I always counted the days? On the Monday before I began my campaign for permission to visit my mother. I had been to see her twice the past year since I had proved myself capable of riding on the bus, taking charge of my suitcase, and getting off at the right station. I could read signs now. I was a "young lady."

The next month we had an unexpected visitor on Mr. Sweeney's day. My youngest aunt arrived in hysterics holding a sobbing child, my cousin Jennie Sue. They handed her over to me and retired behind closed doors. Worn out with sobbing, Jennie Sue fell asleep almost between sobs. I put her on the sofa and went close to the door, though my aunt's voice would probably have reached me even if I had been another room away. She made it plain that she was determined to get a divorce, that she "had taken all she could," and no one could talk her out of it. My grandparents agreed to keep

Jennie Sue while my aunt went west and they talked soothingly to her, expecting her, I believe, to be more rational the next day. She was not and departed on the train for Reno to be gone six weeks.

It was summer vacation and I had almost sole charge of Jennie Sue, sometimes much against my will. She followed me everywhere on her short plump legs, imitating me in everything as best she could—insisting on drying the silver when I washed dishes, putting napkins at places when I set the table, holding a book before her when I read. Once I smacked her hand because she wrote in my book while I was writing on paper.

She was not with me that Saturday when Mr. Sweeney's flivver came in sight because I ran quickly around the side of the house and up to my room, leaving her in the yard. I stared out of the window which was up to let in the morning air, so, of course, I could hear too. Mr. Sweeney opened the gate just in time to meet Jennie Sue who was attracted by the arriving car.

"Well, hello, sweetie pie. Now, who are you?"

"I'm Jennie Sue. I'm four," she confided, holding up four fingers.

He bent, kissed the fingers, swung her up to his shoulders, and marched to the door with her while she giggled delightedly. I heard the murmur of voices below and finally grandmother called to me that Mr. Sweeney was here and wasn't I going to come down and say "Hello." Reluctantly I went down to find him holding Jennie Sue on his lap, his chin resting on her curls, his arms folded around her middle.

"Hey, where've you been so long? Come here and howdy me," he greeted me, taking one arm from around Jennie Sue and beckoning me with it. "My, I've never seen anyone grow the way you have. It seems just like yesterday when you were the size of this little cutie." He tried to put his other arm around me. I went closer to him but not that close. I realized it would never do to show how near to heaving I was. "I'm going to pour you some coffee," I said, getting a cup and bringing the pot from the stove.

"She's getting to be a real help. She's been taking care of the little one all week," grandmother said.

"Yes indeed, a real young lady. And this one here—a little angel is what she is."

I doubt if he noticed that I didn't go near him, so absorbed was he with Jennie Sue. I could look at him with her and realize how he had been with me, almost as if I were seeing a movie in which

I had starred. As for her, she kept putting her fingers over his mouth when he talked so that his words would kiss them and she put her face against his chest. I wanted to yell, "You are not her daddy! She will never have a daddy again! Quit touching her!"

I brooded over her for the rest of the day. Aunt Susan would get a job and leave her here all the time for me to take charge of after school and she would always be here for Touch-up Sweeney's visits. Poor child—to miss a daddy all the time—just having somebody touching her. And grandmother didn't even know. She would *let* him. Well, I wouldn't.

I knew then what I had to do. Jennie Sue was only four and didn't know enough to thank me. She didn't know how long she would have to live without a daddy. She imitated everything I did. Should I put poison in a cookie for her while I ate a good one? It might taste so bad she wouldn't eat it. Should I put a pillow over her face like the lady in the movie? She might wake up and scream, then later when I did it right, somebody would remember. Could I push her up real high in a swing so that she would fall out and break her neck? Maybe someone would guess that I did it on purpose.

The thing is, I was still only half serious. Understand, I knew it was the right thing to do, but I wasn't sure I could do it. I had to do it right the first time. You can't do it half one time and half the next. Then everything just sort of fell right for me. The water had been tasting funny, so grandfather had men dragging around in the well to see if something was dead was down there and they went home to supper and didn't close the top to the well.

It was dark when I thought of catching lightning bugs around the back. Jennie Sue and I got some mayonnaise jars. Honestly, I hadn't even thought it all out. I stepped up on the well platform and looked down just because the top was open. Jennie Sue just naturally came too and stood on tiptoe looking down.

"Look way down and see the moon shining on the water," I said. She pulled herself up until her feet were not touching the platform at all. I simply up-ended her. She didn't scream or struggle. The hardest part was waiting a while before running in and pretending it had just happened.

No one thought of blaming me. It was so easy that I could hardly believe I had managed it and for a couple of days I found myself still making plans. The only important result to me was the effect it had on grandmother. She blamed herself and claimed she must be getting too old to manage a child, so mother decided to take me back to the city with her. After all, I would be in school most of the time.

Jennie Sue would never suffer—never wake up in the night to find her face wet with tears for her daddy, never have to see her cousins riding away with their daddies, or miss him in the evenings at daddy time, or have secrets that only a daddy would want to know—and not have a daddy to tell them to. Jennie Sue was safe forever. But what about him? It was not fair that he should go on hugging, squeezing, touching everyone. But what could I do?

The answer came to me one night. I woke up knowing what to do. I couldn't get him near a well, but I could write, couldn't I? And I knew where to write from the many receipts he had given grandmother. One of the first words I could read was Sweeney, C. L. Sweeney. Later I could read the names of his office and his employer. I never forgot anything about him.

I poured my heart out to his employer on a piece of mother's stationery, but I realized that would not do. Finally I wrote a short note on half a sheet of tablet paper. Addressing his boss, I wrote: "I think you ought to know Mr. C. L. Sweeney touches all the girls on his paper route. He touches them everywhere." And I signed it: "One Who Knows."

A few weeks later grandmother wrote, "You will be sorry to hear that nice Mr. Sweeney doesn't work for the paper any more. He gave up his job and moved away. I don't know where He never said a word to us."

That was long, long ago. They don't have many wells any more, do they? But we can all help in other ways. We can all write. And the telephone is a godsend. Don't call the person himself. He will just argue and threaten to sue. Find out who his next-door neighbor is or call his boss and call from a drug store. They might pretend that they don't believe you, but they'll think about it, you bet. I urge you all to pay attention. They might look nice like daddies. But before it's too late, tilt the page. Take another look.

Timothy Childs

Is Anyone There?

Timothy Childs was born in Los Angeles in 1941, and is a fifth-generation Californian. But he and his wife, Terri, "have kept on the move, living in seven cities in four countries during the ten years of their marriage." Mr. Childs' first novel, COLD TURKEY, was published in May 1979 by Harper & Row (a Joan Kahn book) . . .

It is 1981, and there are nightmares that are peculiarly, perhaps uniquely, 1981. But in these violent days, nightmares have broken out of their former limits of time and darkness. Now there are daymares that are peculiarly, perhaps uniquely, 1981. Will the daymares persist past 1981? Or will they be caught, caged, and returned to their former time zone? . . .

My life is truly cursed.

I couldn't run, not in Beverly Hills, not in my last good suit. Eleven ten by my fine gold watch. Perspiration trickled down my back, sure to leave stains. Eighty-eight degrees on the day before Christmas. Ridiculous. I couldn't run. Running would have been so undignified.

Faster, pavement jarring my ankles until they felt like stumps. The sidewalk was choked with shoppers, their arms clutched around high-stacked Christmas packages. I glared them from my path. At the corners I kept stabbing at the pedestrian buttons, trying to make the traffic lights change faster.

Finally, the Slater Tower Building. Twenty stories high, dark windows, a plaza. A little fountain in the plaza. Workers were rushing out of the building, full of tiresome Christmas cheer, going home early to cook their Christmas turkeys. I couldn't afford a turkey sandwich, after six months without work. My fine gold watch said eleven fifteen. I would be twenty minutes late. My life is truly cursed.

Three snickering girls pushed past me into the elevator. One held a glass of eggnog that threatened to overflow on my fine leather briefcase. Drinking at that hour. Probably file clerks. They prattled all the way to the seventh floor, every word pulling at my neck muscles. As I left the elevator, the three clerks tittered. I swung around quickly to see if they were laughing at me. But the elevator doors had closed.

Down the hall. Two massive doors on which the words:

Suite 700
WARD & ARMSTRONG
Mortgage Brokers

were written in raised steel letters. I opened the door and entered, my excuses rehearsed.

Silence. No one there to hear my excuses. To the left of the waiting area were five secretarial desks, including one for the Receptionist; opposite was a row of offices, each with its door open; to my right, another row of offices, disappearing down a hallway.

No sign of life.

Three of the desks looked very orderly, as if their occupants had left for the Holiday, but the other two had papers on them. On and around them. A folder had fallen from the Receptionist's desk, strewing papers over the chair and the floor. The telephone receiver was off the hook, its dial tone changed to an angry, high-pitched alarm. A most unpleasant noise. I replaced the receiver and sat down in one of the waiting-room chairs.

Someone would surely come soon.

Silence. Only the gentle rush of the air conditioning and a tiny rattle from one of the entry doors. I could have walked off with the entire office, had I been a thief, which I am not. Highly inefficient. I was obviously needed to correct a few things at Ward & Armstrong.

I looked around at the offices: wood paneling, deep carpets, rich fixtures. Even the ashtray on the table next to me was impressive: heavy crystal. And walls covered with oil paintings. Of course, they could have been prints; these days it's so hard to tell the real from the fake.

Still no one came.

I noticed a scratch on my fine leather briefcase. Probably from the file clerks. I licked my finger and rubbed the scratch, making it less noticeable. Then I opened the briefcase and withdrew a résumé for Mr. Phelps. The résumé had been prepared by an executive-placement agency I had been foolish enough to retain. I was nearly an executive in several of my jobs. For an exorbitant fee the agency supplied me with 50 copies of the résumé—professionally prepared—and sent me on a dozen interviews, none of which resulted in a thing. I had wasted money and time. *Six months* of my time. Of my life! For nothing!

A deep breath. Crumple the shreds of a torn résumé into a ball and shove it between the seat cushion and the back of the chair. Another deep breath as the pounding slowed. I started to close my fine leather briefcase, then reached inside and let my fingers caress the raised letters of my specially designed bronze nameplate. *Edward T. Creary.* In bronze. How well it had looked on my desks, how well worth the expense. Even if the others had laughed behind my back.

With Mr. Phelps it would be different . . . I watched him read my résumé. His eyes met mine with respect.

"Mr. Creary, you are a master of many skills."

"I have had a certain success."

He calculated rapidly on a yellow legal pad, writing with a gold pen. I vowed to have such a pen. A pink tinge blushed his cheeks when he turned again to me.

"I can't offer to pay you what you're really worth, because that would unbalance our budget, but—" He had to swallow before continuing. Embarrassed. "But would thirty thousand a year seem insulting?" . . .

Still no one. From far below on the street came the faint scream of a siren. Strange to be so peaceful, there in the waiting room. Seven stories below, awaiting my return, was a jungle of traps and sirens.

But no one came. Only air rushing, a ticking, pecking rattle. Empty desks with papers strewn. It was beginning to get on my nerves. I remembered a movie I saw years ago about an atomic attack. New York looked the same as before, except all the people were gone. Newspapers blowing through the streets. It was a silly movie; there would have been bodies.

My fine gold watch said 35 minutes past eleven. Eleven thirty-five. Time to show some initiative. I stood up and walked to the hallway. No sign of life.

"Hello?" No answer. "Hello! Is anyone there?"

"I am here. Is someone there?" The half-heard voice seemed to come from a corner office.

"Yes! I have an appointment with Mr. Phelps! About a job!" I felt absurd, shouting out my business to someone I couldn't see. Very undignified.

He emerged from the corner office and strutted toward me, a little smile on his face. On his little face.

He was 50, nearly bald, stubby.

"Mr. Phelps, you say. He is in the Board Room at the moment. Everyone is there; except me, of course." Seedy black suit, plain white shirt, narrow black tie. An outfit I might have owned 20 years ago. Not a good impression for an employee of Ward & Armstrong to make on their newest executive.

"I had an appointment for eleven. The traffic was impossible. I've been waiting here since ten after. No one came."

He peered up at me through thick wire-rimmed glasses. "Most of the staff are off today. It is the day before Christmas, you know. Everyone else is in the Board Room, except me. I'm the President, you know."

What luck, the President! "I'm honored to meet you, sir."

He shook my hand with his fingertips. "Why don't the two of us talk a little before you see Mr. Phelps."

I took my fine leather briefcase and started to follow him. "Someone left that phone lying off the hook, so I replaced it." Showing initiative.

"Ah, yes, thank you for putting it back. At times Miss Collins can be quite careless."

His office was grand. He sat in a high-backed leather chair, behind an antique desk. On its green leather surface stood an elegant bronze stallion, galloping. Next to it an ashtray, two telephones, and a triple pen set. I'd never seen a triple pen set. At the other end of the room, four chairs and a couch, grouped around a glass-topped coffee table.

I sat down. In front of me was a plastic nameplate: *Malcolm A. Dodge.* My bronze nameplate was far more impressive. I glanced at the leather-framed photograph of Mrs. Dodge. A lovely woman.

He coupled his fingers and slowly cracked the knuckles on both hands. Always the smile.

"You must have a résumé."

I took another copy from my fine leather briefcase and handed it across the desk. He read from the first page.

"Creary. Edward Terence Creary. Forty-two years old. With Consolidated Mortgage until, let's see, about six months ago." He pulled the triple pen set a few inches closer and looked critically at it. Then at me. "How did you happen to leave Consolidated?"

"A personality conflict." And it had been, with old Stafford, the

Vice-President. He disagreed with my handling of Miss Branch, who wouldn't stop calling me Eddie. Perhaps it was a bit severe, striking her. But she'd been given plenty of warning. Discipline.

"Yes, yes, personality conflicts can occur. I understand that very well." Mr. Dodge had the distracting habit of clearing his throat as he talked. He reached over to shift the angle of the bronze stallion before turning back to the résumé. "You had been with Consolidated Mortgage, let's see, almost two years."

Two long years, and then to be discharged without a word of thanks. Thinking of it made my fists knot. Of all the injustices done me in my previous jobs that was the worst. Not a word of gratitude.

"You seem to have a broad background in the mortgage business, Mr. Creary. Would you describe yourself as being—what shall I say?—*loyal*; yes, loyal to your employers?"

"Oh, yes, sir. I consider loyalty to be most important."

"Loyalty is most important to me, Mr. Creary, especially just now." He'd gone suddenly pale. Tiny beads of perspiration popped out on his bald head. "You see, I have only become President of Ward and Armstrong today, just today. I must build a staff that is loyal to me."

I was quick to reassure him. "You can certainly count on me, Mr. Dodge. And may I offer my congratulations on your promotion."

He relaxed a bit. "Thank you, thank you. It was not easy, you know. There was considerable opposition to my advancement, despite my thirty-five years with the firm, but I convinced them in the end. In the final analysis, hard work . . ."

He rambled on. A queer man. On the telephone Mr. Phelps had said they needed an assistant loan officer. Fifteen thousand a year. An almost private office and secretary. Thinking of it made me miss some of what he had been saying.

". . . and so, I would want you to remember these things, should you decide to work for me."

My mind snapped back. "Oh, yes, sir. I will."

"Good, good. I think you will be a welcome addition to my staff." He clapped his hands and grinned with pleasure, exposing an uneven row of gray and yellow teeth. "You shall be my Vice-President, at an annual salary of, shall we agree, fifty thousand dollars?"

I was afraid he'd see my hands tremble. Vice-President! I'd never occupied so dignified a position. And $50,000 a year! My response was a weak stammer. "That's very generous. I promise you won't be sorry."

"I'm sure of it, I'm sure of it. Your office will be right next to mine. Now I must take you to meet the staff—those few who are here today, of course."

My feet floated above the thick carpet as he led me down the corridor.

At last the position that so long eluded me! We passed several private offices, the mail room, a small library, and a file room with banks of loan folders. Vice-President! At the end of the hall was a door with a sign on it: *Board Room*. Mr. Dodge opened the door for me to enter.

In the center of the Board Room was a long, gleaming conference table. Five leather chairs on each side of it, an eleventh at the head. On the table were two telephones and several of the heavy ashtrays. A notepad and pencil were carefully positioned at each chair.

Four of the staff were there. Three sat at the table. The fourth—a young woman—lay face down on the carpet, her arms stretched out toward the door. She must have been reaching for it when he shot her.

They were all dead.

My life is truly cursed.

I staggered back, colliding with Dodge, which made me recoil again. Lurching forward, I nearly tripped over the outstretched woman. A nightmarish stillness saturated the room, broken only by a strange, choked, whimpering noise. I looked wildly around to see if one of them could somehow be alive.

Then I realized the whimper was coming from me.

"Unswerving loyalty, Mr. Creary, unswerving loyalty." He held the pistol casually, not pointing it at anything in particular. Not yet.

Dodge cleared his throat with a harsh bark. "Staff, I want you to meet my new Vice-President, Mr. Edward Terence Creary." Then to me: "This is Miss Collins, nearest you, and that is Mrs. Melnick. Mr. Phelps, the gentleman you came to see, is over there. Mr. Ward is at the head of the table. Everyone else is off today. It is the day before Christmas, you know."

I nodded at each corpse as he pointed at it, trying to speak, my throat packed with chalk. Mrs. Melnick and Mr. Phelps were slumped over the table. The girl on the floor was Miss Collins. Mr. Ward had his head thrown back and his arms spread wide apart. A bullet had pierced his forehead. He looked grotesque. The air stank of blood.

My knees were jelly.

"Some of the staff were adamant in their opposition to my promotion, but I convinced them." Dodge snarled toward the body at the head of the table. Mr. Ward had died with terror on his face. Dodge spoke to him—to it—sharply. "Ward, I want that proposed budget on my desk by three this afternoon. By three at the latest."

He twinkled at me in satisfaction as he gestured toward the door. Somehow I obeyed.

I stumbled down the hall, away from the Board Room and its corpses, my brain beginning to clear. My only chance was to stay calm. At least the gun was gone from his hand. We stopped at his office while I got my briefcase, then he took me next door.

"This will be yours, Mr. Creary. I hope that it suits you?"

Under any other circumstances it would have suited me beyond my wildest dreams. Ultramodern aluminum desk, the kind with no drawers. Handsome. On the desk, one of these sculptures composed of plastic balls hanging from wires. Out the window, a fine view of Beverly Hills. Not as impressive as the President's office. But distinguished in every aspect.

The rise in my fortunes was monumental, even if it might only last a day.

"It's very handsome, Mr. Dodge. I hope the previous occupant won't object to my taking it."

"Object? Oh, no. This used to be the office of Mr. Phelps, and I've explained the situation fully to him."

I searched his face, but he seemed quite serious. Out of touch with reality. He pointed at the desk, to a small box.

"That is the intercom. If I buzz twice, that will mean for you to come to my office."

"Yes, sir. I understand."

He went on cheerfully. "The rest of the staff will remain in the Board Room, should you need to consult them. I'm afraid you will have to work through lunch today. There is so much to do. Yes, there will be no lunch today for either of us. And no sneaking out—I can see the hall clearly from my desk."

His eyes instantly menaced. I had to pacify him. "Oh, no, Mr. Dodge. I'd never do that!"

"Fine, fine. Now I will leave you to get used to your new office."

As soon as he went out of the room I sat down in my new chair. Of course, it was actually Mr. Phelps's chair. Or Mr. Phelps's former chair. Anyway, it was covered in velvet. Deep blue. Beautiful. Under the desk was an electric buffer. I pressed the switch with my toe, setting the polisher in motion. In truth, my shoes needed a shine. I took a cigar from the lacquered box on the desk, clipped the end with the gold tool lying next to the box, and lit it with the matching gold lighter. A smooth flow of smoke began to sooth my nerves.

If only Edna could see me in this office. Edna, who never understood my destiny, who left when Fortune turned against me.

I took out my bronze nameplate and positioned it carefully on the desk. Then I noticed a dial on the side of the desk. I turned it on. Stereophonic music soared from hidden speakers. Wagner.

If only Edna could see me in this impressive office, a Vice-President at $50,000 a year. Getting a shoeshine and smoking an expensive cigar. Stereophonic Wagner. And only yesterday I'd considered selling my fine gold watch to buy groceries.

But, of course, this could never last.

Two short buzzes. I went next door to see Dodge.

He was standing behind the desk, rearranging a book shelf. "Oh, yes, Creary. We must discuss our plans for the new year. Sit down, sit down."

I sat down.

"Now, then. We have problems—small problems—with a few of our loans. They are decent people, but things have just not worked out well, for them or for us." He picked up a thick loan folder from the desk. "Look this over right away and let me know what you think. You may go now."

Not a very polite dismissal.

I took the folder back to my office and closed the door. My chair certainly was comfortable. Another siren passed on the street below. I turned up the music to block out such intrusions. In one of the desk drawers were some cards and a marking pen. I carefully wrote my new title on one of the cards. *Vice-President.* I leaned the card exactly against the center of my bronze nameplate. Until I could order a new one. Then I opened the folder and began to read.

Twenty minutes later I sat back in disgust. Dodge wasn't fit to be President. Of anything. He had approved a quarter-million-dollar loan on property that couldn't have been worth half that much. Sheer incompetence. *Malcolm A. Dodge, Assistant Vice-President.* Mr. Ward was probably going to fire him, so Dodge murdered everyone and made himself President. Assistant Vice-President to President in one day. Quite a promotion. For an incompetent.

I went to his office.

"Well? Well? What do you think, Creary?"

I tried to appear respectful. "It looks bad, to be frank. We'll simply have to foreclose, then sell the property for whatever we can get."

"Not very inspired advice, Creary! Perhaps I made a mistake with you!"

"I'm no good to the firm if I'm not honest."

His eyebrows were two black sponges, soaking up the perspiration that flowed into them. "Not very inspired at all for a fifty-thousand-a-year man!"

He was like all the rest—made a mistake and blamed me. Unreasonable. "I wasn't the one who approved this loan."

Dodge leaped out of the chair. His hand darted toward a coat pocket.

"Maybe things aren't as bad as they look! Must further consider the matter. Approach it a different way!" Words came from me in a gush, as if the force of their flow could stop his hand. "We can meet with the borrowers. Talk over the situation. It's not anyone's fault when conditions change." Dodge was obviously a lunatic; only a lunatic would make a loan like that. Obviously a dangerous, incompetent man. "Something can be worked out!"

Slowly he relaxed back into his chair. He withdrew the hand from his coat pocket. "Yes, that's it; yes, nobody's fault." He smiled, but weakly this time. More form than substance. "You are going to be all right, Eddie."

Why do people have to call me Eddie! Forty-two years old and still Eddie! I fought to retain my composure. "Thank you, Mr. Dodge. I hope I live up to your expectations."

"And you do, Eddie, you do. Go on back to your office now. We will talk about this later."

Eddie. When I got back to my desk I saw that the cigar had come apart in my hand. I lit another and turned up the music. So pleasant there, alone, without that lunatic. So safe. I had to think. Surely I could find a solution to my problem. Executive planning. A Vice-President could do that.

Facts. What were the facts. Dodge was an incompetent who'd murdered four people to become President. He was a threat to Ward & Armstrong. And to me. If I could overpower him and call the police, the Company would be grateful. I might even get a raise.

A tapping from behind me. Intruding on my thoughts. I turned around to see a man on a scaffold, outside the window peering in at me. A window washer. He tapped again, waved, smiled stupidly.

Another drunk on the day before Christmas. I motioned for him to leave me alone. I had to think. He tapped again. Enough. I went to the window and threw the curtains shut. The tapping ceased.

Back at my desk. I might get a promotion or a raise. Perhaps both. I had to catch Dodge by surprise. Somehow. Then I knew how.

I entered his office without knocking. He had his head on his arms, slumped over the desk, as if asleep. He jerked as the door closed behind me.

"I didn't call for you, Eddie!"

"I've had an idea, sir. I wanted to show initiative."

He didn't seem pleased. "I see, yes."

I sat down in my customary chair. In front of me was the cheap nameplate. *Malcolm A. Dodge.* Malcolm. Malc. "Mr. Dodge, who is the Chairman of the Board of Ward and Armstrong?"

He considered a moment. "Why, I suppose Mr. Ward is still the Chairman. He held that position, as well as being President."

"But that's not right, sir." Malc. "You have shown decisive leadership. You should hold the highest place in the Company."

Annoyance became a beaming grin. "You know, Eddie, I absolutely agree. There is no place in this company for the likes of Ward." He clapped his hands in delight.

"Everyone is in the Board Room, Mr. Dodge." Malc. "We should go tell them."

Dodge sat back in the chair and chuckled to himself. "Chairman. Imagine the look on Ward's face. Very good, Eddie. You keep up the good work and I will make you my Senior Vice-President."

How dare he! I deserved at least Executive Vice-President! But I was in control now. Calm. "Why don't we go tell him right away?"

Dodge was already halfway to the door. "Yes, yes, they must be told immediately."

I followed him down the hall to the Board Room. He was still in the lead. For the moment. I nearly laughed aloud at this President—this incompetent—this incompetent President about to be deposed. A brief struggle, tie him up with my belt, call the police. Gratitude.

We entered the Board Room.

"Mr. Dodge, look. Mr. Ward is still at the head of the table. This can't continue."

I made myself speak to the corpse, trying not to see the crimson hole in his forehead. "Mr. Ward, you are no longer Chairman of the Board. You have been replaced. Mr. Dodge must sit in that chair."

Mr. Ward didn't budge. How could he? Being dead.

I stepped over the body of Miss Collins, gesturing for Dodge to follow me. "We'll have to move him forcibly."

"You are right, Eddie. We will move him together." He walked to the other side of Mr. Ward and bent over him.

My chance. I picked up one of the heavy crystal ashtrays. As he took Ward's arm, started to lift Ward by the arm, I hit Dodge on the back of the skull. Hard. He moaned, pitching forward onto Ward's body. Again the ashtray in my hand flashed. Dodge slid to the floor, moaning louder.

I pulled the pistol out of his coat pocket just as Dodge began to scream.

"Traitor! You would rise against me? You—"

"Incompetent! Not fit to be President!"

He was desperately trying to stand. I pointed the gun between his eyes and squeezed the trigger again and again. The pistol was empty. He was on his knees, shrieking.

"I made you Vice-President!"

"Incompetent!"

"After all your failures!"

"Shut up!"

"Judas! Arnold!"

"Malc, Malc, Malc, Malc!"

I threw the useless gun at him and it knocked him back to the floor. He pleaded with me then.

"Eddie, for God's sake, don't—"

But the heavy ashtray was in my hand once more and I was hitting him with it on the head of that fraudulent incompetent presidential head the crystal burning red my hands slipping on the blood and sweat from his dying presidential head until he stops screaming no danger to anyone ever again ever

Silence. Only the rush of air conditioning to calm my nerves as I lie next to Dodge. The dead Dodge. The dead President.

I have never felt so peaceful.

Finally I get up off the floor and wipe my hands on the front of his white shirt. I leave him there next to Mr. Ward. Two former Presidents.

Across the hall is the men's room. Carefully I wash my hands. Very carefully.

I walk down the hall past my old office to the office of the President. I take the plastic nameplate that reads *Malcolm A. Dodge* and drop it into the wastebasket. My bronze nameplate looks at home on a presidential desk.

I sit in the handsome leather chair. It is even more comfortable than my old velvet one. I reach slowly for the telephone.

But I don't dial.

Suddenly I need a cigar.

I go back to my old office and get the lacquered box of cigars, the gold clipper, and the gold lighter. I return and put them on my new desk. I light a fresh cigar and sit back. Satisfied.

Time passes, a lot of time, how much I cannot tell.

Then there was a voice. A faint voice. From the reception area.

"Is anyone there?" the voice asks.

"I am here," I answer. "Is someone there?"

T. M. Adams

Short Week

Your Editor is going to suggest something unusual—something, to the best of our recollection, we have never suggested before. If you want to truly appreciate this gem of a short-short, read it through, then immediately read it again. The second time around (the story is only about 1500 words) you will fully appreciate its brilliant word-play . . . a tour de force . . .

For no reason other than that it was Monday morning, Parker showered, shaved, dressed, and left the house. On the way out of the driveway he nearly sideswiped Fallon's car, still parked there after the disastrous party Friday night: one more reminder, a sort of four-wheeled hangover. It was raining, too.

Ten minutes out he thought he heard his name on the car radio and attempted a bit of fine-tuning, simultaneously contending for the express lane. He won the position but lost the station. Something washed up out of the static eventually, at first only in crests of disassociated phrases. As soon as he realized it was a newscast, the lovingly dressed-up details of an especially brutal wife-murder, he turned it off. The same old thing, he thought, and one station like another. Pulling into one of eight parking spaces reserved for junior vice-presidents at Intertool, Parker tried to imagine the far shores of the coming Friday . . . but no, even Wednesday seemed too distant.

He had skipped breakfast, not feeling like fixing it himself, and hunger always made him oversensitive to noise. Now he had to walk through a dozen open offices to the privacy of his own, somehow enduring the hammering of typewriters and keypunch machines, the unrelenting ringing of the telephones, and the not-quite-random talk talk talk of 300 tongues. Without civil service training, he reflected, it's almost impossible to totally ignore the human voice, even just a snatch of gossip by the coffee machine (". . . . had a little thing going while her husband was out of town—") or a complaint from behind a sports page (". . . . really murdered them Friday

night . . . in the cellar now for sure—"). And now there came a fragment more lethal than these, louder in its phony bonhomie and right
behind him: "Caught you!"

Parker felt a hand on his shoulder and turned to greet Dave Evans,
a tall booming man given to a kind of forced double-entendre that
Parker didn't feel up to handling this morning. "Grim homecoming
for you, boy!" he was saying, or shouting. "Shouldn't have to tell
you, never cut a vacation short."

"What do you mean?" Parker asked unwillingly.

"I mean Fallon! Seems to have decided to take a long weekend,
with you still off. Leaves a hole; now you're back, you'll probably
have to fill in. Man's gone too far! Someone'll have to keep hitting
him over the head until he straightens out. Know what I mean?"

"Yes," Parker said, ears ringing, nausea rising. "Look, I've got to
run."

"Course you do! Catch you later. Take care of Louisa for us"—a
dig in the ribs here, and a stage wink—"if you haven't already!"

Safe in his own office, Parker told his secretary to hold all but
essential calls, and lost himself for a while in paperwork. But eventually the telephone rang.

It was a bad connection, a hollow unplaceable voice: "Are you
going to have that breakdown today?"

Parker stopped breathing. He found himself looking around the
office, as though expecting to surprise someone hiding there.

"Are you going to have that breakdown today?" Again, more patient this time. Of course, of course, it would be Chadwick, who
never said hello or identified himself. He apparently still wanted a
breakdown on the Finetron figures. Parker didn't point out that he
had just returned from vacation, or that he wasn't even due back
until the next day, or that the SEC ruling had rendered Finetron's
position academic. He merely said yes, he'd keep working on it.

"Okay," Chadwick said. "Now, Fallon's gone, so you're going to
have to talk to the detectives . . . Hello, Parker? Oh, right, you've
been out, haven't you? Well, I've decided to see what the detective
agency can dig up on this seller."

"In the cellar?" Parker asked faintly. This connection—

"Yeah, somebody was dumping Intertool in thousand-share blocks
last week, as though they had advance knowledge that the Finetron
merger would go sour. I told Fallon to sic the detectives on the seller;
get some use out of our retainer—"

"Of course, of course," Parker said.

"Can't have one of our people involved in a killing like that, can we?"

Parker closed his eyes tightly. "No," he said.

"Catch you later," Chadwick said, and hung up.

Parker took an antacid and went back to work. For the next few hours he managed to restrict his thoughts to familiar routines. Consciousness surfaced only once. His eyes strayed from a confidential assessment of Finetron inventories to the photograph of his wife that stood on the corner of his desk. "With all my love, until you come home, Lou." Curious, that "until you come home" part; he didn't remember having ever seen it before, much less seeing it every workday for seven years. For a moment it didn't even make sense to him. But of course, of course: she had sent it to him when he was in the service . . . and the Finetron stockholder's report had overstated their assets by some 23 per cent . . .

The next time he was fully aware of his surroundings, he was at lunch with Evans, George MacKenzie from Merchandising, and someone else, who didn't seem to count for much. He had the vague feeling that he had been keeping up his end of the conversation, but he could no longer remember what they were discussing, could no longer pay attention to anything except a voice emanating from two tables away. "Everybody knows about them," the woman was saying, with nerve-dicing incisiveness. "Who does he think he's fooling? I even know where he's keeping her—"

Dish-clatter, or conspiracy, prevented him from hearing more. Somebody was tugging at his sleeve. He turned and caught the end of MacKenzie's question: "—bury her?"

"What?" Parker said.

Impatiently MacKenzie repeated: "Do you think that cost-effectiveness is the only barrier?" Parker just stared at him. Mercifully Evans jumped in, saying, "Well, of course, there's the licensing too. All the new regulations! Sheer murder." And this last sentiment was echoed around the table, even Parker finding himself saying the words . . .

As they reapproached Parker's office, Evans commiserated with him about how hard it was to come back after a vacation, concluding: "Looks like prison, doesn't it? No escaping it, though!" Parker pretended he hadn't heard.

His secretary looked up at him sympathetically—he probably appeared as ill as he felt—but she said, "The detectives are waiting for you, Mr. Parker."

He froze; and slowly, with a rising inflection, he repeated her words.

"Yes," she said. "You know: Mr. Fallon's gone, so you'll have to tell them everything." He had been watching her lips very carefully this time; that was definitely what she had said.

And indeed they were waiting for him in his office, two of them. He seated himself gingerly, cleared his throat, and tried to remember what he should say. Lou's picture caught his eye. "Come home," yes. "I just came home from vacation Friday night," he began, then faltered.

"Yes, your secretary told us," one of the detectives said finally. "Uh, if you're not ready for us yet, Mr. Parker, we can—"

"I'm ready, I'm ready," Parker said. Starting over: "Look, you know Mr. Fallon, don't you? A junior vice-president here?"

"Sure, he's the one we usually report to," the detective said. "His main thing is public relations, though, isn't that right?"

Parker smiled sourly. *Et tu, Brute?* Yes, the more public the better. So I gather.

"Well, as I said, I came home Friday night, the night before I was expected, and found Fallon with my wife. So I took the poker from the living-room fireplace, went back upstairs, and beat them both to death. Did I say that was Friday night? So on Saturday I tried to go for a walk, but already everyone was talking about it, though I couldn't believe that at first; and the radio, too, the radio's the worst. Now, on television they can only hint around at it, if you keep them in line by watching their lips . . . So on Sunday I just sat at home, watched television. And Monday is today. Did I say I buried them in the cellar? I buried them in the cellar. In case you hadn't heard."

The telephone rang. "Excuse me," he said. "You'll have to catch me later." He picked up the receiver and swiveled his chair around to face the window, away from their pale staring faces.

The same hollow voice from the upper air: "We're wondering, when are you going to have that breakdown?"

He hung up slowly. The two detectives were gone, for the moment. He stood and went to the window, adjusted the louver to let in air and sound. A news-vendor on the street below shouted something about murder, and the pigeons on the sill sang, "Lou, Lou, Lou." Enough, Parker thought. Surely they could all knock it off now.

John F. Suter

The Oldest Law

First, about the book, Melville Davisson Post's UNCLE ABNER: MASTER OF MYSTERIES, *a cornerstone in any definitive detective-story library or collection: the book was published by D. Appleton, New York, in 1918, and remained in print in its original hardcover edition for more than 20 years. The first English edition did not appear for 54 years—Tom Stacey, London, 1972.*

Second, about the quality of Post's tales of Uncle Abner: Howard Haycraft, in his MURDER FOR PLEASURE: THE LIFE AND TIMES OF THE DETECTIVE STORY, *1941, wrote that "posterity may well name Uncle Abner, after Dupin, the greatest American contribution to the form."*

Your Editor, in his THE DETECTIVE SHORT STORY: A BIBLIOGRAPHY, *1942, wrote that "*UNCLE ABNER *is the finest book of detective short stories written by an American author since Poe."*

Anthony Boucher, in his Introduction to the 1962 Collier reprint of UNCLE ABNER, *wrote: "I envy anyone who here discovers* UNCLE ABNER *for the first time. He is about to read the best American detective short stories since Poe."*

Edmund Crispin, in his Introduction to the first English edition, in 1972, wrote: "The Uncle Abner stories remain undated to this day, chiefly because they are an early, and a very distinguished, corpus of historical detective fiction . . . Abner is a superb reasoner."

In the light of these judgments we did not believe that anyone would have the courage (or foolhardiness) to accept the challenge, to dare "take a shot" at writing a pastiche of Post's Abner. But thinking back, we realized that some writers (notably Michael Harrison among them) have ventured to successfully imitate Poe's Dupin, and many have rushed in to write reasonable facsimiles of Doyle's Holmes, so why not a joust at Post's Abner? Well, John F. Suter dared—and delivered.

Here is the first of a new series about that great champion of justice, the "protector of the innocent and righter of wrongs," the

264

"voice and arm of the Lord," stalwart, rugged Uncle Abner, Virginia squire of the Jeffersonian era, the first-published truly American detective, the first truly native American detective, excepting only the American Indian . . .

It was a time of change. We could not fail to reap benefit, many said. My Uncle Abner agreed, but would not say if only good would result or if troubles might come which would outweigh the good.

I tried to get him to discuss it as we rode our horses to get Thomas Harper, the County Clerk, just before dawn that morning early in spring. The railroad already passed through Wheeling, to the north. Now a spur was to be laid through our area, eventually reaching the Ohio River, to the west. This would permit cattle to be taken to the big markets without losing weight on a drive. We could ship out coal, timber, and grain. I found it exciting when I thought of it.

But when I wanted to talk of these changes that morning, Abner merely said, "Rufus depends on you now for much of his farm work. How will these things affect that?"

I had grown into this responsibility, even as my father grew older, but I had not foreseen the things which were coming. I said as much.

"We must consider each thing as it comes," said my uncle. "We should now be considering why Randolph asked me to meet Harper very early and ride with him to the courthouse."

I had no answer. My uncle had asked me to come with him because he knew that the soil was still too wet to turn and that my father could easily handle the other work. If Abner had not divined Squire Randolph's purpose, I could not.

Few people were stirring along the road, although the sky was paling rapidly. The only activity we saw was at Randall Dorsey's blacksmith shop. The forge already glowed, and a steady clanking sounded. There were two of our neighbors waiting outside the shop, and one was inside with his horse. Three others were turning away.

Although the white in my uncle's hair and beard was now more noticeable, Abner still seemed as one who might have been moulded in that very forge, or another like it. The chestnut he rode could almost have been sired by the great horse which had been his companion when I was a boy, so that the pair seemed to present an unchanging picture.

My uncle glanced across at me. "Randolph could expect to meet Harper this morning at the courthouse. He has been unable to see the man at all for two weeks, for Harper has been in Pittsburgh. His return was expected late last night. Yet Randolph wants me to meet him early and ride with him to the courthouse. Why?"

I shook my head, but I felt that no answer had been truly expected of me.

"Something has happened while Harper was away," Abner said, fixing his eyes on the road. "And Randolph does not want him to talk to anyone who has a hand in it before he does. That must be the way of it."

It was not a long ride to Harper's place. He had a modest acreage of several pastures, some timber, and a small section of hilly land bisected by a steep ravine. Since Harper was the County Clerk, he farmed little, contenting himself with a few beef and dairy cattle and some poultry. His house was a neat, white-painted, two-story frame which sat close to the road.

We tethered our horses, Abner's chestnut and my roan gelding, where they could drink from the wooden trough near the barn. At the front door of the house Abner's knock was answered by Margaret Harper, a short, stout woman with plain features.

"Why, Abner!" she said in surprise. "And Martin. It's early for you to be out. Do you want to see Tom?"

"If we might."

An apologetic look crossed her face. "He's not in. One of the cows must be out and has strayed up onto the hill. He's gone to bring her in. Will you come in for coffee until he comes back?"

Abner seemed not to have heard the invitation. "Does he often have this trouble?"

"Why, no. Almost never. Tom was amazed when he heard the cowbell back on the hill a while ago."

"So should I be. Tom builds good fences." Abner turned to me. "Martin, you and I might ride up to help bring that cow in."

As we rode away from the yard toward the hill, I could hear the irregular tonking of the cowbell in the distance. There was something odd about it, and it made me frown. Then I realized: it neither came closer nor went farther away. The beast might be grazing, of course, but where was Harper?

I started to mention this to my uncle, but he was glancing intently at the ground, which was soft. I looked down and could see the hoofmarks of Harper's horse, but that was all.

There was morning mist as we approached the hilly tract. A small pond lay at the foot of the hill, and white vapors from the water had spread up the slope and into the ravine which flanked the right side of the hill. The sun, just rising at the hill's top, made long, slanting shafts in the mist in the places where the trees let it shine through. Down in the ravine I could hear the piping of the peepers, the tiny frogs of early spring.

As we urged our horses carefully through the dead brush, Abner shook his head impatiently.

"A strange cow which makes no sound but the clanking of its bell. Why do we not hear Harper or his horse? See, they came this way."

We mounted higher until we were more than a hundred feet above the bottom of the ravine. Then the mist thinned to mere wisps, and I could see empty woods before us. There were only the spruces, the sweet gums, the maples, and the stalks of the brush, all bare and leafless. The spruces alone were green.

Then I saw that the woods were not completely empty. Ahead, to our right, a horse stood, its saddle empty. There was no cow, although I could still hear the bell. It was very close.

"The cow—" I began.

"There is no cow," said Abner, raising his right arm. "There. Look up."

I stared where he pointed. Near where the horse stood there was a ledge or rock, at the edge of a straight, high drop into the ravine. A silver maple grew by the left side of the ledge, one long branch extending over the rock. Attached to the branch above the center of the space was a cowbell, sounding when the gentle morning breeze stirred the branch.

I started to urge my horse toward this strange thing.

Abner's massive hand closed on the gelding's bridle. "Wait," he said. "Where is Harper? And look at his horse. It only stands on three legs."

He turned his head this way and that, then faced the ledge.

"Harper!" he called.

There was no answer.

He dismounted and walked slowly toward the horse, a young bay stallion. I saw that he was right—it did, indeed, favor its left foreleg. I saw, too, that Abner paid less attention to the horse or the bell than he did to the ground. He stooped once and picked something up, examined it, and carefully put it into his pocket. Then he walked to the ledge and looked down into the ravine.

"Harper!" he called, as before, then waited. Again there was no answer.

He turned aside and walked to and fro near the ledge. Once again I saw him pick up something. Finally he walked to the side of the horse and began to soothe it.

"Now come here, Martin," he said. "I want you to look at this animal's hoof while I hold his head."

I dismounted, tethered both our horses to a nearby beech, and came to the stallion's side. The beast was distressed, but Abner had quieted it and was holding firm.

I raised the bay's left foreleg carefully and gripped it much as Randall Dorsey, the smith, might have done. When I looked at the hoof, the reason for the horse's lameness was clear. A prolonged piece of metal protruded from the tender part of the foot, and the hoof was bloody.

I told Uncle Abner about the curious thing I had found.

"A caltrop," he said. "A Devil's tool, in this case. I thought you might find it. Now, Martin, you are strong. Take my glove, then grip the prongs and pull hard."

He passed his right glove, of heavy leather, to me. I donned it, reached down to grip the protruding metal, and pulled with all my strength. The bay would have plunged with the pain had my uncle not curbed him. The metal object came free, and the bay grew quieter.

I examined the thing. It was of iron and consisted of four prongs so arranged that no matter how it fell, three prongs would rest on the ground and the fourth would project upward. The points were almost needles, and the edges were sharp. Each prong was between one and two inches long. Three of the prongs were bright; the fourth was bloody.

I held it out to my uncle, who glanced at it briefly and put it into his pocket.

"I picked up two more," he said, his voice wrathful. "Now, look at the bell. It hangs just higher than a man can reach, even sitting in his saddle. Harper would want to cut down the bell, else how would he know when a cow really was out? He would ride to the ledge and raise himself in his stirrups. On the ledge would be three of Satan's instruments, placed where the horse would be sure to step on one. Then—"

He turned and then began to lead the bay gently toward our own horses

"Martin," he said. "Get the bell. Then we must go down to the ravine."

We were both silent as we came to the courthouse, with its white plaster pillars, later in the morning. I had completed the unpleasant task of carrying Thomas Harper's body back to his house across the front of my saddle. My uncle, after leading the lame bay to the barn, had taken the burden of telling Margaret Harper how we had found her husband. Both of us were in a somber mood.

We had just tethered the horses when I looked up and saw Squire Randolph coming down the steps of the courthouse. He moved slower nowadays, and there were pouches under his eyes. He still cherished his affectations, but he had lost none of the respect he commanded as a Justice of the Peace.

"Abner," he called, "did Harper not return? Or is he following you?"

My uncle looked up, his eyes bleak as January sky.

"Harper did not return. He is at his house, but he will not be following us. You asked me to find him this morning, and we did. We came upon his body at the foot of a small cliff in the ravine on his land. His neck was broken."

"Did you see anyone else?" Randolph asked.

"That is a strange question," Abner replied. "We did not, although it was clear that he had been led into a trap. A fall killed him, but that fall was planned."

Randolph's face was heavy with sadness.

"Harper was needed to help settle a case. The disputants are in my office now. It would seem that one of them might have caused this terrible thing. I had foreseen interference, and I asked your help. But you saw nobody."

Abner seemed to grow taller. "Randolph, I think we should talk to these people. It is true that we saw only Thomas Harper's body, but the image of his murderer's mind was all around."

Randolph nodded. "Mr. Emerson says there is no den in the wide world to hide a rogue. How does he put it? 'Some damning circumstance always transpires.' "

Abner was beginning to mount the steps. "He had only to look to Adam and Cain for his examples." He glanced sidewise at Randolph. "This morning someone attempted to ignore the oldest law. If that person is in your office, we shall know it."

There were three persons already seated at the big oak table when

Randolph, still puzzled by Abner's last remark, showed us into his office. Two of them I knew; the third was a stranger.

Everyone knew Randall Dorsey, the blacksmith. Not only his chair, but the room, seemed too small for him. He had removed the superficial grime of his trade, but his horny hands were gray with ground-in dirt. Flying sparks had singed his brown beard in spots. His eyes seemed to have carried some of the banked fire of his forge with them.

At his side sat his sister, Anna Blackhurst. She was in her mid-forties, but the widow's black she wore detracted in no way from the appeal she had for any man who ever saw her. Her figure had scarcely thickened. Her auburn hair had no gray, and it had barely darkened. Her milky skin was unlined, and her green eyes were clear and penetrating.

For us, her neighbors, she had been the preserver of tales and legends as far back as my memory went. She could summon up for children the fairies, the elves, the leprechauns, and the gnomes. Frontier history was as familiar to her as her next-door neighbors. The Indians themselves knew no more of their lore than she. I still remembered the day when she shocked many women by appearing at school in buckskin shirt and trousers. She was recreating for us the famous exploit of Anne Bailey, when that frontierswoman rode through nearly 100 miles of hostile country for ammunition when Clendenin's Fort was besieged. All the same, Anna Blackhurst never completely won back her standing in the community.

As a Justice of the Peace, Randolph often settled disputes of many types. When the issues were beyond his jurisdiction, he acted as a sort of Special Commissioner of the Circuit Court. As such, he lacked a judge's authority, and his decisions could always be appealed. He was known, however, to be able and fair, and few appeals were taken. This reduced the number of the Circuit Judge's cases, and he could dispose promptly of litigation requiring jury trials.

Randolph waved a hand. "You know Mrs. Blackhurst and Randall Dorsey, Abner. This young man is a stranger. Let me introduce you to Nathan Dillworth."

My uncle looked at the young man curiously, and no wonder. Ephraim, the oldest of the local Dillworths, operated a busy still, among other things, and he was no better than he should be. The Dillworth most remembered was Lawrence. His greed for land had twice led him to clash with Abner. The second clash had ended in his hanging for murder.

The young man stepped forward. "I might be unfamiliar to you all, but my roots are here. My father was Gideon Dillworth."

Abner nodded in recognition. "I remember him. He left here for Baltimore nearly twenty years ago. He had a wife and a small boy. He was a sign painter, I recall."

He studied young Dillworth, who was tall with thick, black hair and a sweeping mustache. He was lean and appeared to be keeping a ferocious strength in check. His most striking feature was a hook which had replaced his left hand.

"And what do you do, Nathan Dillworth?" Abner asked.

"I was a cavalryman until my horse fell on me and crushed my left wrist," Dillworth said. "Now I am an actor."

"Were you ever sent to fight Indians?"

Dillworth laughed. "I have never seen an Indian. The accident happened when I had just finished training."

Randolph clucked with impatience. "And we are attempting to settle a matter of land ownership. Shall we be seated?"

When we had taken our places, Randolph placed two folded pieces of paper before Abner.

"Here are two deeds to a piece of property," he said, settling back in his chair. "Read both and tell me what you think. Be sure to examine everything."

I could tell that Abner considered protesting that he was no lawyer, but he said nothing. He knew that Randolph valued his opinion.

He read slowly and carefully. When he had finished both documents, he placed them side by side and glanced from one to the other. Finally he turned them over and examined the writing on the back of each.

"These deeds are both to the same piece of land," he said finally. "They were drawn about fifteen years ago. The property is a tract of two hundred and fifty acres, sold by Oliver McCoy. One deed is made to Gideon and Flora Dillworth. The other is made to Richard and Anna Blackhurst. Yet one deed must be worthless, for the two are identical."

"Not quite," said Randolph.

Abner looked again at the papers. "Not quite, that is true. The Dillworth deed is dated three days earlier. In all other respects, the documents are twins—the same lawyer, the same notary—why, even the recorder's statement on the back as to the number and page of the record book is the same."

Randolph stroked his jaw. "And this is impossible."

"Not entirely," Abner said. "Oliver McCoy could have bilked Richard Blackhurst, who was given the later deed. This is unlikely. It was not in McCoy's nature to do this. Besides, the fraud would never have passed Morgan Roberts, his lawyer, or Morgan's clerk, who made out the papers and notarized them."

He looked hard at Randolph. "What does the record book show?"

Randolph sighed. He picked up a large ledger-type of book which was in front of him and opened it. Without a word, he pushed it to Abner.

My uncle consulted the deeds for the page reference, then glanced at the book.

"The page is gone!" he said. "It has been cut away with a sharp edge. It might never have been missed until a time such as this came."

This provoked Randolph into a summation of the situation as it stood. One of the deeds had to be false, but it was difficult to say which one. The later dating of the Blackhurst deed might make it suspect, but the Dillworth deed might have been dated earlier to throw suspicion the other way. There were no witnesses to testify one way or the other. Oliver McCoy, his lawyer, and the law clerk were all dead. The dead law clerk was shown as notary on both deeds. The fact of fraud had been established by the missing page from the record book.

"That is why I wanted to talk to Harper," Randolph said. "He had a prodigious memory. He might have recalled whose name was on the copy in the records. He might even have remembered who asked to look at the book. That person could have removed the page."

The table vibrated to the slap of a heavy palm.

"There was no fraud done by our family," growled Dorsey. "My sister is as honest as anyone here. So was her husband while he was alive."

He turned to his opponent. "Dillworth, I don't know you. I did know your father, and I had thought well of him. Now I think he was cut from the same cloth as some of the others of the same name."

Young Dillworth paled. "You can never support that."

The smith leaned forward. "Your father was a sign painter. He could have had the eye and the hand to be a forger. And he came back here once, fifteen years ago. He could have cut that page from the book then."

Dillworth's jaw was set. "My father had the honesty you claim for your sister. As for Blackhurst, I have been told by many of your neighbors that customers in his store had to be wary of short weight and scamped measure when he was alive."

Anna Blackhurst's eyes flashed. "You defame a man who cannot defend himself."

"My father has no better defense against your brother," said Dillworth, indicating the smith. "And my mother's a widow, like you."

Dorsey raised his hand to thump the table again. Dillworth saw it and brought his own left arm down so that the hook at the end of it cracked sharply against the wood. My uncle's mouth tightened in displeasure at such tactics.

Anna Blackhurst smiled ruefully and dropped a handkerchief on the surface of the table. "But it is such meager land. Why should my husband have risked going to prison over it?"

"My father knew there was coal under it when he bought it," Dillworth replied. "He always said that its value would increase. I have learned, in Baltimore, that the railroad will pass within a quarter mile of the property. The coal will now be more valuable because it will be easier to transport. What my father knew, Blackhurst could have known."

"My husband's judgment was poor," Anna Blackhurst said. "He bought land for the sake of owning it."

Dillworth turned to Randolph. "You spoke of Harper, the County Clerk. Where is he? If he could help, he should be here."

Randolph made no reply. Instead, he gestured toward Abner.

My uncle reached into his pockets. "Two of us have seen Harper this morning—Martin and I," he said. "Before we discuss that, let us all look at these."

He set out on the table the cowbell and the three sharp-pronged objects. The point of one of these was still stained with the blood of Harper's horse. The other two were clean, bright metal.

Dillworth leaned forward and drew one of the pointed things to him with his hook.

"Caltrops," he said wonderingly. "Where did you get these?"

My uncle was watching him, and a flicker of surprise crossed his face. "You recognize these things?"

Dillworth pushed it from him. "A cavalryman should know them. Many a charge has been undone by these wicked things. It is said that Napoleon met with them, to his cost."

"Not only Bonaparte," Abner said. "Thomas Harper encountered these four objects this morning and paid for it with his life."

Amid shocked exclamations, he went on:

"At first light, someone hung this bell on a branch, to lure Harper into looking for a stray cow. It was hung at the edge of a small cliff. To complete the trap, these Devil's tools were strewn near the bell, where a horse would step. Harper's horse did step on one. The blood is still to be seen. Harper was thrown over the cliff. His neck was broken."

There was silence at the table. It was plain that everyone remembered what Randolph had said about Harper's memory and knew what the murder implied.

Anna Blackhurst broke that silence. "I propose a test. Squire Randolph, will you send for a candle?"

Randolph rubbed the side of his nose, where the tiny broken blood-vessels showed. "To what end?" he asked.

The widow's green eyes flashed. She stretched out her right hand, slender and graceful, but clearly strong. "Let us have a trial by ordeal, Mr. Dillworth and I, as the Indians would do. I am willing to expose my good right hand to the flame to prove my innocence. Is he?"

Dillworth went pale. "You know well that no man would face a woman in such a test."

"There is no need for such foolishness," Abner said sharply. "By ignoring the oldest law, Harper's killer has stepped into plain view."

Randolph cleared his throat. "That is the second time you have referred to a law which escapes me. A Virginia law? Something carried over from England? The Sixth Commandment? Or the Tenth?"

"All those might be involved," replied Abner. "The Sixth and Tenth Commandments are, I am certain. As to the rest, I do not know. The law which I mean is older than any of these."

"It goes back to Adam, I suppose," said Randolph.

"It is older than Adam."

"Impossible!" Randolph snorted. "There is no law named before the commandments made to Adam."

"It is not named, that is true," Abner agreed, "but it is written in everything which was created. Think, Randolph: the Lord decreed that mountains should crumble, rocks should break, the sands of the desert should powder, all living things decay. From all this came the dust. From this dust Adam was formed. Now do you read the law?"

"It is still unclear."

"Once again—it is stamped on every created thing and cannot be broken. This is the law: all things must change."

Randolph nodded. He could not fault Abner's explanation. "And by naming Harper's murderer you will also name the forger?"

"By no means," said Abner. "The forger is different. I suggest that the forgery was done by Morgan Roberts' law clerk. No other person could have had the original document long enough to do it. No person here could have produced the necessary form for the deed."

"Morgan Roberts—" Randolph began.

"Had no motive," Abner finished. "He was an old man, and the land involved seemed of little value. Where was his gain?"

"I can hardly remember his clerk," Randolph reflected. "McGraw. Joseph McGraw. A sickly man. He died young. He had few attractive qualities while he lived."

Abner turned to Dillworth. "Dillworth, why did your father leave here for Baltimore?"

The ex-cavalryman was surprised. "To earn a living."

Abner stared at him. "That completes it."

He gestured toward the three caltrops before him and spoke to Randolph and the three disputants.

"I spoke of the oldest law, and how Harper's murderer thought to ignore it. It is at work here."

He touched the three caltrops. "That law decrees that everything must change. What are we told in the Sermon on the Mount? Lay not up for yourselves treasures upon earth, where moth and rust doth corrupt. What, then, is rust?"

His question brought only silence.

He answered it himself. "Rust is nothing but the oldest law at work. Now, look at these three of Satan's instruments. One is stained only by the blood of Harper's horse. The other two show not the faintest blemish, not a pinpoint of rust. All are newly made."

He turned to young Dillworth. "Dillworth, when you showed familiarity with these things, I became unsure of the picture which had formed in my mind. There were things which stood in your favor, but you could have brought these objects with you. Even so, they would have shown rust somewhere, if only faint blackening."

Dillworth made no answer. He lifted his good hand and let it fall to the table.

Randall Dorsey started to rise from his seat. "There's no man's blood on my hands, in spite of this made-up law of yours!"

"No, Dorsey, I don't believe there is," said Abner mildly. "You could not have been at Harper's place this morning. Martin and I both saw you hard at work when we passed your smithy."

Anna Blackhurst laughed, and I could hear nothing but music in it. "Then you must be saying that I did all the scheming for the land, that I stole out in the last shades of night to take a man's life. Abner, I must remind you that it is not I with theatrical connections. I am not the one skilled in pretending."

"You have many skills," Abner said gravely. "You know the ways of the Indian, and you know the ways they have been fought. How would Dillworth know, when he was raised in Baltimore?"

"You become more confusing, Abner," she laughed. "First you talk of old laws, then of Indians."

"It is simple enough," Abner said sternly. "You heard how Harper died. The ruse with the bell is a redskin's trick to lure a settler from his cabin. The settlers, in turn, used the deadly steel tares to penetrate moccasins and cripple prowling enemies. You knew these things. I have heard you tell of them."

I, too, heard her voice talking of them, in the days when I carried a wooden hunting knife.

She raised her head and thrust out her chin. "Who paid Joseph McGraw to forge a deed to the land? Dillworth's father had money. I had none."

"Dillworth's father had little money," Abner replied. "Why did he go to Baltimore? Only ten minutes ago I was told 'to earn a living.' "

Abner's presence suddenly seemed to increase, dwarfing even Randall Dorsey's.

"Joseph McGraw was an unloved man. And not all payment is in money. If you want an example, I give you Delilah."

Still she did not yield. Reaching out, she swept the caltrops the length of the table. "Still, to prove your ancient law, you must say that I made these things. That is impossible."

"Then I have a question," said Abner. "Is your brother Tubal-cain or Cain?"

Dorsey suddenly shot to his feet. His voice shook. "Cain I am not! I said that no man's blood is on my hands, and that is true. She said she wanted them to show in school, and I thought it was the truth. I always believed the deed to the land was a true one. But I will not defend murder."

He looked down at Abner. "I made the caltrops for her. Yesterday."

Stanley Ellin

The Ledbetter Syndrome

*Critics are not always unanimous in their judgments, but we
know of no critic who does not share Julian Symons' critical view
of Stanley Ellin. In* MORTAL CONSEQUENCES (1972), *Mr. Symons
wrote: "[Stanley Ellin's] work is a landmark in the history of the
crime short story"* . . .

As Chief Clerk of the county's Hall of Records, Mr. Ince reigned
with benevolent inefficiency over a pleasant domain which
Women's Liberation had either passed by or not yet arrived at. The
domain, on the top floor of the county courthouse, was a spacious
room cluttered with filing cabinets and metal book-racks and with
a well-worn counter where the public was served. On the counter
at appropriate intervals, hand-lettered signs indicated where the
public was to present its queries about *Births & Deaths* or *Marriages*
or *Property Records (Deeds & Abstracts).*

A staff of three serving under Mr. Ince provided the advertised
services. Miss McCurdy and Miss Schultz, both Clerk, Grade 2, were
oldtimers on the job. Mrs. Rogers, Clerk, Grade 5, was a relative
latecomer. A widow, she had been a native Chicagoan, assistant to
her struggling shopkeeper husband there for the twenty years of
their marriage. After his unexpected death by heart failure, she had
emigrated westward to the placid county seat of Kandia Falls to
share life with her already widowed sister and eventually, when
what little money there was had run out, had taken the necessary
civil service examination and wound up as a member of Mr. Ince's
team.

So there they were, the four of them tucked away under the occasionally leaky roof of the courthouse, getting along with each other
very well indeed. Cheerful dispositions were what their leader
wanted around him on the job, and the ladies generally obliged. This
imposed little strain on them since they all admired him intensely,
a robust, high-spirited man and certainly the least demanding and
most tolerant of supervisors.

277

And, as they sometimes had occasion to remind each other, this was a long-suffering soul who, with hardly any complaint, had to contend with a thankless marriage. How natural—and how saddening—that after a particularly bad session at home he should be led to seek solace in the bottle and so plainly show the effects at his desk the next morning. The more reason then to put on those bright and smiling faces for his comforting.

They were wrong in one regard.

What they did not know, because Mr. Ince kept the secret clutched tight to his bosom, was that when he turned to the bottle it was to drown nothing more or less than the frustrations of the failed creative artist. A devotee of murder mysteries, he had, over the long years, sent out a score of cleverly plotted murder tales to publishers from coast to coast. Those evenings when a cherished manuscript would appear in his mail on the rebound, the familiar *Sorry* appended to it, were the bad ones for Mr. Ince, the mornings after even worse.

But of course, as his ladies could attest, these hangovers were occasional small dark clouds passing through their sunshiny working days. Most often it was the sunshine that prevailed.

Then along came Mr. Ledbetter.

For some reason, people like to believe that in a small town everyone knows everyone else, which is a long way from the truth. The truth is that in a small town like Kandia Falls—population 20,000—everyone knows *about* everyone else who may be worth knowing about. Thus when Mr. Ledbetter suddenly appeared in the Hall of Records one fine morning, all present knew enough about him to be greatly surprised by this visit.

Mr. Ledbetter was rich, reclusive, and, at age fifty, as total a bachelor as one could be. Your true bachelor of fifty is seldom a big jolly fellow with carefree ways. Far from it, he is likely to be spare of build, prim of manner, and with a disposition to hypochondria.

So it was with Mr. Ledbetter, for good reason. An only child, the last of his line, delivered to his astonished and delighted parents after they had long given up hope of becoming parents, he had been an ailing little creature, swathed almost to smothering in the cotton-batting of their adoration, privately educated so that he could be kept away from any possible contamination. When in the fullness of their years his parents died, the son took one quick look at the world he would have to contend with from the presidential suite of the Ledbetter National Bank, then placed the bank's affairs in the hands of capable surrogates and fled back to the spacious confines of the Ledbetter estate, a Victorian mansion surrounded by acres of lawn and garden on the far outskirts of town near the waters of Kandia Falls itself.

There, nursing a neurasthenic shyness, the estate in charge of a trusted houseman and whatever staff he chose to muster, Mr. Ledbetter devoted himself to a solitary life of gardening, extensive reading, coin collecting, and, of recent years, genealogical investigation of his forebears. Although he never entertained at home and was rarely seen in town, there was nothing of the misanthrope in him. An appeal to him by any respectable local cause would, if delivered by mail, be answered more than generously. In the end, although almost invisible to the community, he came to be well-regarded by it. Even the most calculating of those unmarried ladies who had seen in him the prize of a lifetime came to view his remote image with kindliness once they understood that in this lottery there would be no tickets sold. That's the way he is, poor soul, they told each other, and took comfort in knowing they were all in the same boat.

Now here was Mr. Ledbetter standing at the counter of the Hall of Records and bearing a formal letter of introduction. The letter was from the State Commissioner of Records himself, was addressed to Mr. Ince, and was brief and to the point. Every possible courtesy was to be extended to Mr. Ledbetter, all possible assistance was to be provided him. The underlining of the *every* and the *all* gave the message an almost menacing authority.

No need for that. Mr. Ince was delighted with this turn of events, a personal contact with the town's most sought-after and elusive citizen. At his desk, railed off at the far end of the room, he patiently extracted from his tight-lipped visitor the nature of his business. In a nutshell, it was that Mr. Ledbetter was now engaged in preparing a definitive history of his once-extensive family from that time, a century before, when they had first homesteaded in the county and helped found the town of Kandia Falls.

So, said Mr. Ledbetter, to make sure that every detail of the history was accurate, he must rely on these public files. Would need them at his fingertips for a few weeks. If that could be arranged without difficulty—

It could, indeed. On the strength of the letter from the Commissioner, a small table was commandeered from the laboratory of the County Farm Agency across the hall. A well-padded chair was carted up from the courtroom clerk's office downstairs. Room was made for these furnishings under the large window overlooking the town square, where any available sunlight would be behind Mr. Ledbetter's shoulder while he was at work. An added advantage to the location was that it was a good distance from the counter, thus assuring the historian a certain amount of privacy at his labors, and for this he was outspokenly grateful.

It took only a few days for all hands to familiarize themselves with their guest's routine. Ten o'clock each morning he would arrange the contents of a swollen briefcase on his table—notebooks, charts, and index cards—and go to work with a glassy-eyed concentration, sometimes approaching Mr. Ince with a list of required documents and plat books. Only Mr. Ince was approached, no one else. At noon there would be a break for lunch, a sandwich and a small Thermos of tea extracted from the briefcase, and then it was back to work with a vengeance. Four o'clock to the minute was departure time.

Mr. Ince, who had at first welcomed the arrangement, quickly came to detest it, for sound reasons. He had always run his department on the logical assumption that what you didn't do today was probably not worth doing tomorrow either. Now faced by someone across the room with a direct pipeline to the State Commissioner, he had to at least go through the motions. A gregarious spirit, he used to take pleasure in extended visits to old acquaintances in other departments. Now he was nailed down to his desk and, what was worse, the bottle locked in its bottom drawer could not be called on for support when needed.

Then there was the way Mr. Ledbetter remained so conspicuously aloof from the ladies on the staff, suggesting nothing so much as a Pilgrim Father on guard against a trio of threatening Jezebels. Since Miss McCurdy and Miss Schultz were well on in years and, to put it kindly, exceedingly plain of feature, and since Mrs. Rogers, while somewhat more pleasant-featured, was almost comically short and tubby, they might have found this rather flattering. But they did not. They were too level-headed for such nonsense. What they did feel was a mounting resentment which, only out of regard for Mr. Ince, they tried to keep tightly bottled up.

The result, of course, was the collapse of the department's morale. Once the happiest of havens, the Hall of Records now became almost funereal in atmosphere.

To ease this situation, Mr. Ince several times deferentially asked Mr. Ledbetter to call on the ladies for information retrieval rather than lay all dependence on him. Each time, Mr. Ledbetter demonstrated a maddening stubbornness in his ways. "No, Mr. Ince. I prefer it this way."

"The ladies are extremely competent, Mr. Ledbetter."

"I am sure they are. But I prefer your services."

No solution there. The one and only solution to everything, Mr. Ince morosely told himself, would be provided by time itself. After all, it was only a matter of a few weeks before this interloper took his leave for keeps.

Indeed, after a few weeks, each as nerve-racking as the one that preceded it, Mr. Ledbetter's requests for documentation did become more and more infrequent. One day there were no requests at all. The historian, lost to the world, simply spent that day examining his notes, now and again nodding sober appreciation of them. Mr. Ince took pleased notice of this. Definitely, from the look of it, the moment of deliverance was near.

He went home that evening in comparatively high spirits. There, his wife, whose face was not often wreathed in smiles, greeted him with a face wreathed in smiles. The reason became clear when she handed him his mail, which she was honor-bound not to open. The envelope on top was from the publisher to whom Mr. Ince had sent his last novel, a wickedly contrived murder mystery where the least likely suspect, a gentle spinster, was, in fact, the murderer.

Mr. Ince opened the envelope with trembling fingers. Always before, it had been the bulky manuscript itself which had been returned to him, a rejection slip attached to it. Never before had a publisher acknowledged receipt of a manuscript in this form. What else could this signal but an acceptance? At the very least, keen interest.

Mr. Ince read the letter. *Sorry, but your novel is unacceptable. However, you neglected to enclose postage for its return. If you would kindly—*

When he gingerly seated himself at his desk the next morning the ladies instantly recognized the symptoms. Miss McCurdy hastily brought aspirin, Miss Schultz brought a glass of ice water, Mrs. Rogers brought an empty paper cup for the one treatment in which he had any faith, a strong dose from the bottle in the desk. Some may argue against this hair-of-the-dog treatment, but, as Mr. Ince saw it during these crises, if all it offered was a quick and merciful death, so much the better.

By the time Mr. Ledbetter made his appearance the ladies were back at their duties, and Mr. Ince, elbows on desk and throbbing head buried in his hands, was brooding over the outrageous stupidity of publishers who didn't recognize masterpiece when it was planted right in their hands. He put aside the subject as Mr. Ledbetter approached, for once not bearing the familiar briefcase. Mr. Ince felt a tiny spark of gratitude find its way through his monstrous *katzenjammer*.

Mr. Ledbetter seated himself beside the desk. He seemed extraordinarily pleased with the world. "Fine weather," he remarked.

"Very," said Mr. Ince with an effort.

The amenities attended to, Mr. Ledbetter got down to business. "You must know how helpful you've been to me in my project."

"Glad I could be."

"And I haven't made any problem for you, have I? Taking up space here?"

"No problem." Mr. Ince could see this was going to be one of those long farewells. "There's plenty of space here."

"Yes, that's how the Commissioner seemed to feel about it. I had him on the phone last night about my work plan. He saw it your way. Said to move right ahead with it."

Mr. Ince tried to grasp this. "Move ahead?"

"Well, I'm about to start on the writing of the history itself in a week or two. A publisher has just contracted for it. The State University Press."

Envy pierced Mr. Ince's bowels like a sawtoothed blade. "You mean your book is definitely going to be published?"

"Oh, definitely. I've already received part payment for it. And I've been so productive here—this workmanlike atmosphere, I suppose—that it struck me as wisdom to simply remain at that table until the job is done. There are too many distractions at home, you understand. None here. So for the year or two required—"

"You said a *year* or two?"

"At least. After all, this is to be the comprehensive study of literally dozens of people. And what complex and colorful people." Mr. Ledbetter's voice became rich with scorn. "Believe me, you won't find their like nowadays. Nothing like them."

Mr. Ince stared at this insufferably self-assured, self-satisfied bane of his life through bloodshot eyes. Oblivious to his suffering, Miss McCurdy and Miss Schultz were at the counter casually tending to trade. Mrs. Rogers was at her desk, vigorously banging staples into some documents.

A madness seized Mr. Ince.

He leaned toward Mr. Ledbetter. "Can you keep a secret?"

"Yes, of course," Mr. Ledbetter said in some surprise.

"Well, then"—Mr. Ince aimed a forefinger—"see that little lady there? Our Mrs. Rogers?"

"Yes."

"A widow."

"Oh, I'm sorry."

"*She* isn't."

"I beg your pardon?"

"Happened five years ago in Chicago," said Mr. Ince, wildly improvising on his most recently rejected masterpiece. "Married to a big brute who liked to knock her about. One night she just picked up his shotgun and, cool as a cucumber, let him have both barrels. Blew his brains out."

Mr. Ledbetter looked stunned. "That woman?"

"Right."

Mr. Ledbetter was visibly paler. "But she's employed here. I mean, after something like that—"

"I told you, cool as a cucumber. Tried for murder, put on a weepy act, and the jury let her off scot-free. Justifiable homicide. It all came to me by mistake. A confidential report that should never have been released. *She* doesn't even know I know about it."

Mr. Ledbetter swallowed hard. "Incredible."

"Colorful, I'd call it. Colorful. And complex." Mr. Ince put a warning finger to his lips. "But remember. I have your word that this is as far as it goes."

"Yes," said Mr. Ledbetter weakly.

Mr. Ince watched with satisfaction as the historian departed on what were unquestionably shaky legs. Then he took the bottle from the desk drawer. The very least he owed himself was a victory toast.

His satisfaction lasted until he woke the next morning, a sense of doom now bearing down on him like an express train.

He clutched his head as he considered his plight. A joke, of course. That's all it had been. But what in heaven's name had led him to play any such joke on a pompous ass who had the ear of the State Commissioner? If Mr. Ledbetter spilled the beans, there would be, at the very least, a thorough investigation of the office management here as reprisal, and it was not a management that could bear even cursory investigation. And there were those retirement benefits and the pension which in a few years were to free Mr. Ince to a full-time vocation as author. What would happen to them?

Just as bad, what about Mrs. Rogers herself? Let the word get out, and hungry lawyers would gather like sharks, slavering over this airtight case of slander.

First the departmental trial, then the criminal trial—there was the future. Or was it the other way around? Either way, it was the same future.

And what defense could be offered by the accused? Intoxication on the job? A mental disorder?

The one and only hope was that Mr. Ledbetter—now a perambulating time-bomb—had been sworn to secrecy and would abide by his oath. The odds on this, as Mr. Ince weighed them carefully, seemed favorable. Meanwhile, there was going to be a drastic change in office management, a cleaning up, reorganizing, and disciplining which, in the vent of an investigation, might have a soothing effect on the investigators.

Might.

Heavy-laden with his cares, Mr. Ince entered the office to be immediately surrounded by the ladies full of high excitement. They had a story to tell, and what a story. Miss McCurdy narrated it, Miss Schultz embellished it, and roly-poly Mrs. Rogers confirmed it along the way with smiles and nods.

It seemed that as soon as Mrs. Rogers had arrived home from work yesterday she had received a call from Mr. Ledbetter, an invitation to dine with him at the Kandia Falls Lodge, no less. She had been much taken aback, had hesitated, and then, as Mr. Ledbetter persisted, she had yielded. So there she had been, seated at the very best table in the very best dining room in town, a place patronized only by the very best people, and didn't they goggle at this unprecedented sight being offered them.

Even with that embarrassment, however, it had been a most pleasant time, so pleasant, indeed, that there had been an invitation to dinner tonight as well, and Mrs. Rogers had guilelessly accepted it on the spot. Plainly, guile, and whatever strategy it might dictate to the skilled matchmaker, was not for Mrs. Rogers.

At his desk, Mr. Ince sat hunched up in misery brooding over this undreamed of and catastrophic development. Irony of ironies, he himself had played Cupid to the couple. He had provided Mrs. Rogers with her credentials. Because Mr. Ledbetter, that confirmed bachelor, that supreme misogynist, having rejected every genteel and proper lady who ever pursued him, had now been knocked right off his pins by the image of a smiling, cool-as-a-cucumber murderess. On second thought, or even third or fourth, why not? Lucrezia Borgia had never lacked for suitors, had she?

With a panicky feeling that time was of the essence in establishing his second line of defense, Mr. Ince gathered the ladies together and coldly advised them that from now on they would be sailing aboard a very tight ship. He then explained at length what, in terms of the Kandia Falls Hall of Records, a very tight ship was. Miss McCurdy and Miss Schultz received this grumpily, plainly feeling betrayed by an old friend. On the other hand, Mrs. Rogers was vague in response, euphoric in manner, her thoughts evidently far away.

As the office underwent its transformation in the days that followed, the reason for the euphoria became obvious. Mr. Ledbetter was conducting a whirlwind courtship of his Lucrezia Borgia. All her available time was claimed by him. Even his precious book had been laid aside while he plotted new diversions, new excursions for her pleasure.

There was never any real question of where the courtship was heading; the only question was when it would get there. To Mr. Ince it was the waiting for the inevitable that was ulcerating him, and all the hard work he was sharing with his staff couldn't ease the pangs. Too imaginative for his own good perhaps, he kept visualizing that scene once the marital vows had been taken.

A bedroom scene. The Ledbetter bedroom.

The new Mrs. Ledbetter: "Why are you staring at me so strangely, dear?"

Mr. Ledbetter: "Because now that you're mine, there's something I dare to ask you. Mr. Ince confided to me the fascinating story of how you did away with your first husband. What I've been wondering—"

That was as far as it went each time. The rest was too grisly to contemplate.

What all this was doing to him was finally summed up by the long-suffering Mrs. Ince who told him in some heat that he was becoming impossible to live with. Miss McCurdy and Miss Schultz, toiling to bring order to dusty and long-forgotten office files, eschewed the words but let him know through expressive body language how heartily they agreed with this sentiment. The sole consolation was that Mrs. Rogers, toiling away as valiantly as her colleagues, seemed to be living in a world of her own, and it was

only fitful consolation. Sooner or later, Mr. Ince warned himself, the
wedding announcement would pop up in his mail, and into his mind
would pop yet another replay of that nightmarish bedroom scene.

The announcement was not delivered by mail. Close to lunch hour
one noon, it was delivered by Mrs. Rogers herself.

Mr. Ince, hard at work deciphering some waterstained birth cer-
tificates, became aware that she was standing beside him silently
demanding his attention. The proximity made him nervous. He sat
back as far as he could on his chair. "Yes?" he said warily.

Mrs. Rogers explained apologetically that this was goodbye.
Really goodbye, her formal resignation from the Service now on its
way to Personnel. Because to avoid public commotion, she and Mr.
Ledbetter were slipping away in very few minutes to be wed out of
town and so begin a long honeymoon abroad. Even the girls—the
ladies always referred to each other in the plural as "the girls"—didn't
know about it yet. Indeed, the longer the news was delayed, the
better.

"I see," said Mr. Ince numbly. "Of course." He tried to rise to the
occasion. "Well," he said, "good luck to you. And to Mr. Ledbetter."

"Thank you. But there's a little favor I must ask. It has to do with
that strange story you made up about me."

Mr. Ince gaped at her. "He told you about it?"

"Last night. He was," said Mrs. Rogers, "most sympathetic."

Mr. Ince flung his arms wide in appeal. "Believe me—" he stam-
mered. "I assure you—"

"And I told him," said Mrs. Rogers gravely, "that this subject was
just too painful for me. I made him promise never to mention it
again. Never. Not to me or anyone else. Now will you make me that
same promise?"

Mr. Ince found himself incapable of speech. But he could nod his
head. He nodded it in a daze.

"Thank you," said Mrs. Rogers. She suddenly leaned forward and
gave him a quick little peck on the cheek. "Oh, I do thank you for
everything," she whispered in his ear, and then she was out the door
and gone.